OVERWATCH

OVERWATCH

A THRILLER

MATTHEW BETLEY

EMILY BESTLER BOOKS

—

ATRIA

NEW YORK   LONDON   TORONTO   SYDNEY   NEW DELHI

ATRIA BOOKS

An Imprint of Simon & Schuster, Inc.
1230 Avenue of the Americas
New York, NY 10020

First Emily Bestler Books/Atria Books hardcover edition March 2016

EMILY BESTLER BOOKS / ATRIA BOOKS and colophons are trademarks of Simon & Schuster, Inc.

For information about special discounts for bulk purchases, please contact Simon & Schuster Special Sales at 1-866-506-1949 or business@simonandschuster.com.

The Simon & Schuster Speakers Bureau can bring authors to your live event. For more information or to book an event contact the Simon & Schuster Speakers Bureau at 1-866-248-3049 or visit our website at www.simonspeakers.com.

Interior design by Kyoko Watanabe

Manufactured in the United States of America

10 9 8 7 6 5 4 3 2 1

Library of Congress Cataloging-in-Publication Data is available.

ISBN 978-1-4767-9921-6
ISBN 978-1-4767-9924-7 (ebook)

*This novel is dedicated to all Marines and members of
the Armed Forces who served in Iraq, who sacrificed for
us and often paid the highest price of all in the service
of our country. No matter how the landscape changes,
your service will not be forgotten. Semper Fi.*

o·ver·watch **1.** The process of watching from a high position another group of soldiers who are involved in a military activity and giving them support if necessary.

—Macmillan Dictionary

PART I

FIRST CONTACT

CHAPTER 1

ANNAPOLIS, MD
29 OCTOBER 2008

Logan West opened his bloodshot green eyes as he emerged from unconsciousness. Light pierced his vision, and pain lanced through his head like a sharp knife. His forehead throbbed relentlessly as the brightness slowly dimmed.

He was facedown on the carpeted floor of his basement, his left arm stretched out above his head. He turned his wrist to look at his watch. It was almost one thirty in the afternoon.

I remember the first whiskey sometime around six o'clock, but there's no way this is from only last night. Oh God . . .

With a dawning sense of horror, he realized he'd lost at least forty hours. *A whole day? I've never blacked out that long before. It's getting worse.*

He struggled to his knees, his right arm fully extended, bracing himself for a fall that didn't come. A wave of nausea washed over him. *This is going to be a bad one,* he thought. He felt the acrid bile rising in his throat when he heard a disembodied voice from across the room. "I was wondering when you were going to wake up. I've been waiting all night."

The voice had the effect of ice-cold water thrown in Logan's face, instantly suppressing the nausea and clearing his cloudy mind. He turned his head to look at the intruder, his mind feverishly working to regain its bearings.

The man was smiling as he leaned against the long marble-top bar fifteen feet from Logan. He appeared to be Hispanic, in his late twenties or early thirties. His hair was black and cropped closely, almost in a military manner but without the sides shaved to the skin. He wore a white long-sleeved thermal tee shirt under a black polo, as if trying to hide his muscular frame. His dark-brown eyes curiously assessed Logan, and although the man appeared relaxed, his overall demeanor presented a different picture. A neon sign flashed in the darkened street of Logan's mind. *This man's a professional.* And then . . . *More importantly, he's a threat.*

A multitude of questions ricocheted in Logan's head. None of them mattered. Logan knew the intruder wasn't here to nurse him back to health. "Who the hell are you?" He wobbled on his hands and knees.

"That's not important," the man responded. The smile faded to reveal the hard interior beneath the cool facade. "But what is important—extremely important—is that you have something we want. Let me rephrase: *need.*" Logan's unease grew at the man's tone. "And as soon as you get your sorry ass off that floor, you're going to tell me where it is." The certainty in the man's voice triggered the final alarms in Logan's head.

Logan West, relapsing alcoholic, was still a man who, once committed to anything—a plan, a promise, an ideal—was relentless in its pursuit. He evaluated a situation so rapidly that his former platoon sergeant had repeatedly accused him of acting recklessly; however, in each of those former situations, Logan's judgment had always proven correct and above reproach. He just understood and saw things before others did.

Unfortunately, that was before alcohol had forced its insidious way into every aspect of his life, including his decision-making abilities. Had he been completely sober, the rational part of his mind might have stopped him, but Logan West hadn't been himself for months, and this afternoon was no different. This time, his platoon sergeant would've been correct. He acted before thinking.

He launched himself across the basement floor like a sprinter out of the starting block. His speed caught the intruder off guard—but only slightly. As Logan covered the distance in four long strides, a long blade appeared in the man's right hand.

Logan was almost upon the man, his left shoulder raised and his right arm at his waist, both hands in fists. As he gained momentum, he moved his head to the left in a quick feint, hoping the man would draw back and provide an opening Logan could exploit. Otherwise, plan B was to plow into the man as hard and fast as he could.

Instead, the man violently flicked his right arm upward in an arcing uppercut motion. Logan, surprised by his miscalculation—*not the first one of the day*—saw the blade rush past his face. Even as he moved his head away, he felt a searing pain race across his left cheek. His mind registered the soft *pat . . . pat . . . pat . . .* of blood droplets cascading to the carpeted floor.

Then the sound was gone as his 210-pound frame crashed squarely into the assailant's chest and forcefully slammed his back against the marble countertop. Logan heard the man grunt, his breath expelled in a sudden gasp, and Logan seized the momentary opening.

He delivered a vicious short punch to the inside of the man's right wrist, causing his hand to open reflexively. The knife fell to the carpet and softly bounced away, landing near the bench press machine of Logan's multistation gym.

Now disarmed, the man lowered his arms to protect himself as Logan assaulted his ribs with a furious onslaught of violent punches.

Logan sensed the tide of battle distinctly turn in his favor. He reached upward and grabbed the back of the man's head, intent on delivering a knee to the man's face to swiftly end the confrontation.

The attacker sensed his intent and countered. Rather than try to ply Logan's arms from his head, he quickly snaked his right arm over Logan's left arm and under the right one. The man's left palm struck his own right hand with an upward blow with enough force to break Logan's grip, flinging Logan's arms up and away from him. *The smart, defensive move of a trained professional,* Logan thought.

The wounded intruder stepped forward and quickly delivered a side kick that squarely connected with Logan's stomach. Logan stumbled backward, and his legs struck the seat of the pull-down station of the gym. He felt himself falling, and he grabbed the pull-down bar still attached to the pulley's cable suspended over his head. His fall abruptly stopped, and Logan teetered precariously, twisting in the air from side to side.

Logan glanced at his enemy—how he now thought of the intruder—as he dangled from the pull-down bar. He recognized the change in his thinking, but he didn't have time to contemplate the psychological implications of it. To his dismay, his enemy had moved closer to the dropped knife as Logan had fallen backward. In another moment, he'd have it—as well as the tactical advantage.

Logan did the only thing he could. As the man dove for the knife, Logan regained his balance, reached up, and unhooked the carabiner that secured the pull-down bar to the cable. He grabbed the bar with both hands and wielded it above his head like an awkwardly shaped sword, a heavy weapon forged from the top of a wide parallelogram. He stepped forward and swung the bar downward with all his might.

The attacker was prone on his stomach, crawling toward the knife with his hand outstretched, when one end of the metal bar violently collided with the back of his neck. He didn't have time to register the fact that the end of his life had arrived.

Logan heard a sickening *crunch!* like popcorn being stepped on with a hard-soled shoe, and then the intruder sprawled forward, his spine severed. Logan watched as the man's legs kicked spasmodically, his lungs shut down, and he began to suffocate.

Logan stared impassively at the dying man. *You brought this on yourself.* After a brief period, the man's body stopped moving. Silence engulfed the basement in the aftermath of the battle.

The adrenaline rush that had swept away his hangover suddenly subsided, and Logan felt the all-too-familiar effects of his self-destructive behavior return. He realized he was breathing hard, and he forced himself to take slow, deep breaths. He was still thinking only one step at a time. Now that the fight was over, he needed to clear his head and figure out who the dead man was.

He bent over slowly to prevent the accompanying dizziness he often felt after a hard night's drinking. He grabbed the man's left arm and rolled him over onto his back. The dead man's eyes looked at him accusingly. Logan didn't care. Something else had grabbed his attention.

The left sleeve of the thermal tee had been pushed up his forearm during the fight, revealing a tattoo of a pair of .50-caliber bullets crossed in front of a skull. *You've got to be kidding me. Who the hell was this guy?*

He'd seen a tattoo like this on one of his Marines in Fallujah. The young sniper's favorite weapon had been his Barrett .50-caliber sniper rifle, and the sergeant had been eager to broadcast it to the rest of his team.

They'd initially ribbed him with copious sarcasm when he'd received the tattoo. Fortunately for all of them, the sergeant had proved to be a deadly, accurate shot. After three days of heavy fighting in Fallujah, he'd earned the right to wear the ink proudly. No one said a word about it afterward.

Logan turned his thoughts to the present. The dead man lying in his basement wore tactical boots, had possessed a military demeanor, and was illustrated with a killer's tattoo. It was the knife near the dead man's hand that told Logan that his attacker was a skilled professional. *Of the pay-for-hire kind,* he thought. It was matte black with a ribbed handle for an improved grip during hand-to-hand combat.

His world tottered again. Logan felt another wave of nausea overtake him. He sat down on the basement floor as the withdrawal symptoms set in, and he knew they weren't going to go away this time. He needed a drink to alleviate their severity. But first, there was one thing even more important.

I have to call Mike.

————

WASHINGTON, DC

At six foot two inches and close to 220 pounds, Special Agent Mike Benson hunched over his desk. He scrolled through the latest National Counterterrorism Center intelligence report on a laptop that felt tiny in his massive hands. His phone suddenly rang, the only noise in his private office.

The ringing was a welcome relief. He could only process so many threats to his country at one time. Most of them were the result of erroneous or faulty intelligence, *thankfully.* Unfortunately, it seemed like every extremist group associated with Al Qaeda was in the planning stages of a major operation against either the US homeland, US embassies worldwide, or US allies. It wasn't a good time to be a Westerner overseas.

He removed his hand from the mouse and picked up the phone. "FBI, Washington, DC, Field Office, Special Agent Benson."

"Mike, it's Logan. I don't know what you're doing, but I need your help, and I need it *now.*"

At the word *now* and the tone with which Logan used it, alarm bells sounded in Mike's head. He immediately knew it was serious. *So much for the NCTC.*

It wasn't an exaggeration to say that Mike owed Logan his life from their time in Iraq before the surge. "Just reading some bullshit report. Where are you?"

"At home . . . the Annapolis one. How soon can you get here?" The urgency in his voice heightened Mike's level of tension.

Mike looked at the time on his computer. It was 1:35 p.m. Traffic out of DC wouldn't be too bad, especially moving outbound toward the capital city on the west side of the Chesapeake Bay.

"Give me forty-five minutes or so. Anything I need to know beforehand?"

"Yeah. Come alone and don't tell anyone . . . at least not yet." Logan paused. "It seems I'm in a bit of a bind, but at least I'm better off than the dead guy in my basement." He said it as matter-of-factly as if he were reciting a dinner menu.

Logan didn't give Mike a chance to respond. "See you soon," he said and hung up.

Mike stared at the receiver in his right hand, thankful Logan had abruptly ended the conversation. He hadn't had time to formulate a response—let alone a thought—before the phone went silent.

He'd once vowed to Logan that no matter what the cost, he'd be there for him. As he looked at the phone, he realized he was about to test that commitment. Dismissing from his mind the number of laws he was likely about to break, he got up from his desk and moved toward the door.

What the hell now, Logan? I thought we left all the dead guys in the desert.

CHAPTER 2

Logan hung up his cell and put it away. Just then, another phone began to ring. It was coming from the dead man. Other than rolling the man over, he hadn't disturbed the body. He knew better.

He'd decided to wait until Mike arrived to search the man for two reasons. First, he wanted a witness before he moved anything in his basement, which was now a crime scene. Second—and more importantly—Mike would likely see a piece of evidence Logan's untrained eye would overlook. *And right now, Logan, you need all the help you can get.*

Just as quickly, another inner voice questioned his resolution. *How much harm can you do? You already killed him. Maybe you can find out why if you answer it.*

He really didn't want to touch the phone, but he only had a few seconds to make a decision. Answer the phone and see who it was, or ignore it and pray the FBI's forensic team could exploit it for evidence?

How much worse can it get? He wasn't a sit-on-the-sidelines kind of man. He bent down, reached under the body, and pulled the phone from his back left pocket. Mike was going to be even more pissed than he probably already was.

"*Hola,*" he said in a muffled voice, hoping the dead man spoke

Spanish. He was somewhat surprised when a male voice with a Hispanic accent asked, "Roberto, do you have him?"

That answered one question. Whoever this was, he wanted me alive. But why? The dead man—formerly known as Roberto—had been dispatched to kidnap him. He must've assumed Logan would be easy prey, especially if he'd been conducting surveillance on him and had seen him in a drunken stupor.

Logan smiled malevolently. Even though he knew he was in a serious situation and likely facing hard questioning from local law enforcement, he was still somewhat pleased with himself. *Someone sent this asshole to get me, and even after emerging from a blackout, I took him out first. Not bad for a relapsing alcoholic.*

Logan knew the man on the phone wasn't going to be easily fooled for long. He took the direct course of action—the path he worshipped, often to his own detriment.

"Sorry, this isn't Roberto. I'm not sure where he is right now— spiritually speaking, I mean—but I know he won't be taking any more calls." He waited for the response.

The man paused before he spoke, but when he did, he was eerily calm. "Mr. West, I assume it's you. Roberto would never have given his cell phone to anyone, which means I can also assume that Roberto is no longer among the living. That's quite a shame since Roberto was one of my better men. Not the best, mind you, but good enough."

"Well, apparently he wasn't that good, asshole." He wanted to provoke a response, but the man wasn't taking the bait. The man continued in the same calm voice, as if they were having a friendly discussion like two old buddies.

"Too true, Mr. West. Too true. You know, I warned him not to underestimate you. Unfortunately for him, he did. I think he thought that since he was former Special Forces, he could handle you. I guess pride really does come before a fall."

This guy wasn't easily provoked. Okay, so I can't ruffle his feathers. Logan let out a slow breath. "So let's cut to the chase, shall we? What do you want from me? Obviously, it's something you thought I wouldn't give you, or you wouldn't have sent your former employee here. So what is it?"

The other man started to speak, but Logan cut him off, "Sorry. One more thing before you tell me your sob story, asshole: Can I have something else to call you? My wife tells me I swear too much, that it's become worse in the last few years. So if you don't give me something else, I'm just going to continue with my own pet names for you—such as 'fuckhead' or something cuter—against my wife's wishes."

The other man laughed softly. "Very colorful, Mr. West. I wouldn't want you to betray your wife's wishes now. So please, call me Juan."

"Fine, Juan. What do you want?"

There was a pause. Logan didn't break the silence. He waited. "I want an artifact that your team acquired during your tour in Fallujah. It's a flag, to be precise. One of Saddam Hussein's flags of Iraq that you or a member of your team now possesses. Do you know what I'm talking about?"

Logan didn't have it but he knew who did, and he sure as hell wasn't going to let this man know it, at least not without trying to glean some information from him first. He had to be smart or Juan would easily see through his ploy. He looked at his watch. *I've got plenty of time before Mike gets here.*

"What's so important about a flag? You know you can order one online? Seems it would be a lot cheaper and easier than coming after me for it. My prices are rather steep, as Roberto here can attest." Logan waited for a response. He sensed Juan growing agitated. He was right.

"Enough jokes and small talk, Mr. West. Do you have the flag or

not? If not, don't waste my time . . . or your *wife's* for that matter."
A chill ran up Logan's spine.

"What the hell does that mean, motherfucker? You definitely
don't want to go where you're going. And now that I think about it,
I think I'll stick with calling you 'asshole,' asshole."

"Let me be perfectly clear, Mr. West. Either you give me what I
want, or you find it for me. Otherwise, you'll never see Sarah again.
I don't want to, but I'll have one of my men hurt and then kill her.
Please don't test my resolve." Juan paused, the words hammering
Logan like shots to his chest. He said it matter-of-factly, and Logan
didn't doubt he'd do it.

Logan closed his eyes as the dark rage tried to overwhelm him.
The fury, combined with his physical state, created such a blinding
pain in his head, he thought his skull might fracture into a thousand
tiny pieces.

*Get ahold of yourself, Logan. If you can't think straight, you'll make
mistakes, mistakes that might get Sarah hurt or killed.*

He'd seen mistakes kill careful men before. In Iraq, a Marine
had spray-painted "Complacency Kills" on a concrete barrier near
Al Qaim, a city on the Syrian border. All too true, it was a constant
reminder to be ever vigilant.

When he finally spoke, his voice was barely audible. An observer
might have suddenly mistaken the good-looking man with an
athlete's physique and chiseled facial features for the devil himself,
green eyes sparkling furiously within a dancing mask of pure, violent
hatred.

"Listen very carefully, Juan. I'm going to find you, I'm going to
stop you, and then I'm going to kill you after I've spoiled your little
game. You'll be seeing me soon."

Logan was already leaping up the basement stairs as he hung up
the phone. He stuck it in his cargo pocket as he dialed Mike with
his personal cell phone in his other hand.

Mike answered immediately. *He's expecting me.* "Mike, meet me at Sarah's house now, specifically, at the entrance to the community. I think—scratch that—I *know* she's in trouble . . . serious trouble. These people just upped the ante. I'll call you from my car. You better grab our tactical gear. We're going to need it. Talk to you in three minutes," he said and hung up.

He prayed Juan's threat was just a bluff, another way to get him to give up the flag. He had to know that if he harmed Sarah, Logan would never do what he wanted. Unfortunately, the logic didn't calm the dread he felt.

The day had rapidly spiraled out of control. If he had any chance to get out of this mess, he had to take it now before Juan could make the next move. *It's my turn, asshole.* He had to get ahead of whatever storm was coming before it consumed the only woman he loved. *I'm coming, baby. Hold on.*

CHAPTER 3

RURAL MARYLAND

Sarah West fumed over her soon-to-be ex-husband. Logan had dropped Daly off with no notice. He'd told her he was going out of town, but when she asked him if everything was okay, he'd lied to her. She knew it, but he'd insisted he was fine.

He told her he was going to ski Whiteface Mountain in Upstate New York. He said he needed to "clear his head" and that "cold air and fresh snow might help."

She was certain something was wrong. She'd tried calling him several times since he'd left, but with no luck. He hadn't answered. That in itself wasn't uncommon, but she'd sensed something different about him after he'd left. He seemed more distant than when they'd been married, if that was possible.

Sarah had thrown herself into her work for the last three days, working feverishly on her housing crisis article for *The Economist*. Unfortunately, the article, her daily runs, and quality time with Daly, their three-year-old golden retriever, still hadn't diminished the frustration she felt toward Logan.

She'd immersed herself in some serious house cleaning, hoping it might distract her from her concerns. It failed . . . miserably. She was furious that even now, when she was about to file divorce papers, he continued to weigh heavily on her mind. It was ludicrous.

Cooking had been her next diversion. As she placed a chicken parmigiana in the lower oven, she felt Daly paw her right foot imploringly, as if to ask, *Where's mine?* She looked down and smiled, scratching behind his ears. He grinned and tilted his head to one side.

"What's that, big guy? You already had your lunch. Sorry. This is for me for later."

Daly whimpered and placed both his paws on her thighs, his sleek face open in a goofy and loving smile.

"Okay. Okay. How about this? Let me go check the laundry upstairs, and then we'll head out back until this chicken's done. Sound like a plan?"

Daly barked once, removed his paws from Sarah's legs, and scampered over to the patio door that opened onto the back deck. His paws click-clacked on the hardwood floor as he moved. He stopped at the door and sat on his haunches, looking back and forth between the gigantic backyard and Sarah, waiting expectantly.

"I'll be right back. Just give me a minute."

Daly barked one more time in acknowledgment. *Okay. I'll be here.*

As Sarah walked through the kitchen, she admired the rolling hills and woods that extended in all directions. It was a view of which she never tired. She fought the urge to stop and stare, as she often did at this time of day.

The setting was serene, unlike the chaos and emotional maelstrom that had been their lives until she'd finally given Logan an ultimatum in March of 2006. "Deal with your drinking, or I'm out. I can't stand it anymore."

Unfortunately, Logan had chosen to ignore the problem until she'd finally kicked him out of their house. Sarah was eternally relieved that Logan had finally gotten sober—for his sake—but by then, too much damage had been done for their relationship to right itself.

The five-thousand-square-foot home on twenty acres of what she called "suburban countryside" had initially served as their own private refuge from the outside world. It sometimes felt like it was a million miles away, when in reality, it was only miles from Route 40, north of West Friendship, MD. She was within an hour by car of Baltimore, Annapolis, and DC.

Still, when they'd first moved here after Logan separated from the Marine Corps, it had been a nice fantasy for both of them to imagine they were completely secluded, protected from the horrors of the outside world that Logan knew too well. Unfortunately, the horrors had been in his head, and he couldn't run from them, no matter where they lived.

She couldn't believe it had already been four years, but a lot had happened since Logan's honorable discharge. Logan still refused to talk about what had so fundamentally changed him in Fallujah. He'd walked away from a stellar career in Force Recon, the elite of the elite as far as the Marine Corps was concerned.

She'd been to the funerals with him, and what little he did tell her was enough to prevent her from asking more questions.

For some reason, Logan blamed himself and his headquarters for his men's deaths. The ironic part was that whatever had happened had made her husband a hero. He'd been awarded a Navy Cross, but he hadn't wanted it. He told her he didn't deserve it, that he'd failed to keep his Marines alive, that he'd been deceived into doing something that was a disaster he should've seen coming.

Sarah didn't think he could've done anything in reality, at least not from what John Quick had told her. But it didn't matter. Logan carried the guilt like a physical weight threatening to break his back. Psychologically, it had.

He'd promised to tell her the full story someday, but that had been four years ago. His drinking had escalated and resulted in his breaking that promise—one of many, now that she thought about it.

To shroud the situation with even more mystery, Logan had actually been provided with full retirement benefits even though he'd only served ten years. No one received that type of compensation, especially from the Marine Corps or any service in the Department of Defense.

Logan had tried to reject the benefits, but the Marine Corps had insisted. Lieutenant General Jack Longstreet—now the commandant of the Marine Corps—had visited their home one evening several months after Logan had returned from his deployment. She knew General Longstreet had been with Logan in Fallujah. Their conversation had lasted less than thirty minutes. When the general left, Logan refused to discuss the visit, but he did acquiesce to the benefits package.

It was only several months after that visit that Sarah discovered Logan was donating each pension check directly to a fund established for children of fallen Marines who'd served in Iraq. She hadn't been surprised.

Logan was independently wealthy, the heir to a small fortune that he never flaunted. His humility was always evident, even though he had more than one reason to be proud. It was one of the attributes she'd loved about him . . . before the drinking began to destroy the man.

She crossed through the hallway to the foyer and turned to the stairs, failing to look out the sidelight windows that framed the heavy oak double front doors. As a result, she didn't see the four men moving up the wooded driveway.

CHAPTER 4

Logan fought to contain his panic. He'd been trying to call Sarah every few minutes from the car. He was still twenty minutes away.

Logan called Mike again. "She's not answering. What's your ETA? I'm about twenty minutes out. If I don't get killed by one of Juan's hired thugs, this fucking hangover will do the job for him."

"Christ, Logan. You sure you're okay to do this? I can have HRT there and staged within an hour. Just say the word." Mike paused before continuing. "Hell, brother, I probably should. You know that. But it's Sarah, and it's your call."

Logan knew the FBI's Hostage Rescue Team members were the most elite unit in the country for this type of situation. Most were former operators and trigger pullers from the Special Ops community, including Delta, the Navy SEALs, and Green Berets. Still, this problem was his, and he refused to allow the FBI to jeopardize his wife—*soon to be ex-wife*—until he knew what was going on. *She's probably fine. Could be any number of reasons she's not answering.*

"No way, Mike. Let's hope everything is okay at Sarah's, but if it's not, we do this ourselves."

Mike knew Logan wouldn't yield, and no matter what laws he had to bend, he'd back whatever play Logan had in mind.

"You got it, brother. I just hope we're in time. See you in twenty."

———

RURAL MARYLAND

Sarah was upstairs in the hallway laundry room. She loved the convenience of it on the second floor instead of in the basement. She'd just pulled her load of workout clothes from the washer when she heard the *beep-beep-beep* of the alarm system. A door or window had just been opened.

Had Logan decided to pick up Daly without calling? What the hell was he thinking? She now had one more offense to add to his growing list.

She was about to call out when she heard Daly scrambling across the kitchen toward the direction of their garage, growling and barking as he ran.

It wasn't Logan.

She started to move to the railing overlooking the foyer when she heard two loud gunshots reverberate throughout the house. *Noooooo!* She stifled a scream as her mind registered that the intruder had just shot their beloved dog.

She froze in her tracks as a toxic mixture of fear and grief smashed into the pit of her stomach. The panic gripped her, and her heart accelerated wildly. She was cemented to the carpet, transfixed by her horror.

She heard Daly yelp in pain and surprise, followed by a thump as his sixty pounds fell to the kitchen floor. She sank to the floor, temporarily overwhelmed by a paralyzing sadness.

Sarah had a chilling realization. *Whoever was in the house was dangerous. If he shot our dog, he'll likely shoot me as well.* She had to move. Fast.

Now wasn't the time to grieve for Daly. That would come later. She wasn't going down without a fight.

After marrying a Marine, a Force Recon one for that matter, there was no way in hell she was going to allow herself to be a victim. Her grief was replaced by an ember of fury that grew brighter with each moment.

Sarah took two breaths to stop the shaking from her initial shock. She moved quickly and quietly to their master bedroom.

The entrance to the large bedroom had two doors. She carefully closed the right one behind her, leaving it open half an inch to prevent the latches from making even the slightest sound. She propped the left open halfway, allowing only a partial view of the bedroom from the hallway.

As she moved to the closet, she heard voices downstairs. They spoke in Spanish, a language she didn't speak or understand.

This is unreal. This can't be happening. Then she thought of Logan. Regardless of the current state of their marriage, she heard his voice in her mind, firm but silently encouraging her. *Keep moving or you're going to die.*

She moved into one of the oversized walk-in closets, the one that had belonged to Logan before he moved out. In a back corner of the closet on the middle shelf she found what she was looking for—her husband's Benelli M2 tactical shotgun.

He'd left it for her when he'd moved out. He'd shown her how to use it and said he didn't need it since he was taking his pistols. He'd said, "Save it for a rainy day," giving her a wide grin. She didn't think he'd still be smiling if he knew she was actually about to use it to fight for her life.

She grabbed the black, menacing shotgun by the pistol grip with her left hand and pulled the cocking lever backward slowly—just as he'd shown her—to confirm it was loaded. She saw a shell in the chamber and exhaled in relief. *This was real.*

She couldn't recall what Logan had loaded it with, but he'd told her, "Hon, if anyone ever comes into this house, and you shoot him with this, he's not getting out." He'd smiled when he said it, like most gun owners, proud of what their weapons could do but never really expecting to use them. She just hoped she'd live long enough to let Logan know how effective his shotgun was.

She grabbed the spare box of shells from the shelf, although she doubted she'd have time to reload. Each shot had to count.

She moved back into the bedroom and lay down on the floor on the left side of the bed, lining up the shotgun's sights on the small opening at the entrance to the bedroom. She flicked off the safety and waited.

CHAPTER 5

Juan hadn't told Cesar that there was a dog in the house. He knew Cesar had been terrified of dogs from childhood, where he'd grown up on the outskirts of Ciudad Juárez. Wild dogs had roamed the streets of his neighborhood in the evenings. Cesar and his friends had been chased by the predatory packs on more than one occasion. It had been just one more dangerous aspect of living near Juárez.

When Cesar entered the house through the side door near the garage and the yellow dog leapt at him in defense of its home, Cesar had panicked and fired two shots with his Glock 9mm pistol. The first one had missed and struck the wall on the other side of the kitchen, but the second round caught the dog in the left shoulder and knocked it to the floor.

As Cesar moved past the dying animal, he looked down and saw the dog following him with its gaze, blood leaking from the gunshot wound down its fur to the floor. The dog was still defying him with its last moments, as if to say, *This is my house. You don't belong here.* The dog's eyes closed, and it shuddered one last time.

Cesar knew the West woman was home, but there was no sign of her in the kitchen. It was a big house—much bigger than he'd expected—and he knew they'd have to search it carefully.

Their instructions had been to capture her, no matter what. Juan had emphasized that point.

"At all costs, Cesar. It's critical that she be kept alive." If the boss wanted her alive, then so be it. They had their orders, and they never deviated from them.

Juan Black compensated them greatly for their specialized work, but Mr. Black also had a ruthless way of maintaining order if his instructions weren't followed precisely.

He thought of Marcos Rivera. The image of his head lying in a box, his face peeled away so that it actually rested on top of his black hair, wasn't a pleasant one. Cesar was a hard man, but Juan Black still scared him.

Cesar turned to the other three men with him and spoke in Mexican-accented Spanish. "Angel,"—he pronounced it *AHN-hell*—"you're with me. We'll go upstairs. Antonio, you and Tomas check the rest of this floor and the basement. Again, no one kills the woman. Her husband is too important. If she's dead, he won't cooperate. Understand?"

Antonio and Tomas nodded and moved into the dining room, adjacent to the kitchen. Cesar knew both men would do precisely as they'd been told. Like Juan Black, Cesar also knew a thing or two about disciplining subordinates.

Cesar moved to the foyer, Angel following and watching the area behind them. Silence. *The bitch must be hiding. Her dog was braver than she was. Like all women, a cowardly whore . . .*

Cesar's mother had abandoned him when he was seven, leaving him to care for his alcoholic father. His views of women had been formed at a young age. It was one of many reasons he preferred to be alone, refusing to compromise with a member of the inferior sex.

They moved up the curving staircase, making as little noise as possible. They reached the top, and Cesar turned right, spotting the entrance to the master bedroom. The door was ajar. *I'll bet she's cow-*

ering in the corner like a scared little girl. "Search the other rooms. I'll take this one." Angel turned left and crept down the hallway.

Cesar raised his pistol in front of him as he moved toward the open doorway. He smiled at the thought of the pleasure he'd have once he captured the West woman. *I'll find you. You can hide, but I'll find you. This is going to be fun.*

———

Sarah heard the man moving down the hallway. He was quiet, but the soft rustle of his shoes on the plush carpet revealed his presence. The footsteps stopped outside the bedroom door.

She struggled to control her breathing and heartbeat. Her world felt as if at any moment it would turn on its axis, and she'd pass out into oblivion before she had a chance to defend herself. She blinked hard and squinted her eyes, focusing on the door . . . waiting.

She knew the moment was upon her as she heard steady breathing on the other side of the door. She suppressed an urge to scream at the intruder just to shatter the maddening silence. Instead, she concentrated fiercely on the opening, the sight of the shotgun aimed where she assumed his chest would be. She intended to make sure whoever was on the other side didn't get a second chance to hurt her. She was playing for keeps.

———

Cesar hesitated outside the master bedroom. Through the opening, he saw another door leading to a large bathroom. Light from a skylight reflected off the surface of a glass shower. He heard no movement. *She has to be here.* He could feel it.

He wanted to hurt her, but he knew the mission outweighed his own selfish desires. He could at least terrorize her while he had her captive, if nothing else but to remind her of her place in a world of men. First though, he had to find her. He entered the bedroom, his Glock raised in front of him with both arms, searching for his target.

As he stepped across the doorway, his eyes glanced to the right into what appeared to be a gigantic closet. *Americans were so spoiled.* He saw shelves of sweaters and racks of hanging blouses, skirts, and dresses. It only made him resent her more.

Cesar took another step as he turned to the left, and he immediately realized he'd made a fatal mistake. He froze midstride. *She's been patient, like a predator waiting for her prey. I misjudged her . . . bitch.* His mind reeled at the knowledge that he'd been lured into a trap by a woman. He opened his mouth to shout when the woman pulled the trigger on the ugly shotgun aimed directly at him. He only hoped the pain would be brief.

———

Sarah saw the barrel of the Glock before anything else. *This monster killed my dog.* With that thought echoing in her head, she felt another wave of calm wash over her. As he moved into the room, she recognized a thick black mustache, and slick, jet-black hair parted on the left side.

He looked into her closet with disgust, which further sealed his fate. He moved farther into the room and turned toward her. She waited for the right moment. He finally spotted her lying down next to the bed.

As soon as her blue eyes locked on to his dark-brown ones, his eyebrows rose in surprise, and she felt a small chill of satisfaction knowing she'd outsmarted him. Without hesitation, she pulled the trigger on the Benelli. *This is for my dog, you sonofabitch. You're done.*

The thunderous roar of the shotgun blast echoed and was magnified in the enclosed space of the bedroom. Her ears rang, but there was no other sound. *Oh my God. I can't hear.*

More important, her aim was true. She watched the gunman take the full brunt of the shotgun triple-aught buck load—what Logan had tactically decided would do the most damage in close quarters—in the chest. Eight .36-inch balls shredded his clothes and turned his chest into a bloody pulp. At a range of less than ten feet, three of the balls tore holes in his heart, immediately stopping it and the blood flow to his brain, killing him instantly.

As the shotgun ejected the empty shell, Sarah watched the gunman's body bounce off the closed door and crumple to the floor facedown on the carpet. Blood slowly began to soak her carpet, blossoming on the fibers the way a paper towel absorbs a dark liquid.

Fortunately, she didn't have time to process the fact that she'd just taken a life. Through the ringing in her ears, she faintly heard a second intruder shouting in Spanish, racing down the hallway toward her.

She tried to remain calm and focused. She knew if she moved, she'd reveal her position and the second intruder would have the advantage.

Logan had often talked about how people in movies and TV shows always made the wrong choices when chased or trapped in a house. It was a soapbox she'd tired of but was grateful for at the moment. "If you're ever trapped in a room, just keep shooting as they come in. Unless they're coming armed with flash-bang grenades and assault weapons, you have the advantage. If there's more than one, they'll know you're there, but you still have the upper hand. It will suck, but it's the only play." She was about to test Logan's theory.

The second intruder stopped outside the bedroom doors. His partner's body was visible through the doorway. She was sure that was why he'd stopped shouting.

As he tried to figure out what had happened, Sarah remained still and silent. Her finger was on the trigger. She prepared to squeeze it a second time.

The second gunman suddenly spoke, startling her, causing her to lose her focus momentarily. "Mrs. West, let me be blunt. We are not here to kill you. We need you as leverage to persuade your husband to help us. Cesar—the man you just shot—obviously underestimated you. I won't do the same. We can wait here all night if necessary. It will serve the same purpose, since you're trapped. If you move, I'll see you." She knew he was right.

"If you come out now, this will go much smoother. It's going to end the same, no matter what you do. My orders are not to kill you, but I will shoot you if you leave me no choice. If you want to stay there, that suits me fine as well. You have nowhere to go and can't do any harm from there. Like I said, Mrs. West, we have all night. More men are on the way. There's nothing you can do. One way or another, you're coming out of that room. Count on it."

More men? My husband? She had killed this man's partner, and it hadn't even fazed him. *Who were these people?* She knew it didn't matter. She only had one move left, and she had to make it quickly. She exhaled again, aimed at the slightly ajar door panel and pulled the trigger a second time as she silently prayed for help.

BOOM!

Luck was on her side—or at least, not on the gunman's—since the second shotgun blast shattered the door panel into small fragments of splintered wood. The shards mixed with the buckshot and created a lethal cloud of wood and lead that struck the second intruder on the upper left torso. Several large splinters tore into the side of his neck, piercing his carotid artery. Blood splashed onto the carpet in a crimson waterfall.

Sarah heard the gunman fall to the floor. *Logan would be proud.* She waited for the ringing in her ears to subside. She didn't hear any sounds in the house, but she couldn't be sure it was empty. It was a risk she was willing to take. She knew she had to get out of the house now. If reinforcements really were coming, she wanted to be as far away as possible before they arrived.

She quickly rose to her feet, keeping the shotgun in front of her with her finger on the trigger. She moved to the doorway, past the first gunman's corpse and into the hallway.

She saw the second gunman, lying in his own blood, which continued to pump from the side of his neck, his dark eyes vacant. *Why were these men after Logan?*

She didn't have the luxury of time to contemplate. She needed to leave. *Now. And fast.*

As she sprinted down the hallway and down the spiral staircase into the foyer, it never occurred to her that there might be two more men in the house, professionals waiting patiently for her to come to them.

CHAPTER 6

When Antonio and Tomas heard the first shotgun blast, they were in the basement on the opposite side of the house. They'd been clearing the first of two guest bedrooms connected to a gigantic common area that served as an entertainment area and fitness center.

When the shotgun blast reverberated through the walls and floors, the men exchanged a wary glance. Both immediately knew something unplanned had just occurred: neither Cesar nor Angel carried a shotgun.

Antonio thought he heard a voice shouting upstairs, but it was extremely faint. The floors and insulation separating them dampened the speech to an almost inaudible level. "Let's go," Antonio said.

The two men exited the bedroom and moved through the common area with a single purpose. Once up the basement stairs, they'd entered the hallway outside the kitchen.

A second shotgun blast startled them once more. Both men froze. Neither spoke. They were too well trained to reveal their position.

Antonio whispered, "Give it a minute. We wait here until we hear something else." The men positioned themselves on either side of the hallway entrance to the kitchen, waiting for any sign of movement.

Antonio stared at the dead dog on the floor. He was a mercenary and paid handsomely for his services. As a result, he compartmental-

ized his personal feelings on a job like this one. He wasn't supposed
to know the details of their mission, but he'd overheard Juan and
Roberto talking.

He knew what they were doing would change the political balance in the Middle East. He didn't care. The money trumped everything—politics, ideals. None of it mattered to him. So it was ironic
that he felt a twinge of remorse at the sight.

Antonio had owned a yellow Labrador as a boy. It had been his
closest friend until he was twelve years old, when the dog had somehow escaped the confines of his family's fenced-in backyard. The dog
never returned.

He'd desperately wanted to believe the dog had been picked up
by another family, free to live out its existence. Unfortunately, Antonio knew the world was a different place. Things like that didn't
happen in Mexico. There were no fairy-tale endings. More than
likely, the dog had been killed by a vehicle, or worse.

Quick footsteps from the front staircase shifted Antonio's attention from his troubled memories to the present.

Neither man moved, their dark eyes fixed on the kitchen entryway. *Wait for her . . . a few more seconds.*

Antonio heard soft shoes strike the hardwood floor of the foyer.
There was a squeak as the West woman turned sharply and moved
toward the kitchen. And then for some reason, she suddenly stopped
in the hallway.

Antonio wondered what had happened. *Did she hear us?* Then
he realized why she'd stopped, and he felt a moment of sympathy
for this woman he didn't know. She'd seen her lifeless dog lying in
a pool of blood on the kitchen floor, and the sight had stopped her
cold in her tracks.

He heard a stifled sob of grief, but then she regained her composure. Oblivious of the two men, she walked into the kitchen toward
her fallen companion.

Antonio waited for her to reach him before he acted. As soon as she entered the kitchen in front of him, shotgun held in front of her in both arms, Antonio lashed out and covered the distance between them in one stride.

She'd heard the rustle of his clothes, but it was too late to react.

Antonio snaked his right arm around her throat and locked his right hand into the inside of his left elbow. He placed his left hand on the back of her head and squeezed.

The suddenness of the attack forced her to drop the shotgun, which fell loudly to the hardwood floor. Unlike them, she was not a trained soldier.

As Antonio secured his grip behind her head, he heard a clatter as something else hit the kitchen floor. He looked down and saw that she'd dropped her cell phone. It was in the process of making a call.

"Turn that off, Tomas," he hissed to his partner as he applied more leverage to the back of her head. "She's trying to call someone."

Tomas quickly bent down and picked up the phone. He saw a small picture of her husband, Logan West, smiling back up at him. *Even on a small screen, this was a fearsome-looking man. It was in his eyes.* Before Logan could answer, Tomas pressed the "end" button and disconnected the call.

"It didn't go through. I think we're okay."

Antonio grunted acknowledgment and squeezed harder. She never had a chance. A gasp escaped her throat. Before she could scream, Antonio's iron forearms and biceps cut off the circulation of blood to her head. Even with no oxygen, she continued to fight, surprising him. *She's stronger than I thought.*

Instead of underestimating her, which had obviously been fatal for the other team, Antonio applied more pressure. He was as calculating with his use of force as a doctor prescribing an especially dangerous medication. *Just a little more . . .* and after an additional ten seconds of struggling, the West woman finally went limp in his arms.

CHAPTER 7

Logan was parked and waiting. His was the only vehicle in sight. He'd pulled off at the end of a service road just inside the community entrance. There was a guardhouse, but it wasn't staffed during the day. All residents owned electronic key cards that provided twenty-four-hour access.

He exited the vehicle and forced himself to stand still as he waited for Mike. Now that the initial hangover was finally subsiding, withdrawal symptoms had begun. He'd started trembling approximately twenty minutes ago.

Out of desperation and necessity, he'd grabbed a bottle of Maker's Mark as he ran out of his house. As he waited, he swallowed a few gulps of the smooth brown liquid.

He felt the immediate warm rush as the alcohol hit his stomach. After a painful moment of nausea, the familiar sensation he was physically addicted to became the dominant feeling. His thirst temporarily satisfied, he concentrated on his breathing as the alcohol coursed through his system.

Within a few minutes, the shakes diminished in intensity. He was ashamed that it had come to this, that he'd used whiskey to avoid severe withdrawal. Unfortunately, he didn't have the luxury or time to suffer through the various stages of sobering up. He had to be as clear-minded as possible for what was coming, his aim true and without hesitation.

If someone did have Sarah, Logan knew she'd be counting on him. No matter what he'd done to her in the past, he wasn't about to let her down again. If that meant using the same thing to save her life that had wrecked their marriage, so be it. *Sometimes you do have to make a deal with the devil.*

The isolation of the gated community was an advantage for Logan and Mike. There was no traffic at this time of day. It was still a few hours before the evening rush.

The fact that there were only twelve homes in the entire community also played in their favor. With approximately a half mile between each home, the chances of a neighbor's seeing anything was remote.

A dog barked from across a field behind him. *Must be from one of the other homes. No strays out here.* He didn't know which neighbors owned dogs, since neither Sarah nor Logan had made an effort to meet any of them. Seclusion had been a main attraction of the location for both of them.

He thought of Daly. He hoped his loyal retriever was okay. Other than his wife, the dog had been the only other thing he'd truly loved in his life in recent years. Daly had helped preserve his sanity, even when he'd been trying to self-destruct in an alcoholic rage. No matter what he said or did when drunk, he'd never hurt his dog. On more than one occasion, Daly had brought him back from the brink of some very dark places.

He looked up to see Mike's dark-green Toyota Land Cruiser pass through the gate. Logan had given Mike a key card for emergencies. Now was definitely one of those times.

Logan moved to the back of Mike's Toyota as it stopped behind his own Land Cruiser. Mike cut the engine and stepped out to join him at the rear of the vehicle, where Logan had already opened the hatch to pull out the assault gear Mike had brought with him.

Mike looked hard at Logan without speaking, anger and concern mixed on his face. He noticed the fresh wound on Logan's left cheek.

"Jesus, Logan, you okay? That looks like hell. You need anything for it? I have my med kit."

Logan shook his head, gestured to the trunk of Mike's SUV, and said, "Mike, I'm fine. The only thing that's going to make me feel better is what's in here and what I'm going to do with it."

Mike nodded. He knew it was pointless to argue or ask questions, at least right now.

"Fair enough. As for Sarah, first we need to get eyes-on. Then we can figure out how to handle it. Until we get an idea as to who's inside—if there is anyone—we can't just go in guns blazing. We have to figure out who the fuck they are and what they really want." He touched Logan's shoulder to get his attention. Logan snapped his head around and glared at him, an impatient intensity on his face, green eyes blazing.

"Logan, depending on how many men there are, we have to take at least one of them alive. We'll need him for information, especially on this Juan character or whatever the hell his name is. The more information we get, the better this whole thing goes. I can contact my uncle to find a secure location where we can sort this out with the appropriate security and methods." His words hung in the cool air. He prayed that Logan saw the logic in his reasoning. He was relieved when his friend finally spoke.

"We do it right, Mike. If we can, take at least one—if not more—alive, but if I think for one second that Sarah might be in danger, I'm shooting to kill, and you know I don't miss—even if I am hungover as all hell." The whiskey was working its magic. He was starting to feel somewhat normal. *Normal for a bingeing alcoholic who just woke up from a two-day blackout,* he thought.

"One last thing," Logan went on. "We approach the house from the back and conduct a solid recon from a distance. And then we wait until just after the end of dusk before we make our move. It'll provide us with the most cover and the best chance of success."

"Good plan." Mike grabbed his own bag from the back of the SUV. "You know, Logan, you're going to have to figure out how to stay sober once and for all. You had what? Seven? Eight months? I don't know what happened." He paused, redirecting his thoughts. "You can tell me later. First, let's make sure your wife is safe."

Having established the ground rules, Logan relaxed a little bit as he looked across the surrounding environment. Even though there was no one in sight and the only sound he'd heard was the call of one lonely dog, he still felt exposed in the middle of his rural neighborhood.

"Deal . . . when this is over." His voice hardened. "But now, down to business. What toys did you bring?"

Mike smiled. Jokes were good. It meant Logan was in that focused state of mind all trained killers possessed for this kind of work.

"Weapons first," he said, as he opened the first of two black bags. "I brought you a suppressed HK MP7—we upgraded from the MP5—with a reflex sight I mounted myself. It's zeroed out to three hundred meters, but for close quarters, someone as trained as you could probably put a grouping on a quarter at anything out to fifty yards. You also have your Kimber Tactical II forty-five, also with a suppressor." He handed the weapons to Logan.

"No suppressor. Won't need it. Neighbors might hear shots, but they'll assume it's someone hunting." Logan detached the narrow tube from the end of the weapon. "If I have to shoot, I want it loud. The noise might give me a slight tactical advantage in such a confined space, although I doubt it. If these guys are trained like the asshole at my house, it won't make a difference, but you never know."

Mike continued with the inventory. "You also have two flashbangs. I didn't know what your plan was, so I brought them just in case you *didn't* want to kill everyone." Logan smiled at the remark.

"Where's the fun in that?"

Mike ignored him. "And for the final touch, your Force Recon Mark II fighting knife. I remembered the one you had in Ramadi." He paused at the graphic memory of an insurgent with his throat cut and bleeding to death inside a stairwell. He blinked his eyes as if to remove it from his mind.

"But first, put this on so you can carry all this shit." Mike handed Logan a black tactical vest with several pockets and loops for the various weapons. Logan slid his arms into the vest and zipped it up. Underneath, he wore the neoprene short-sleeved fitted black undershirt he'd put on at home.

"It's perfect. Matches my tee shirt. And Sarah tells me I have no fashion sense. Can you believe that?" he said, deadpan, while he secured the grenades and knife to his vest.

There was a nylon holster for the pistol on the left side of the vest, positioned low and at an angle for fast access. Logan holstered the Kimber.

"You're killing me, Logan."

"Not you, Mike. Whoever's inside my house," he said seriously. Then, to emphasize the point, he looked at Mike and added like a chided child, "Only if I have no choice. I know."

Mike glanced at Logan as he handed him the last item in his bag—a tactical communications secure personal radio. "Here's the throat mic and earpiece. The radio is one-hundred-twenty-eight-bit encrypted. No one will hear us, even if they're trying to."

Logan secured the throat microphone around his neck. "Feels similar to the ones we used in Force."

"I know. That's why we're using it now."

"You know the way to a man's heart, Mike. What did you bring for yourself?"

Mike smiled and grabbed a large, black canvas rifle bag. "My personal weapon for accuracy—the Israeli Tavor STAR-21, complete with a bipod and Trijicon four-times magnification ACOG scope. Bottom line—if you need me to make a precision shot, this is the baby to do it with. I may be a fed, but I'm still one of the best shots in the FBI. Satisfied?"

Logan looked from the weapon back to Mike and saw the quiet confidence exuding from him. "Absolutely. Let's go. Like I said, we'll approach from the back where the woods can provide some cover. Once we're in position, we'll wait. Unless they're using night-vision goggles, they'll never see us coming. We should be there in approximately fifteen minutes, and we'll have about another two hours before sunset."

Mike closed the hatch on the Land Cruiser and locked the vehicle. Logan turned back to him. "One more thing. I don't have the time to express my full gratitude to you right now. I know what you're risking. I appreciate it more than I can say." He smiled wickedly. "Let's just make sure it's worth it."

Both men checked their weapons and gear and then quickly jogged across the road into the woods beyond.

CHAPTER 8

Antonio and Tomas were nervous. It was nearing five o'clock, and Roberto should've called by now to confirm he'd captured Logan West. Antonio was accustomed to operational uncertainty after his time in Iraq and Somalia, but if he didn't hear from Roberto in another fifteen minutes, he'd have no choice but to try and reach him.

If that fails, I may have to call Mr. Black. He shuddered at the thought.

Tomas had searched the entire house for the flag. After the first search turned up nothing, Antonio ordered him to do it a second time, with the same result. It wasn't in the house.

Antonio knew that was why they needed the woman alive—to apply leverage on her husband. He'd either give them what they wanted or watch his beautiful brown-haired wife die. It was his choice.

Tomas hadn't disturbed Cesar's and Angel's corpses. He left them where they fell, after confirming that neither one had any type of identification. Antonio planned to take the bodies when they left, but if something else went wrong, he was prepared to leave them behind. It was the team's standard operating procedure, but these kinds of missions often went sideways.

No shit. Cesar and Angel are dead. This job's definitely gone sideways.

Sarah West had posed no problem since she'd regained consciousness and found herself duct-taped to a kitchen chair, her hands zip-tied behind her.

Her initial reaction had been as he expected. She'd cried briefly when she saw the pool of blood on the kitchen floor where her dog had died. She knew he was dead, but they'd removed his body to try and lessen the trauma.

Tomas had carried the dog's corpse out the sliding glass door into the backyard, where he'd placed the dog in a shadow near the side of the house.

Antonio hadn't expected her *second* reaction. Instead of screaming or begging for them to release her, she'd only said in a low, defiant voice, "I don't know who you are or what you want, but if this has anything to do with my husband and he finds you, God help you both. He's going to kill you."

Antonio was amused by her display of bravery but only shook his head as he said, "Mrs. West, your husband is likely already in our custody. And as for God, I've been doing this long enough to know that there is no God."

Sarah didn't respond. She didn't want to give him the least amount of satisfaction.

"You're right on one count though. You *do* have no idea what this is all about, and unfortunately, I'm not about to tell you. Hopefully, this will end well for all of us. It all depends on your husband."

The calmness in his voice was unsettling. Sarah replied, "Go fuck yourself." She then closed her eyes and lowered her chin to her chest as all three of them continued to wait, the West woman for her husband, and Antonio and Tomas for Roberto.

The next hour proved uneventful, the only excitement occurring when the backyard flood lights turned on unexpectedly as darkness engulfed the gigantic expanse behind the West house.

Sarah told them they came on every night and remained on a

timer until eleven o'clock. She said the lights helped keep the abundant wildlife at bay, especially the curious raccoons known to chew through trash can lids or screen doors in hopes of finding a treasure trove of garbage.

Tomas approached the large bay window every few minutes and gazed into the backyard, as if he expected a wild animal to emerge from the darkness and charge the glass.

Antonio glanced at his watch again. A few more minutes and he'd try Mr. Black. Neither he nor Roberto was answering the phone, which distressed him.

He looked up and saw the West woman staring intently at him, as if she knew something he didn't. Her stare made him uncomfortable. He looked away and continued to wait.

CHAPTER 9

"I'm in position, approximately forty feet from the bay window, out of their line of sight in the shadows. I can see Sarah. She's tied to a chair in the middle of the kitchen." His wife looked haggard but not defeated. *That's a good sign.* "Motherfuckers . . ." His voice trailed off in quiet fury.

He needed her to be alert. When he assaulted his house, a place he'd called home for several years, she couldn't panic and do something rash. That was the greatest danger in the coming moments, but Logan knew he couldn't plan for every contingency.

The reality was that fear and panic usually led to the tragic deaths of many innocent hostages. Sarah was tired, but at least she still had her faculties.

He saw no sign of Daly. Logan prayed that they'd locked Daly up in the garage or in the basement, but all he heard was silence. Daly wasn't barking, which likely meant . . . He refused to let his mind go there.

He took a deep breath, suppressing the hot rage he felt in his chest. He *had* to compartmentalize his emotions or he'd make a mistake. Like panic and fear, mistakes were often killers.

"No sign of Daly. You know what that means." Mike didn't respond. "I'll take one alive, but if Daly's dead, only one lives, and that one is going to wish he didn't by the time I'm through with him."

Mike knew his friend was dead serious. "Roger, Logan. We get Sarah, and then we'll figure out where Daly is. I know what he means to you. As for the bad guys, I see two gunmen in the kitchen. So far, that's all. You have eyes on both?"

Mike was in a prone position approximately one hundred yards away, next to a fallen tree out of the reach of the flood lights. The tree had been a casualty of the freak fall storms the area had endured. Fortunately for Mike, Logan had been too busy to deal with the deadwood. Now it served as the ideal concealment.

"I see one standing near the window, but I don't have eyes on the other. Where is he?"

"He's next to your island countertop." Mike stared through his scope. The image of the man filled his view. "Looks like he's trying to decide whether or not to make a phone call. Fifty bucks says he's calling his buddy, Roberto. Too bad Roberto can't answer." He heard Logan issue a subdued grunt of satisfaction.

"Well . . . I don't know what happens in the afterlife, but in a few minutes, he may very well be able to check with him in person. So here's the deal." Logan West briefly outlined his plan to rescue his wife from two killers occupying his kitchen in rural Maryland.

When he was finished, he moved around to the side of his house into the three-car garage. The middle bay was still open, the only occupant his wife's Audi sedan.

———

By 6:15 p.m., Antonio's unease had grown into a full-blown state of concern. "Tomas, I'm calling Mr. Black again. Roberto should've had West in custody hours ago. Something's wrong. If Roberto and Mr. Black don't answer, we're leaving immediately and taking her

with us. We go back to the safe house and wait. Mr. Black or someone else from the company will contact us, but we can't stay here
any longer."

Antonio hit the green talk button on his phone. He looked up
at Tomas to confirm he'd heard him. Tomas opened his mouth to
speak, but before he could respond, the kitchen's silence was violently interrupted. Multiple events happened simultaneously, and
none of them were good for the two mercenaries.

The bullet from Mike Benson's STAR-21 rifle shattered the bay
window. Fragmented glass cascaded to the kitchen floor as the bullet struck Tomas in the left temple. The rear left quarter of Tomas's
head exploded outward as small chunks of skull and brain hit the
floor, spraying Sarah's legs and the chair with a red mist. Tomas's
body crumpled to the ground, and his pistol fell from his hand and
bounced across the room, coming to rest along a baseboard under
the smashed window.

As Antonio processed Tomas's death, his first thought was to use
the West woman. *I have to grab her and use her as a shield, or I'm dead
too.* With his only thought now focused on survival, he reached for
his Glock 9mm pistol on the countertop.

———

Logan had been silently waiting in the garage outside the kitchen
door. The gap between the frame and the door was backlit from the
kitchen lights and revealed no dead bolt. He'd minutely turned the
doorknob to confirm it was unlocked.

Mike had then given him the countdown. "Okay, Logan. On my
count . . . three . . . two . . . one."

As Mike Benson exhaled and pulled the trigger on the Israeli
rifle, Logan West had simultaneously thrown open the door and
leapt into his former home.

———

What Logan saw as he entered the kitchen would've momentarily frozen a normal man, but Logan West was anything but normal, even under the influence of alcohol.

His preternatural ability to function both mentally and physically under the most stressful situations had served the Marine Corps exceedingly well. He'd once been dubbed "Wild West" because of his bold decisions and the extreme lengths he'd go to in order to accomplish a mission. Now he used those same traits to try and save his wife from an unknown enemy that had suddenly invaded their lives.

Thoughts flashed through Logan's head at breakneck speed. *Sarah's alive . . . lots of blood on the floor . . . not hers . . . must be Daly's . . . one dead gunman . . . second one reaching for a pistol . . . neutralize and keep alive . . . can't take a shot . . . Sarah's in the line of fire.*

As Logan processed the information, he chose the only option at his disposal. The gunman's eyes widened in surprise and anger at Logan's unexpected arrival, and his hand closed on the black pistol.

In a blindingly fast movement, Logan dropped his own pistol from his right hand and stepped forward with his right foot. He unsheathed the specially crafted fighting knife from his vest and hurled the balanced blade at the intruder, twisting his torso and extending his right arm.

His aim was precise. The knife buried itself in the back of the man's arm. He screamed in pain and fury.

Logan closed the gap between them and delivered a blow to the man's exposed right side. He was rewarded with an audible *crack!* as one of the ribs broke, and the gunman doubled over.

Logan thought he was collapsing from his injuries, the fight over. He was wrong.

Instead of falling to the floor incapacitated, the mercenary executed a sweep with his right leg, catching Logan off guard.

It was a move Logan would've expertly avoided under normal circumstances, but his hangover had dulled his reactions and he'd underestimated the stamina and determination of his attacker.

The man's heel collided with the outside of Logan's foot. Logan was knocked off balance, and he fell to the hardwood floor, rolling backward. He pulled out of the evasive maneuver and fluidly moved into a crouching position on the balls of his feet.

He looked at the man before him, reassessing his enemy. What he saw momentarily shocked him. *Who was this guy?*

The man stood tall in defiance and leered at him. His weapon was firmly gripped in his left hand in a knife-fighting position, the blade pointed down toward the floor. It dripped with his blood since he'd pulled it out of his right arm after knocking Logan backward.

"You must be Logan West," he managed to hiss through gritted teeth. "I was wondering if you might show up. We should've had you hours ago. I knew something had to be wrong. In fact, we were just about to leave."

The man was breathing heavily, but Logan had already underestimated him once. He wasn't about to do it again. Logan knew he was a professional, just as Roberto had been, trained in hand-to-hand combat and still a significant threat.

Logan glanced at Sarah, who stared at him in disbelief. She hadn't uttered a word since his dramatic entrance.

"Don't worry, Mr. West. Your wife is unhurt. My men gravely underestimated her. She killed two of them," he said in a matter-of-fact tone.

Logan was both impressed and proud at the courage Sarah must've shown by defending herself.

"Where's my dog?" Logan asked.

"Unfortunately, the dog wasn't so lucky. One of my men—one of the dead ones—panicked and shot him when we came in. It's dead. For that, I'm sorry." He sounded sincere, which only angered Logan more.

"You don't get to be sorry," Logan growled, outrage seeping through every word. "You shouldn't have been here at all. I know what you want, and it's not here. This has all been for nothing."

Antonio moved slowly toward Logan. "That may be so, but I do know one thing. If you'd wanted me dead, you would've shot me as you entered. But since I'm still alive, it means you want to know what I know." The man smiled. "It's a good plan, but it's never going to happen. If the flag isn't here, I'm sticking with plan B."

"What's plan B?" Logan asked.

"Kill you," he said matter-of-factly. "And when that's done, I'm taking your wife with me back to my organization. She may still be useful."

Logan stared impassively as he listened to the man's words, which hung in the air. Logan finally revealed the devil within and allowed a small smile to form on his lips.

"What is it with you and your team? Do you really believe I'm just going to roll over and let you go? I don't know who or what you think I am, but you guys picked the wrong fight. It's the same with your asshole boss."

At the mention of Mr. Black, Antonio raised his eyebrows.

"That's right, jackoff. I talked to Juan after I killed your friend. So guess what? As of a few hours ago, he knew your team didn't have me. You know what that means, don't you?"

Logan watched the realization dawn on the man's face, but he stated it just to rub salt in the proverbial wound. "He hung you and your team out to dry. He *knew* I was going to come here. He could've warned you, but for whatever sick reason, he didn't. And you know what else? I'm *glad,* because now I get to take care of you myself." The smile fell from Logan's face, revealing the lethal predator he was.

"So here's the deal. You have one chance to drop my knife. If you don't, the pain from that wound is going to feel like a massage when I'm done with you. I guarantee it."

Antonio heard the hardness in Logan's voice. He knew this was a serious man. There was no point in carrying the conversation any further. His choice made, Antonio inched forward, the sleeve of his right arm darkening with blood. The menacing knife glinted in the kitchen lights, its intent clear.

Antonio moved within striking range. Logan nodded and said, "Fine. But don't cry about it later. And don't say I didn't warn you. Now let's finish this so I can untie my wife."

Without hesitation, Antonio swiped his left hand up and across Logan's throat. Antonio was fast, but the blade missed by several inches as it flashed by his face.

Antonio had intended to miss—it was part of his feint—but before he could deliver the killing blow and bring the blade back toward Logan, stabbing him in the side of his neck, Logan West countered *that* move before it even began. *How could he be that good?* Antonio didn't get a chance to contemplate further.

Logan wasn't surprised. With the gunman's right arm out of commission, he knew Antonio would have to catch him off guard with some kind of feint. The man would expect him to block it.

Instead, Logan tilted backward, away from the attack. He waited until the blade whistled toward his throat. He then stepped into his attacker's space and planted his right foot as the blade swished by inches away. He hooked his right arm vertically inside the knife's arc, stopping its deadly momentum. Logan grabbed the attacker's wrist and turned away from him. He pulled the man's arm over his right shoulder and yanked down on the wrist with both hands. The force broke all three bones in the man's elbow, simultaneously tearing the ligaments and tendons.

The killer crumpled to the kitchen floor and writhed in agony. Logan stood over him and said, "I told you that knife wound wasn't the only pain you'd feel today. I'm just getting started."

Logan hit him at the base of his skull, knocking him unconscious and temporarily stopping the pain.

CHAPTER 10

Logan knelt beside Daly's corpse as tears formed in the corners of his eyes. *This dog brought me back countless times when I thought I was lost.*

Logan wasn't an exceptionally emotional person, but kneeling there next to his loyal companion, he was suddenly filled with a deep sense of sorrow, an ache that penetrated the hardened shell of his soul. He couldn't imagine his life without Daly, but now he was gone, killed by one of the evil men who'd attacked his home and held his wife hostage.

His tears stopped as his grief subsided, slowly turning to a cold rage he planned to utilize. Sarah had already avenged Daly's death. God knew what Logan would've done to that man were he still breathing. *At least there's one left alive . . .*

"Logan?"

"Yeah. I'm okay. You know I valued Daly more than a lot of the people I know? He was family. And now he's dead. And that asshole inside is going to tell me why. I hope you're prepared to let me work. They brought this fight to me, and I have no problem getting down in the mud with them. Whatever's going on has to be extremely important to these people, and we need to know what it is." He looked up at Mike as he said, "My interrogation techniques aren't exactly government-approved. You okay with that?"

Mike shrugged his shoulders and said, "I have no idea what you're talking about. As far as I know, that man sustained all of his injuries when you subdued him."

"Good. Now let's do this. My hangover's killing me."

———

Antonio awoke to find himself tied to a chair in the kitchen, his hands bound together in front of him with duct tape. Some kind of cord was wrapped around his chest, securing his upper body to the chair.

His mind cleared slowly. His brain registered pain along his entire left side. He drew in a short breath and involuntarily let out a low muffle of agony.

The position Logan had tied him in resulted in constant pressure on his wrecked left arm that was as vicious as any torture method Antonio had witnessed. Pain coursed through his head. He started to pass out again.

Slap!

An open hand smashed into the side of his face. "Hey! Don't fall asleep yet! We've been waiting for you to come back to us."

Antonio tried to focus on the voice, but his vision was blurry from the tears the slap had produced. He blinked his eyes, and light assaulted his senses. He squeezed them shut again.

"Your eyes are overly sensitive to the light right now. It's from the concussion I gave you when I knocked you out. It'll pass. Just open them gradually. It'll help. Trust me. It once took me two weeks to recover from an IED blast that flipped my Humvee in Iraq. Had to wear glasses the entire time. It sucked."

Antonio slowly opened his eyes. The light dimmed in the

kitchen. He squinted and looked up to see a large black man adjusting a sliding switch on the wall. The man stared at him intently. The West woman sat at the kitchen table and watched him, an obvious look of disgust on her face. He finally looked directly forward and into the face of Logan West.

Logan glared down at him with dead, emotionless eyes, cold pools of emerald green that revealed nothing. Antonio felt as if he were being scrutinized by a reptile. The fresh scar on the left side of West's face added to the menacing visage. *What did I get myself into?* Doubt finally crept into his mind as he wondered what was next.

"Good. That's better. Now I'm a direct man, and I'm not going to bullshit you and tell you 'Everything's going to be okay.' It's not." Logan paused to let that sink in.

"So here's the deal. I'm going to keep this simple since you're in need of medical attention; however, your answers will determine what kind of attention you get. You have two choices," Logan continued, his hard gaze continuing to unnerve Antonio. "One, tell me what the flag is for and whom you work for, or option two, don't tell me what I want to know, and I'm going to hurt you more than you can possibly imagine, even with the injuries you have right now. I promise you. I know you're trained, and you probably think you can resist or mislead me. You can't. You'll break." The certainty was evident, stated matter-of-factly.

Antonio stared at this man, hearing the calm conviction in his voice. He'd try and hold out. *Maybe Mr. Black had already called in a second team.* Maybe that's why he hadn't answered the calls. Maybe another team was already on the way. He just had to make it through the next few minutes.

Antonio coughed and spoke one word, "No." He stared at Logan, who stood there quietly, as if he hadn't heard Antonio's response. He opened his mouth to repeat it, but he never got the chance.

Logan West delivered a ferocious knife-hand blow to Antonio's shattered left arm. It happened so quickly, Antonio's mind didn't register it until after the fact. The sensory overload was too much for his already exhausted body. He shrieked as every nerve ending he had cried out in agony, his audience watching impassively. He passed out.

———

Antonio slowly emerged from unconscious darkness. Fresh panic gripped him. *I can't breathe! Where am I? What's happening?*

He opened his mouth to scream, but instead he swallowed cold liquid. He choked and gasped as his lungs struggled for oxygen.

He was underwater. *No! He's going to kill me!* A fresh wave of panic gripped him. He had to get free! His lungs burned as their remaining oxygen was depleted. Panic overpowered all other thoughts but one—survival. *I have to breathe!*

He felt a pressure on the back of his neck. It was a hand, holding him tightly. He couldn't see, a fact that only amplified his fear. His terror heightened, all his nerve endings completely exposed to every sensation. He had to make this stop.

Thoughts of his father suddenly flashed through his head. He'd watched him drown in a flash flood when they'd crossed the border into Texas. He'd been twelve years old at the time. He and his mother had been helpless to save him, and his father had been swept away. The possibility of suffering the same fate was unbearable.

He lost all grip on reality. His body slumped. His mind still craved air. *If I get air, if I can breathe again, I'll tell him what he wants.* He realized he might not get the chance. Antonio felt himself slipping away, a buzzing sensation growing in his head. *I'm going to die.* The finality sank in, and his mind gave in to the inevitability of his impending death.

The faint light at the edges of the blindfold faded into darkness.

In his mind, he cried like the little boy who'd watched his father drown, his whole world shattered. Then, nothing.

———

Sound roared into his consciousness. Antonio found himself vomiting water and bile. He wept as he realized he was alive. He didn't care about anything else.

He was facedown in the corner of the master bathroom. He trembled from the exhaustion, but he didn't care. He was breathing fresh air.

He heard Logan ask, "Are we done? Or should I keep going? I actually thought you were dead for a moment. If we continue, you likely will be." It was as unsympathetic a voice as any Antonio had heard in his lifetime. He knew this man would kill him.

Antonio didn't look up. He couldn't take the sight of those merciless green eyes. "No more. I'll tell you what I know."

Rough hands gripped him as fresh pain shot through his body. Logan propped him up against the bathtub. He was finally forced to look into the face of Logan West one more time.

The eyes never changed. The predatory gaze blazed at Antonio as Logan said, "See? That wasn't so hard, was it?" Then he smiled.

Antonio looked down at the wet floor. He felt Logan's gaze burning into his skull. *I was a fool to think I could stop this man.*

"Well, then. I think we finally have an understanding. You know it starts all over if I even suspect you're lying?"

Logan leaned down and spoke directly into Antonio's face, his hot breath only inches away. "I seriously want to kill you, but I know I need you alive. If you fuck with me—even for a moment—my friend here is not going to stop me. *Comprende?*"

Antonio vigorously nodded his head. He'd do anything to get away from this man.

Logan's tone suddenly changed, as if what had just transpired was just a minor inconvenience. "Now that that's out of the way, let's get down to brass tacks, as they say. What's your name?"

Logan looked at Mike, who'd already taken out a notepad and pen from a pocket inside his jacket.

"Antonio Morales." He paused for a moment. "I work for a man named Juan Black. He's a freelance contractor and enforcer for the Los Toros cartel. He has an office in San Antonio, but I honestly don't know where. I'm not supposed to even know about it."

Logan and Mike exchanged a quick glance. The Los Toros cartel had arrived on the Mexican drug scene within the last few years. What they lacked in longevity they'd made up for in extreme violence. Unprecedented horrors appeared on the news day after day.

Antonio continued. "My team does—did—a certain type of work for him. We hit rival cartels that Los Toros identified as 'problems.' This job was something else. It was our first job inside the United States."

Logan interrupted him. "I think you made a bad career decision somewhere along the way, Antonio. You're lucky I didn't kill you. In my book, you definitely deserve to die." He waved his hand dismissively. "Regardless, next question is a two-parter. Think you can handle it? But you can't phone a friend," Logan said sarcastically.

Antonio was beginning to believe Logan West was a little crazy in addition to extraordinarily dangerous. He coughed and waited for the first question.

"Which unit were you with? I know you're former military. Roberto had a tattoo on his left forearm of a fifty-caliber ammo band. You've got that nifty red skull with a beret on it." Logan pointed to the man's right forearm. "It tells me you're a former Green Beret. Either that or you just liked the tattoo. So tell me, Antonio,"—and he leaned in to emphasize his interest—"what is a former Green Beret doing working for a drug cartel? But before you answer, part two is this: what were you supposed to do with my wife after you captured her, assuming that I never showed up and spoiled the party?"

Antonio knew there was no point in denying it. "Each of my team, including myself, was dishonorably discharged from the military. I was a Green Beret with the Fifth Special Forces Group at Fort Bragg. I got drunk at a unit function and struck my commanding officer. The asshole deserved it—he told a joke about illegal aliens and Mexicans—and I broke his jaw. Landed me two months in the stockade before I was kicked out. I know Tomas—the dead man in the kitchen—was with the Seventy-Fifth Ranger Regiment and that he had two DUIs. He claimed the MPs were after him because he'd put one of them in the hospital in a bar fight. I'm sure he did, but it still sounded like bullshit to me. The truth is he probably just got caught driving one too many times lit up. I have no idea what unit Roberto was with or where Juan found Cesar and Angel. They just joined my team three days ago in San Antonio. Juan told me to take them on this operation. So I did."

Logan shook his head, as if he couldn't believe what he was hearing, even though he knew Antonio was telling the truth. It was utter insanity. "Okay. I get it. You're all big, bad former Special Forces types. But how the hell did this Juan Black manage to find you? That's what I really want to know."

"I have no idea. He never told us how he obtained our names, but I assumed someone gave him my military records. I don't know how, but he knew things about me only the military knew. Once I accepted the job, I never asked. I liked my life." Antonio waited for a response. There was none. He continued.

"I received a phone call out of the blue several months after I was discharged. I was desperate for money, and this man—Juan Black— offered me one hundred thousand dollars for one week of work. I knew it was for a cartel, but he insisted the wet work never targeted innocent civilians, only other cartels. I needed the money. So I took the job. As simple as that." There was no point in sugarcoating what was an ugly truth. He was a paid mercenary, plain and simple.

"So what the hell are you doing here looking for an Iraqi flag?" Logan growled.

"Juan sent us here for one reason, to find the Iraq country flag you confiscated on a mission in Fallujah in 2004. If we didn't find it, we were to take your wife hostage and use her as leverage to force you to find it. Tomas searched the house before you arrived. He found nothing. We already had your wife under control and were waiting for follow-on orders from Roberto. Since it'd been several hours since I'd last heard from him, I was getting ready to leave with her when you arrived."

Logan stared at him for a moment before he spoke. "I guess it's good that I got here when I did, then."

Antonio didn't respond.

"What's so important about an old Iraqi flag? And don't tell me you don't know. You have to know something."

"They didn't tell us. Only what I overheard. Roberto was on the phone and talking too loudly. He said something about 'thousands of innocent lives' and that 'it would be worth it for what they did to us.' Those were his exact words. I didn't ask. I swear."

Logan looked at Mike again, concern on his face. This time, Mike asked the question. "Do you know if these innocent lives that are going to be lost are here or overseas?"

"I have no idea. I swear to God. If I'd asked, I'd be dead right now."

Mike looked at Logan and said, "We need to talk. Let's get this piece of shit out of your bathroom and down to the kitchen before the cavalry arrives."

"How long did your uncle say they'd be?" Logan asked.

Mike looked at his watch. "Should be any minute now."

Logan nodded. "Fair enough. If anyone's going to help us sort this mess out, it's him."

Antonio was confused as he looked at the two men. His confusion was replaced with pain as Logan and the other man suddenly jerked him to his feet. As he was roughly dragged downstairs, he screamed the entire way.

CHAPTER 11

"Logan, you look awful and smell like whiskey. What the hell happened? I thought you'd been sober for the last six or seven months." Sarah stared at him, expecting a response resembling the truth but not all of it. Trustworthiness hadn't been one of his strong suits in their relationship over the past few years.

Logan looked at Sarah. He struggled to find words that could accurately convey his emotions. He was full of sorrow at the loss of Daly, rage at the intruders, and disgust with himself. *How do I explain that?*

He wasn't an expressive man. Conversations like this one weren't easy for him. He almost preferred getting shot to discussing his feelings.

He contemplated his response when he remembered that one of Alcoholics Anonymous's Twelve Steps said something about "honesty." After everything that had occurred, there was no point in denying the truth.

"I went on a two-day binge. It started two nights ago. Two days ago was the four-year anniversary of my last operation in Fallujah. I thought I could handle it, but then I started reliving the events in my head. I didn't want to talk about it. So I chose the easy option like a coward. I drank myself into a blackout." He paused as he looked around the kitchen. "Guess it wasn't such a good choice."

Both Sarah and Mike knew what had happened on that last mission—at least the most important part. The faces of his fallen Marines burned brightly in Logan's consciousness.

The pain was evident on his face as he spoke. "I'm not making any excuses. I was trying to drink myself into oblivion, for at least a few days. When I dropped off Daly,"—his voice broke as he thought of his dead dog, and tears welled up in his eyes—"I knew I was going to go back to my house to start drinking."

Sarah put her head in her hands as he continued. "And because I couldn't face my personal demons, Daly is dead. And there's nothing I can do about it. And now I have to carry that guilt with me." He stopped again to gather himself. He expected no sympathy from Sarah. He didn't deserve any.

He was surprised when she said, "Logan, you didn't choose for these bastards to invade our house. If Daly had been with you, he could've been killed at your house. I blame you for a lot of our issues, but Daly's death is not yours to carry. It's not your fault."

The shame from his decision to drink was almost too much to bear. Sarah's forgiveness only increased the humiliation he was experiencing. *Never again will I put her or anyone I care about in a position like this. Never . . .*

He gathered his bearings for a moment and breathed deeply. "I cannot honestly and in any words I know express how sorry I am for what happened." He saw the acceptance in Sarah's face and let the rest pour out.

"As for the last two days, I blacked out completely. I honestly don't remember a thing. I woke up this afternoon in the basement on the floor. There was a man, one of these mercenaries, with me. I killed him. I called Mike to ask for help, and as soon as I hung up with him, the dead guy's phone rang. I decided to answer it, hoping to get a clue as to what this was all about." He looked at Mike, expecting a rebuke.

Instead, Mike said, "Makes sense, considering the situation."

"It was a man calling himself Juan—apparently this Juan Black—these assholes' ringleader. He asked me about a flag from Iraq. When I told him I didn't have it, he said I'd better find it for your sake, which is when I called Mike again. We came over, parked near the entrance to the neighborhood, and . . . well, you know the rest."

Sarah looked at him, processing everything he'd just told her. He sensed her outrage at the violence that had been brought to their lives.

"I'm just glad I could send two of them to hell, especially the one who killed Daly."

"Sarah, I'm seriously impressed. Most people would have collapsed under the fear and pressure. What you did is the epitome of courage under fire, hon. No cliché in this case."

"Well, it helps that I'm married to a Marine." The use of the present tense wasn't lost on Logan. "You may be an arrogant alcoholic with some serious personal issues, but when it comes to self-defense, I always paid attention. I waited in the bedroom for them to come to me. It was the smart choice since they had to find me. If I'd known there were two more, I'd probably still be up there right now. You were right about that part too."

For the first time that day, Logan's face broke into a genuine smile. "I told you so."

———

The three of them sat around the kitchen table, which had miraculously remained unscathed during the assault. It was a little past 7:00 p.m.

Antonio was bound, gagged, and blindfolded in the dark outside in the backyard. Logan had tied him to a tree. As he did so, he'd whispered, "We'll be inside waiting for the cavalry. You'll be fine out here . . . unless the local bears get you. Why do you think I installed the motion-sensor flood lights? Have fun, asshole." He'd punched Antonio in his wounded arm and walked away.

"What now? The number Antonio used for this Juan Black is now out of service. No way Antonio has another means to reach him. I'll bet only Roberto had a backup comms plan with him, but he can't tell us what it is, and even then, since Juan knows he's dead, that'd be no good as well."

Mike interrupted. "Our forensics guys are excellent. They'll get as much information—more than you think—from the number Roberto used. Trust me."

Logan nodded. "Okay. As for the second issue, I know where the flag is and who has it. Remember John Quick, my platoon sergeant from Iraq?"

Mike nodded. "He was almost as dangerous as you are."

"Even more so, in a few ways. Anyhow, I'm pretty certain he took it on that last operation after we survived. We were all tired of seeing those fucking flags in their execution videos. He took it as a trophy from that site—as a reminder. I just wish we knew what the hell was so important about some goddamned Iraqi flag."

Mike was about to respond, but his cell phone rang. He answered it and gestured to Logan with a "wait-one-minute" signal with his left hand. He listened intently to the speaker on the other end.

"Okay, sir. Got it." Another long pause. "And Logan's house in Annapolis has been secured? No police?" Another moment of silence. "Excellent. Let the forensics team tear it apart." He mouthed to Logan, *Sorry, man,* and kept talking on the phone.

"Also, Logan has the dead man's cell phone here. As soon as the other FBI team arrives, I'm getting them out of here and down to Quantico. We can let the digital forensics guys see what they can exploit off the phone. We have a name, Juan Black, likely an alias. He has answers we don't. He operates out of San Antonio as a hired gun for the Los Toros cartel. We'll also need to activate another team. I need to call you back. Give me five minutes."

Mike looked at Logan and Sarah. "That was my uncle." Jake Benson was the assistant director of the FBI's Counterterrorism Division, which had existed for decades and then received limitless funding and resources in the wake of the 9/11 attacks.

Jake Benson had been the special agent in charge of the New York City Field Office when the towers had been brought down. His office's response to the attacks and the relentless operational tempo had made him and his agents legendary throughout the Bureau. When the last assistant director retired in 2006, the director of the FBI had contacted Jake directly and appointed him to the new position. Jake hadn't actually had a say in the decision. It had been directed, which was all that mattered in the Bureau's hierarchy.

"So where does John live now? If there's another mercenary team heading his way, we need to warn him."

The look on Logan's face was sinister. "If retired Gunnery Sergeant John Quick is even fifty percent of what he used to be before retiring, they're the ones who are going to need the help."

"That's all well and good, Logan, but again, where is he?"

"Outside of Helena, Montana. He moved there to enjoy retirement by hunting and fishing. I haven't talked to him since. The good news is that his place is secluded. He'll see them coming for miles. The bad news is that if he needs help, he's not going to get it right away. Like I said, there's no one else around for miles. I have his address in my email somewhere. I'll log in with Sarah's laptop and get it to you after we get our friend out back prepped for his trip to Quantico."

Mike nodded. "I'll take care of Antonio. You get the address. He's two hours behind us. So it's still daylight there . . . Shit! Denver handles Montana, but the closest field office is Salt Lake City. Even if the office sends a chopper—and it will when my uncle calls—it's going to be a few hours away from him. He's on his own, Logan, at least for now. You have a number for him that we can at least try and call to warn him?"

"It's in the email as well, but unless John started doing meth and eating Twinkies every day, he'll be fine. He's one mean sonofabitch. His hand-to-hand skills are ridiculous. He makes me look like a Girl Scout, seriously."

"That's a very scary thought, my friend."

"You have no idea."

———

Fifteen minutes later, Mike was once again on the phone with his uncle. "I'll call you on the way to brief you further. One other thing, I need the FBI jet fueled and ready out of Reagan. We may have to take a trip to Texas to follow up on the Juan Black lead. Call you on the way back to Quantico, sir. Thanks."

Mike spoke to Logan and Sarah. "He's going to brief the White House and the directors of both the FBI and Homeland Security in a few hours. I have to call him back after we leave here, which we'll do as soon as our team arrives. There's another one already at your house. We're keeping this from all local law enforcement for now. It's officially under wraps until we know what the hell's going on."

"Smart move," Logan said.

"It's the only move right now—we're flying blind. We also have a transport team coming to take Antonio back to Quantico for further questioning. Hell, after what you just put him through, he'll probably be so relieved, he'll tell us anything we want."

Sarah suddenly asked, "So what's going to happen when the team gets here? I heard what you told your uncle, but what about me? I'm not leaving here." She'd just survived a vicious attack on her home, and there was no way she was leaving what she'd killed to protect.

"Think about it. Whoever these men are, they're not coming back. This Juan Black has to assume that the flag is either not here or will soon be under federal protection. If he knows all about Logan, then he surely knows about his connection to you, Mike. And he definitely has to know about John."

Mike smiled. "I always knew there was a reason I liked you more than Logan. And you're absolutely right, but I'd still feel more comfortable if you weren't here. Having said that, it's your call. If you do stay, in addition to the forensic team, which has to process this crime scene, you'll also have a four-man detail from our HRT. After all this, I'm not putting regular agents here. Again, it's your call."

Sarah looked from Logan to Mike. "I'm staying here. When your guys are finished with the house as a crime scene and have removed the bodies, I want to clean up. I *need* to." She looked imploringly at Logan. "I know you're devastated by Daly's loss, Logan, and I know you'll deal with it in your own way, but I *have* to do this. It's my way of coping. I'm not changing my mind."

No one spoke for a moment. Then Mike said, "Okay, Sarah. I only have one small request for you, if it's okay. It's going to be one long night for Logan and me, and your man here is fighting a vicious hangover, if not alcohol poisoning. I'm going to get him an IV when the team gets here, but in the meantime, do you have any coffee? I'd do it myself, but we need to go move our guest out front while we wait for the other agents."

"Of course. I'll make sure it's strong." She pushed herself away from the table and stood up, placing her right hand on Logan's forearm. She squeezed gently, as if to reassure him that it would all work out. The tenderness both relieved Logan and added to his guilt. *How could I have done this to them? She should despise me, not comfort me. I don't deserve it.*

Mike interrupted his thoughts. "Logan . . . Logan? Let's go get that piece of shit out front so we can pass him off as soon as the transport team gets here."

Forty-five minutes later, the forensics and transport teams arrived, followed by Logan's and Mike's vehicles, driven by FBI agents. They'd picked up the SUVs on the way into the neighborhood, surprising the night guard with their badges and weapons.

The agent in charge—a big, blond-haired man in his late thirties who looked like an Oklahoma State football player—had been directly briefed by the FBI director. His instructions were specific, and he intended to follow them.

Mike and Logan sat on the front steps and greeted him when he exited the unmarked car. Mike said, "I presume you're Special Agent Turner?"

The man responded, "I am, and please call me Charlie. I've been briefed. The director's instructions were clear. You have whatever you need. I've got a four-man forensics team"—he gestured to a group of youthful-looking agents, two men and two women, unloading equipment from a dark government SUV—"waiting to comb this place for whatever evidence there is. Also, one of my agents found a rental car parked on the other side of your neighborhood about two miles away. I ordered him to do a vehicular sweep after we came through the gate just to make sure these assholes didn't have any lingering support in the area. We'll have a forensics team on it soon."

"Nice work," Mike said.

"Thanks. I see you have the suspect." He didn't know what else to call him.

He looked at the blindfolded, bound, and gagged mercenary, feet tied to his hands behind his back with a small, thin nylon cord.

"Looks like he's not enjoying himself. Good. Sounds like he deserves it." Despite his wry smile, there was no humor in his voice.

"If Logan here had his way, that asshole would already be dead. He's lucky, and he knows it. He'll cooperate out of gratitude, if nothing else."

Special Agent Turner grimaced. "Our interrogators at Quantico will work on him. They'll be able to pull everything out of him, even details he doesn't realize he knows." He turned to face Mike. "You know how good those guys can be. You may have even trained some of them—from what I've heard, at least."

Mike didn't respond. He'd spent a portion of his early years in the Bureau's Counterintelligence Division. He'd specialized in interrogation techniques that some politically correct bureaucrats referred to as "questionable" and "harsh." In Mike's experience, the methods were extremely effective tools.

"Anyway, on to the second point of order—there's an FBI HRT team from the Salt Lake office inbound via a Gulfstream to the Helena Regional Airport. Once they're on the ground, it's going to be another half hour to Mr. Quick's house. It's going to be close to seven thirty his time. No one's been able to reach the number you provided, Mr. West," he said looking at Logan. "The cell's either off, or he's not answering for some reason. I'll let you know when the team touches down. After that, I'll update you after they get to his house."

"Sounds good, Charlie. Logan says if this Juan Black did send a team, they might actually be the ones in need of help." Special Agent Turner raised his eyebrows, slightly skeptical.

"Believe me, Charlie. If Logan says he's that good, he is. Regardless, you'll be able to reach me on my cell. It's going to be one long night. Hopefully the HRT can secure Mr. Quick and the flag. Otherwise, we're playing catch-up, which doesn't seem like a good idea when dealing with mercenaries and Mexican cartels."

Mike scanned the busy agents preparing to work. He realized only the forensics team had arrived with Turner. "What about the protection detail? I called that in after I spoke to my uncle. Mrs. West has decided to remain here. There should be no further threat, but after what she's been through, I let her make the call. She killed two of them herself."

"So I heard," the agent said, nodding approvingly. "Quantico is sending a four-man detail. I have no idea who they are, but I'm sure they'll be adequate. DC knows how important this is, and no one is going to let anything else happen to Mrs. West. They should be here within an hour or so."

Special Agent Turner pulled out a notebook and verified that he'd covered each item. He looked up and said, "Did I miss anything?"

"No, Charlie. You got it all. Thanks for the support. We'll be out of here as soon as Logan handles a personal matter." Mike looked at Logan, who turned and joined Sarah on the front steps.

There was just enough time to take care of Daly before they left. Logan and Sarah walked toward the side of the house, all resentment and anger wiped away as they braced themselves for one final task. They were going to bury Daly in the backyard that he'd loved and where they'd spent the most time together as a family.

Mike looked back at Turner. "Charlie, I'll be inside until we leave. Please let me know as soon as you hear something."

Special Agent Turner said, "You got it. I'll get my agents processing the scene while we wait." Without further delay, he turned to his young agents and barked instructions. Special Agent Benson was right. *This is going to be one long night.*

CHAPTER 12

The man known as Juan Black stood looking out his office window, his athletic silhouette contrasting darkly against the ambient light that entered the room from the city. His impatience was visible on his tanned features. The more time that passed, the more impatient he grew.

Roberto's death had complicated matters. Since he'd been the team leader, he was the only one with orders to contact Juan directly. Juan, of course, had all the team's numbers and could contact each member if he needed, but he'd decided not to because of the sensitivity of the operation.

Since Roberto was dead, the team was on its own. It was why he hadn't answered the earlier calls. He didn't want any more connections between himself and the debacle in Maryland.

Speaking directly to Logan West had jeopardized all of them. He was acutely aware of the federal government's ability to track people through their cell phones. Even though his men used digitally encrypted devices, he didn't want to risk it. So he continued to wait.

This helplessness is what the staff officer assholes back in the rear must've felt when their teams were on an operation, he thought, reflecting on his former life. *No wonder they were always pissed off.*

As he stared into the San Antonio skyline, a shadow appeared in the doorway. Its owner remained motionless until Juan turned and acknowledged him.

The man, a trusted aide and trained assassin, said, "Sir, no more phone calls from Roberto's team." He was one of the few men in the organization Juan trusted to actually provide counsel.

"It's just past twenty hundred on the East Coast. Something has obviously gone wrong. Fortunately, none of the team members knows the significance of the flag. Only Roberto had an idea, and fortunately, he's dead, according to Mr. West."

Neither man knew that Antonio, now captured and in custody, had knowledge of operational details that could compromise them.

Juan interrupted him. "If something has gone wrong, I pray that all of Roberto's team is dead. Who really knows what he told his men or what they knew." It was a statement, not a question.

The aide continued. "At least they're not our only chance for success. Carlos just sent us an update. They're in position but are waiting for full darkness before approaching the house. He said it was 'too exposed' to approach during the day. The target would've easily seen them coming."

The man looked at his watch. "They should hit the house in approximately thirty minutes. Carlos—per your orders—knows to take Mr. Quick alive."

The aide knew the tactical details of the operation but was also aware that Juan Black cared only for results at this point. "I'll let you know as soon as I hear something, sir." Just as quickly as he'd arrived, the man turned and vanished from the doorway, leaving Juan alone with his thoughts.

The weather was changing in San Antonio. Juan hoped his luck would as well. If this operation succeeded, he'd be financially secure for the rest of his life and free to retire anywhere on the planet . . . in a country with a nonextradition status, at least.

It all comes down to Carlos's team. Maryland is a dry hole. He knew there was no way they'd succeeded. He would've heard something by now from the Company. Cain's source in DC would've been briefed by the FBI, which was no doubt involved by now.

Juan had been informed about Mr. West's personal relationship with Special Agent Mike Benson. It had been a factor in deciding whether or not to move forward. Ultimately, Juan had determined the risk to be acceptable. *I could've been wrong.*

If Carlos failed, Juan would contact Cain at midnight. That wasn't a call he wanted to make.

No matter what the outcome, Juan knew that by tomorrow morning, all US law enforcement and intelligence agencies would be using every available resource to search for him. Even though he'd thoroughly compartmented this operation by ensuring the teams were not aware of each other's existence, he knew he'd still have to evacuate his office within a few hours.

He planned to relocate his operations center south of the border, where a secure facility with adequate protection was already established for him. The alternate location had been predesignated and was known only to himself and Cain.

The Los Toros cartel valued his services. As a result, the cartel kingpin hadn't asked any questions. In fact, the cartel wasn't even aware that Juan's true employer was Cain's Company—it wasn't an official name but what they called this effort—and that his work for the cartel was only a means to an end, a legitimate and lethal cover story.

If the cartel knew the truth, his life expectancy would be shortened dramatically. Juan didn't think the head of the cartel would find out; however, just to be safe, he planned to be on the other side of the world before the success of the operation exploded its way into the global headlines.

He looked at his watch for a third time since his aide had left. *I despise waiting.*

As the minutes ticked by, Juan contemplated the current state of world affairs. The only variable was the degree of the response and where it would be directed. No matter what, the country would fall.

Failure wasn't an option. They'd never have a better opportunity than now to exact their revenge. Even though their mission was personal for Cain, Juan lived with righteous anger and outrage too, personal mementos from his time in Iraq. He knew the deaths of the innocent served a higher purpose. It was unpleasant and morally repugnant, but unfortunately, it was necessary. This was their one and only chance. It was now or never. The United States had failed to act for too long.

But we won't. Not anymore.

CHAPTER 13

HELENA, MONTANA

Forty-two-year-old retired gunnery sergeant John Quick had built the large A-frame house on a small, isolated lake in the middle of a secluded forest. The house was connected to the lake by a fifty-foot pier that he'd personally constructed and joined to the back deck, which stretched the length of the house.

The lake itself was no more than two miles in diameter and surrounded by thick trees that grew within a few feet of the entire bank. In mild weather, he could easily swim from one side to the other without worrying about riptides or changing currents, two things from his Force Recon days that still sent shivers up his spine.

Even though the location was considered to be the outskirts of Helena, there wasn't another living soul for miles in any direction. He'd scouted the region thoroughly when he'd decided to move to Montana. He wanted as few distractions as possible. He'd seen the chaos and evil that pervaded the so-called civilized world, and he wanted none of it.

The combat he'd experienced and the horrors he'd witnessed had taken a steep psychological toll, ultimately leading to a divorce from his first wife only halfway into his career. For now, he just wanted to be alone. Someday he might try to reconnect with society, but first he had to reconnect with himself.

The house faced due west across the lake. It provided a prime vantage point for the sunset every evening. The lake didn't have a name, probably because no one ever visited.

Even though the dense woods that encircled the lake provided a formidable ring of protection, there was enough space between trees that he could walk and hunt in any direction he chose. It was perfect.

His path to this specific place still perplexed him. He believed all major events in a person's life occurred for specific reasons, that there was some sort of organized sense behind all the chaos. Unfortunately, his own personal reasons for being continued to elude him.

All he knew for certain was that after twenty-three years in the Marine Corps, multiple combat tours to Afghanistan, Iraq, and a few other countries with no official US presence, he preferred the solitude and complete independence his new home afforded him. It calmed his essence, which had been a violent and churning source of unhealthy anger for longer than he cared to remember. He was certain he'd made the right decision by moving to Montana.

He'd spent the day—one of countless many—on the lake in his small boat, catching two nice largemouth bass. One of the fish had just found itself served up as dinner, grilled and blackened with a nice lemon-butter concoction.

As the sun began to set a little after six o'clock, he built a fire in the circular open-hearth fireplace that occupied the center of his living room. It was where he spent most of his time relaxing and contemplating his life's journey, often staring out the gigantic plate-glass window into the beautiful scenery beyond.

The fire was his after-dinner relaxation. He placed the six logs he'd cut into a leaning pyramid construction. He hit the automatic lighting switch—there was no sense in doing everything the hard way—and a stream of gas hit the pilot light, igniting the logs. He smiled at the ease with which the wood burned.

He turned the gas switch off when the fire was self-sustaining and moved to his reading chair adjacent to the twelve-by-fifteen-foot window that occupied one side of his living room.

The chair was one of the few furnishings present in the gigantic two-story space. The other pieces of furniture included a dark mahogany dining room table and an oversized brown leather couch. He sat his athletic 180-pound frame down and took a sip from the single-malt Scotch that had been waiting on a small end table next to his chair.

It was his evening ritual as day faded into night, all thoughts and concerns washed away with the promise of a new tomorrow. The tranquillity of the moment was as close to a sense of peace that he could attain. No grenades, mortar rounds, or IEDs exploding near him. No *crack!* as rounds ricocheted overhead.

Most importantly, no screams from wounded or dying Marines . . .

He closed his eyes and was still, soaking in the silence as the sun concluded its ritual disappearing act. He suddenly opened his eyes, the dark-brown orbs focusing on the dusk outside. *The silence . . . it's too quiet. No crickets, frogs, or other nightlife.* The normal sounds that accompanied night conquering the fading daylight were absent.

In his experience, preternatural quiet was usually followed by extreme violence. Before the thought had fully registered in his mind, he was already moving toward his study.

Could be a bear. Last thing I need is a hungry grizzly looking for food. He'd heard enough stories of giant bears breaking into homes. The news media seemed to think bear stories were funny. Out here, he sure as hell didn't.

In his study, he opened a dark-brown cabinet and retrieved a .45-caliber M1911, fitted with special night sights and a polymer nonskid grip. He grabbed the holster belt and slid it around his waist, securing the thigh rig around his leg by snapping two clips together. He reached for his shotgun but then paused as he thought, *If it is a predator, maybe I can take it down and mount it on my wall.* He'd only hunted elk thus far but hadn't kept any of the heads for trophies.

Thinking he'd like to make a quiet kill, he grabbed two more tools of his current trade: a full-sized KA-BAR hunting knife and his Excalibur Vortex crossbow, equipped with a green illuminated reticle scope.

The crossbow packed an extremely powerful punch at 330 feet per second. With Horton Carbon Strike arrows, one shot usually resulted in a clean kill.

To the casual observer, he appeared to be prepared for combat, but John just considered equipping himself to be smart planning. "Sweat saves blood" was one of his favorite slogans, but so was the undeniable "Semper paratus," or "Always prepared." When venturing out into the wild Montana darkness, he definitely intended to be.

He attached the KA-BAR sheath to the left side of his holster belt, slung the quiver of arrows over his back, and moved to the living room.

As he entered the room, he turned off the light switch, bathing the room in a glowing orange that emanated from the fireplace. He stood on the right side of the window, out of sight from any creature lingering outside between his house and the lake. He waited as his night vision adjusted. To ensure that no ambient light affected his vision, he walked over to the fireplace and separated the logs, spreading them apart to diminish the fire to an incandescent glow.

The shadows from the fading coals danced across the room as he remained motionless, counting the minutes until his eyes were fully acclimated for the night outside. *Might as well have as much of an advantage as I can before I go out there.*

Carlos Quintana was a patient man. He hadn't survived this long in the world of the cartels without knowing precisely when to act. His timing was impeccable and had served to save his life more times than he remembered. The current job was no different.

The junior man—Erik—had suggested they break into the target's house and wait for him to return from his day on the lake. Carlos had momentarily considered that option but then dismissed it.

"If this man is as good as his military record indicates, he'll notice anything out of the ordinary, and we lose the element of surprise. There's no point in escalating the confrontation and creating an unnecessary risk. Instead, we wait until he's had his evening drink, and when he goes to bed, we move in . . . quietly." The others had agreed, and that had been the end of the discussion.

So when all light inside the massive living room suddenly vanished, Carlos was surprised. He looked at his watch. It was too early.

His man on the west side of the small lake—a skilled sniper named Edward—had an excellent viewpoint and radioed that he'd just lost visual on the target inside the house. He'd seen the outline of the target walk over to the fireplace and then . . . darkness.

Edward said through his radio, "I can see a glow from the fireplace, but nothing else inside the room."

"Roger. Notify me if you see anything else." *Had he seen or heard us?* Carlos didn't think so. He and his men had been in their positions for almost thirty-six hours.

The four-man team had parked its unregistered SUV five miles away on a deserted access road in dense underbrush on the other side of the lake. The road had a gate that had been padlocked. After they cut the lock off, they'd replaced it with an old lock of their own, one that had intentionally been beaten to reflect wear and tear and hopefully not raise any suspicion to the casual observer. Their SUV was concealed with trees and branches and was invisible unless someone literally walked into it.

In addition to Edward on the west side of the lake, Carlos's other team members, Erik and Hector, were positioned on the east side of the lake. Hector was Carlos's specialist for entering any type of building virtually undetected. The small and lean man with short black hair was a former Mexican army commando who'd fled Mexico for Texas after his unit was betrayed by a local politician and ambushed by a corrupted army unit working for a drug cartel. Only Hector and one other member of his squad had survived. As a result, Hector despised both the Mexican government and the cartels.

Hector had been referred to Juan Black and had landed on Carlos's team three years earlier, where he'd proved himself an invaluable asset. Hector asked no questions about the source of their funding. He didn't care. All that mattered was the vengeance he delivered to the cartels as personal payback for all they'd wrought.

Hector was the main player for this operation, and Erik was his personal security and additional firepower in case things didn't go according to plan—as was often the case.

When the lights suddenly went out in the living room, Carlos had ordered Hector and Erik to remain in place for another thirty minutes before approaching the house. He looked at his watch. The thirty minutes was up.

Carlos peered through his night-vision binoculars, hoping to spot Hector and Erik moving from their hide site five hundred meters away. Since he'd been in his own vantage point three hundred meters to the northeast of the house, he knew precisely where to look. He wasn't disappointed when the blurry figures of two camouflaged men began to creep toward the objective.

Once they reached their assault point, he'd have them remain there for another thirty minutes before entering the house through the study window he'd reconnoitered earlier in the day. It was the easiest—and safest—point of entry, since it was on the first floor and the farthest room from the target's bedroom.

Carlos had wanted originally to conduct the raid in the middle of the night, but Juan had insisted it happen as soon as it was dark. There were other constraints that Juan had to account for, and the longer Carlos and his team took to accomplish their mission, the greater the chances the entire operation could be jeopardized.

Juan had emphasized to him that failure wasn't an option. That reminder was a hovering presence in the back of Carlos's mind. He'd seen what happened to those who failed Juan Black. He didn't intend to become one of them—an example in death.

———

After thirty minutes, John Quick's eyes were fully adjusted to the darkness. He reached for the brushed-nickel handle of the large sliding back door when movement to the north side of the lake, no more than a hundred meters away, stopped him dead in his tracks.

What the . . . ? He could've sworn he saw something move and then suddenly stop. His years of night patrols in the woods, mountains, and jungles of foreign countries had honed his peripheral vision into a deadly warning instrument that had saved himself and his Marines on more than one occasion. Instinctively, he lowered his hand from the handle, positioned himself to the left of the picture window and sliding doors, and waited.

Two minutes later, two shadowy figures in camouflage carrying what appeared to be assault rifles moved a few feet through the trees and froze once again. The figures assumed prone positions near a fallen tree he'd planned to use for firewood.

He didn't panic. He'd been in peril numerous times and was no longer prone to irrational fear; rather, he immediately recognized the threat.

John was a trained sniper and had once stalked a South American president through a field with minimal cover and concealment. He'd remained in his hide site with his spotter for two days, at one point less than two hundred yards from the president's guards. The CIA ended up negotiating a deal with the dictator, and John had never received the order to eliminate the target. So he and his spotter had backtracked for another painful twenty-four hours before reaching their extraction point. The dictator never knew how close he'd come to taking a 7.62mm round through the temple.

I'm trapped. Whoever the hell it was outside his home had to be professional. He hadn't suspected anything out of the norm over the last few days. Maybe he was a little complacent from his self-imposed solitude, but he was still dangerously perceptive. *If these guys are that good, they'll have men on the other side of the house and on the front. Shit. I have to figure out something fast.* Then he smiled as he recalled words once famously uttered by Chesty Puller, one of the Marine Corps's most iconic and legendary officers: "We're surrounded. That simplifies the problem."

An idea occurred to him as he recognized his best option. He even allowed himself a small smirk at the thought. There was one exit they *hadn't* covered.

———

Hector was restless. His ghillie suit was irritating him again. He hadn't worn it for this long since Colombia, but even *that* mission was shorter than this one. He forced himself to ignore the discomfort, even though he was fairly certain that a tick or two had lodged itself in his upper thigh.

He just wanted to get this operation over with and get the hell out of Montana. He preferred the hot Texas climate to this cool fall weather.

The sun had set over half an hour ago. He and Erik had moved as close to the house as the situation permitted. They had an excellent line of sight into the living room and the side door. The target must've gone to bed early. Neither Carlos nor Edward had seen any movement from their vantage points once the dim glow from the fire had vanished.

Hector scanned the house methodically, working his way from the top down and left to right with his night-vision binoculars. *Nothing.* "Carlos, are we cleared?"

At the other end of the radio, Carlos contemplated his options and the risk involved if the target was aware of their presence. *What did the change in his evening routine mean?* He could only guess. *Was there any way the target knew they were there?* He didn't think so, but it was better to be safe when dealing with situations like this one.

"Wait another ten minutes just to be sure. Then proceed as planned. I'll move into position to cover the front. Begin radio silence until you have him or the flag. Out."

"Roger." Hector looked over at Erik, who was waiting for instructions. "We're a 'go' in ten minutes. Mark the time now."

Erik adjusted his camouflaged boonie cover and turned back to train his eyes on the house. The countdown had begun.

———

John Quick moved smoothly through the water, producing no sound or ripples. He never expected that the years of operational experience in exotic locations such as Lagos, Nigeria, or the coast of Somalia would pay dividends in Helena, Montana. Life continued to be full of little surprises.

He had no idea who these men were, but he'd immediately assumed hostile intent. As a result, he operated under his own rules of engagement. *I have guns too.*

When he realized that all three sides of his home were likely covered by fire, he'd immediately dropped below the bottom of the picture window and crawled to his basement stairs near the hallway to his kitchen.

Once in the basement, he'd secured his M1911 in a Ziploc bag he'd grabbed from his basement workbench. He'd placed it in the back of his trousers in his waistband. It was his weapon of last resort.

If he hoped to even the odds and give himself a fighting chance, he had to operate as quietly as possible, which meant no gunshots until they were absolutely necessary.

He'd then exited the basement through a small window leading directly under the back deck. When he'd built the deck, there'd been at least two feet of clearance between the ground and the bottom of the deck surface. It was all he needed.

He'd slithered under the deck until he'd reached the cold surface of the lake and slowly submerged himself, careful to make no unnecessary movements.

There was no way any of the hostiles—as he thought of them—had seen him enter the lake and move underwater to his planned exit point 150 yards to the north of his house. It was 50 yards behind the two men he'd spotted.

So here I am again. Unbelievable . . .

He exited the lake as quietly as he'd entered. Once he was on dry ground, he unslung his crossbow and stalked his prey from behind. He used the night-vision scope on his crossbow to guide him.

He moved quickly and quietly. His eyes focused on the location where he'd last seen the two men stop and assume prone positions. *There.*

He saw the barrel of an assault rifle—it resembled an M4—approximately twenty feet in front of him. The figure holding it slowly materialized in the darkness.

John held his breath and tensed every muscle. He prayed he was still undetected. *Nothing.* He exhaled quietly, the water drying on his skin.

He needed to close the distance by at least another ten feet before he could act. He slowly placed one foot down at a time, ensuring each landed softly on the dirt.

His right eye focused through his scope on the figure on the right, while his left remained open and watched for any sign of movement.

He was within striking distance. He planned to move only a few more feet and draw his .45—he'd removed it from the plastic bag and reinserted it into its holster when he'd exited the lake—with his left hand and cover both men, the one on the right with the crossbow and his partner on the left with the M1911.

He never got the chance. As he placed his left foot down, it made contact with a twig on the forest floor, breaking it in half. *Crack!*

John froze midstride, the crossbow raised and aimed directly at the back of the neck of his target.

The prone man on the left immediately turned his head, but before he could finish the movement, John spoke quietly.

"If you continue to turn that head of yours, you're not going to have it much longer."

The man froze. His partner visibly stiffened in the darkness. The pale light from the crescent moon illuminated his hand as it reached in front of him for an object that John couldn't see.

"Asshole, if you move even one more inch, I'm going—" John didn't finish the threat.

The intruder on the right had hoped to catch John off guard by acting instead of allowing the situation to unfold. The move might've worked on an amateur, but John Quick was a trained killer who wasn't surprised by much. It was stupid, but he'd seen other men make similar foolish moves, usually moments before they died. *They always think they're faster than they really are.*

He pulled the trigger of the Excalibur crossbow, releasing the carbon bolt, which rocketed through the night with a *swish* at an incredible 330 feet per second.

The bolt covered the distance in the blink of an eye and pierced the left side of the man's neck with a loud, wet *thwack!* The bolt missed the carotid artery but tore through his windpipe and trachea as it exited his neck. The man began to choke and suffocate on his own shattered windpipe, the high-pitched wheezing sound echoing through the forest like the cry of a wounded animal.

As soon as he'd fired, John knew his aim was true. He also knew he didn't have time to draw his .45. So he made the only move he could. He dropped the crossbow and lunged toward the other man, who was struggling to turn around. John drew his KA-BAR from its sheath.

The man rolled away in an attempt to put some space between him and his attacker. John moved in at an angle and closed the distance.

He took one more step and then launched himself into the air, his left hand in a fist and his right hand holding the knife in a combat grip, blade turned down and parallel to his wrist.

He landed on top of the dark figure, his left forearm striking the man in the upper chest. The blow knocked him backward to the ground as John landed on top, pinning him underneath. He brought the knife up from his side to slash upward at the man's left arm, hoping to sever the axillary artery.

The man instinctively anticipated the knife's movement and brought his left arm down on top of John's wrist, deflecting the knife attack to the side. He struck John on the left side of his head with his right fist, trying to knock him over and off him. *Damn. This guy is good.*

The punch succeeded, even though its impact was minimal. John rolled off the man and to his right. He landed on his feet.

He faced his opponent, who was now also standing and holding some type of blade that flickered in the moonlight. *Great. So much for my tactical advantage . . .*

Neither man spoke. There was nothing to be gained by it. Both men understood the stakes involved. This was a fight to the death. There was no room for negotiation.

John knew this man was extremely well trained, a professional soldier of some kind. Unfortunately, the fates had brought him to John's home with bad intentions, which was all that mattered in the end. *Kill or be killed.*

Even though he knew it was pointless, John said, "One thing before we begin: your name?" The man paused, surprised at the question. He smiled in the dark, his white teeth flashing momentarily.

"Hector." He paused and added, "You're good, Mr. Quick, but I'm better" in a thick Spanish accent.

"Okay, Hector. We'll see about that."

Hector began to circle clockwise, and John moved toward him. Both men searched for an opening, trying to determine the other's weakness. Hector acted first.

As John was still a few feet away, Hector threw a feint to John's face with the knife. He immediately followed the feint with the real strike, which was a spinning back kick that landed flush on John's chest and knocked him off his feet.

John rolled backward when he landed on the ground, springing back to his feet as his momentum carried him away. He stood up just in time to watch Hector charge him with his knife now in his left hand.

Now on the defensive, he waited until Hector closed the distance and moved to deliver a thrust to his chest. John spun to his right and caught Hector's forearm. He turned violently and flung Hector face-first into a nearby tree. Hector's face smashed into the bark, and his nose shattered, bleeding profusely. In the dim moonlight, the blood formed a black mask.

John retreated to a safe distance as Hector pushed off the tree in frustration and leapt backward. He brought his right arm backward in a slicing arc, hoping to catch John with the blade.

John had expected something like this, and all Hector struck was thin air. As the knife sailed through the crisp Montana night, John stepped in under its arc, low to the ground. He placed his left foot outside Hector's and delivered a crushing blow to Hector's ribs. He felt at least two ribs fracture as the blow knocked Hector off his feet and flat on his back on the dark forest floor.

John pulled his right arm back, fully extended as if he were delivering a pitch. His arm reached the top of its arc as he bent his left knee and dropped the weight of his body. He lowered his center of gravity to gain momentum, the knife in his right hand flashing through the night, light flickering across the lethal blade. He plunged the knife into the center of Hector's chest, piercing his heart and killing him instantly.

John waited until Hector's body was still and the postmortem tremors ceased. He withdrew his weapon from Hector's chest and wiped the blood on the dead man's trousers. He moved to a tree in the direction of his house, crouched down, and waited.

He knew he wasn't alone. He just hoped he'd evened his odds. The sounds of the fight had carried through the trees. Whoever else was out there likely now knew that their plans had gone horribly wrong. It would only take a few minutes to figure out exactly how.

———

As soon as Carlos heard the commotion, he knew the target had somehow eluded them and passed unseen through their surveillance perimeter.

He scanned the last location he'd seen Hector and Erik, one hundred meters to the north of the house. Through his night-vision goggles, he saw two figures circling each other in the middle of the sparse trees. He recognized Hector's silhouette, but he didn't wait to watch the fight ensue.

He knew Hector was superbly trained, but John Quick was just as lethal. *It's the perfect diversion.* His thoughts were on the flag, not Hector's welfare.

Without a moment's delay, he sprinted through the woods toward the house. He prayed Hector could delay Quick for at least a few minutes.

As he ran, he heard a thump and a muffled grunt. Either Hector or Quick had just hit the ground, and hard from the sound of it. Still, perhaps the battle had bought him enough time to find the flag and rendezvous with Edward on the west side of the lake.

He hit the front walkway and suddenly halted at the base of the porch to stifle the sounds of his movements. He crept up the three steps to the front porch and tried the doorknob. *Locked.*

He knew it would be, which he found amusing considering the isolated location of the house. He pulled out his lock-pick set and opened the door after an easy thirty seconds of maneuvering the small tools. He smiled. *Even a dead bolt was child's play to a skilled professional.*

He entered the house and paused, orienting himself to his surroundings. He stood at a small entryway. A faint glow from the smoldering fire emanated from the end of the hallway. Beyond was the kitchen and gigantic living room with the enormous window and view of the lake.

He walked down the hallway and entered the kitchen, moving quickly through and beyond it. He stepped into the center of the living room and scanned the walls. *Nothing . . .* as he'd expected. He turned to his right and entered the study.

Their reconnaissance hadn't provided any intelligence on this room since the shade on the study window was always closed. The room was extremely dark. He turned on a small, tactical flashlight and swept the room from left to right. *Jackpot!*

Suspended on the right wall above a hardwood desk was a four-foot-by-six-foot Iraqi national flag. It had three horizontal stripes of red, white, and black in descending order, with three green stars in the center white stripe. It was the version that Saddam Hussein had created in 1991, with the words *Allahu Akbar* written between the stars, reportedly in Hussein's own hand.

Carlos yanked the flag off the wall, laid it flat on the floor of the study, and looked on the back of the lower left-hand corner. A wave of relief washed over him as he found the ultimate object of the operation. It was really there. *Thank God.*

He radioed Edward. "I have it. I'm coming out and moving toward you. Do you have eyes on Hector, Erik, or the target?"

"Negative. I can't tell what happened at this distance. When the fighting stopped, there was only one man standing, but I can't tell who it is."

"Roger. Neither Erik nor Hector has checked in, which tells me it's probably Quick. I'm coming at you full speed. I need you to cover me. If you see any movement from their location, shoot to kill. We're running out of time. Be there in a few minutes. Out."

Carlos jogged his way back to the front of the house. He paused—he'd forgotten something. He looked down and then back toward the kitchen. He completed one last task, opened the door, and sprinted down the steps and into the woods toward Edward.

He never looked back, but as he was approximately 200 meters from the house, he heard a succession of shots from Edward's location. He hoped his school-trained sniper had hit his target.

———

John watched his house, deliberating his next move. He was crouched behind a tree, blocking the line of sight of any shooter who might be watching from the other side of the lake. He had to assume there were more men, but he also had to be cautious or he'd get himself killed.

After a few minutes of no sound or movement, he heard his front door open. The sound of faint steps reached him as they made contact on his porch and then the gravel driveway, moving quickly away from him. Someone had just been inside his home. *What in God's name do these people want with me?*

He decided to move closer to the house. He was certain that there were no more men left on this side of the lake. He'd have detected them. Most importantly, he needed to identify the additional threat and eliminate it.

He moved slowly, creeping his way toward the front of his house *Crack!*

He heard the gunshot across the lake a full second before the bullet ricocheted off the tree immediately to his left at the approximate height of his head. He dove to the ground as bark splintered in all directions from the round's impact.

He looked to his right. He saw a second muzzle flash and heard another shot. This time the round struck the tree in front of him but lower. *Motherfucker's bracketing me, figuring I'll be near the ground.*

He maneuvered his body as low as he could. A third shot scattered dirt from the forest floor two feet behind him. He realized the shooter couldn't actually see him, a small relief given the circumstances.

Even though he was on the ground, he was still in perilous danger. The sniper was hoping to hit him with a lucky shot, and John knew that if he remained in this location, the sniper would likely get it. So he did the only thing he could and began to low-crawl as quickly as possible, not stopping to look in any direction but forward—to his house and cover.

After twenty harrowing meters, he realized that the shots were still striking behind him. *He thinks I'm still there.*

He didn't wait to see if the shooter would discover he'd moved. *Have to get to the front left corner of the house. Then I'll be out of his line of sight.*

The only problem was the last thirty feet between the edge of the trees and his home. The area was cleared because it was where he parked his Ford F-150 pickup truck, which was there now. Other than the car, there was no cover or concealment in this small no-man's-land.

He reached the edge of the trees and paused to catch his breath. His adrenaline was pumping furiously since it'd only been seven or eight minutes since his initial encounter with Hector and his partner. He forced his breathing to slow.

He looked across the lake and saw several flashes as more rounds impacted his previous position. The shooter was several hundred yards away, but he thought the shots might be moving closer to the house. He didn't think he was in immediate danger—at least for the next thirty seconds.

He knew that if he could reach his study and his gun rack, he'd turn the tables on the shooter across the lake. His modified Remington 700 rifle was loaded and ready. His plan was to move upstairs to his bedroom unseen, open a window just enough to provide a clear line of sight to the sniper, and end this cat-and-mouse game.

First, he needed his cell phone from his kitchen counter to dial 911. He hadn't even thought about it before he left the house through the crawl space.

He took one last deep and slow breath, crouched into a semi–runner's starting position behind the tree, and leapt from cover. *I've had better ideas than this one,* he thought as he sprinted across the gravel driveway.

He waited for a bullet to knock him to the ground and send him plummeting into oblivion. Neither happened.

He reached the front of his house, steadied himself, and crept along the wall until he saw his porch and front door. The door was ajar.

He immediately realized it could be a trap. There could've been two men inside, one of them sprinting away in order to draw him back to the house, only to be ambushed by the remaining man. *Or the house is empty, the assholes got what they came for, and I have no fucking clue what that is.*

At this point, John figured it was fifty-fifty either way, but in order to find out, he was going to have to go inside.

He drew his M1911 from its holster and moved up the steps. He stopped outside the door, realizing the shooter on the other side of the lake had ceased firing.

Were they on the way back here? He had to get to his rifle and his cell phone. He'd been relatively lucky so far, but he didn't want to push it.

He shoved open the door and saw varying shades of black. The glow from the embers had vanished since the fire was almost completely extinguished. His front hallway was pitch-black. He could see the light of the night sky entering through the picture window in his living room. He stepped into his hallway and moved toward the living room.

He realized his mistake as it occurred. He'd moved too quickly. Had he slowed down, his left leg might not have made enough contact with the filament wire running six inches above his floor and across the hallway.

Oh no.

He heard a metallic *ping* followed by a louder *clack*. He recognized the sound of a pin popping out of its slot and the release of a safety lever, which landed on the floor. *Grenade!*

John Quick spun on his heels, turning 180 degrees in a blur of dark motion. He lunged for the doorway and prayed that the grenade's fuse would last long enough to provide him an extra second to clear the porch.

He sprinted through the door and was halfway across the porch when he thought, *I'm not going to make it.*

He clearly saw the edge, knowing that if he could reach the ground below, he'd likely be safe from flying shrapnel and debris.

He took one more step and dove into the air, hoping he'd judged his leap accurately. As he sailed across his front porch, the remaining part of the fuse burned, detonating the 6.5 ounces of Composition B explosives.

The explosion in the confined space of his hallway was tremendous. The concussion wave from the grenade was magnified by the walls and doorway. The blast split the front door in half and tore both pieces off their hinges, sending the giant wooden planks rocketing across the front porch.

For a moment, he thought he was going to land in safety on the gravel below. *I have enough time.*

As he sailed through the air, he momentarily saw his silhouette illuminated by the flash of the explosion, a dark shape elongated across the edge of the porch and down the steps.

In that moment, the image reminded him of an old black-and-white negative, captured in some abstract and surreal world. Then the top half of the door smashed into the back of his head, propelling him over the edge of the porch. He didn't feel the impact as he somersaulted over the edge and tumbled down the steps, coming to a sudden halt on the gravel below.

As he lay on his back and looked up at the night sky, his only thought was, *I guess I didn't have enough time.* The surrounding blackness closed in on him, and he thought no more.

CHAPTER 14

Carlos and Edward were jogging their way through the deep woods to the staged SUV when the booby-trapped grenade exploded. Both men abruptly halted, and Edward looked over to see Carlos smiling.

Edward asked, "A booby trap? Nice touch."

"I just hope it killed him. That man is one tough hombre. Let's go. We need to be out of here before company arrives. We're not safe until we're on the highway and heading south to the airport. Hopefully the explosion bought us some time and will cover our tracks."

They resumed their pace, weaving in and out of trees, leaping over fallen limbs as they ran. Carlos focused on his breathing and kept moving through the thick underbrush.

Nothing can stand in our way now.

———

John Quick opened his eyes to find himself lying on a cot in the back of an ambulance. *At least I'm not dead . . . yet.*

He heard several voices outside the vehicle. He turned to look, but the full brightness of the ambulance caused more pounding pain in his head. He squeezed his eyes shut tightly.

"Aghh . . . that hurts like hell," he said to no one in particular.

Surprisingly, a voice responded from the door of the ambulance. "Relax, Mr. Quick. You suffered a severe concussion. Your eyes are going to be extremely sensitive. You're lucky—"

"To be alive. I know," John interrupted. "Not the first time either—*and* with a concussion. Not my first rodeo, so to speak . . . unfortunately."

He squinted and slightly opened his eyes to see a twenty-something, baby-faced paramedic looking at him intently, gauging his physical well-being.

"Three questions, son. One, how long was I out? Two, what the hell happened? And three, what's your name?"

"It's David, Mr. Quick. I'd say you've been out for at least an hour or so. We arrived on the scene after the FBI called it in. It's a little after eight o' clock. As for what happened, Mr. Quick, I have no idea. I'm just a paramedic, but it looks like you had yourself a small war here. Let me find an FBI agent for you. Back in a sec."

Before John could ask any more questions, David jumped out the back of the ambulance and disappeared.

His eyes slowly adjusted to the light, and the first view John had through the back of the ambulance was of the front of his house—or at least what was left of it. The porch railing was shredded, most of the individual posts were gone, and the remaining ones were barely hanging by splinters. Parts of the porch surface itself had been stripped: some sections were vertical, as if someone had physically pried them up with an invisible, enormous crowbar. The most impressive damage was the enormous hole where his front door had once hung.

Not only had the door been blown completely off its hinges, but all the framing was destroyed as well. He saw the top half of the door lying in the grass several feet from the front steps, and he instantly realized what had happened and how close he'd actually come to the afterlife . . . again.

I am lucky to be alive. That could have taken my head off or even sliced me in half. Good Lord . . .

His thoughts were interrupted when a serious-looking man in a dark-blue FBI field jacket appeared at the back of the ambulance. He wore a bulletproof vest underneath the lightweight jacket. The man's black hair was combed back and fixed in place. It reminded John of that L.A. Lakers coach from the eighties who won all those championships, although he couldn't quite remember his name under the current circumstances.

"Mr. Quick, I'm Special Agent Jack Thorton. You're lucky—"

"I know. I know," John said dismissively. "Another concussion. Sucks. The kid told me as much."

The agent continued. "Anyhow, at least you're going to be okay." He paused as another agent out of view said something to him John couldn't understand.

"Listen, Mr. Quick. There are several things I need to tell you because the men who did this are gone, minus the two that you killed, of course. But before I do, I have to ask you a very important question: did you have an Iraqi national flag from your time in Fallujah? And if so, where is it?"

John studied the face of the agent. He was sure he'd misheard the man. *My head must be more fucked up than I thought. An Iraqi flag?*

"Say again, Agent Thorton? A flag? You've got to be kidding me."

"I wish I were, Mr. Quick. I'm not, and this is deadly serious, as you now know. Do you have it?"

This entire situation felt preposterous and surreal to him, but he answered nonetheless. "I do. It's in my study on the wall."

Agent Thorton turned and spoke to the agent out of John's sight. "Check the study now. It should be on the wall if it's still here."

He turned back to John as the other agent ran inside the house.

"Okay. Here's the deal. You're not the first one attacked today. This same organization—they're somehow connected to the Los

Toros cartel—tried to kidnap your former commanding officer, Logan West."

John raised his eyebrows. "How'd that work out for them?"

"Not so well. He killed a man in his Annapolis home."

"Not surprising," John said.

"Well, they then tried to hold his wife ransom. They got her, but only after she killed two of them herself."

"Good for Sarah," John said.

"Mr. West—after he survived the attempt on himself—called Special Agent Mike Benson. I believe you know him?"

"I do. Sounds like quite the fiasco."

"It was. Special Agent Benson's uncle just happens to be the assistant director for counterterrorism. Mr. West and Special Agent Benson then proceeded to rescue Mr. West's wife. They left one gunman alive."

John sat up and smiled. "That asshole's lucky. So where are Logan and Mike now?"

"On their way to Quantico. All we know is that these men were looking for that flag you had inside your study. I say 'had' because I'm guessing it's already gone. The bottom line, someone or some organization has launched a serious campaign to get that flag, and we're still struggling to figure out why. The surviving gunman stated that the flag is critical to some attack and mentioned the loss of—and I quote—'thousands of innocent lives,' but he didn't have any more details." He paused to allow John to process the gravity of the situation.

"Jesus. I knew these were serious men. The one I killed with my KA-BAR—his name was Hector; he told me so before I killed him—was a professional and trained in hand-to-hand combat. He was good. Really good." *Just not as good as I am,* he thought matter-of-factly and without a trace of arrogance.

The second agent suddenly reappeared from the house and shook his head, confirming Special Agent Thorton's suspicion.

"As I thought. So now that we know the flag's gone, can you tell me exactly what happened?"

John recounted everything that occurred, including the fact that there'd been at least two more men, the sniper and the man whom John had heard exit his house. *He'd had the flag in his possession as I heard him leave. Damnit.*

When he finished, Special Agent Thorton removed a BlackBerry from a cell phone holster on his belt, dialed a number, and waited.

"Sir, he's awake. The flag's gone. Mr. Quick killed two of the attackers. At least two more were here, but they escaped with the flag."

He paused, staring at John. "Okay, sir. Will do. I'll hold."

After a brief moment, he said, "Roger. Here he is," and handed the phone to John. "It's for you."

John grabbed the phone and placed it to his ear. His head still throbbed from the concussion.

"This is John Quick."

"Still alive, are you? So much for your retirement . . . I think your peace and quiet just went away with the assholes that tried to kill you and blew up your house."

John smiled broadly at the sound of his friend's voice.

"Logan, your concern is overwhelming. I'm touched. But I hear you had your own excitement today." His sarcasm switched to genuine concern. "You and Sarah both." He paused and continued. "Seriously, brother, I'm glad you're okay. This is some crazy shit, even for us. Any idea what the hell is going on, other than some assholes screwing up our retirements?"

"Funny you should ask. As a matter of fact, the FBI is in the process of questioning the man I captured. I'm down in Quantico right now with Mike Benson. Remember him from Iraq?"

"Of course. How is he? Guess he had your back today. Glad to see even a fed can get dirty once in a while."

"He definitely did. He shot one of Sarah's captors through our kitchen window. It was a nice shot. You would've appreciated it," he said, complimenting John's own formidable skills as a marksman.

"Sounds like it."

"Anyhow, we should know more after the interrogation is over. In the meantime, I have a proposition for you. Are you sitting down?"

John sighed. *Here it comes.* "Man, I'm in the back of an ambulance. I was knocked out by a booby-trapped grenade inside my front door. So yes, I'm sitting down. Why is it that every time I seem to get blown up, it involves you?"

Logan laughed, relieved that John at least had his sense of humor intact. "Must be my special karma."

"It's definitely something," John said.

"So here it is: how do you feel about consulting with the FBI on this case? I've been asked to assist in an official capacity as a private contractor."

John remained silent, waiting for more before he responded.

"I kid you not. Obviously, you remember Mike, and Agent Thorton probably mentioned his uncle. Well, his uncle called me directly and asked for our help. He figures the more manpower, the better, especially since several of the men we're up against are former Special Forces."

John interrupted him. "These guys definitely were. I killed one of them in a knife fight, and trust me, he was no amateur."

"It's why he wants us on the team. We have experience dealing with these guys. He also knows what happened with his nephew in Ramadi. He read the details of that classified operation. The bottom line is he thinks we can help. I told him I'd ask you, but that it was your decision. I'm already in."

Logan paused to let John decide for himself, although he already knew what John's answer would be.

"Do I get a company car? Looks like my SUV took some shrapnel in the explosion, and I'm going to need a new one."

Logan laughed. "A company car is the least of it. We have the full resources of the FBI. You're actually going to be legitimate, which is one scary thought."

"Just as long as I don't have to wear a suit. No offense, Agent Thorton."

Thorton just shook his head, raising his eyebrows. "None taken."

"You can wear anything you like, but I need you to pack a bag now. Pack both warm- and cold-weather clothes. Agent Thorton has to get you to the airport. I'll see you in San Antonio tomorrow morning."

"San Antonio? What the hell is in San Antonio?"

"A drug cartel enforcer. The bad guy we captured gave us that information. The FBI is working on the cell phones we retrieved as well," Logan said.

"Drug cartels? Special Forces mercenaries? Any more good news?"

"Yeah, John," Logan responded seriously, "If we're lucky, we'll get some payback on these motherfuckers. They came after me, killed my dog, and held my wife hostage. No way they get away with it—not as long as I have a say in it."

John closed his eyes. "I'm sorry about Daly, Logan. I know what he meant to you." After a moment, he went on. "I'm with you. We'll put a stop to whatever the hell's going on. I'll go pack right now. Be safe and see you soon."

John recognized the righteous, controlled rage in Logan's voice. It concerned him, not for Logan's sake, but for the sake of the men they were now hunting. He'd heard Logan talk like that once before, in a deserted compound in Fallujah after an ambush by insurgents weeks before Operation Phantom Fury had started.

When Logan was finished, not one insurgent had remained alive. That operation had removed any semblance of mercy Logan West might've reserved. They'd all seen the true evil men were capable of that day, and Logan had been forced to accept the fact that the only successful strategy to defeat those insurgents involved eliminating them completely.

John had no issue with it, but what had impressed him was how quickly Logan had transformed. The enemy had awakened the true warrior in Logan West, and he'd fully embraced it as if he were Ares himself. It was as if Logan had been made for a singular and lethal purpose. *God help whoever's behind this, because Logan will kill them all.*

He walked back into his home to pack his clothes and weapons. He thought again about that last ill-fated mission in Fallujah, fully aware that it'd been four years ago that both his and Logan's fates were altered forever.

The mission had ultimately resulted in his early retirement and Logan's "medical retirement," which he knew was a smokescreen and a failed attempt by the Marine Corps to somehow appease Logan's sense of moral outrage at the events that had transpired.

He shook his head as he walked through the gaping hole that had once been his door. He and Logan were back in business. *Some things never change.*

CHAPTER 15

THE GREEN ZONE

BAGHDAD, IRAQ

29 OCTOBER 2008

Cain Frost paced back and forth across his office deep inside the Green Zone. He waited for confirmation that his team had retrieved the flag.

The suspense was maddening as his attempts to control his emotions failed. He was a caged tiger, intense concern rippling across his hardened face.

At five eleven, he wasn't an imposing figure, but closer scrutiny revealed a lithe, fit, and capable man who moved with the ease and quickness of a trained fighter. Each movement was executed with maximum efficiency.

His short black hair looked like it'd been tousled by the wind. A closely trimmed black beard, combined with the prestige of his position, afforded him a degree of credibility among the Iraqi generals and politicians he interacted with on a daily basis.

He wore a crisp white button-down shirt and a pair of ironed and impeccably tailored khaki trousers. The ensemble was completed by a pair of tan Oakley combat boots that had more in common with cross-trainers than actual boots. They were built for quickness in a rugged environment, which perfectly characterized Iraq.

He looked around the office, his icy blue eyes analyzing his surroundings for the umpteenth time. He appreciated the sparseness of personal mementos, the only one a picture of him with his brother from when they'd played football together at USC, before the world and the injustice it dished out had pulled them into its crushing vortex.

The two brothers had been a living dichotomy, two forces moving in opposite directions, yet inexorably connected. Steven had been the idealist, the one who thought individuals could change the world; Cain, the realist. He'd seen the truth at an early age. Ironically, it was Steven who'd shown it to him, albeit unintentionally.

When Cain was fifteen and Steven seventeen, they'd taken their annual family trip to Wisconsin. Their father owned a successful metal manufacturing company in Akron, Ohio, and every summer, the family piled into the family van and drove up to the Door Peninsula for two weeks of boating, water-skiing, and fishing. It was on the way home that their world had changed.

Two hunters, returning from a long day of drinking and hunting, had crossed the double yellow line and struck the Frost van head-on. Cain and Steven had been in the rear row of seats, engrossed in an intense game of travel Connect Four. The impact flipped the van on its side, and Cain had been trapped under the middle row. The vehicle had caught fire, and Steven, somehow unscathed, had managed to free Cain and drag him to safety.

As Steven made his way to the van for their unconscious parents, the surviving passenger had stumbled out of the wrecked pickup, still drunk, and just stared at the van. *The coward didn't even try and help.* Before Steven could reach the van, it exploded into flames and smoke.

The image of that remaining hunter, swaying like a drunken boxer as his parents burned, was seared into Cain's soul as the epitome of all human selfishness and cruelty. For Cain, the moment had crystallized his world into one singular reality—Steven was now his entire family, his constant. Amid the carnage and smell of burning gasoline, he'd vowed that no one would ever take that away, the way his parents had been violently torn from their sons' lives.

The two brothers had learned diametrically opposed lessons from the same traumatic event, fundamental changes in their characters that revealed themselves as the brothers grew into young men.

Steven became convinced that one man could make a difference, change the world. By saving his brother, he'd unlocked that part of himself that wanted to help others and actually *believed* he could. On the other hand, Cain's belief system solidified around himself. There was no God. It was a cruel world where bad things happened to good—not just good, but wonderful, loving, full-of-life—people. It was a world where careless men killed innocent people, a world where you had to increase your odds of surviving through preparation, discipline, and training.

Cain focused his efforts on supporting his brother, making one personal sacrifice after another. Steven had thought it was out of love. Cain had even deluded himself into thinking the same. But in the end, not even he could prevent the inevitable. The world was full of horrors, a world where weak men did nothing while evil men walked free to do the devil's bidding.

Well, that's about to change, Cain thought as his Iridium satellite phone rang and broke the repetition of his pacing. He walked over to his desk, picked up the phone, and pressed the talk button.

"Yes?" He waited, his body tense.

Relief from the confirmation surged over him like a wave. He sat down and sank into the luxurious leather of his desk chair. All assets were finally in place; the operation was about to commence.

Thank God. We're almost there, Steven. By this time tomorrow, I'll have it, and then vengeance will be ours.

The last few years of endless searching and planning were about to pay off. He couldn't believe their victory was nearly at hand.

The irony of Logan West's and John Quick's involvement was almost too much for him to bear, but he intended to make the most of it. Their failure years ago only deepened his hatred for them. Intellectually, he understood they weren't responsible, but his rage overshadowed rational thought when it came to his brother.

They'd been there. They could have done something. They should have gone sooner.

If only he'd known the flag was in their possession, he might have made a few different decisions. Regardless, he wasn't one to second-guess his choices. There was nothing to be gained from self-doubt.

If nothing else, the years of searching had provided him the opportunity to create the largest private security firm in the world. It earned hundreds of millions in profit from security contracts worldwide, not just in Iraq and Afghanistan.

HRI—Hard Resolutions Incorporated—was a globally recognized firm that provided security and "peace of mind" to US government officials entrenched in foreign policy and global military matters.

Even the current president had personally thanked him for his contributions to the stability in Iraq, following the success of the surge. He'd recently received an invitation for lunch at the White House. He hadn't responded with a proposed date, since unfortunately, once this operation was over, he doubted he'd be welcome back into the United States, let alone at 1600 Pennsylvania Avenue.

At least I'll have justice, and that's all that I need.

He closed his eyes and said a prayer to his brother, hoping that if some type of afterlife existed, Steven appreciated what Cain was doing to change the course of history in the Middle East.

PART II

THE SANDBOX-PART ONE

CHAPTER 16

Captain Logan West sat in the small conference room surrounded by plywood walls and camouflage netting that hung from the ceiling.

His impatience slowly transformed into a gnawing anger he struggled to control. Four hours wasn't enough time to plan a successful assault-and-rescue mission on a suspected insurgent compound, especially based on the questionable intelligence the CIA liaison officer had just provided.

Captain West had been summoned to the Tactical Fusion Center—referred to as the TFC—to receive a brief from a CIA officer who'd flown in from the Green Zone on a Black Hawk helicopter only an hour ago. He'd been at the gym and was already pissed off that his afternoon workout had been interrupted.

"You've got to be kidding me, right? With all due respect, I don't care if it's Saddam Hussein himself hiding in this house. I need more than a few hours to prepare my Marines, especially when you're telling me you have no idea how many insurgents are at this place, what kind of defenses they have, and even more importantly, who the target is. And don't forget the fact that this house is in the middle of nowhere, with no good avenues of approach."

When Captain West finished stating his objections, he glared at "James." He was certain it wasn't the agent's real name. The agency had a ridiculous habit of using cover names, even when it wasn't necessary. Even when everyone who dealt with the "Other Government Agency" jokingly made fun of the institutional rigidity, the leadership at Langley continued the practice, ever in denial that anything they did might be silly or needless. *The alias was always something generic and stupid. James, Bob, what-the-fuck-ever . . .*

"Captain West, all I can tell you is that our source, a very reliable one, informed us that a high-value target—reported to be one of Saddam's henchmen—is using this house as a bed-down location while he operates throughout Al Anbar Province. If we don't go there tonight, we're going to miss him."

Captain West shook his head. *I can't believe this shit.*

"I understand your frustration," James continued, "but General Longstreet has committed any and all resources to us for this mission, and that includes *you* and your Force Recon platoon. You know as much as we do."

His icy gaze arrogantly told Captain West everything he needed to know about this man. Dropping the name of the First Marine Expeditionary Force commanding general was intended to intimidate him. Unfortunately, James didn't know Captain West very well.

"Don't worry, James. I'll be talking to General Longstreet as soon as this little prep session is over. I'll see what he has to say about it before I do anything. You understand me?"

James shrugged. "Do what you have to, Captain West, but it's been decided."

"If he orders me directly, obviously, we'll do it, but I'm telling you now, James, if this is some bullshit mission, I'm holding you personally accountable, you understand? I won't put my Marines in harm's way for some half-assed ghost chase, especially when we're only weeks away from retaking this godforsaken city."

There was no mistaking the threat behind his words. Logan's loyalty to his Marines and his steadfast resolve to protect them was paramount. He'd taken his officer's oath seriously.

"We leave at twenty-one hundred hours. Here's a hard copy of the intel." James handed Captain West a red folder with the word *SECRET* printed across the front cover in big capital letters.

"I suggest you study it and prepare your men." Before Captain West could respond, James turned and briskly walked out of the small conference room.

Captain West turned and looked at the other man in the room, Gunnery Sergeant John Quick. His platoon sergeant had sat silently throughout the entire exchange but spoke up now that they were alone.

"Sir, that is one gigantic asshole. Those CIA types are arrogant as hell. Think they know how to run operations, although most of them never get their hands dirty."

He shook his head and ran his right hand through his crew-cut brown hair as if to convince himself this conversation hadn't occurred. He finally looked at his commanding officer, stood up, and asked, "What do you want to do?"

Captain West formulated his next move as he exited the conference room with Gunny Quick at his side.

"Gunny, you go prep our boys. If our good friend James invoked General Longstreet's name, I'm sure we're going to have to suck this one up, as much as I don't like it."

As they reached the entrance to the TFC, Captain West suddenly stopped. The move surprised both Gunny Quick and the young lance corporal providing security at the front desk.

"Make sure everyone has plenty of water and ammunition. Borrow two M79s from our SEAL friends. Pack a couple of Claymores and some explosives. This part of Fallujah is a known safe haven for insurgents, and as much as I detest clichés, I have a bad feeling about this one. I want us as heavily armed as possible. I'll be back at the Cantina as soon as I see the general. Take this with you," he said as he handed over the folder James had provided. "Any questions?"

Captain West read Gunny Quick's face, trying to sense any doubt or hesitation. There was none. Both were trained and dedicated professionals, poised for action. They might not like the mission, and they definitely didn't trust the CIA, but orders were orders.

"Negative, sir. I got it. See you when you're finished."

———

In the central part of Camp Fallujah stood a fortified facility that had once been the living quarters of an Iranian dissident group leader. Captain West knocked loudly on the metal door that served as the front entrance to the current resident's quarters.

After four knocks, the general's aide—a serious-looking major, shorter than Captain West but just as fit—opened the door and asked, "What can I do for you, Captain West? The general's getting ready to head over to the COC for his afternoon operations brief." The camp's combat operations center was where all tactical, logistical, and air support operations were coordinated.

"Major Carter, I'm sorry to bother him, but I really need to speak to him right now. Please tell him it's about this mission tonight." Major Carter looked confused, his brow furrowing.

"I didn't think we had any missions going tonight. We're in an operational—" He was interrupted by a voice from a distant part of the quarters.

"Let the captain in, Jack. And then I need you to head over to the COC and let them know I'll be a few minutes late." He laughed and added, "It'll give them a few more minutes to come up with another Chuck Norris saying."

It was a long-standing tradition that had somehow taken on a life of its own over the past several months. At the end of every brief, the operations officer included a short saying that spoke to the true lethality of the action hero. It was even rumored that the deputy commanding general was trying to coordinate a visit from the man himself.

As Captain West entered the quarters, spacious by Iraqi standards, General Longstreet said, "You know what they say, 'Chuck Norris is the reason Waldo is hiding.' Now leave me and the captain alone, and I'll see you over there. Thanks, Jack."

Major Carter didn't hesitate. "Roger, sir." He exited the building, nodded at Captain West, and closed the door behind him.

Captain West looked at the general, who at fifty-two years of age was an intimidating figure of a man. His barrel chest showed through his green tee shirt. He didn't have his camouflage blouse on, and he was holding a towel in his muscular left arm. His salt-and-pepper hair was slightly damp, and Captain West realized the general must have just returned from an afternoon PT session. His fitness was legendary, a carryover from his days at First Force Reconnaissance, time which included some extremely sensitive missions behind enemy lines in the immediate days before Operation Desert Storm.

The general spoke first. "Logan, I know why you're here, and I'm sorry to tell you, son, that this operation is on. This one is coming straight from the Green Zone in Baghdad. Hell, I'm not even sure how much they're not telling *me*. All I know is that a phone call was made by the director of the CIA to Baghdad, and I received a phone call from General Harding earlier this afternoon. This mission has the highest priority. I know it's last minute, and it's dangerous as hell, but it's a go."

Captain West was stunned. *The commanding general of all forces in Iraq had called? This is crazy.*

"Sir, I'm not sure what to say. The intelligence is sketchy at best. That CIA asshole said it was a HUMINT source and not corroborated by SIGINT or anything else for that matter. On top of that, we're supposed to be in an operational pause—like Major Carter said—and weather isn't going to permit any UAV support. We're basically on our own and going in blind. *And* into an insurgent-infested hotspot. It's not going to be pretty, sir."

"Logan," General Longstreet said. *He used my first name. It's a done deal.* "My hands are tied. I know it sucks, but if anyone—and I do mean anyone—can do it, it's you and your Marines."

Captain West paused, and General Longstreet sensed he had something else to say. The general waited patiently. Finally, Captain West spoke, his voice steady and calm.

"Sir, I'm your asset. I do what you tell me. I just needed to hear this one from you. I guarantee we'll get this target if he's there, or die trying—although I prefer it to be the former, sir." He managed a wry smile.

"Sir, if you'll excuse me, I need to attend to my men. Gunny Quick is already prepping them, but I need to memorize the file the CIA gave us and brief the Marines one last time."

"Listen, Logan." *There it was again.* "I trust your judgment, especially after what you did for me in Ramadi," he said, referring to a meeting with the FBI and local tribal leaders that had gone horribly wrong. Logan and his Force Recon Marines had ultimately rescued General Longstreet and the FBI liaison officer from a guaranteed flight home in body bags. "More importantly, I trust your loyalty to your Marines." The general let the gravity of the compliment sink in. A moment passed.

"Now get the hell out of my quarters and let me finish getting dressed. Good luck, son." With that remark, the general reached out and shook Captain West's hand firmly, looking him squarely in the eyes as he did so.

Captain West had almost reached the door when the general added, "I have faith in you, even more so now than I did on that day in Ramadi. Just remember that. I do. Every day I'm still breathing."

"Thank you, sir."

Captain West exited the general's quarters, briefly wondering if he'd see the general again. He looked at his watch, his thoughts interrupted by the time.

Fifteen thirty? I need to go. I'm burning prep time and daylight.

———

Captain West entered the Cantina and assessed the scene in front of him. Even though the lack of planning weighed heavily on his mind—an operation like this usually required at least twenty-four to forty-eight hours for adequate preparation—he was encouraged by the intensity and focus he saw on the faces of his Marines.

The Cantina was First Force Reconnaissance's combat operations center, nicknamed the Cantina out of pure irony, since there was a zero tolerance policy for the use of alcohol by any US forces in Iraq. Located in the southern part of Camp Fallujah, it provided easy access to Highway 1 just south of the camp. The highway curved to the north and connected at a cloverleaf exchange to Route Michigan, which led west into the heart of the city.

The structure had once been used as some sort of storage facility, but it was more than adequate for Captain West's purposes. All mission planning was conducted inside its walls.

Gunny Quick looked up. He stood over the table in the center of the room with the contents of the intelligence folder spread out before him. Next to him were First Lieutenant Kyle Williams and his platoon sergeant, Staff Sergeant John Lopez. Both men watched as Captain West moved to their side of the table.

"So what do we know about the target location? Is any of this information worth a damn?" Captain West asked.

"Sir, for a bunch of bureaucratic spies, they've given us everything we need; however—and all kidding aside—this is going to be tight. Take a look."

Gunny Quick grabbed one of the satellite images printed on a regular sheet of paper in black-and-white and placed it in front of Captain West. He bent over to scrutinize it more closely.

"It's in the southern outskirts of the city. It's an isolated compound that has two single-story houses about three clicks west of Highway One. Looks like our best approach is via Humvee. There's a series of dirt roads off One right here."

He pointed at a military grid map that depicted several dotted lines intersecting Highway 1 approximately two kilometers south of the cloverleaf intersection.

Gunny Quick continued. "The problem will come when we get close to the target. As I said, it's isolated. There's nothing around it for five hundred meters in any direction. Additionally, it looks from this satellite photo that there's some kind of perimeter wall. I can't tell how tall it is, but it looks taller than I am. The whole place is one big square. There appear to be two openings, one in the northwest corner and one in the southeast corner. And between the wall and the building is approximately thirty meters of open ground." Gunny Quick paused to let the information sink in.

Captain West clenched his jaw and let out a barely audible sigh. "Perfect. So if there are guards—and we have to assume there will be—they'll have plenty of chances to detect us, either approaching across the big, open space or at the wall entrances. Even if we scale the wall and the guards hear us, we're sitting ducks. Fan-fucking-tastic . . ."

He continued to study the photos and map. Finally, he looked up into the faces of his Marines. He knew they expected him to have a plan. He was their leader, for better or worse. So far, he hadn't let them down.

"Okay, here's the deal. I see only one option, and it's not going to be pretty. We're going to pull a Rommel."

Captain West intentionally stopped to see if the reference registered with his Marines. He saw Gunny Quick smirk, his brown eyes amused by the idea. The looks on the faces of Lieutenant Williams and Staff Sergeant Lopez told a different story.

"I'm disappointed, Williams. Don't they make you read at the Basic School anymore?"

Lieutenant Williams didn't know how to respond. "Only pop-up books, sir."

Captain West laughed. "Fair enough. I didn't think you could read anyhow," he responded, to the amusement of the two staff NCOs.

"Okay. All kidding aside, I know you all know who Erwin Rommel was, the famous commander from World War II who led the Germans' tank campaign in North Africa; however, what most people don't think of is Rommel's time as a junior officer in World War I, which earned him multiple decorations for heroism. As a result of his exploits, he published a book called *Infantry Attacks*, which outlined several of his successful tactics. For us, the key one is the good old diversionary attack, which is precisely what we're going to do tonight."

Captain West outlined his plan, which included sixteen men, four Humvees, and the element of surprise. When he was finished, he looked at the clock hanging on the wall. The red digital display informed him it was already 1630. *This is moving way too fast.*

"Any questions?" Each of them knew the risks, as well as his specific responsibilities.

"One, sir," Gunny Quick said. "What about James? We can't have a civilian slowing us down. He may be CIA, but I don't trust the bastard."

"I already thought of it, Gunny, and you're right. I'll deal with him at the eighteen hundred brief with General Longstreet. He won't be coming with us. Any other issues?"

The silence confirmed there were none. Captain West added,

"Good. Now get your men prepped. Ensure they have a hot meal and are rested. I have a few things to attend to, and I'll see you all back here at twenty hundred."

––––––––

COMBAT OPERATIONS CENTER
1745 LOCAL HOURS

Captain West stood against one side of the gigantic two-story combat operations center, immersed in an intense conversation with James. Even now, in the face of Captain West's verbal onslaught, the CIA operative somehow managed to retain his arrogant demeanor.

"James, I don't care what you want. Take it up with General Longstreet. He approved my request fifteen minutes ago. He'll be here shortly. The bottom line is this—my men and I are doing this operation, but we're doing it my way, and that doesn't include you. I'll see you after it's over for the debrief."

Captain West abruptly turned and walked away, leaving James to stand there alone in stunned silence as the general's staff filed into the room in preparation for the brief.

Later, as he left the conference room, his mind examined each detail of the operation, dismissing all thoughts of James or the CIA. Had he known it would be the last time he'd see James in Iraq, he might have handled the situation differently. In fact, if Captain West had even remotely suspected the way the operation would ultimately unfold, he likely would have drawn his .45 pistol and shot James point-blank in the face.

CHAPTER 17

Captain West was confident they had at least a puncher's chance of pulling this operation off successfully.

He looked over the west wall of the camp and saw the city of Fallujah, several kilometers away, sporadic lights flickering in the darkness. Random civilian and military vehicles moved along Highway 1. He hoped the light traffic would disguise their destination.

Even the dense cloud cover that precluded the support of an unmanned aerial vehicle—a UAV—now seemed to favor them. The lunar gods had blessed his Marines with only six percent illumination, which was enough for them to use their night-vision monocles but not enough for the enemy to observe their approach with the naked eye.

A light breeze brought a touch of coolness to the air, a pleasant reminder that the winter months would soon break the unbearable daytime heat.

He heard Gunny Quick approach him from behind.

"Sir, we're ready to move out when you are."

Captain West turned to him and scrutinized his battle-hardened

Marine. Gunny Quick's expression reflected Captain West's own feelings about this mission. *We can't afford any mistakes.*

Satisfied, he responded, "Let's roll," repeating Todd Beamer's final words on United Flight 93. The significance was not lost on Gunny Quick, and he nodded approvingly.

Both men entered the lead Humvee. Captain West sat in the front passenger seat; Gunny Quick behind the driver—Sergeant Tom Avery, a compact twenty-seven-year-old Marine on his second tour in Iraq with Force Recon. In addition to being a team leader and Captain West's Humvee driver, he was also a fluent Arabic linguist.

Gunny Quick tapped Sergeant Avery on the right shoulder, waved his gloved right hand forward, gave him the go signal, and sat back.

Sergeant Avery looked at Captain West, nodded once, and flipped the ignition switch to start the vehicle. He shifted gears and proceeded slowly toward the south entrance of Camp Fallujah and into hostile territory beyond.

CHAPTER 18

Twenty minutes later on Highway 1, three Humvees rolled to a stop at a Marine checkpoint 2,500 hundred meters from the cloverleaf intersection. Jersey barricades filled with sand were positioned every 100 meters along the road in a configuration that created a simple maze. It forced vehicles attempting to leave the city to slow down and navigate their way through it before reaching the Marines and their mounted heavy weapons, which included a .50-caliber Browning machine gun and a Mk 19 (called a "Mark 19") 40mm grenade launcher.

On the east side of the road was an aluminum building with three sides and a roof. The combat engineers had erected the structure, which housed the communications equipment the Marines required to maintain contact with their headquarters in Camp Fallujah. It also had electricity and fed that power to spotlights aimed in the direction of the city.

Multiple checkpoints like this one were located around the city of Fallujah in order to prevent insurgents from fleeing before the upcoming offensive.

Captain West smiled inside the lead vehicle as it stopped. The checkpoint provided the perfect cover for the first phase of the mission. Any insurgents observing the vehicles approach would assume they were either resupplying or relieving the Marines manning the checkpoint.

And that's if they can even see past the lights. I'm not taking any chances, though.

Captain West exited the vehicle and approached the senior Marine, a tough-looking African-American staff sergeant who stood in the middle of the road. He'd obviously been expecting their arrival.

Captain West reached him as he nodded his head in respect since salutes were forbidden by the Marine Corps in any combat area of operations.

The staff sergeant said, "Sir, I was told you'd be staging here for a sensitive mission, not to ask any questions, and to await further details from you. How can we help?"

Captain West pulled the staff sergeant over to his vehicle and explained the mission as briefly as possible. He used the map he'd prepared for the operation.

To the casual observer, it appeared almost as if he were a wayward tourist, lost and asking directions. When he finished, the staff sergeant looked at him, nodded again, and turned toward three Marines standing behind him.

"Detail, in the shack!" he said. The three Marines rapidly walked to the aluminum structure. The staff sergeant followed.

Moments later, the lights at the checkpoint went dark, the gigantic spotlight bulbs glowing in the blackness of the Iraqi night. The lights remained off as the staff sergeant yelled, "What the fuck is going on in there, Jackson? What the hell happened? Do I have to do every mother-loving thing myself? I asked you to repair the radio, not shut off the fucking power. For God's sake!"

For the next forty-five seconds, he screamed at the Marines inside. His loud display served as a diversion for the fifteen Force Reconnaissance Marines who used the darkness to mask their movements as they exited the three vehicles on the right side of the road.

They quickly moved to the back of the aluminum structure and linked up with Captain West.

Within ten seconds, he had full accountability of his men. They jogged fifty meters back down the east side of Highway 1, crossed back over the paved surface, and moved off into the black night toward their objective.

Captain West guided them from the front, and his team of hardened warriors followed, the only sound the soft *thud-thud-thud* of weather-worn combat boots and the occasional rattle of ammunition-filled magazines. They were long gone before the lights of the checkpoint turned back on.

———

Just before 2200 local hours, they reached their final staging position in a shallow wadi five hundred meters south of the compound.

As Captain West conferred with Gunny Quick, Lieutenant Williams, and Staff Sergeant Lopez, the remaining Marines provided security on the lip of the shallow ditch.

They double- and triple-checked their gear, acutely aware that in Iraq the slightest mistake could be the difference between life and death. A misplaced magazine or loose snap could easily get one killed in the heat of combat.

Captain West looked at his watch.

"Kyle, you know what you have to do, but not until twenty-three hundred on the dot. I'll do a final comms check with you at twenty-two fifty. At twenty-three zero two, Gunny and I will infiltrate the southeastern entrance with Sergeant Avery and his team. We hit the first building, hopefully with complete tactical surprise since any bad guys should be distracted by your fire. If we find the target, we'll grab him and leave the same way we entered while you continue with the small arms fire. We should be in and out in less than five minutes. As soon as we're clear, I'll contact you on the radio. Any questions?"

Again, there were none. "I got it, sir. They'll never know what hit them," Lieutenant Williams said as he stood up.

Captain West looked up at the confident Marine officer. He had complete faith in his abilities to execute a direct action mission but also knew operations never went as smoothly as planned, especially in circumstances like these.

"Kyle." The use of the Marine's first name caused him to look back at his commanding officer. "No fucking around. We keep it clean, and we keep it short. We're on our own out here. You understand?"

Lieutenant Williams heard the concern in Captain West's voice and said, "No worries, boss." Then he added, "That's why I have Lopez here . . . to keep me on the straight and narrow." He smiled broadly. "We got this one, sir. We'll be in position and ready to rock 'n' roll."

Lieutenant Williams turned away and moved off to gather his Marines and confirm the plan one last time. Captain West turned to Gunny Quick.

"Gunny, I seriously do not like this one fucking bit. There's something about it that just feels out of whack."

"I know, sir, but the lieutenant is sharp, and we're not too bad ourselves. We'll be fine."

Lieutenant Williams finished briefing his men. They stood and waited for him to move out. Before he did, he looked back at Captain West one last time, nodded, turned away, and disappeared into the night, his Marines in trace behind him. Captain West watched as the shifting shadows swallowed them one by one.

CHAPTER 19

ENEMY COMPOUND
2255 LOCAL HOURS

Captain West and Gunny Quick scrutinized the dark compound for any sign of life. There was none, a fact that made both Marines considerably nervous.

From their vantage point in some isolated underbrush two hundred meters south of the compound, all that was visible was the ten-foot-high perimeter wall. It appeared to be rough and built from gigantic square stones haphazardly put together with mortar.

In the southern face of the wall was the opening the satellite photo had captured. In the right section was an iron gate that was currently shut and probably locked. The buildings inside were completely hidden by the walls and darkness, with only the flat rooftops visible above the stone perimeter.

The movement to their staging position had been uneventful. The only incident occurred when Lieutenant Williams reported that one of his Marines thought he'd seen the flicker of a light five hundred meters to the northwest. The team had immediately frozen in its tracks and dropped to the desert floor, searching the horizon for movement. Other than the outline of a building more than a thousand meters away, there was nothing.

Captain West's team was now staged and ready to infiltrate the compound as soon as Lieutenant Williams launched the diversionary assault.

Lieutenant Williams's men had been in position since 2245 local time. They formed a semicircle approximately one hundred meters long that began in the middle of the northern wall and ended on the western wall. All fire would be directed at the northern entrance within ten meters of both sides.

Captain West had ordered Williams to prevent any fire into the compound, especially once he and his assault team had entered from the south. The last thing Captain West needed was a friendly-fire incident. *This mission is already dangerous enough.*

He looked down at his watch one last time. 2259. *Showtime.*

"Gunny, as soon as I break cover, you follow."

He turned his head to the left and repeated the same order to Sergeant Avery and his three Marines.

———

At precisely 2300, a grenade launcher initiated the assault, blowing the gate at the northern entrance completely off its hinges. The gate came to rest in a pile of twisted iron just inside the entrance.

Lieutenant Williams's men unleashed a sustained volley of fire that shattered the eerie quiet of the Iraqi night. The onslaught of lead included 5.56mm ammunition from several M4 assault rifles, two M249 Squad Automatic Weapons, two Remington assault shotguns for sound effects, and one M79 grenade launcher that fired 40mm high-explosive grenades.

The gunfire echoed throughout the compound and reverberated off the tall perimeter walls. The northern side of the compound was illuminated in a cacophony of intermittent flashes from each muzzle, as if gigantic strobe lights were aimed at the compound, flashing to the sound of the guns.

———

Captain West had watched the illuminated second hand on his watch laboriously tick by, as he waited for it to reach the twelve o'clock position.

As soon as the hand pointed straight up and the gunfire began, he broke from cover and sprinted across the two hundred meters of open ground in less than fifty seconds. Gunny Quick and the other four Marines ran close behind him.

He reached the southern gate, placed his hands on the cold metal, and felt the explosions from the grenades vibrating through the iron. He checked the lock, only to discover the gate wasn't secured.

What the hell? This was supposed to be an insurgent hideout.

With his nerves on edge, Captain West pushed the gate open. It swung inward, the loud creaking masked by the deafening gunfire.

He stepped through the opening and peeled off to the right. His eyes looked over the scope of his M4 to the inside of the compound. What he saw triggered alarms inside his head that shrieked almost louder than the thunderous gunfire.

There was absolutely no movement or light of any kind inside either building in the compound.

This is very fucking bad.

Gunny Quick, Sergeant Avery, and the other three Marines—Staff Sergeant Rick Hayes, Sergeant Matt Helms, and Sergeant Keith Baker—entered the compound behind him.

Gunny Quick's reaction was the same as Captain West's, and he shrugged his shoulders as if to say, *We're here now. Might as well get on with it.*

Captain West whispered, "I know," turned, and started moving in a fast combat walk across the open space toward the first building, his weapon raised the entire time.

The gunfire continued on the other side of the compound.

The first building was constructed of concrete, square in shape, and approximately forty by forty feet. There was one door placed in the center of its southern wall. Two small, barred windows were carved into each side. A small stone patio led to the entrance, and Captain West and his Marines moved into a tactical stack on both sides of the door.

Captain West reached out with one gloved hand and turned the doorknob to the right. Like the gate, it too was unlocked.

He looked up at Gunny Quick, directly opposite him on the right side of the doorway. He held up his right hand and three fingers and began to drop them one by one. Gunny Quick grabbed the doorknob with his left hand. When Captain West lowered his last finger, Gunny Quick turned the knob, and Captain West burst through the door, the flashlight under the barrel of his M4 piercing the darkness inside.

Gunny Quick and the other Marines were inside within seconds.

Sergeant Baker was the last one to go through the door. As he stepped inside and rushed to the right, he plowed into the back of Sergeant Helms.

"What the hell, Matt! You trying to get us killed?"

Then his eyes adjusted to the low-level illumination provided by the flashlights. He saw what Sergeant Helms and the rest of his team were transfixed by, instantly wishing he hadn't. His mind cleared, and he thought, *Oh God. What have we stumbled into?*

———

The nightmarish sight in front of them looked like it was pulled straight out of a gruesome horror movie. The sporadic movement of their tactical flashlights flickering across the room somehow made it more macabre.

The continuous din of automatic weapons outside made it difficult for Captain West to process what he saw. He continued to look though, as if the longer he stared, the more he might be able to understand what kind of monsters were capable of the kind of evil on display in front of him.

The building was an enormous space with one purpose—to serve as a modern-day torture chamber, equipped with all the requisite accommodations.

The floor was linoleum where Captain West and his Marines had entered, but the back half of the house contained an area of tile at least fifteen feet wide and ten feet deep. The back wall was also built of tile.

Jutting out of the back wall in two different locations, approximately eight feet apart, were two large metal carabiners, each holding a series of chains. It was what was connected to the chains that had stunned his trained Marines into a temporary daze—two naked bodies.

The body on the left seemed to be Caucasian, but they could only discern that fact from the light-skinned torso. The head was missing.

The dead man was propped into a sitting position. Someone had placed a hook in the ragged hole at the neck behind the spinal column in order to keep the body from falling forward. The arms were raised out to the sides, held up by a thick rope tied to each wrist. The rope had been thrown over a crossbeam in the ceiling to elevate the body. The man's torso had multiple lacerations and bruises. His legs were splayed out in front of him but ended in bloody stumps where both feet had been roughly hacked off.

The worst thing about it, the thing that Captain West would never forget no matter how hard he tried or how much he later drank, was what the torturers had done to the man's genitalia. Where the man's crotch was supposed to be was in fact a gaping, red hole.

The body on the right was just as disfigured. Although the corpse did have its head, its face was a red mask of blood.

The man appeared to be of Middle Eastern origin, with a darker complexion than the body on the left. It too was naked and propped up against the tiled back wall, its arms outstretched and raised in a similar fashion to the corpse on the left. Both feet were also missing, but instead of the genitals, both hands had been removed.

As Captain West turned away from the horror, he heard Gunny Quick ask, "What the hell is on his face?"

He looked back at the dead man as Gunny Quick moved closer to inspect the second corpse. Captain West stared at the man's face. He realized with a righteous sense of outrage what was wrong with it. *It wasn't just bloodstained.*

Gunny Quick realized it too. "Good Christ. Someone cut off his face." He said it again, as if to convince him it was real. "They fucking cut off his face, sir."

He looked at Captain West, whose own expression was one of pure outrage and fury at the perpetrators of this heinous act. The look of intensity in his eyes was something the gunnery sergeant had never seen before in his commanding officer. He understood it completely.

Captain West broke the trance. Even though it felt like they'd been in the house for minutes, it hadn't even been one.

This is getting worse by the second. We have to move.

"Gunny, you and Sergeant Avery check the other house, but I'm willing to bet there's no one there, at least no one alive. I need to get Williams on—"

That was all he said as they heard the dull *thud! thud! thud!* as at least a dozen mortar rounds were fired from somewhere nearby.

"Oh, shit. They're sitting ducks out there!" Captain West screamed.

His worst fears had been realized. The ambush had been triggered, and there was nowhere to hide.

PART III

REMEMBER THE ALAMO

THE ALAMO, SAN ANTONIO, TEXAS

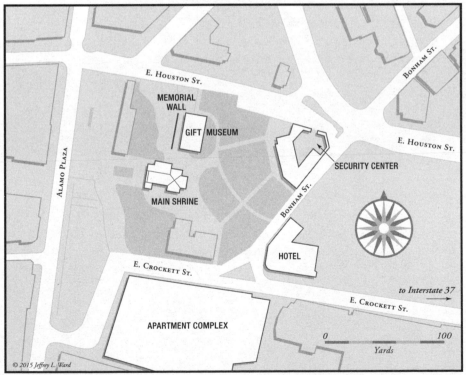

E. Houston St.

MEMORIAL
WALL

GIFT MUSEUM

Bonham St.

E. Houston St.

SECURITY CENTER

Alamo Plaza

MAIN SHRINE

Bonham St.

HOTEL

E. Crockett St.

to Interstate 37

E. Crockett St.

APARTMENT COMPLEX

0 — 100
Yards

© 2015 Jeffrey L. Ward

CHAPTER 20

The Alamo Plaza was a living testament to the paradox of modern civilization. An isolated fortress that served as the last stand for a group of honorable men who started the Texas Revolution was now surrounded by buildings, streets, highways, and the finest shopping and dining San Antonio had to offer.

Carlos figured if Davy Crockett knew what the Alamo looked like today, he might've let Santa Anna have it, revolution be damned.

He looked out into the plaza in front of him as he sat on a bench along the curved walkway running through the heart of the memorial plaza. He scrutinized the civilians that passed on the street.

His honed observation skills had paid dividends throughout most of his adult life, but this morning, he'd fought hard to concentrate on the task at hand, especially wary after the fight at John Quick's house the night before.

He'd run the scenario through his mind over and over on the private charter flight that had carried him and Edward from Montana to San Antonio. The only conclusion he could reach was that they'd somehow overlooked an exit from Quick's house. How and where? He'd likely never know, but the fact that he'd lost two good men hurt his pride.

And my reputation to boot, if I don't deliver the package . . .

He took several breaths and refocused his concentration on the small details of every person in the grass courtyard outside the Alamo Church. He looked for odd mannerisms, movements, and facial expressions—anything that might indicate trouble.

More importantly, law enforcement, federal or otherwise . . .

It was midmorning, and tourists and visitors were arriving at the Alamo, a place revered by Texans for the heroics of two hundred defenders who fought to the death against the Mexican general Santa Anna.

The legend was that when Colonel William B. Travis, the commander of the Alamo at the time of the Mexican assault, had drawn a line and asked for all men willing to make the ultimate sacrifice, only one man failed to step across it. Carlos figured that was the only smart man in the bunch. Everyone else had died.

Sure. Glory has its benefits, but what good are they if you aren't around to enjoy them?

He shook his head at the thought as he continued to watch the wide-open area for anything out of the ordinary.

The encrypted email he'd received that morning from Juan Black had informed him that he was to deliver the flag to a man who would contact him at the Alamo. He'd been instructed to enter the church at ten minutes past ten a.m. and wait near Davy Crockett's buckskin vest.

A man—he had no idea who or what he looked like—would approach him, greet him with the code phrase Juan had provided in the email, and Carlos would turn over the flag he'd recovered from John Quick's study. Clean and simple.

Carlos pulled out his cell phone and sent a text message to his four-man team providing security just outside the Alamo. "Heading inside. Wait for confirmation."

In his line of work, Carlos always had a backup plan. If things went sideways—like last night, for example—he'd need the team to provide cover for a hasty departure.

Juan Black had again emphasized how important it was that he successfully hand over the flag to the contact, going so far as to practically order him to guard it with his life until it was out of his custody. "No one gets that flag. You understand? Not the police, not the FBI, *no one*. If I find out you failed me, it's the end of you."

He stood up and walked toward the church, the large semicircular door looming in front of him.

He despised the FBI. If he had to kill a few feds to get the job done, so be it. A smile formed on his usually stern face, creating the illusion that he was just another enthralled tourist captured by the spell of the Shrine of Texas Liberty.

He reached the door, opened it, and moved inside to wait. He hoped this deal would get done and he could get the hell out of this city and into Mexico, where he knew he would be safe.

CHAPTER 21

Less than a block away in the downtown San Antonio Post Office just north of the Alamo, a group of weary and battle-hardened men struggled against fatigue from the previous night's activities.

Logan West and John Quick sat at a rectangular table in a nondescript conference room. They waited for Mike Benson to update them on what the FBI interrogators had obtained from Antonio Morales, the lone survivor from the assault on Logan's home.

Mike had told them the FBI technicians were pulling all the metadata off the phones they'd recovered. They were conducting some kind of analysis to search for patterns and similarities.

Logan's muddled brain—thirsting for more caffeine while Mike described the analysis—had blocked him out while he was speaking. Mike's explanation reminded Logan of his days in the TFC in Fallujah. He'd understood the concepts of signals intelligence—commonly referred to as SIGINT—but the technical details eluded him. A Second Radio Battalion operations officer had once tried to explain it to him. When the Marine major had concluded his brief, Logan's only thought had been, *Just tell me where they are, and I'll take care of the rest.*

He was smart enough to know what he didn't know, and the finer technological points of SIGINT had definitely fallen into that category.

Logan looked at John and asked, "How's your head?"

John took a sip from the white ceramic coffee cup filled with dark government brew and said, "I'll be better when we know what the hell is going on. This is some seriously crazy mess we're in."

Logan laughed. "Tell me about it. But like I used to say, we're in it to win it, right? Someone else started this carousel, but I'll be damned if someone's going to tell me when to get off."

The smile was gone. Only steely resolve remained in Logan's bright-green eyes, which contrasted with the dark, garish wound that ran down his cheek.

"Fair enough, brother, but God only knows how this is going to turn out. These are people with significant resources and money. You don't just launch a two-pronged operation thousands of miles apart without serious leverage or power. It just doesn't happen."

"Well, hopefully the techs can make some sense of it all, including what was on that flag that's worth all this trouble."

Logan was about to add another quip, but the door to the conference room suddenly opened to reveal Mike standing in the doorway, a look of urgency on his face.

"We just got a hit on a cell phone that the lead tech thinks might be related to the team at your house, John. It's a number that one of the cells recovered at Sarah's had contacted within the last few days. And here's the best part—and you're not going to believe it, swear to God—it's active right now, and the motherfucker is across the street at the Alamo as we speak. Saddle up."

"You're not going to tell me to get on a horse, are you?" Logan said half-seriously. "If so, I didn't bring my cowboy boots. So you might be out of luck."

"What? You need an invitation? Let's go get this asshole before we lose him. I still can't believe he's right across the street. Guess it's true what they say."

"What's that?" John asked.

"Sometimes it's better to be lucky than good."

Mike exited the room as Logan and John scrambled from the table to follow him to the underground garage and armory.

———

Carlos's patience had finally worn transparently thin. It was nearly 10:15 a.m., and there was still no sign of the contact.

He'd been standing and studying Davy Crockett's vest for more than five minutes. A security guard near the exit watched him. Was he suspicious about the tan Blackhawk backpack he wore over his right shoulder? Nowadays, all security personnel seemed to be paranoid, but who really wanted to blow up the Alamo anyway?

If his contact didn't show in the next few minutes, he was leaving the church to find a safe location and contact Juan via email. A hand suddenly grasped his left elbow, followed by a low voice.

"To the victor go the spoils, and Mr. Crockett was definitely not one of the victorious."

To which Carlos responded, "No, but his glory will last forever in this shrine."

"Indeed, sir, indeed," the man replied, confirming he was Juan Black's promised contact.

Carlos turned and studied the man's face. He appeared to be in his midtwenties—younger than Carlos expected—but his eyes had that calculating glimmer of a man older and wiser. He had short, blond hair, all one length, a mustache that curled down the corners of his mouth, and blue eyes that said *Don't fuck with me*.

Carlos had no idea where this man was from or where he worked. He knew it was probably best *not* to know.

"Inside or outside?"

The man responded, "Outside," and moved toward the exit at the rear of the church.

The daily throng was still filing onto the grounds. Pedestrian traffic was light, with maybe twenty or thirty people inside. Later in the day, the number of visitors would rise to well over one hundred at any given time inside the museum.

Both men exited the building and turned left. They walked until they reached the Wall of History, a memorial comprising several gigantic marble panels telling the story of the Alamo. The blond man stopped at the first panel and took off his black backpack, which looked heavy.

Carlos removed his own pack, reached in, and found the Iraqi flag, folded up neatly in a zipped leather pouch. He brought out the pouch, briefly thinking about the lives this artifact had cost him.

Before he could ponder any further, the young man grabbed it, inserted it into his own pack, hoisted it onto his back, looked at Carlos, and crisply said, "Thank you." The man turned around and took two steps toward the southeast pathway that led to the Bonham Street pedestrian exit.

And that's that.

Carlos let out a sigh of relief, his task complete. He turned around and quickly walked north past the Long Barracks building toward his destination, the pedestrian exit to Houston Street.

He glanced to his right. What he saw in the vicinity of the security building momentarily froze him.

What could only be three federal law enforcement officers—he could spot them anywhere—stood with another very serious-looking man with a set jaw, brown hair, and intense gaze. A large African-American man appeared to be the leader. They looked in his general direction, but at more than 150 feet away, he had no idea if they'd seen him and Juan's contact man. He sure as hell wasn't about to find out.

Carlos picked up the pace discreetly and moved toward the Houston Street exit, thinking, *How the hell did they find me?*

CHAPTER 22

Logan visually searched the area between the church and the Long Barracks, slightly out of breath from the sprint they'd just finished after deciding to discard discretion. There was no way to know how long the target would remain at the Alamo.

And if he runs, all the easier to spot him, Logan thought.

They weren't even sure what they were looking for, just hoping for a lucky break. They had no idea what the subject looked like—no age range, nothing. It was a wild goose chase.

Logan remembered one of his Amphibious Reconnaissance School instructors beating into him the mantra Hope Is Not a COA, or "course of action." At this point, he was willing to try hope, Chinese fortune cookies, or even a Native American rain dance if he thought it would provide a tangible lead.

They'd split into three groups: Logan, Mike, and three other agents covered the area near the security house; John and another FBI agent were outside in the main plaza; and two more agents were positioned outside the perimeter wall on Houston Street. All the agents had handheld radios, since they hadn't had time to don their tactical gear. They'd literally grabbed their weapons and dashed across the street.

As Logan studied the crowd in front of him, he looked for anything or anyone out of the ordinary, someone engaged in behavior only a trained eye would spot. A quick look over a shoulder, a fast break through the crowd, anything that might reveal a person's true identity.

All he saw were young couples, tourists, and middle-aged men looking for a midmorning coffee break from their office jobs downtown. He felt discouraged and was about to start over when a movement caught his eye. His head swiveled to where his peripheral vision had detected something.

There!

A young man walking quickly toward a pedestrian exit had grabbed his attention. It wasn't anything he was wearing—khaki cargo pants, loose navy pullover top, black backpack, and hiking shoes—but it was the way he moved. His stride exuded confidence and an intense purpose.

Logan was reminded of something Sarah used to harass him about when they went out to dinner or shopping. She used to say, "Hon, you look like you're on a mission, even at the mall. It's kind of scary." Now here he was, watching a potential suspect exhibit that same type of out-of-place behavior.

He has military written all over him.

"Mike, young blond man at our ten o'clock, moving toward the exit with a purpose. Also, that's an Oakley tactical backpack. I know. I own one myself."

Mike saw him and said, "Okay. Let's move. At least we can stop him and ask him what he's doing."

He radioed to the two agents on the outside, "Get over to the Bonham exit. Now! Possible suspect. Young blond man in twenties, khakis, navy pullover, black backpack. He's going to be outside in about twenty seconds. Move!"

The group of men moved swiftly down the walkway, not quite running but walking briskly enough to gain ground on the man as he drew closer to the exit.

The man was still thirty feet from the exit when he glanced left, directly at Logan. In that quick look, Logan saw a brief glimpse of recognition, and their subtle chase took on an increased momentum.

"Mike, he somehow recognized me. God damn it!" Logan shouted.

Logan broke into a sprint ahead of Mike and the other agents, cutting across the grass to intercept the man.

The man turned back toward the exit and started to run, reaching into his waistband with his right hand as he moved.

Logan held his Kimber .45 in his right hand, angled down and pointed to the ground. He heard Mike shout at the man to freeze, identifying himself as an FBI agent. The sudden commotion caused several bystanders to stop and stare, not fully aware of the danger in their midst.

The man ran, ignoring Mike's shout. Instead, he brought his right arm up across his chest to fire the .40-caliber Glock pistol in his right hand.

Logan sensed the move before it occurred and dropped down to one knee. He took aim at the man, slowly—at least in his mind; to the observer, the motion as he brought the Kimber pistol up to fire was lightning quick.

Crack! The loud snap of a rifle shot from a nearby building shattered the morning tranquillity at the Alamo, events no longer escalating but instead violently exploding out of control.

CHAPTER 23

Thwack!

Mike Benson heard the sniper's bullet strike the FBI agent standing behind him. The powerful 7.62mm round drove downward at an angle and punched an exit wound just below his sternum on the right side. The bullet tore through the agent's left lung and struck the bottom of his heart as it exited his chest. He was dead as soon as he hit the oversized stone walkway.

Panic flew through the crowd like wildfire as visitors realized what had happened. A woman screamed, and Mike heard a man yell, "Sniper! Get down!" He realized it was Logan doing the shouting, now prone on his belly after diving to the ground at the sound of the shot.

The blond man took full advantage of the diversion and ran toward the exit at a full-out sprint.

Mike watched Logan scramble to his feet to pursue him. He radioed for police and medical support for his downed agent, knowing it was already too late as he knelt next to the fallen man.

He heard one of the other agents shout, "Sir, second suspect at two o'clock!"

Mike looked up from the dead agent and saw a dark-skinned

man in a red top and khakis moving quickly toward the Houston Street exit.

"Agent Reynolds, second suspect moving in your direction. Suspect wearing khakis and a dark-red top. Assume he's armed. I say again. Assume he's armed!"

A second shot rang out. *Crack!* Mike saw the bullet ricochet off the walkway near Logan, who was already on his feet and running after the first suspect.

He heard John Quick over the radio say, "Shooter is on the roof of the apartment building across the street to the south! I'm going after him!"

Mike looked at the gigantic, city block–sized apartment complex across Crockett Street, but he couldn't see the shooter on the rooftop. He was about to respond when a series of gunshots, followed by automatic weapons fire, erupted outside on Bonham Street.

From the sound of it, he realized his agents must've encountered a heavily armed backup team. They were likely outgunned and in the most need of his assistance. He knew Logan and John could handle themselves.

This is turning into a goddamn nightmare.

Mike screamed at Logan across the grass and into his radio to ensure John heard it as well. "I'm heading outside through the security building up to Houston Street to assist! John—Logan—good luck! The shooter killed Agent Stansfield."

There was a pause as he controlled the rage starting to affect his voice. "Catch these motherfuckers but try to take at least one of them alive, if possible!"

He turned and looked at the two young agents still with him. He pointed at the older of the two, hoping he had enough experience for what he was about to ask. "Parker, you're with me. Turner, stay with Agent Stansfield's body until the police arrive. We're going to go help Reynolds. Radio me if anything else happens."

Without another word, he and Agent Parker ran toward the security building behind them that led to the Houston Street exit beyond.

Jesus Christ. This is happening too fast.

———

Edward Rodriguez had watched the drop from the apartment building across the street. From his vantage point next to a rooftop entrance in the middle of the building, he'd covered Carlos since his boss had entered the plaza. He'd hoped this would be an uneventful exchange, especially after last night's turn of events.

The former Army Ranger sniper appreciated smooth operations, and this one had been anything but, so far. The money was more than enough motivation for him to do whatever was needed to make this morning's exchange a success, but he still preferred for things to go the easy way. A smooth operation ensured both his safety and financial well-being, which were the most important things to him.

Edward had watched Carlos sit down on the bench, enter the church, exit, and link up with the man at the memorial, all without the slightest hiccup. Once Carlos handed over the flag, Edward had figured the deal was concluded, and he was beginning to disassemble his Remington M24 sniper rifle to return down the stairwell to the street below.

His balloon of optimism had been deflated when he saw the small group of what were clearly government agents enter the plaza from the security building.

He'd waited, silently hoping that they hadn't seen either Carlos or the blond man walk away from each other. Then something had happened—Edward couldn't hear or see what it was from this distance—but it had caused the blond man to run and the agents to pursue him.

He remembered the guidance Carlos had given him: *No matter what happens, this drop has to occur. The success of this entire operation rests on it. Do anything—absolutely anything—to ensure it does. Understand?*

Carlos's words echoed in his head as he drew a bead on one of the agents, exhaled, and slowly pulled the trigger, turning the quiet San Antonio morning into a modern-day O.K. Corral.

CHAPTER 24

As Logan scrambled up from the ground, he watched the blond man disappear through the pedestrian entrance to Bonham Street.

Little fucker's fast . . .

Logan sprinted to the entrance, trying to avoid the pedestrians scattering off the sidewalk as he approached. They shied away in fear, uncertain of his intent.

Logan empathized with them and realized that in the midst of the chaos, they probably thought he was the shooter, since he was carrying a gun and dressed in civilian clothes. He knew he definitely didn't resemble typical San Antonio law enforcement, especially since he hadn't shaved in four days and was operating on little sleep.

He reached the entrance, leaned against the left side of the wall, and peered around the corner onto the street. He was surprised to find that just outside the wall of the Alamo, the morning's activities appeared to be unaffected by the rapidly unfolding violence.

No one out here's realized the sounds were gunshots. Probably thought it was construction or other sounds of the city . . .

Suddenly he heard the distinct blasts of automatic weapons fire originating from the other side of the Alamo. He knew the FBI agents on Houston Street must be engaged with more suspects.

This just gets better and better.

People on the sidewalk, moving casually moments before, stopped, confused by the sound of combat and unsure what to do next. He heard voices raised in concern, one man within earshot of Logan telling his wife, "Maybe I should call nine-one-one?"

Logan looked left and saw nothing out of the ordinary in the slowly changing scenery on Bonham Street. He turned right toward a big, stone corner building across from the Alamo. It was an old, historic hotel and, based on the activity in front of it, a busy one.

The main entrance was just north of the intersection of Crockett and Bonham. Multiple guests waited to check in, their vehicles lined up on the street, facing his direction. Logan's eyes were drawn to one of the valets, an overweight man in his late fifties, pointing furiously toward the corner of the building as he spoke to a member of the hotel staff.

The man appeared to be flustered, as if he weren't really sure what to do. The hotel staffer held up his hands, trying to reassure the valet driver.

Bingo, Logan thought and sprinted across the street.

As Logan ran in between the cars on the street, the hotel staffer noticed him and shouted at him as he ran past, "Hey! He's got a gun!"

As the words echoed across the entrance crowded with hotel guests checking in and out, Logan heard several exclamations of surprise. A few women let out small screams.

Thanks, buddy. Way to add to the situation.

Logan screamed in his command voice—the one he'd used for insurgents and other situations that required an authoritative tone—"Get back inside! *Now!* It's not safe out here!"

He rounded the corner of the building, leaving the hotel guests—including the valet driver and staff member—to scramble for the glass doors to the hotel and the safety inside.

As he turned onto Crockett Street, his blood turned to ice, and time seemed to slow down as he saw the trap his quarry had set for him.

Fast, and smart . . .

Across the street, a black Range Rover with tinted windows was idling in the eastbound lane, the rear of the SUV facing Logan. Both driver's side doors were open. Standing next to each door was a mercenary dressed in dark clothes holding a compact submachine gun—*HKs*, Logan thought—aimed in his direction.

As Logan sprinted around the corner into view, both men raised their weapons and opened fire from a distance of less than fifty yards.

Even as the men pulled the triggers, Logan, having quickly registered the danger, launched himself into the air and dove toward the front bumper of a taxicab parked along the curb on his side of the street.

Speed and momentum were the only things that saved his life. As the rounds from the submachine guns tore into the body of the vehicle shielding him, he realized that if he'd turned the corner cautiously, the men would've easily had the drop on him. Instead, the speed of his arrival had surprised them just enough to cause a momentary pause before they opened fire.

Logan crouched near the front right tire as bullets shattered all the windows of the taxi. He heard a *pop! pop!* as both tires on the driver's side of the cab were punctured by incoming rounds.

After ten seconds of fire, there was a sudden silence as both men reloaded their weapons.

Logan heard loud screams from around the corner, the nearby gunfire finally motivating the passersby to seek cover.

Told you it wasn't safe.

Logan rolled from behind the taxi to his right as he heard the men's magazines clatter to the street. He transitioned into a prone position, his arms up in front of him and elevated off the street.

He knew that neither man was Blondie, the one he needed to capture alive. He aimed at the man standing next to the rear door and fired three shots from the Kimber. All three rounds struck the man in the chest, and he fell backward into the backseat of the Range Rover, slumping onto the floorboards, his weapon and a fresh magazine falling from his hands.

The man near the front door reacted with the calmness of a well-trained killer. Even as Logan's bullets struck his partner, his eyes never left Logan. In the time that it took Logan to fire his first three shots and adjust his aim, the man completed his reload, raised the weapon in Logan's direction, and fired a short burst.

Unfortunately, his aim wasn't as honed as his composure, and Logan fired twice as the man's rounds ricocheted harmlessly off the pavement around him. This time he aimed for the head.

The first round struck the man in the right shoulder—Logan credited the inaccuracy to the incoming fire—but the second round was a direct hit. It shattered the bridge of the man's nose, producing a blast of red mist in front of the man's face before boring a hole through his skull, killing him instantly.

As the man's body crumpled to the street, he heard a man scream from inside the Range Rover, "Go! Go! Go! I need thirty more seconds!"

I'll bet that's Blondie.

Logan leapt to his feet. He saw an arm emerge from the front of the vehicle, grab the handle of the door—now covered in blood—and slam it shut. The Range Rover lurched forward as the driver put the vehicle into gear. The rear tires spun momentarily, then gripped the surface, and the Range Rover shot down the street.

Without a moment's hesitation, Logan pivoted and ran back to the hotel entrance. As he entered the valet area, he realized he was in luck, since most of the guests had now fled inside the hotel. As he scanned the cars for the right one—*There! Perfect!*—he heard a man behind him say, "Are you okay?"

Logan whirled on the man, the Kimber in his hands. It was the valet driver, a terrified look in his eyes.

Logan heard the trepidation in the man's voice and replied calmly, "I'm fine. When the FBI get here—and they will—tell Agent Benson that Logan West—that's me—is in pursuit of a black Range Rover with the blond suspect in it. Got it?"

The valet nodded vigorously and repeated, "For Agent Benson, Logan West in pursuit of black Range Rover with a blond man in it."

Logan nodded and said, "Thanks. Now I'm going to borrow this guest's vehicle." And before the valet could object, Logan jumped into the open door of a metallic silver 2009 Audi A6, complete with the optional sport package and nineteen-inch tires.

He slammed the door shut, pressed the start engine button—the digital key was still in the ignition—and shifted the car into drive. Even though it was an automatic, the 350hp V8 engine propelled the sedan out of the valet area like a rocket, leaving the attendant to stare after Logan in bewilderment.

As Logan reached sixty miles per hour in less than six seconds, he prayed the Range Rover hadn't made it far enough to escape his reach. He wasn't finished with Blondie—not by a long shot.

———

As soon as John Quick had informed Mike and Logan he was pursuing the sniper, he'd sprinted down the cobblestones on Alamo Plaza Street toward the shooter's hide site on top of the apartment building. Agent Price—a man in his late forties and starting to show it—ran behind him, trying to keep pace.

It had only been twenty seconds since the last rifle shot had echoed through the Alamo Plaza, but John knew if the shooter were in the process of disassembling his rifle, he'd be off the rooftop at any moment. He'd succeeded in creating a diversion for whatever transaction had occurred just prior to their arrival.

Someone probably got my flag. That's what happened.

John reached the corner, where the ground turned from rough stone to smooth pavement. He crossed East Crockett Street in a direct line toward the double-door entrance in the center of the apartment building, avoiding the slowly moving traffic as the drivers reacted to the unfolding chaos.

When he reached the sidewalk, he turned back and saw Agent Price approximately thirty feet behind him.

Come on. Come on. Move!

After what seemed like an eternity, Agent Price reached him and leaned over, gasping for breath.

John turned and entered the front door, his .45 in front of him and Agent Price close behind.

The two men stood inside a foyer thirty feet long and thirty feet wide divided by two sets of marble columns. On their left, a doorman in his sixties gawked at them, his cap slightly askew as he stared at the armed men in silence.

Agent Price spoke first.

"Sir, FBI. There's a shooter on the roof. How many stairwells are there?"

The doorman gathered his composure and responded, "There's three here—one dead ahead past the elevators and one at each end of the corridor that runs through the front part of the building. The corridor itself is over a hundred feet long."

"Shit!" John heard Agent Price say, but he was already thinking.

Three stairwells. One near the street—that's no good, get cornered. The middle's too obvious—

"Agent Price, take the middle stairwell. I'll take the one at the left end of the corridor. The one to the right will leave him with no exit, but these two—especially the left one—will give him additional access to other parts of the building if he's cornered. It's what I'd do."

Agent Price nodded. "Sounds good to me."

He turned to the doorman and said, "Sir, get behind that desk and call nine-one-one and tell them to get police to surround this complex. Tell them Agent Price with the FBI asked you to call. Stay down until either the police arrive or you hear us coming. If you hear anyone else, don't move. The man on the roof already shot one FBI agent this morning."

The doorman's face grew pale and then he crouched behind his desk, his words echoing their sentiments precisely. "Oh, God . . ."

John and Agent Price raced down the hallway and reached the center stairwell. Agent Price opened the door and looked at John, ready to speak, when John interrupted him.

"You keep the radio. Watch your ass up there. These fuckers are professionals and nasty. Trust me. Also, make some noise as you go up the stairwell so that he gets distracted and thinks it's the only approach we're using. And then just flush him my way. As soon as you think it's clear for me, fire off three quick shots and get him to move toward me. Hopefully I'll be able to flank him. Good luck."

John nodded, turned, and sprinted down the corridor to the other end of the building, hoping they weren't too late. The hunter in him smiled as he reached the stairwell door, pressed the bar handle in, and stepped into the shadows. He eased the door closed behind him and began to silently climb the steps, landing softly on his forefoot with each step.

I'm coming.

———

Mike tried to request both local and federal backup on his radio as he and Agent Parker ran into the security building through which they'd earlier entered the eastern side of the Alamo.

He slammed the bar down on the door and rushed through, barreling into an armed security guard who was responding to the shots. The guard was flung backward onto the floor.

Mike looked at the man on the ground and then quickly around the room. Another armed guard—a white male with graying hair and a mustache in his early fifties, obviously frightened—moved toward them. A third guard was on the phone, requesting police support.

He didn't bother with introductions since he'd already informed them who he was only a few minutes ago—although it felt like an eternity had passed.

Mike pointed to the man on the ground. "You. Go stay with my fallen agent's body. There's another agent out there with him."

He looked up at the standing guard. "You're with me. We're going outside onto the street. You'd better know how to use that weapon," he said sternly, glancing at the Glock in a holster on the man's right hip.

He turned to the man on the phone. "Tell the police we have a shooter on the apartment building across Crockett Street. I have two men in pursuit. One of the suspects fled south, and I have another man after him. We're heading to Houston Street to assist our agents. Sounds like they're in a war. Let's go!"

He and Agent Parker sprinted through the office and never looked back to see if the security guard was following. The gunfire outside was now sustained, as if both sides were dug in and exchanging concentrated volleys of fire.

I hope Reynolds and Mathews are okay. It's like fucking Iraq . . .

He dashed down the sidewalk and immediately halted as he reached the corner of the perimeter wall at Houston Street. He heard

Parker stop behind him. He quickly glanced around the corner and surveyed the battleground.

A black Toyota Land Cruiser was parked a hundred feet down the street, facing his direction. Two men with assault rifles—one on each side of the Land Cruiser—had their backs to him and were firing up the street toward the position he'd assigned to his agents. Beyond the men, he saw three civilians lying in the street, apparently caught in the cross fire. None of them moved.

God damn it!

As the two suspects ran out of ammunition and began to reload, he heard the distinctive sound of two FBI-issued Glock 22 .40-caliber pistols.

He looked beyond the motionless civilians and saw his men in cover behind a parked taxi along the curb on the westbound lane near the Emily Morgan Hotel. He heard the impacts of their rounds and realized that only one of the weapons was firing in the direction of the two heavily armed men.

What the hell?

He searched the street to find the target of his agent's gunfire. His peripheral vision captured movement to his left. He turned to see the suspect from inside the Alamo—the man wearing the red top and khakis—creeping along the perimeter wall from the pedestrian exit toward the Land Cruiser. One of his agents was trying to keep him pinned down while the other returned fire at the Land Cruiser.

Even though his agents were having some success slowing the suspect down, Mike knew that the man would reach his partners in another thirty to forty-five seconds. His agents were outgunned and didn't have enough ammunition to delay him indefinitely.

Mike had no approach along the perimeter wall toward the shooters. The moving suspect was facing his direction and would likely see him if he broke cover and tried to move up the street.

There has to be something, some way . . .

A dangerous idea formed in his head. It was so bold that even Logan might have balked at it. Mike realized what he had to do and knew he was going to have only one chance to do it.

He turned to Agent Parker and discovered the security guard was nowhere in sight.

Fucking rent-a-cop!

"Here's what's going to happen."

CHAPTER 25

Logan concentrated on maneuvering aggressively through the slow-moving southbound traffic on Interstate 37 as he sped along at ninety miles per hour. The Range Rover and Blondie had gained a forty-five-second lead on him since the chase had started. He was trying to make up the precious seconds with every car he passed on the highway.

Once he'd left the hotel, he'd driven east as quickly and safely as possible and stopped at the next main intersection—actually stopped—right in the middle of it.

Fortunately, traffic had been light enough that he hadn't risked being hit by a careless motorist. The other drivers had spotted the motionless Audi, and all lanes of traffic had halted, wondering what the hell the crazy driver was doing. What he'd been doing was looking for any indication as to which way the Range Rover had gone, and he'd found one.

Approximately one hundred yards south of the intersection on the main cross street of Bowie, he'd spotted a red Honda Accord resting on a curb, both driver's side doors open. The sedan faced the wrong direction. A skid mark zigzagged across the pavement in a large curve and ended at the Honda. Logan recognized at once that the fleeing Range Rover must have run it off the road and into oncoming traffic.

He'd also figured that the Range Rover would likely try to reach a highway to place as much distance between them and the shootout. The interstate was the fastest route.

So he'd floored the accelerator, the thrum of the V8 engine purring beneath the hood as he shot down Bowie Street, looking for the first entrance ramp to Interstate 37. He'd had to turn left onto East Market Street, but once on it, he'd located the entrance ramp and maneuvered the Audi along the shoulder, never relieving the pressure on the accelerator.

By the time the entrance ramp merged with moving traffic, Logan accelerated the Audi to eighty miles per hour and moved into the left-hand lane.

Now he weaved in and out of traffic like a maniac fleeing the police. Cars blew their horns as he flew by some and cut off others. He prayed he hadn't made a mistake.

Logan drove on—twenty seconds . . . thirty seconds . . . forty seconds . . .

Where the hell are they? They have to be close!

His nerves were frayed from the stress and pressure. He had to find Blondie.

Suddenly, he spotted the black Range Rover two hundred yards down the interstate in the right lane, and a wave of relief eased his tension.

Gotcha, Blondie.

He grinned to himself and exhaled, thanking God that his gambit had paid off.

The driver of the Range Rover—not Blondie; Logan knew he was in the backseat—must have thought they'd made a clean getaway. He drove the SUV at a smooth sixty-five miles per hour, hoping he was inconspicuously hidden amid the morning traffic. Had anyone bothered to look closely, they might have wondered what the red stains on the driver's door window were, not realizing it was a dead man's blood.

Logan pumped the brakes and slowed the Audi to seventy-five miles per hour, moving into the middle lane of the interstate to the left of the Range Rover. He had a plan, but he needed to close the distance to execute it.

He inched the Audi closer to the target, keeping his eyes locked on the black SUV. Fifty yards . . . forty yards . . . The front end of the A6 devoured the pavement underneath, closing the distance.

When he was less than thirty feet away, he braced himself and did the only thing he could—slammed the accelerator to the floor and executed a well-aimed pit maneuver.

The Audi struck the Range Rover in the left rear wheel and caused the SUV to career from side to side.

Lose control, asshole, and end this now.

He thought the Range Rover was about to veer off the road when the back window lowered and the muzzle of a semiautomatic weapon suddenly appeared.

Oh no.

The man in the backseat—Logan assumed it was Blondie—opened fire on the Toyota minivan directly in front of Logan's Audi.

He saw me coming.

Rather than target Logan's car directly, Blondie intended to create as much carnage on the highway as possible in order to block Logan's path. If it weren't for Logan's preternatural reflexes, it would've worked.

The bullets struck the rear quarter panel of the minivan, shattering the taillights and the back windows. More rounds hit the right rear wheel of the minivan. The impacts shredded the tire, jerking the Toyota violently to the right.

The inexperienced driver panicked as he lost control. In the heat of the moment, he reacted incorrectly, yanking the wheel all the way to the right.

The effect was immediate and dramatic. The minivan turned right ninety degrees, the left side tires digging into the pavement. The vehicle shrieked to a stop and launched itself into the air on its left side. It hit the ground in a shower of sparks and glass and rolled down the highway like a square can at sixty-five miles per hour.

Logan hoped like hell the driver was wearing his seat belt. *Even then, he's going to be lucky to be alive—if he survives.*

The cars in the left two lanes overreacted as they watched the minivan bouncing down the interstate. A dark-blue sedan slammed on its brakes and swerved into the far left lane. It struck the back of a green SUV, which then caromed into the median, hitting it at an angle. The blue car bounced off, its back end spinning around, slicing through the air.

As the massive accident unfolded, Logan had less than one second to react. He slammed the accelerator to the floor and swerved the Audi as far right as it would go.

The Audi shot forward, and the front end missed the flipping Toyota by less than six inches. Logan concentrated on the Range Rover. He failed to see the terrified face of the minivan's driver staring at him upside down as Logan sped by.

Logan heard additional thumps and metallic crunches as more vehicles were drawn into the chain reaction. Outraged at the mayhem and wake of destruction Blondie was leaving through downtown San Antonio, he felt a deep wave of concern for the drivers, but he knew he had to focus on Blondie.

Logan planned to find out what Blondie thought justified all this reckless violence. After he did, he'd make him pay for it—*dearly.*

Logan was directly behind the Range Rover as both vehicles accelerated down the freeway. The Range Rover had no chance of outrunning the A6, but Logan knew he had to be smart about his next move. After what had just happened, he knew Blondie wouldn't hesitate to use civilians as disposable obstacles.

Logan pulled halfway into the left lane to see what lay ahead on the interstate. It wasn't what he expected. The intersection of Interstates 37 and 10 formed a gigantic cloverleaf mixing bowl, with multiple exits and entrances that weaved over and under each other.

As both vehicles streaked toward the cloverleaf and entered its enormous tentacles, Logan calculated his options. Once again, only one stood out.

He pressed the accelerator to the floor and swerved back to the right shoulder of the interstate, dangerously close to a median concrete barrier. There was nowhere else to go. They'd entered the cloverleaf and were traveling on what was essentially a bridge that traversed the entire suspended structure, its entrance and exit ramps mixing in the bowels below.

The Audi reached one hundred miles per hour. As the A6 shot forward, Logan pulled along the passenger side of the Range Rover. *Now!*

He slammed the front left corner of the luxury sedan into the right rear wheel of the speeding SUV as Blondie lowered the right rear window to shoot at Logan with an assault rifle. The maneuver was executed in less than a second. Blondie never had a chance to pull the trigger.

The SUV's rear wheel was compressed inward with the force of the impact. The disc brake automatically engaged, shrieking as it attempted to completely stop the Range Rover's momentum. The vehicle was suddenly redirected toward the shoulder's concrete barrier at close to ninety miles per hour. It was traveling too fast to stop.

Logan slammed on the Audi's brakes as he watched his handiwork unfold before his cold gaze.

The Audi skidded sideways down the interstate, rubber burning as the oversized tires gripped the concrete. As the sedan whipped by the Range Rover, Logan watched the SUV strike the barrier head-on, smash through the concrete, and fly off the top of the cloverleaf overpass.

The A6 skidded to a halt on the asphalt. Logan heard one loud *crash!* as the Range Rover's front end struck the road fifty feet below and then flipped forward, careening off an entrance ramp and leaping into the air once again.

The Range Rover fell another forty feet before it landed on its back end. The force of the landing crumpled the gas tank, which instantly exploded as a spark ignited the fuel. The Range Rover was blown in half as it slid westbound in the eastbound lanes of Interstate 10. The flaming front end separated from the back half, and the two parts of the SUV raced down the highway intent on beating each other to some invisible finish line. Both halves finally ground to a burning halt, two twisted piles of charred and flaming wreckage.

Logan jumped out of the Audi and reached the edge of the overpass just in time to see the two halves stop on the pavement far below. He watched the carnage as he heard other drivers stop their vehicles and run over to offer assistance.

He remained oblivious to them as he watched the flaming SUV. No one walked away from a crash like that . . . ever.

I hope John or Mike got one of these assholes alive. We're running out of bad guys.

———

John reached the top of the ten-story stairwell without incident. He paused at the door to the rooftop and listened. He knew Agent Price would be entering the roof within a few moments. He hoped like hell they'd made the smart choice in splitting up. If not, they'd both pay for it soon enough.

The door was steel with another bar lever that would open it outward. He desperately wanted to crack the door to glance out, but he knew doing so would likely tip off the shooter to their presence. So he waited.

Come on, Agent Price. Let's get this show on the road.

His .45 was ready, his finger extended and off the trigger. His thumb rested on the 1911's safety. He concentrated on his breathing and forced himself to lower his heart rate.

Crack!

The high-pitched report of the sniper's rifle reverberated through the metal door.

He's close, maybe only a few feet away to the left. Ready . . . ready.

Like a dinner bell calling him home, three deeper shots sounded, fired by Agent Price. *Time to act.*

In one fluid motion, John quietly depressed the door handle with his left hand. As the door swung out and to the left, he followed through with his right arm and leg, the .45 leading the way around the edge of the door.

The shooter was kneeling a few feet away, directly in front of him. He wore cargo pants, a short-sleeved white polo, and hiking boots. John couldn't discern any of his other features since he also wore sunglasses and a Texas Rangers baseball cap.

Nice touch.

He had to try and keep this one alive. He slid the 1911 into the waistband at the small of his back.

A little less than one hundred feet away, John noticed the center rooftop entrance door as it swung back and forth on its hinges. Agent Price was nowhere in sight. He hoped he hadn't been struck by the shooter's bullet.

John wasted no time. He stepped toward the man with his left foot, but as he let go of the door, the handle reset itself.

Click.

He knew the shooter had heard the sound. Without hesitation, he rushed forward to close the distance before his target could react. John was fast, but so was the sniper.

Before John reached him, the shooter dropped the rifle and rolled onto his back. He brought his right arm up and around toward John.

He's good. Where do they get these guys?

By the time John reached him, a .40-caliber Glock pistol was aimed almost directly at him. The man pulled the trigger, but John had anticipated the move and stepped forward, pivoted, and swung his right leg up in a short roundhouse kick, connecting squarely with the man's pistol before the weapon discharged.

The force of the kick caused the man to reflexively open his fingers and release his grip, and the Glock skidded several feet on the roof before coming to rest at the base of a large HVAC unit.

Even as the gun slid across the black surface, John allowed the momentum of his kick to carry his body forward. He planted his right foot and turned his body to the left—his back momentarily exposed to the shooter—and brought his left knee up and then kicked straight backward in a vicious mule kick. His target was the shooter's jaw, which was level with his blow since the shooter was still sitting on the rooftop.

Unfortunately, the shooter—now unarmed but with both hands free—blocked the kick with his left hand and pushed John's leg to the right. The man rolled away and onto his feet.

As John's left foot touched the asphalt, he pivoted on his right foot and turned his body to face the shooter, who was now in a crouched combat position within arm's reach.

Déjà-fucking-vu. Was it really last night I was in this same predicament?

The sniper stepped forward with his left foot in a feint, hoping to divert John's attention away from the right front kick he aimed at John's chest. John didn't react to the feint, recognizing it for what it was.

Instead, he delivered a vicious punch to the right side of the man's knee, hoping to incapacitate him as quickly as possible.

The man let out a muffled groan and fell forward as pain shot up his leg. He rolled away from John and scrambled to his feet, moving toward the dropped Glock lying on the rooftop.

John closed the distance in three large strides. Before the shooter could grasp the weapon, John grabbed the back of his shirt with both hands and pushed hard, using his momentum against him.

The man toppled forward and landed on his right arm, somehow managing a combat roll forward away from John. He was close to the edge of the rooftop, along the side that overlooked the inner courtyard of the apartment building. He glanced over the edge before turning to face John again.

Guess there's no easy way out.

John stepped toward him, intent on ending this fight, but the man reached down and withdrew a three-inch fixed blade from a concealed sheath strapped around his right hiking boot under his cargo pants.

Great. Not again.

Unfortunately, John wasn't carrying his KA-BAR this time. He'd left it in his pack in the FBI office since he hadn't expected another close-quarters encounter like last night's.

Guess that was a bad call.

All John saw was a brief smile; the Rangers cap and sunglasses—somehow still on his face—concealed everything else.

"You want me to take him down?" John heard Agent Price shout from somewhere close by.

Thank God he's okay.

Agent Price had picked himself up from the rooftop and had made his way toward the two men locked in combat. He was thirty feet away on the other side of the HVAC unit.

John's eyes never left his opponent. "No," he yelled back, "I got him."

"Do you now?" the man said in an amused way.

"Indeed I do, asshole."

John reached for the 1911 from the small of his back and gripped the barrel of the weapon, the pistol grip facing outward.

The man issued a laugh, his head bobbing up and down, a moving and fluid target. He moved toward John, the sun glinting off the short blade in his right hand.

John remained exactly where he was and allowed him to come closer.

The sniper moved quickly and threw a left-hand punch toward John's stomach. John deflected the blow with the pistol. As his mind registered how easy it was, he realized his mistake.

The man raised his right arm and brought the knife down in a quick arc. The blade cut a deep gash into the back of John's forearm, the shock of the wound reflexively forcing him to drop the 1911.

The pain was surprisingly sharp and intense, as well as familiar. He'd been cut before.

I must be getting old, he thought, as blood dripped to the surface of the roof.

John, though wounded and bleeding, still retained his warrior's focus. Rather than allow the bastard to gain more confidence—which was often the deciding factor in a hand-to-hand confrontation—he delivered a back fist that struck the man squarely on the jaw.

He reeled backward from the force of the blow, shocked at the power behind it.

John pressed forward and ignored the pain in his right arm. He stepped toward the shooter and delivered a left punch to the man's ribs. He was rewarded with a loud gasp as he found the mark.

The mercenary stumbled backward, but remained on his feet. John grabbed his right wrist with his right hand and the back of his right shoulder with his left. He pulled down with as much strength as he could muster and delivered a powerful knee to his torso that shattered four ribs.

The man roared in pain and sprawled backward, the knife clattering to the rooftop.

That should do it.

John walked toward the fallen man, but then he realized something wasn't right. He looked around. The end of the fight had carried them back *toward* the big HVAC unit in the middle of the roof.

John's eyes darted over the rooftop, looking for it, but not seeing it.

No Glock.

He knew with a sense of dread what was about to happen. The man had fallen near his pistol.

As the man moved, John dove away toward the area where he'd dropped his 1911.

This is going to be close.

The shooter pointed the Glock toward John. In fact, he'd landed directly on it and had grasped it with his hand beneath his body.

John tried to locate his own weapon. He frantically searched but couldn't find it.

Where the hell is it?

His mind processed the fact this killer had him dead to rights. He was likely going to die in the next few seconds. He closed his eyes, his back to his executioner. He just hoped it would be quick—*no pun intended, one last joke.* He smiled briefly and waited for the end to come.

As he resigned himself to his fate, two loud reports came from his left. The first bullet struck the shooter in the left temple. The second bullet smashed into the top of his head and ripped away his skull and the Rangers cap, splattering blood and skull fragments across the running HVAC unit. The Glock fell from his limp hand, and his body collapsed to the black surface.

John looked away from the man's death throes to see Agent Price not ten feet away in a traditional Weaver stance, the barrel of his own Glock aimed at the shooter.

John said, "Thanks, Agent Price. Nice shots." He looked back at the shooter's body, now still.

What a mess.

"You better call this in," John said.

He stood back up and looked down at the gash on his right forearm. He'd had worse. He looked around to see his 1911 only two feet behind him.

How did I miss it? Almost had him . . . Mike's not going to be happy.

He bent down and retrieved his weapon.

Way too close . . .

———

Mike turned to Agent Parker as the exchange of gunfire in front of them continued. They were waiting. When the two shooters stopped to reload, Mike would make the first move of his plan—or what he remotely considered a plan.

This is crazy. I'm going to get myself killed.

Then he looked again at the motionless bodies of the three civilians caught in the cross fire, and all his doubt was wiped away. He knew he'd only get this one chance.

I'm going to make them pay.

Agent Parker was ready, his weapon pointed down the street. The suspect in the red top and khakis who'd fled the Alamo when the first shots rang out slowly crept toward his mercenaries near the sidewalk. Fortunately, his attention remained focused up the street on the FBI agents. He hadn't noticed either Mike or Agent Parker—*yet.*

Houston Street was now deserted of all civilians. They'd either fled back inside the safety of the Alamo—once again a refuge—or down side streets to escape the gun battle.

Both shooters emptied their last rounds into the taxi providing cover to his agents. As the first man pressed the magazine release and dropped the clip to the ground, Mike bolted from cover—Agent Parker on his heels—toward the middle of the street. He sprinted straight toward the front of the Toyota, completely exposed.

Mike's shoes made little noise as he gained ground on the shooters. More return fire from the FBI agents kept the men's attention fixed away from him.

I hope I don't get shot by my own guys.

Both men completed their reloads and fired once again toward the taxi. The suspect was fifteen feet away, almost to the safety of the SUV. Once he reached his men, he'd be gone.

Agent Parker stopped in the middle of the street—weapon aimed toward the SUV—to provide cover should either man turn toward Mike as he approached. Neither did.

Mike skidded to a halt twenty-five feet from the shooters, far enough in front of the vehicle to provide a clear line of sight to both men. He raised his weapon and steadied his aim amid his rapid breathing. An old marksmanship adage popped into his head as he sighted on the man on the left.

Slow is smooth; smooth is fast.

He centered the Glock's sights on the back of the first shooter's head, exhaled smoothly, and pulled the trigger.

Mike was a former marksman instructor at Quantico, and at such short range, it was almost impossible for him to miss. He didn't.

The round struck the back of the man's head above the base of his neck, severing his spinal cord instantly. The round exited his mouth, shattering his teeth along its fatal path. His limp body pitched forward, all muscle control gone. He slumped against the open passenger's door before hitting the ground, his assault rifle clattering to the street.

As the first man fell, Mike switched targets to the second shooter, who now, seeing his partner fall and blood spatter on the driver's door window, realized that the shot had come from behind.

He turned to his right, the barrel of his assault rifle swinging down and backward as he pivoted to face the new threat.

Agents Mathews and Reynolds, having seen Mike ambush the two shooters from in front of the Toyota, broke cover toward the initial suspect who was only feet away from the SUV.

Agent Mathews was closer, and Mike heard him scream, "Freeze! FBI! Drop your weapon *now*!"

Mike didn't have time to see the suspect's reaction, since his eyes were locked on the second shooter.

Mike acquired center mass on the man, choosing to take the easier shot since the man was turned sideways and his profile provided less of a target. He prepared to pull the trigger when a sudden salvo of bullets impacted the ground around him, kicking up splinters of concrete that pierced his pants but miraculously missed him.

What the hell?

Somehow he'd missed a third gunman on the north side of the street.

His focus remained on his target.

I'm taking you first before your friend gets me, asshole.

He prayed Agent Parker might help with the third shooter before he, Mike, was killed, but it didn't matter. He pulled the trigger as his target turned toward him, his weapon rising toward Mike. It was too late.

Mike's first shot struck him in the right side of his chest and shattered a rib as it laterally tore through his right lung and lodged in his back.

Mike fired again, even as the man recoiled from the first shot. The second round struck him in the left side of his chest, punching a hole through his other lung and exiting his torso.

As the second man fell backward, Mike heard a pistol firing somewhere behind him.

Thank you, Agent Parker.

Mike watched as his target landed on his back and sprawled out on the concrete. He gasped for breath as his mortally wounded body shut down from lack of oxygen.

I hope it hurts. You deserve it.

When the man lay still, dead, Mike looked over to the sidewalk where the suspect had been trying to make his escape. He saw Agent Mathews with a knee in the middle of the man's back as he hand-cuffed him and Agent Reynolds provided cover.

It's over. Thank God.

He turned and looked back up the street, where a third shooter lay on his right side, his legs twisted underneath him.

He glanced at Agent Parker to thank him. He was parallel with the dead third shooter, but he pointed farther up the street from where they'd come.

What the hell's he pointing at?

And then Mike saw the object of Agent Parker's gesture: a security guard stood in a front stance on the sidewalk on the same side of the street as the third shooter.

You've got to be kidding me. And I thought he ran away.

The security guard he'd thought a coward had just saved his life.

Mike could see the shock on the man's face. He'd just killed another human being, albeit an evil one. The guard finally lowered his weapon.

Mike walked toward the man. As he passed Agent Parker, who was moving toward the SUV to check the dead men, Parker said, "I never saw the shooter, Mike . . . Never fucking saw him."

Mike nodded and said, "He got the drop on both of us. Forget it. That man just saved my life. Hell, both our lives. Check on those assholes and please make sure they're dead."

"You got it."

He approached the security guard, who sat down on the curb, visibly shaken from the rush of adrenaline and the events that had just transpired.

The sound of sirens grew louder as police from several downtown precincts finally arrived at the multiple crime scenes.

The guard stood to meet Mike as he approached. He'd regained some of his composure. Mike reached out his hand, and the security guard responded by gripping it. "What's your name?"

"Dale," the older guard said.

Mike nodded. "Mike. Mike Benson." He paused. "Well, Dale, thank you. You just saved my life. Not only do I owe you that, but I also owe you an apology. I thought you bailed on us. I was wrong, and I'm sorry."

He pumped the man's hand up and down and locked eyes with him to ensure Dale understood his sincerity. Dale smiled and acknowledged the bond that had just been forged between them, a bond men who survived combat understood but rarely talked about. Then the moment passed, and Mike lowered his hand.

"Listen, Dale. The cops are going to want a statement from you, and I'm going to be tied up. This whole thing is part of something much bigger and more dangerous, and we don't have the full picture yet."

Dale said, "Good Lord. This was bad enough."

"I know. This whole thing is crazy." Mike paused as both men surveyed the carnage on Houston Street. He continued. "When this is over, I'm going to find you, and I'm going to take you out for a beer and a Texas steak. Deal?"

Dale laughed. "Since I'm fairly certain you're not from around here, I'll pick the place."

Mike nodded. "Sounds good. Just wait here for an officer. I'm going to go check on my agents."

Dale sat back down on the curb, his weapon now holstered.

Mike walked away, his mind already focused on the logistical nightmare ahead of him, but suddenly he stopped and said, "Dale, I almost forgot. How the hell did you see him? Neither of us did."

Dale shrugged, almost embarrassed. "I was behind you as you ran out of the building, but as I came down the steps, I somehow lost my balance and fell. I dropped my damn gun, which bounced down the steps and away from me. By the time I got my sorry ass back up, you two were already at the corner. When I finally got to my gun, I bent down to pick it up, and as I stood back up, I caught a flash of movement across the street. I moved closer for a better view and I realized it was another man with a rifle. He was closer to us, for some reason, and was working his way back up the street, I guess using the parked cars for cover. Either way, I realized he'd see you two pretty soon. So I made my way over to his side of the street, somehow without him seeing me. When you made your move, he saw you like I thought he would. I got as close as I could, and as he opened fire, I fired at him."

Dale let out a breath and looked at the dead shooter. He looked back at Mike. "I guess there are some things you never forget. I spent four years in the infantry in the Marine Corps in my early twenties. Used to shoot all the time, but never like this. But all that kept running through my head was a voice from long ago saying, 'Lance Corporal Dawson, make every shot count.' Crazy, huh?"

Mike recalled his own thoughts minutes ago as he shot the two suspects. "Dale, not crazy at all, my friend. Not one bit." And then he added, "Amen for the Marine Corps, Dale. Amen."

As he walked away, he heard Dale quietly say, "Semper Fi."

That about sums it up, Dale, because without a little faith, something awful is going to happen—and soon.

CHAPTER 26

It was past two o'clock. Both local and federal law enforcement continued to process the crime scenes, and back at the FBI offices inside the San Antonio Post Office building, Logan, John, and Mike were huddled around the same conference room table where they'd been before the shooting and dying had started.

"Jesus Christ. What a mess," Mike said.

Logan and John were physically exhausted after the morning's activities. They stared into oblivion, the last twenty-four hours finally taking their merciless toll on them. Fatigue had set in, and Mike's words barely registered.

The San Antonio Division special agent in charge had recalled all FBI personnel from the University Heights office, and downtown San Antonio now swarmed with local, state, and federal law enforcement. Multiple FBI forensics teams were in route from Quantico, but even with a private government charter, they wouldn't arrive until early evening. Until then, the best local teams available were processing the scattered scenes and combing the fiery wreck of the black Range Rover for any shred of evidence.

When the shooting had finally stopped, there were eight dead gunmen and three dead civilians, the latter all caught in the cross fire on Houston Street. Miraculously, no civilians had died in the massive crash on Interstate 37. The suspect from the gun battle on Houston Street had been placed in custody. He was undergoing interrogation as they waited.

Mike continued. "My uncle just got off the phone with the director, who has to brief the president at the White House in the next thirty minutes. I told him everything we know, which right now is jack shit. The Range Rover that you obliterated and the Toyota I shot up were legally registered—you'll love this—to names and addresses that don't exist. The local police went to the addresses. The streets are real, but there are no houses or buildings with those numbers. Same thing for their identities. Somehow, these guys were able to register vehicles and obtain legitimate license plates with false identities and—here's the best part—it didn't raise any red flags at the DMV."

"I'm not surprised," Logan said, drinking a Gatorade one of the agents had provided. He was still trying to rehydrate from his recent binge. "These guys are heavy hitters with serious resources and professional training. Wouldn't surprise me one bit if they were all former military or Special Forces." He shook his head in disbelief, green eyes flashing. The slash on his cheek had scabbed over, darkening the ugly wound. "And we're not any closer to figuring out what this is all about. Unbelievable . . ."

John spoke up. "Well, the one thing we do know is that whatever was on that flag was worth killing for. Obviously, it wasn't just a flag. I've been trying to rack my brain as to what it could be, and stop me if you think I'm crazy. Remember"—he chuckled before continuing—"I was blown up and knocked unconscious last night. The only thing I can come up with is that it was either an invisible map or it contained directions to someplace or something vitally important to these guys." He paused as he looked from Mike to Logan. Neither laughed. He continued.

"If it were a geographical map, you'd think we would've recognized it. I'm betting it contained encrypted directions or a code to something. But what? That's the real sixty-four-thousand-dollar question. Unfortunately, sounds like the flag burned up with that blond-haired sonofabitch."

Mike nodded. "It did, but once the fire department put out the blaze and recovered the bodies, they also found the remnants of a laptop and what looks like some kind of printer."

"A printer? What the hell did he have a printer in the car for?" Logan asked.

There was a moment of silence as all three men pondered the question.

"Wait a second. Nowadays all printers do more than just print," John said. "Hell, I have an all-in-one in my office in Montana. I'll bet you anything that he scanned the flag or part of it into the printer and transmitted the image to the same someone who is behind this entire mess."

"And I thought you were just some Unabomber-wannabe backwoods loner. Will wonders never cease?" Logan said.

"But that's a good thought," Mike interjected. "The local forensics guys are still combing over the wreckage as we speak. I'll let them know to look for any signs of a wireless internet card or anything else that might come in handy. Once my guys get here, if there's anything they can retrieve off the printer-scanner or the laptop, they will. They're the best at what they do."

Logan nodded and then asked, "What now? I'm sure I'm not the only one who could use a shower and some sleep. No joke, I'm dead on my feet."

"Me too. Those bastards who blew up my house interrupted my Scotch last night, and I could sure use one right now." John looked at Logan and said, "No offense, brother."

Logan smiled and responded, "None taken. I think I've finally had enough."

John nodded in silent approval.

Mike smiled and said, "Already ahead of you, boys. There's a Marriott downtown that's close, nice, and offers a great government rate, of course. I already booked us rooms. I'll have one of my agents drive you both over there to get some sleep. I'll be close behind, but first, I have to update my uncle and let him know what we think about the flag. *And* I want to pop in on the interrogation. Maybe he'll give us something; maybe not. He still hasn't told us his name yet . . . arrogant fucker. Either way, I want to talk to him. We were able to get his phone, and the police techs are running it through their own digital forensics processing. We might get lucky and find something on it."

Logan nodded and said, "Sounds like a plan. Hopefully, no one declares war on us again until we're well rested. I feel like I aged ten years overnight. I also need to call Sarah and let her know I'm okay. She's got to be worried, especially if she's watching the news."

The three men stood up to leave, and as they walked out the door, Mike voiced a concern that'd been worrying him since the shootout at the Alamo. "Just between us, the longer this goes on and the longer we're in the dark, the more nervous I am about the endgame."

"I know," Logan said. "I have a bad feeling about this too. If we don't figure it out, I don't think today's casualties will be the last. I just hope it's not another nine eleven."

John said quietly, "We all do. Let's just not let it get that far, then. Once we identify these assholes, we hit them first, and we hit them hard."

Logan looked at him, bone weary. "Always."

CHAPTER 27

CAMP FROST, BAGHDAD
30 OCTOBER 2008
2200 LOCAL HOURS

Cain was in one of his remote offices in the main HRI compound southwest of Baghdad, near Baghdad International Airport, his home away from home. He watched intently on his satellite television as the US national news ran nearly nonstop coverage of the events that had unfolded in San Antonio. Some of the gun battle had been captured on video by a bystander's camcorder. It was captivating footage, gunshots and screams mixing and echoing across the urban setting, but Cain's thoughts were elsewhere.

After it'd become apparent that the United States was going to be bogged down fighting an insurgency in the middle of major sectarian violence between the Sunnis and Shia, Cain Frost had seen the writing on the wall.

In 2005, he'd created his first major—and still the largest—private security base in Iraq between Saddam Hussein's Al-Faw Palace and the airport. From his base of operations, his security personnel had continuous access for resupply from the airport, as well as easy ingress and egress routes to the former Baghdad Airport

Road, renamed Route Irish after the airport was captured in 2003. In addition to serving as a connector between the airport and the Green Zone, Route Irish also provided access to Highway 1, referred to as Main Supply Route Tampa.

It was the ideal location for his purposes, especially on days like today. When he'd received the information that Juan's team had obtained the flag from John Quick's home, he'd immediately called Scott Carlson, his chief of operations, former Delta Force operator, and CIA case officer, to place the security convoy on a one-hour alert.

Cain had traveled to Camp Frost as soon as Scott informed him they'd received the scanned image of the flag, complete with the serial number.

He'd locked himself in his office, forced himself to sit calmly at his desk, and proceeded to decrypt the map coordinates with the key he'd obtained in 2006 from a now-deceased former insurgent who'd been working with both the Iranians and Al Qaeda in Iraq.

Deciphering the code had been easy, almost unsettlingly so. The key the insurgent leader had devised had been logical, but only one who knew the basic mathematical formula to the key would be able to decrypt it.

The serial number read 313657292749. He'd then reversed the order, broken the number into a series of six two-digit numbers, and finally subtracted fifteen from each one. It'd taken him less than one minute, providing him with the coordinates 34 12 14 42 21 16.

The ease with which he'd converted the number ("decrypted" really was too much of an overstatement) made him pause and reflect on the irony. *Over two years of laborious work, all to prepare for one moment that was over in seconds.*

He was accustomed to complex tasks, and the simplicity of the coordinates and the key were almost too much for his strategic mind to comprehend. He'd plugged the coordinates into Google Earth on his desktop, but unlike the task of converting the number, the location displayed had shocked him.

He'd expected the item to be in western Al Anbar Province. He'd been told as much, but he'd also expected it to be isolated, in the middle of nowhere, marked by only a cluster of five large rocks that had been placed in a pentagonal configuration sixty feet from each other, just as he'd been told. His source had said that he could walk in an invisible line from any rock to the center of the configuration, and there he'd find the item.

He double-checked the coordinates and looked at the surrounding area to find the Haditha Dam less than one mile away.

You've got to be kidding me.

As he sat at his desk, he stared at the numbers. Cain had seen the interrogation video. He was fairly certain the Iranian had told the truth; torture could be an effective technique. Unless the Iranian had lied to his people, Cain Frost and his private security force were on a collision course with the Haditha Dam and its protectors.

Acutely aware of how close he was to his objective, he called Scott into his office.

Before he could talk, Scott said, "We have a problem."

Indeed it was—an unforeseen act of defiance by Mother Nature. Cain had planned on wasting no time. He'd waited long enough, and he could barely contain the physical urge to push forward now that the goal line was in sight. He knew he'd become consumed by his quest for revenge, but he couldn't control himself. His brother hadn't deserved to die the way he did, and it was now his sworn duty to ensure those responsible paid for their crimes and suffered, hard.

Unfortunately, his revenge was going to have to wait a little longer, all thanks to the weather.

A gigantic cold front had rolled across from the west, picking up sand and dust as it gained momentum. It had blanketed most of Al Anbar Province in one enormous dust storm. All air operations had ceased, and even convoy support had become almost nonexistent, except to units deployed outside the wire requiring a ground medevac. Visibility was limited to less than one-eighth of a mile.

As much as Cain wanted—physically *needed*—to get his forces moving, he knew the conditions would only create chaos and likely decrease his chances of success. He was too smart to make such an amateur mistake. His plan was complicated and would take several days to execute, but the delay was unavoidable.

Scott had told him the sand and dust might clear tomorrow. If that turned out to be the case, Cain and his men would depart as soon as there was enough visibility.

Fucking Murphy's Law . . .

It was too early to sleep; instead, he studied the blueprints of the dam and tried to anticipate everything that might go wrong. Given the proximity of the dam, the city, and the fact that a Marine Corps regimental combat team was providing security for both, a whole lot could *definitely* go wrong.

Cain Frost hoped that when this was over, he'd never encounter another Marine again.

He shook his head to rid himself of the distraction and focused once more on the task at hand.

In addition to the interrogation report, his personal laptop, and the list of personnel and resources accompanying him, a map of Iran lay open on his desk. On the map was a circle around the southwestern city of Ahwaz, known in intelligence circles as the location of the Fajr military base, home to the tactical headquarters of the Quds Force.

Keep your eyes on the prize, Cain. Eyes on the prize . . .

PART IV

THE SANDBOX-PART TWO

CHAPTER 28

FALLUJAH, IRAQ
27 OCTOBER 2004

The gunfire outside abruptly stopped. A deafening silence ominously fell over the entire area as trace echoes bounced off the interior of the compound walls.

Captain West screamed into his tactical throat microphone, "Williams, get inside the compound! It's an ambush! Get to cover now! *Move!*"

He stared at Gunny Quick as moments later Lieutenant Williams screamed back, "We're moving now!" There was a pause. "We've got company! Several vehicles coming from the west from the direction of that building in the distance."

Captain West heard Lieutenant Williams screaming at his Marines to move inside the compound. He prayed to the God that all fighting men facing death know too well, prayed that there was enough time before the first rounds landed.

Lieutenant Williams shouted at Staff Sergeant Lopez, "Lopez, get inside! *Now!*"

Those were the last words Lieutenant Williams ever uttered. The first 82mm high-explosive mortar round landed within a few feet of him. The mortar shattered the silence with a tremendous explosion, killing the lieutenant and one of his team leaders, their bodies flung aside like rag dolls.

Staff Sergeant Lopez was twenty feet away when the round that killed his commanding officer detonated. He miraculously remained unscathed by the shrapnel. Chaos surrounded him like a thick cloak, and he didn't have time to think.

He couldn't hear anything since the world had gone suddenly quiet: the mortar round's concussion had blown out both his eardrums. All he knew was he had to get the rest of his Marines inside.

He looked to his right and saw Staff Sergeant Jeremy Simpson screaming at him and waving, but he couldn't understand him. *We have to get inside,* he thought, but he couldn't get the words out.

Suddenly, he was blown off his feet as the remaining rounds began to rain down along both sides of the compound. The lethal mortar fire slaughtered the Marines caught in the open with nowhere to go and no time to react.

Lopez now lay on his back as he realized that he'd been hit. Both legs had been severed above the knees, and his back was broken.

I feel no pain.

He looked up at the night sky. He thought about his wife and son back in Jacksonville, North Carolina. His last conscious emotion was the love he felt for them both.

Then he was gone, but not alone. Death had come to collect his entire squad outside the compound.

CHAPTER 29

As soon as the mortar fire stopped, Captain West bolted for the door on the side of the building. He hoped some of his Marines had survived, but he knew the odds weren't good. *It had been perfectly executed. They were watching us the entire time.*

He grabbed the door handle and turned to Gunny Quick. "You and I are moving straight to the north entrance to see if we can help. We do *not* leave the compound until we have a better idea of what the fuck is going on out there. We're more valuable to our men alive than dead. Understand?"

Gunny Quick didn't hesitate. "Absolutely."

Captain West turned to Staff Sergeant Hayes. "Hayes, you four enter the other building. Ensure there are no more surprises. I'm willing to bet it's clear. The mortars were the real show. Then join us at the entrance. Take no more than thirty seconds. Got it?"

Staff Sergeant Hayes nodded his head and moved out.

Captain West turned back to Gunny Quick. "Let's go."

He pushed down on the door handle and swiftly exited the building. He realized as he moved that the sounds of incoming mortar rounds had been replaced by small arms fire.

I hope my guys are holding their own.

Moments later, they arrived at the front entrance and peered around the edge of the wall, unobserved. The scene before them exceeded their darkest fears. Unspeakable carnage lay outside the walls, and the horrors were still in progress.

Captain West restrained himself from running through the gate with guns blazing. The action would've temporarily satiated his bloodlust, but it also would've ended with his and Gunny Quick's certain demise.

I'm no good to them dead, he tried to reason with himself, but a part of him yearned for violent retribution, practicality be damned.

Six vehicles were arranged in a semicircular pattern where the Marines had been positioned. The pickup trucks were commonly referred to as "technicals," since each one contained a .50-caliber machine gun mounted on its hood and was manned by both a driver and a gunner. But these weren't military vehicles. The gunners all wore dark, civilian clothing.

It's an insurgent group.

That fact alone told Captain West all he needed to know about his enemy. They would attack ruthlessly and with zeal. He'd come to expect nothing less in Iraq.

He forced himself to compartmentalize his thoughts. It worked, barely. His mind shut down on his emotions like a steel trap. The outrage was replaced by a cold fury, a tsunami of raging will, the likes of which he'd never experienced.

I'm going to find a way to kill them all.

The gunners methodically fired into the kill zone where his Marines lay wounded, dead, or dying. The machine gun fire from the .50-caliber weapons finished the job the mortar rounds had started.

They never had a chance.

In addition to the gunners, more than a dozen insurgents walked among his fallen Marines. He watched as the one who must've been the leader—a short, stout man with a beard and bald head, a pair of sunglasses on top—stopped over a body.

Captain West couldn't see who it was, but he stiffened as the man drew a sidearm from a holster under his shoulder. He realized in horror what was about to happen, but before he could do anything, the insurgent shot the fallen Marine in the head.

Captain West closed his eyes to quiet the rage that yearned to consume him. He had to be smart, or he was going to get the rest of them killed.

"Sir—sir—Logan!" Gunny Quick whispered.

The use of his first name brought him back to the present and away from his fury. He looked at his closest friend, mentor, and trusted advisor.

"I know what you're thinking, but we can't. If we go out there, then they died for nothing. We need to stay alive to avenge them."

Captain West knew Gunny Quick was right.

"Right now, they don't know we're here. We've only got a few minutes before those fuckers decide to enter the compound and realize they're not alone. We have the element of surprise, but only for a few minutes."

Captain West looked at Gunny Quick, who'd once again read his mind. He managed a small, savage smile.

"I know. More importantly, I know how we can hurt these motherfuckers, or at least take as many of them as we can with us."

He outlined his plan. "Set a Claymore fifteen feet from the entrance and run the wire back to the other house where Hayes is. Wait at the entrance. I have to go inside and talk to our Marines. Hayes might've found something. This was an orchestrated attack, and those assholes outside are not some ragtag bunch of bad guys. They were expecting us, and I need to know why. If they come in before I come back out, wait for as many as you can before you trigger it. Make them pay."

"Roger, sir. See you in a few minutes."

Gunny Quick took off his small Oakley backpack, set it on the ground, and removed a Claymore mine.

Captain West turned around after taking a few steps, "And John, if possible, save that short motherfucker outside for me."

Gunny Quick nodded and returned to the business of preparing the Claymore.

CHAPTER 30

When Captain West entered the second building, the first thing that struck him was the layout. It was set up exactly like the first one, a large, open-spaced structure. The only difference was its purpose.

The insurgents had used it as their living quarters. The back row was lined with several cots—US military–issue ones—and a round wooden table with six chairs stood in the kitchen. In the left corner of the building was a toilet surrounded by a five-foot-tall wall to provide a semblance of privacy.

Captain West spotted Staff Sergeant Hayes, Sergeant Helms, and Sergeant Avery standing at the kitchen table, fixated on an item blocked from view.

"Hayes," he called out, "what did you find?"

Hayes turned around, his face ashen, and said, "Sir, I was just about to come find you. You need to take a look at this." His eyes were wary as he asked, "What about our boys outside?"

The machine gun fire had stopped, and an eerie silence had fallen over the compound.

"Staff Sergeant Hayes, I need you to compartmentalize right this second. This whole thing was a fucking trap. Our Marines, our friends, they're all dead. They never had a chance." A mix of emotions ran across the young staff sergeant's face. Captain West thought he might lose it.

"Listen to me, Hayes," he said solemnly but firmly, "we grieve for them when we get out of this mess. But in order to do that, we have to be smart. Do you know why?" Captain West didn't wait for an answer. "So we can kill those motherfuckers outside and make them pay for what they did. You understand? I need you with me."

Staff Sergeant Hayes nodded his head vigorously, trying to quell the grief he felt for his lost friends.

Before Captain West could say anything else, Sergeant Helms moved away from the table, exposing the item that had so transfixed him. It was a human head, resting in the middle of a plate in the center of the table.

That solves that mystery, Captain West thought.

The sight of the head didn't faze him. In his current mental state, nothing short of the Second Coming would've had an impact.

But what did grab his attention was what was carved into the blond man's forehead. It explained everything he needed to know, a violent epiphany laid out in flesh. In jagged gashes three inches tall was spelled "CIA."

James, you sonofabitch. You'd better pray I die here.

The real objective of the mission was suddenly obvious. It wasn't intended to capture one of Saddam's henchmen. It was a rescue mission to save a captured CIA officer. James had manipulated all of them to do the CIA's dirty work. He'd sent them straight into an ambush, and now ten of his Marines were dead because of it.

How could I be so stupid? He played me. Hell, he probably knew I'd kick him off the mission. He's as insidious as the insurgents outside, maybe worse. At least outside, I know who my enemy is.

Unfortunately, before he could extract answers from James, he had to keep his Marines and himself alive.

Captain West spoke with a tone of command intended to focus

his Marines on the task at hand. "We're about to have company. We only have a few minutes. We're making a stand here first, and then we'll fall back to the other building."

He issued his orders, his three Marines absorbing the details. It forced them to concentrate on their responsibilities and not on their fallen comrades.

"Sergeant Avery, run back to the rear entrance and make sure there are no insurgents back there. If we're lucky, there won't be. Set a Claymore fifteen feet from the entrance and run the wire back to the outside of that door."

He pointed to the other entrance to the building, which faced south and provided a view of the southeastern entrance to the compound.

"You stay outside, and when the shooting starts, if they try to use that entrance, kill as many as you can. The Claymore will let me know they're coming from that way. If we come flying out of this building, be prepared to run with the wire to the other building. Understand?"

Sergeant Avery responded, "Got it, sir. Kill as many as possible. I absolutely fucking understand," he added for good measure.

"Sergeant Helms, radio the COC in Fallujah and see how fast they can get CAS out here. I don't give a fuck about the cloud cover. Tell them we need a couple of F-15s, or better yet, A-10s. They should scramble from TQ. Tell them we have ten KIA and need rotor CASEVAC immediately. That should give them a sense of urgency. Stay in here and keep the radio silent until you hear from me on the internal," he said, referring to his throat microphone.

Captain West looked at Staff Sergeant Hayes. "I want you to set up in the doorway in the other building. If they make it inside the compound, they'll be focused on us in here. Most importantly, you need to wait until I open up. We're going to trigger a Claymore first and wait for the second wave before we go to guns. Once I engage, kill everything with the SAW that comes through that doorway," he said, pointing at the light machine gun Hayes carried.

"Gunny Quick and I will be outside this building, waiting for the bastards."

Captain West started to move but then stopped as if he'd forgotten something. He turned to face the two young Marines.

"We have close to twenty insurgents with six technicals supported by indirect fire. They're well trained, and we fell right into their trap. They killed our friends and brothers, even executed those that weren't immediately killed. When they realize we're here, they're going to do the same to us. And quite honestly, I can't fucking wait for them to try. These are evil men who did this. Now it's our turn. No mercy, no hesitation. Not one of them leaves alive. Understand?"

His tone conveyed their sentiments exactly. They were with him to the bitter end.

Sergeant Matt Helms summed it up. "We kill them all or die trying."

"That's exactly what I had in mind, Sergeant." Captain West turned and walked out into the night to join Gunny Quick in the calm before the second fierce storm of the night.

CHAPTER 31

Abdul Sattar wiped a sweaty palm across his bald head. It was a tic he'd formed at a young age, one that told the others he was pleased with both them and himself.

These Americans are so stupid. How could they truly believe they could occupy our country without suffering heavy casualties, especially at the hands of our holy warriors?

The ambush had been child's play. Abu Omar's mortar fire had been precise, and he had ten dead Americans to bring back to Abu Musab al-Zarqawi as trophies. The leader of Al Qaeda in Iraq would be pleased and reward Abdul Sattar and his men with more weapons and ammunition for their righteous cause.

It was al-Zarqawi who had orchestrated the operation. Their spiritual leader had received information on a CIA officer who was a member of an American task force hunting him. He'd lured the CIA agent and his driver out of the Green Zone in Baghdad by ordering one of his men to act as an informant and feed the CIA false information about weapons of mass destruction located near Fallujah.

The meeting had occurred off the military base and south of Camp Liberty. The CIA officer had foolishly believed his safety was "guaranteed," but in this war, there were no guarantees.

Al-Zarqawi had kidnapped and smuggled the CIA officer to this location, tortured the man himself, and cut off his head when he'd finished with him. He'd then decided to use him for bait—and as an example.

Al-Zarqawi had wanted to actually participate in the ambush, but Abdul Sattar had insisted he remain in Ramadi, safe from the Americans and free to continue planning his attacks.

The genius of al-Zarqawi's plan had borne fruit and provided more opportunities to exploit the Americans, displaying their weaknesses for all to see. A video of ten dead American "soldiers" would spread fear into the hearts of their enemies.

Abdul Sattar smiled at the thought, watching his men quickly move the bodies to the pickup trucks.

He looked at his watch. It was only 11:08 p.m.

Allah be praised. We are blessed in triumph.

Although he was grateful for the victory, he was still surprised at how easy it'd been. What he couldn't figure out was why the Americans had fired upon the compound. Had someone inadvertently stumbled upon their safe house and decided to stay the night, forcing the Americans to act hastily? He couldn't imagine any Iraqi male staying in the killing house once he'd seen what was inside.

He didn't know, and he didn't care. All that mattered was that he retrieved their corpses and left before American reinforcements arrived.

"Ziad!" he shouted to a taller, gaunt man dressed in a black jogging suit.

"We need to go! The Americans will be missed at some point, and we cannot be here! Hurry up!"

Ziad barked orders to the rest of the freedom fighters. The words had the desired effect as they redoubled their efforts to get the bodies and gear loaded on the trucks.

As he watched the retrieval operation, one question continued to nag at his brain. *What were the Americans shooting at?*

He decided he *did* care and needed to know. He wasn't concerned about the bodies inside since he knew they'd ultimately be discovered—were, in fact, intended as a message—but his personal curiosity finally outweighed his sense of urgency.

He turned back to his second in command. "Ziad, take three men and search the compound. I know we left it this morning and no one has been here, but I just want to make sure. These men were shooting at something, but the dead do not reveal their secrets, no? Maybe something spooked them. Who knows?" he said matter-of-factly.

Ziad didn't question the order. He nodded his head and ordered the three closest men to join him.

They grabbed their AK-47s from the front of their pickup truck. They looked at Ziad expectantly, loyal followers waiting to do their leader's bidding.

Ziad spoke. "We're going to quickly search both houses just to be sure no one else has been inside, and then we get back here to finish picking up these dogs. We don't have time to waste, understand?"

All three men nodded. *"Allahu Akbar."*

Each had been with Abdul Sattar for more than a year and had participated in multiple operations against the Americans. It was the only response.

"We'll be back shortly," Ziad said to Abdul Sattar, and then added with a smirk, "Don't leave without us, brother."

Abdul Sattar smiled and said, "Never, brother. Allah has shined on us this glorious night, and we'll celebrate our conquest together later. Now go!"

CHAPTER 32

Captain West was a statue, completely focused on the entrance thirty meters away. He lay prone, shrouded in shadows along the east edge of the house, his SOPMOD M4 aimed at the doorway. Gunny Quick lay next to him, the trigger for the Claymore mine in his hands.

Captain West knew they were too close to the mine to safely detonate it. He just hoped the edge of the house would shield them from the backblast and ricochets of the seven hundred steel balls that would be traveling at over 1,200 meters per second.

God, help me get us out of this one alive, he silently prayed, more for his remaining Marines than himself.

His prayers were suddenly interrupted by the appearance of a man in a dark jumpsuit who slowly moved through the entrance into the compound. His weapon was up and ready as he searched the area.

Fortunately, Captain West and Gunny Quick were concealed in the darkness.

The man was followed by three more insurgents, all in dark clothing and carrying AK-47s. As soon as the last one entered the compound, all four fanned out in a single line, approximately twelve feet across, and slowly moved toward the entrance of the house.

Wait for it. Wait for it.

Captain West never had to utter a word. Gunny Quick was a master of timing. He chose the precise moment to squeeze the lever on the detonator. Captain West closed his eyes as he heard the *clack*.

Please let me at least survive the initial blast.

The Claymore exploded with a thunderous roar.

BOOM!

The flash of the explosion blinded the four insurgents milliseconds before the hundreds of one-eighth-inch steel balls tore dozens of holes through their flesh, piercing vital organs and shattering bones.

Captain West kept his eyes closed. Even with his gloved hands over his ears, he still heard the balls ricochet off the north wall and careen crazily throughout the front of the compound. He heard several impacts as steel balls impacted the front of both buildings.

When the whizzing of the projectiles ceased, he opened his eyes and saw four figures in tatters on the ground.

Burn in hell, assholes.

He looked at Gunny Quick to make sure he was unhurt by the flying steel. His platoon sergeant had already discarded the detonator and had his M-4 trained on the entrance. Captain West smiled at the quickness with which his second in command had switched weapons.

Always have to be one step ahead of me. Well, now the real fun begins.

———

Allah had been by Abdul Sattar's side, for he'd walked away from the entrance to the compound and was thirty meters away, talking to one of his men, when the explosion occurred.

Three of his men weren't so lucky. They were in the direct pathway of over two hundred steel balls that shot through the entrance and riddled them and the pickup truck behind them with ragged holes.

The remaining fighters initially stood shocked by the explosion before they regained their senses and dove to the ground for cover as they'd been trained to do.

Abdul Sattar searched for signs of the enemy. There were none. In fact, a deathly silence had fallen over the entire compound. The only sound was a constant stream of fluids leaking from the destroyed pickup truck to the dirt below.

We're not alone.

Abdul Sattar rose to his feet and screamed at his men to grab their weapons. He motioned for Farraj to join him.

He reached into a jacket pocket, pulled out a gray cell phone, and punched a speed dial number, talking quickly to Farraj as he waited for the call to connect.

"Farraj, Ziad must be dead, Allah rest his soul. You are now in charge, do you understand?"

Farraj, a man in his midtwenties who was a fierce fighter, nodded, encouraged and proud to lead the remaining holy warriors.

"What will you have me do?" he said, addressing Abdul Sattar with complete deference.

"That was either a booby trap, or more Americans entered the compound before we arrived and are inside right now. I need you to take three more men and enter two by two through this entrance. This isn't going to be easy. You and your best shooter go in second. If the Americans are waiting, they'll hit the men in front of you and give you a chance to locate them and return fire. If you meet no resistance, check both buildings and get back here. We're running out of time."

Farraj nodded, unconcerned about risking the lives of two of his men. They would only see Paradise sooner. They served God's will. What would happen would happen.

Inshallah.

"Good luck," Abdul Sattar said.

He wondered if he'd just doomed Farraj to an early grave. He'd just lost seven good men. He only had eleven left, including himself. He couldn't risk more, but he had to find out who was inside the compound. His curiosity was getting the better of him, but he couldn't help himself. He *had* to know.

Suddenly, a voice spoke from the phone, and he heard Abu Omar. His thoughts switched to his next move. If indeed Americans remained alive inside, his dark mind had plans for them they most certainly would not enjoy.

CHAPTER 33

Captain West and Gunny Quick waited. Sergeant Helms informed him over the team channel that the COC in Fallujah had contacted Al Taqqadum, but direct air support was still twenty minutes out.

Probably trying to find the pilots at some base bar. Fucking cowboys . . .

Captain West wasn't really counting on the air support. He knew their fates were going to be determined within the next few minutes, one way or another. What that fate would be was still a mystery.

How the insurgents responded to the mine that had just killed four of their men would be the determining factor and was the only question that mattered. He hoped the leader was wondering why there'd been no additional gunfire from the compound after the explosion. He knew the bald man couldn't be certain Americans were actually inside.

Captain West's breathing was slow and steady. His pulse remained at its normal resting rate. He realized that he'd entered *mushin,* a combat state of mind he'd once read about in a book on Zen while he was earning his first black belt in karate in college.

He had no fears, thoughts, or distractions. He was completely focused on the doorway, prepared to react with maximum lethality.

There's my answer.

The first man through the door appeared apprehensive. He paused as he saw the mutilated remains of his comrades. Captain West thought he looked like he was expecting to be shot at any moment.

Not quite yet, but soon.

A second man followed. He focused on the building immediately ahead of the entrance.

Captain West aimed through his reflex scope center-mass at the man on the left. He knew Staff Sergeant Hayes would target the insurgent on the right.

He exhaled as the two men stopped. He was moments away from slowly squeezing the trigger when two more men suddenly appeared through the entrance behind them.

The new men moved to the other side of the first pair and directly toward the other building and Hayes's position.

Captain West immediately recognized his opportunity when all four insurgents inadvertently positioned themselves in an L formation. They presented perfect silhouettes and had exposed themselves to both fields of fire.

Now or never . . .

Captain West squeezed the trigger on the M4, firing controlled automatic bursts, first at the man on the left end of the L formation, and then at the others.

His aim was precise. The first salvo of rounds struck the insurgent in the chest with a wet *thwuck! thwuck! thwuck!* as the bullets pierced flesh and shattered his breastplate. One round tore through his heart, ending his life instantly. He crumpled to the ground as the second controlled burst struck the top of his head, shattering his skull into several pieces and tearing a chunk of his brain away for good measure.

Both Staff Sergeant Hayes and Gunny Quick had been prepared for Captain West to initiate the ambush. Once he did, they opened fire.

Gunny Quick dispatched the second insurgent on the right with a burst to the chest and one to the head. He fired early on the second burst, and one round ripped apart the insurgent's throat, spraying blood into the air as he dropped his AK-47 and fell in a dead heap to the sand.

Staff Sergeant Hayes, bloodthirsty for revenge after what the insurgents had done to his friends, pulled the trigger of the SAW. He unleashed a salvo of more than fifty rounds in less than ten seconds, strafing back and forth between the two murderers facing him.

The devastating fire struck the men in multiple places from the upper legs to the lower face. One round shattered the jaw of the insurgent on the right, leaving a bloody hole where the lower half of his face had been moments before. Both men fell to the ground to join their dead comrades. Blood poured from the four bodies and pooled around each, forming a thick mixture of blood and sand.

Captain West surveyed the scene. His breathing and heartbeat remained calm and controlled.

Well, now he knows we're here. Eight down, at least ten more to go. Let's see what you do now.

He tapped Gunny Quick on the shoulder as he spoke into his throat microphone.

"Eight enemy KIA out front. Everyone inside the building with Sergeant Helms. Avery, keep the back door open so you can see the south entrance. Hayes, cover the north entrance from the doorway. But both of you make sure you're *inside* and under cover. This is where it might get a little dicey."

A wolflike grin appeared on his face. "By the time this is over, we're going to kill them all. Let's get inside. We need to prepare for the next attack."

Gunny Quick moved from the prone position and stepped around the corner to the entrance of the structure.

What the hell do you have up your sleeve now?

He glanced back at the eight bodies strewn across the compound. He realized his commanding officer was hell-bent on exacting revenge. The raw malevolence in his leader's voice was undeniable.

Thank God we're the good guys, he thought, almost pitying the killers outside the compound who had no idea they were dead men walking.

———

Over a thousand meters away in a clearing surrounded by small trees, Abu Omar orchestrated the next volley of fire from his four 82mm mortar teams.

Their position was on the other side of the building Lieutenant Williams had spotted at the beginning of the operation.

As a result of its placement, there'd been no way the American forces could've spotted it, even during the day. All had unfolded precisely as Abdul Sattar had intended.

Abdul Sattar's instructions had been clear. He didn't want to disappoint his spiritual leader and military mentor.

A former math teacher in Ramadi before the occupation began, Abu Omar performed the calculations in his head. He double-checked them, and when he was positive the numbers were correct, he summoned his four teams and issued specific instructions.

Within minutes, the gun adjustments were made. Abu Omar stood in front of all four teams and held his right arm up in the air. When the teams were ready, rounds in hand and suspended over the mortar tubes, he dropped his right arm.

With a loud *thump!,* four high-explosive rounds were launched at the compound, rocketing through the night toward their intended targets.

PART V

RUN FOR THE BORDER

CHAPTER 34

The loud knocking on Logan's hotel door painfully latched onto his consciousness and dragged it to the surface. He'd been having a nightmare—one he often had since Fallujah—where he was alone and trapped in a house in the desert, all of his Marines dead, their bodies standing like toy soldiers around him in a circle. Their eyes were white, and their mouths moved, but no sound came out.

Thud! Thud! Thud! Something awful was coming.

Logan opened his eyes and shook his head, the images still visible in his mind's eye.

All right already . . .

"I'm coming!" he shouted, and forced himself to sit on the edge of the bed.

His entire body ached from the previous forty-eight hours, but at least his system had purged the remaining alcohol.

Pathetic. What was I thinking?

He was an alcoholic, and he hadn't been thinking at all. All he'd cared about was numbing the emotional pain and guilt that consumed him like a ravenous animal.

Even though logic told him it hadn't been his fault, he still second-guessed his decision to accept that mission in Fallujah on such short notice and with limited intelligence. He should've known better. Instead, nearly his entire team had been killed, and each day he saw another sunrise only reminded him of that fact.

"Logan? Hurry up. We need to move!" Mike shouted through the door.

"Give me a second."

He stood up from the bed and pulled on a fresh Under Armour tee shirt he'd purchased on the way back to the hotel the day before. He was already wearing new boxers to replace the ones he'd worn for thirty-six hours. He'd thrown out the entire wardrobe since it stank of sweat and blood.

Fresh clothes equal a fresh start, he thought and smiled at the cliché.

He walked to the door, opened the dead bolt, and removed the chain. He turned the handle to allow Mike to enter and walked to the bar to turn on the room's coffeemaker.

As he filled the tank with fresh water and closed the oval coffee package inside the filter, he asked Mike, "What's so urgent?"

"First, how do you feel? I know you're fit as hell, but even you have your limits."

Logan smiled and looked at Mike. "One hundred percent better than I did two days ago. Other than being sore, I'm good to go. Don't worry about me. What did you get from the drop man?"

Mike nodded, obviously relieved Logan was on the mend, both physically and mentally. "From him? Nothing. He lawyered up. We ran his prints through every database we have in federal, local, and even military law enforcement. This guy's a ghost. Whoever he was before he started working for this organization, we'll never know, at least not in time for it to help us. That information's gone, wiped clean somehow."

Logan scoffed and said, "I'm not surprised. Whoever's in charge of this operation has gone to great lengths to ensure nothing leads back to him or his gang of thieves."

"I know, but it's just not that simple to hide a person's identity. You have to have people inside the Department of Motor Vehicles, law enforcement agencies, and even the Intelligence Community. Hell, if you want to create new identities, then you have to have someone in the Social Security Administration who can provide you with real SSNs that will pass scrutiny. And all of that takes two things: money and power."

"So where does that leave us?"

"Like I said, we have nothing from the suspect; however, his *cell phone* is another matter entirely. While you were sleeping, our tech guys finally arrived from Quantico, *and* they were able to process his cell phone. We had a warrant issued on its contents before the techs even arrived. The phone company was able to provide call detail records, and we found out that our golden boy made a series of calls and texts to the same number—and get this—they started one day before the attacks on you and John."

"Is that so?" Logan said as he raised his eyebrows.

"It is. And once the techs had the new number he called, we were able to get another warrant to obtain that number's data, including locational information. And here's where it gets good. Are you ready for this? Whoever was using that phone left San Antonio two nights ago. The last hit we had from the phone was here downtown in an office building. We sent agents to it, and it's now empty."

"Jesus. These guys have been one step ahead of us the entire time. I'm getting seriously pissed off about it."

"It gets better. So the owner of that mystery phone received another text—we don't have what it said; it was encrypted—before the shootout at the Alamo. And this is the *really* good part. He must've left San Antonio and entered Mexico through Nuevo Laredo, because the phone's now approximately fifty miles west of the city. Once we realized he left US territory, we obtained an order from the FISA Court in record time in order to keep the lawyers happy. Because the locational data was obtained using multiple cell towers, we don't have an exact location, but we were able to pinpoint it to within one kilometer. And since it's Mexico, I talked to our friends in the DEA at the El Paso Intelligence Center. They provided us with satellite imagery of the area, and they think they know where he is. It's a Los Toros cartel compound."

Logan shook his head. "Jesus. I guess there really is a purpose for lawyers after all. I'm just glad I went into the Marine Corps. You know I once actually considered law school?"

Mike looked at him in disbelief. "Will wonders never cease? You know you can't shoot people in a court of law, right?"

Logan laughed. "It was when I was a little more idealistic, when I thought everyone had the same rights. Not so much anymore. Looking back on it, I definitely made the right choice. We're often our own worst enemies with how we tie the hands of our folks, be it CIA, Special Forces, or whoever. It's a wonder to me that we haven't been hit again with another attack on the scale of nine eleven."

He stopped himself before he continued. "Anyhow, enough of the soapbox. Back to the matter at hand. We should've figured as much regarding the cartel. Antonio—the asshole I politely questioned at my house—told us his boss, one Juan Black, worked for the Los Toros cartel. I'd bet you dollars to doughnuts it's Mr. Black using the cartel as his own personal refuge."

"I agree. And since he's our only lead, I've already briefed my uncle, who in turn informed the president directly. I've been ordered to tell you this before I continue—we're keeping this information extremely close-hold. As soon as the president found out that our only lead was in Mexico, he called the Mexican president. I have no idea what was said, and honestly, I don't care. What matters is that we've received approval to run a small, tactical operation on Mexican soil. There's only one catch."

Logan raised his eyes expectantly as he sipped his coffee.

"How's your Spanish?"

"*Yo quiero* Taco Bell," Logan said with a straight face. "What can I say? I took Latin in high school and college. Benefits of a classical education—not much use, though, south of the border."

"I kind of figured as much. I always knew you were too smart for your own good."

"Sarah constantly reminds me of that exact fact."

"Now that's the real brains of your operation. Regardless, I don't think we'll be ordering takeout, but we will be working with the Fuerzas Especiales, the Mexican naval special forces unit."

At this information, Logan perked up.

Mike continued, "From what I've been told—which is very little—they're the Mexican equivalent of our SEAL teams. They've been tasked with hunting the cartels since Mexico declared war on them in December of 2006. The Mexican president wanted to ensure he has a team to keep tabs on us, and they're supposedly the best Mexico has to offer. We have the lead, but they'll be supporting. And this specific unit is reportedly as good as they have."

"Our own little coalition of the willing, huh?"

"I'm afraid so. My uncle told me—and I quote—'Whatever it takes, Mike, you have it.' And this is what it's going to take right now."

"I pray these guys are as good as you say they are. Okay. Enough small talk. I'll go tell John. How soon before we leave?"

"One hour. It's only a hundred fifty miles to Nuevo Laredo, but we're landing at Quetzaltcoatl International Airport. The FES—it's what they go by; short for their motto, which translates into 'Force,

Spirit, and Wisdom'—will meet us there. Grab all your gear. You're not coming back here."

"Mike, in case you didn't notice, I barely have one backpack of stuff, but I'll make sure I don't bring my Coach bags."

Mike's voice was laced with thick sarcasm as he said, "It makes me cry knowing you know what Coach is. Seriously, brother, I'm concerned."

"Hey! Now I'm offended. I'm a very cultured individual," Logan said in mock offense. "And one more thing—you really know how to fuck up a perfectly good morning. Now get the hell out of here so I can call John and shower. Now that I've had my beauty rest, I want to get my game face on."

The grin on Logan's face chilled Mike as flashes of the Big Bad Wolf popped into his head. The healing wound didn't help. *Except I think he's more dangerous than that goddamn fairy-tale monster,* Mike thought.

CHAPTER 35

QUETZALTCOATL INTERNATIONAL AIRPORT, MEXICO
31 OCTOBER 2008
1100 LOCAL HOURS

They stepped off the US government Gulfstream jet onto the tarmac in a secluded part of the airport. The day was gradually warming up. At this time of the year, the inviting weather lured tourists from all over the United States to the still-welcoming parts of Mexico, the parts that hadn't been corrupted by the extreme violence of the drug cartels.

Logan figured it had to be in the midsixties as the sun provided an additional layer of heat. White wisps of clouds crept lethargically across the sky.

Minus the violent cartels, corrupt law enforcement, and horrible economy, not a bad place to visit, Logan thought.

All thoughts of weather vanished from his mind as his attention was drawn to the sight laid out before him one hundred yards away inside the nearest hangar. The large rolling doors were slightly ajar, just enough to provide Logan a glimpse of movement inside. A Mexican man in his late thirties or early forties stood outside the opening, beckoning for them to join him.

John said, "Must be the welcoming committee. I expected a red carpet and champagne—not for you, of course, Logan."

Logan mumbled, "Asshole."

John grinned and said, "Trained by the best, my friend—again, that not being you."

Mike was still amazed, even after all the time he'd spent with both men, at how pointed the jibes between the two continued to be. It was relentless. *Must be a Marine thing,* he thought, not realizing how correct he was.

"Let's go see what they've got for us," Mike said.

As the men crossed the tarmac, they heard the propellers from another plane grow louder in the distance. All three men looked around and spotted the US government C-130 begin its final approach from two miles away at low altitude.

"Here comes the backup," Logan said, referring to the thirteen-man FBI Hostage Rescue Team Mike had requested through his uncle.

"As good as you are, Logan, those guys aren't too shabby themselves. Don't forget it," Mike said.

"A bit sensitive today, Mike? Wake up on the wrong side of the bed or something?" John asked.

"Fair enough. Guess all this world-class travel is getting to me in my old age." He turned back to the hangar and kept walking. "Let's go see who our new friend is."

It was immediately apparent that the man designated to greet them wasn't a member of the FES. His demeanor wasn't that of a hardened professional soldier, but more along the lines of a bureaucrat or politician. His hair was jet black and combed back perfectly, and he wore a pair of wireless square glasses. When he spoke, it was with a haughty tone of superiority.

"Special Agent Benson, I presume?" he said to Mike, sticking out his right hand formally.

Mike shook the man's hand. "Please call me 'Mike.'" He turned his head to acknowledge the presence of Logan and John. "And this is—"

But before he could finish, the man interrupted—not impolitely—saying, "Señors Logan West and John Quick."

He spoke in quick bursts, pausing every few sentences, as if he'd prepared each statement in his head before uttering it.

"I know. I am Hector Ortega, senior special advisor to the president of Mexico. He called me personally this morning after your president called him. He informed me of everything, and his instructions to me were extremely direct and specific. I am to afford you *anything* you need to capture this man who is using a Los Toros compound as sanctuary. I understand you've been briefed on our FES, who will be assisting in the operation."

He paused momentarily, again producing the impression he chose his words carefully.

"You're in charge, and our men have been ordered to follow your instructions; however, I must warn you. This is a prideful group of elite men. When I told them they'd be taking orders from an American FBI agent and two former United States Marines? Well . . . let's just say the response was less than enthusiastic from a few of them. Having said that, they are consummate professionals and will do what is necessary."

"Mr. Ortega, it sounds like your president picked the right men for the job," Mike said after a thoughtful moment. "I can relate to their mentality and appreciate their concerns. I promise you, for this mission to be successful, we're all going to have to work together. This is what we call a 'combined operation.' All that matters is capturing Juan Black alive. Whoever he's working for has been one step ahead of us the entire time, and unless we catch up, the intel we have tells us a lot of innocent people are going to die. As ominous and frankly ridiculous as it may sound, the world will be changed forever. Do we have a mutual understanding?"

"Very well, gentlemen. Please follow me inside," Hector said, and gestured behind him. "We're using the hangar as a mobile command post. Let me introduce you to Commander Vargas so you can get started."

As they entered the hangar, none of the men turned to watch as the landing gear on the C-130 touched down, the wheels squealing on the tarmac. All were too busy appreciating the level of preparedness the Mexican government had demonstrated in establishing the mobile command post, which included two armed guards with HK machine guns who closed the doors behind them and stepped outside to wait for the arrival of the FBI HRT.

Inside, multiple tables had been hastily set up in the middle of the hangar. They were connected to each other and arranged into one large, rectangular workspace. Positioned around the giant table were several military and ruggedized computers, their containers set aside in one corner. A large portable generator—an amazingly quiet one, Logan thought—powered the entire work space. The computers were operated by men Logan assumed were members of the FES team, all wearing dark-green fatigues with a subtle woodland pattern.

Six black Chevy Suburbans were parked inside the hangar. Logan noticed the expertly crafted upgraded armor modifications.

They'd probably stop an RPG. Hope I don't have to find out.

Hector guided them to a computer where—in addition to the operator who moved a wireless mouse over a grainy image—an older man in fatigues stood waiting for them.

"Commander Vargas, the Americans are here," Hector stated. "The FBI team just touched down outside, but please allow me to introduce Special Agent Mike Benson, and Señors Logan West and John Quick. Special Agent Benson, as you know, will be leading the operation."

There was silence as the FES commander's calculating gaze scrutinized each of them, finally coming to rest on Logan, who stood before him. The commander's short hair was mostly gray and shaved into a meticulous flattop. His hard eyes were a dark brown, and a scar ran all the way down his left cheek to his neck.

He's sizing us up. Must be a machismo thing, Logan thought. *I can relate.*

The man's expression was fixed in a seemingly perpetual scowl, but then the commander surprised him and smiled broadly, sticking out his hand toward Logan. He spoke crisp English, with only a faint trace of a Mexican accent.

"Señor West, it looks like we could be twins," Commander Vargas said, pointing to Logan's left cheek. "Although I have to say, I think I'm the better-looking one."

Logan laughed, his skepticism defused by the man's sense of humor.

"In all sincerity, it's an honor. It sounds like you've been an exceptionally busy man the last few days. We were all briefed on the recent events, and from one warrior to another, I respect what you've done. We're also aware of your time in the famed Force Reconnaissance, and it will be our pleasure to assist you in any way we can."

Logan noted the sincerity in the man's voice and chided himself for judging too quickly.

"As you are surely aware, our country has been at war with the cartels for almost two years now. These aren't gangsters or criminals with some code of honor; they're murderous, evil men who should be wiped off Mexican soil for bringing such dishonor and disgrace to our country."

I like this guy already, Logan thought.

"Commander Vargas, I appreciate it, and more importantly, I completely understand it. You know what they say, 'All that is necessary for the triumph of evil is for good men to do nothing.'"

Commander Vargas smiled. "Ah, a student as well. Edmund

Burke. I'm quite familiar with his words, and they're absolutely true. Now that I believe we see eye to eye, let me bring all of you up to speed," he said and turned back to the computer monitor.

He looked back at Logan one more time, smiling as he did so. "And please"—he paused—"call me Cris, short for Crisanto."

Logan nodded his head. "In that case, please call me Logan."

He turned to the monitor, realized what he was watching, and looked back at Commander Vargas. "You've got a UAV up. Excellent. At what elevation is it flying?"

He watched as the image slowly circled a large two-story villa built at the base of a rugged range of foothills. In addition to the gigantic U-shaped house, there was a building connected to it and a large structure that resembled a garage across the driveway. As the camera swung around, he saw a stable with a barn and a riding area. The entire compound formed an upside-down L, with the entrance at the southern tip of the long end and the buildings contained in the area at the top that jutted out to the east. Logan figured the compound occupied at least forty acres, all of it surrounded by a wall.

How high is the wall? he wondered. Because of the angle, Logan couldn't tell, but he was certain it was definitely taller than a man.

"It's an Israeli Orbiter we purchased earlier this year. It's at twenty thousand feet. We've had it on station for two hours, but it can last six more," Commander Vargas said.

Logan looked up in surprise. "A total of eight hours? I thought the Orbiter could only loiter for three to four."

"We had a very talented aircraft maintenance technician modify it to both increase the flight time *and* muffle the sound."

"Very nice," Logan said, appreciating the craftsmanship. "So what have you seen so far?"

"Between satellite imagery, our Orbiter, and rather forceful interrogations of several midlevel Los Toros members we captured, we believe this compound is actually the home of Ricardo 'El Fuego' Ortega," Commander Vargas said. "He got his name from his pre-dilection for setting his victims on fire—alive. He's a regional com-mander and controls everything in and out of Nuevo Laredo. We've been hunting him for quite a while, but due to a number of resource issues, we had no idea where he was."

John was the first to respond. "Wonderful. I love a man with flair—no pun intended. What do we know about his security?"

"Well, Señor Quick, I can tell you one thing. This isn't going to be easy. He has a private security force that lives on the grounds. I'd estimate twenty to thirty men, if not more. I'm sure he also has high-tech detection and surveillance equipment, probably motion-sensor cameras and microphones." Commander Vargas wore a serious ex-pression as he added, "El Fuego is extremely dangerous. He's been at the top of our list for two years now, and he knows it. Like I said, it's not going to be easy."

No one spoke. The clatter of typing and the running generator were the only sounds hanging in the air. Finally, Logan stated the ob-vious. "This isn't an infiltration. This is going to be an all-out assault. Once we're inside, it's going to turn into a shootout. I just hope we can take Juan Black alive, or else we're screwed."

The thought of failing to discover who the puppet master was behind this nightmare sent shivers up Logan's spine.

"Well, then, gentlemen, I suggest we get to it and figure out how we're going to do it. There are a lot of people who will never even know who we are or what we're doing, and they're all depending on us to succeed," Mike said. He didn't need to mention the loss of life that would likely result if they failed. They all knew the stakes.

As if on cue, the doors of the hangar slid open, and the thirteen men of the FBI's HRT Red Team walked in. All activity immediately ceased as each FES member looked at the new additions.

Mike spotted the man in front of the group, a fortyish African

American in khaki cargo pants and a white polo. He wore a goatee and was in superb shape, his forearms rippling as he carried his bags.

Mike broke into a smile and said, "I thought I ordered the best, and all I get is you."

Without even breaking stride, the head of the Red Team said, "Fuck you, Mike. I thought you ordered a pizza." As if it'd been rehearsed, one of the other team members stepped forward holding a large, flat square box. "Did someone say extra jalapeños?"

Commander Vargas looked at Logan, obviously confused by the inside joke. John just shook his head and said, "I don't get it either." Commander Vargas only raised his eyebrows more, and both Mike and the head of the team said, "Fuck you too!" in unison. John let out a short laugh.

Logan smiled at the quick response and said to Commander Vargas, "You know how it is, Cris. We're almost as lethal with our sarcasm as we are with our weapons. It's the same in the Marine Corps."

"Now that, Señor West, I do understand."

As the men gathered around Mike, he said, "Okay, then. Now that everyone's here, allow me to introduce Special Agent Lance Foster, commander of the FBI's HRT Red Team, which specializes in counterterrorism operations and in extremis hostage rescue. Since we're burning daylight, and like I said before I was rudely interrupted," he stared straight at Special Agent Foster, "let's get to it."

CHAPTER 36

The plan was simple, but Logan knew its simplicity belied its danger and difficulty. Operations planned under such circumstances were usually risky, and there was always a surprise or two—rarely good ones. Fallujah flashed through his mind as the planning unfolded.

The isolation of the compound ensured that any vehicles that approached it would be detected. The UAV had spotted El Fuego's lookouts along the roads for several miles in all directions. That left only one option.

The plan called for an air insertion several miles away via helicopters, followed by an all-night movement to the objective. The assault would commence at morning nautical twilight—which was 0545 local time—when the sun would still be six to twelve degrees below the horizon. There'd be enough light for the trained operators, and the faint outline of objects would be visible.

Both Logan and Commander Vargas had recommended a morning assault. The security force going off duty would be tired from the previous night's watch, and the day shift would hopefully still be groggy as they prepared for their day of monotonous work.

Logan knew how mind-numbing hours of security duty could be. The Marine Corps tormented its young warriors with various watches of one kind or another. Logan hoped to catch them at shift change to maximize the confusion and chaos.

Fortunately, Commander Vargas's men specialized in night operations, especially in rugged terrain. The drug war had forced the FES to adapt to its enemy, shifting from maritime operations—although they were just as lethal in the water—to assault operations in urban and mountain terrain, the latter of which happened to be plentiful in both central and coastal Mexico.

The command center would remain at the airport hangar, with Mike in contact with the White House Situation Room during the entire operation. The communications equipment already set up by the FES was encrypted and would provide secure lines of communication.

Additionally, one of the FES operators would fly the Orbiter from his ground station inside the hangar, and the live feed would provide Mike with real-time intelligence he could pass to both Logan and Commander Vargas.

Logan, Mike, and Commander Vargas stood at a whiteboard easel with a gigantic satellite image taped to the top half and a map of the compound area on the bottom half. Both Logan and Vargas were conducting the final briefing to two teams—named Alpha and Bravo for simplicity—both including Red Team members and FES special operators.

Alpha Team was commanded by Special Agent Foster; Bravo Team, Commander Vargas's second in command, Lieutenant Commander Miguel Concepción. Logan and Commander Vargas would accompany Alpha Team and provide tactical guidance as needed. Both teams had one priority: capture Juan Black alive, at all costs. Everything else was secondary.

The toughest part of the plan had been identifying a landing zone for the heliborne assault force. Both Logan and Commander Vargas had agreed upon a clearing seven thousand meters to the east of the compound with no visible road access for miles, at least according to recent imagery. It was surrounded by trees and would provide cover for the two Eurocopter EC-725 Caracal special operations helicopters—call signs Specter 1 and Specter 2—outfitted with sound-dampening technology that muffled both rotors. The helicopters would insert both teams and remain on standby to provide support until the assault was over, at which point they'd fly to the compound to retrieve the teams and the target.

In addition to transporting the assault force, the helos were equipped with two 7.62mm FN MAG machine guns mounted in the forward port and starboard windows, two 68mm side-mounted rocket launchers with nineteen rockets each, and one 20mm pod-mounted GIAT cannon with 180 rounds. If the assault force faced serious resistance, the Caracals could be on station within minutes to provide direct air support.

The terrain between the insertion point and the compound was open ground with sparse vegetation. Fortunately, the forecast called for cloud cover throughout the night and would hide their movements from the untrained observer.

From the insertion point, the assault force would travel together until they reached a predesignated area two kilometers from the compound, where the trees grew thick and provided more cover near the base of the foothills. At that point, Alpha Team would break off and move to the north, its destination the northeast corner of the compound. Bravo Team would move to the southwest corner, where the two parts of the upside-down L intersected, directly behind the garage. Both teams would remain concealed one hundred meters from the compound wall until 0545, when the assault would commence.

Alpha Team would scale the compound wall—an imagery analyst assessed the wall to be between ten and thirteen feet tall—and proceed to the villa. The assumption was that the target, Juan Black, who'd been code-named PANCHO, would likely be on the top floor in a guest bedroom. Once inside the villa, Logan would assume point since he was the only team member who'd actually spoken to the target.

Bravo Team's objective was to secure the garage and proceed across the gravel driveway to secure the building connected to the villa. Bravo Team would also secure the perimeter of the villa itself to ensure the target didn't escape while Alpha Team was inside searching for the target. As an expert in explosives, John Quick would provide demolitions support to Bravo Team.

"Gentlemen, I cannot express to you the gravity of this situation," Mike said. "We have been a step behind these people since this started. Operation PANCHO may be our last chance to prevent this event—likely an attack—that will allegedly plunge the US into another global conflict at the cost of thousands more lives."

Mike paused as the gravity of his words sank in. Stern expressions looked back at him. The time for jokes had passed, and the focus was completely on the mission.

"Unfortunately, what that means is that we have to somehow take the target alive, but since we have no idea what this asshole looks like, Alpha Team, once you get inside the villa, deadly force is not authorized unless you are absolutely certain the man in your sights is not the target. You must shoot to wound, no matter what the consequences."

No one reacted to the order, which had already been discussed by Logan, Special Agent Foster, and Commander Vargas. Each of the team members knew the potential implications of the order—injury or worse to a team member—but each of these men was prepared to take the risks. Logan knew they understood the stakes of the game they were playing. It was a deadly winner-take-all scenario. The score was ultimately tallied in lives lost or saved.

"Once we have the target secured, Specter One will land near the barn inside the riding area and wait for both teams at the extraction point. Specter Two will provide air support in the event that any hostiles are still alive and try to interfere. Alpha Team and the target will leave the compound first on Specter One, and then Specter Two will land and retrieve Bravo Team as Specter One provides air support."

Mike saw several nods of approval.

"At that point, two things will happen. First, Mr. Ortega here will call the SEDENA to notify his government's defense department of the cartel compound's location and order a battalion of Mexican army special forces and Mexican law enforcement to secure it. Second, both birds will return here to base, where Commander Vargas will immediately begin the interrogation of the target."

Several of the men smiled at that comment, although Commander Vargas displayed no emotion. Discussions between Mike, Hector Ortega, and Commander Vargas about what to do with the target had brought a potential problem to the forefront.

Even though both presidents had authorized enhanced interrogation techniques, there was still no guarantee PANCHO would break. Several of the methods the CIA employed often took days to work—sleep deprivation, temperature manipulation, disorientation—but they needed answers *now*. They'd agreed upon a simple solution.

Commander Vargas would conduct the interrogation. Hector Ortega had made a phone call, and the Mexican president had authorized the FES commander to use "whatever means he feels are necessary."

Mike looked at both Logan and Commander Vargas and scanned the faces of the men in front of him. *This is one seriously scary bunch. The Los Toros cartel has no idea what the hell's about to hit them.*

Mike spoke. "Gentlemen, the sun sets at eighteen zero two hours, and you are wheels up at nineteen hundred. Before you make your final preparations, are there any questions?"

No one answered. Each man knew his responsibilities during the mission.

"Very well. Then I'll finish with this: both of our presidents have ordered this operation. My president has asked me to express his gratitude for what your country is doing for us today. He knows the risks involved, and he wanted me to thank you personally beforehand. As he put it"—Mike looked down at a piece of paper he'd written on—"'The public may never know what you do tonight, but I will always know, and I will never forget it. These men you pursue tonight personify evil in our world today. Happy hunting, and God bless each of you.'"

Mike looked up and saw a collection of faces set in determination and reflection. The president's words had the desired effect of providing an additional level of genuine motivation for their efforts.

Damn. Our commander in chief may not be the best communicator, but he does know how to make his point honestly and sincerely.

Even his critics acknowledged that he was a man of conviction. The men in this hangar recognized that fact and appreciated it.

"Okay then, gentlemen. In that case, let's get this show on the road—or should I say, in the air?" Mike added with a smile.

CHAPTER 37

Logan quietly navigated the rough terrain. Alpha Team moved in a wedge formation, with three four-man groups making up each section of the larger wedge. Logan was in the center team of the formation, behind Commander Vargas and in front of Special Agent Foster.

He carried his Kimber .45 and an HK UMP .45 caliber, although he hoped he wouldn't have to use either one inside the villa. His Mark II fighting knife was in a thigh-rig sheath one of the FES members had provided. One of the HRT's dark olive-green flight suits provided several cargo pockets for the other tools of his lethal trade. Over the flight suit he wore a lightweight Kevlar vest outfitted with nylon loops used as attachments for the magazine and equipment pouches. On his head was a FES boonie cover, darkening his face already camouflaged with various shades of paint.

Each FBI HRT member wore a helmet that contained a built-in communications system, but Logan had selected the FES communications setup since it was similar to the throat microphone he'd used in Force Reconnaissance.

John Quick had done the same; however, in addition to his

M1911, he'd picked an M4 carbine from the HRT as his assault weapon. Along with his KA-BAR fighting knife, he carried two Claymore mines, several bricks of C-4 explosives, detonators, and several feet of detonation cord. He loved the explosives but despised the additional weight, since he liked to move quickly and lightly.

Both teams had programmed each other's frequencies into their internal networks, but the standing orders were for only Commander Vargas and Lieutenant Commander Concepción to cross-talk as needed.

The insertion had been executed flawlessly. The helos had encountered no other air traffic during the entire flight. Logan knew it was one thing to operate safely in Iraq, where all aircraft were US-controlled, but it was entirely another thing to conduct a low-altitude helo assault in a populated country that wasn't considered a war zone—*at least not yet*—and contained commercial air traffic.

The only suspenseful moment had occurred minutes after the helicopters had landed and shut down their engines after unloading their passengers. As the men gathered in the clearing, a pair of headlights had appeared on the horizon more than a mile and a half away. The headlights had momentarily traveled toward them and then suddenly turned left, disappearing into the darkness to the southeast.

Logan looked at his digital watch: *0103. Moving quickly . . .*

They'd covered more than four and a half kilometers. They were close to their separation point, where Alpha Team would break off to the north and Bravo Team would continue to the west-southwest. At this pace, they'd be in position ahead of schedule.

Logan was apprehensive at the ease with which the operation was unfolding. He knew from experience that these things never went off without complications. Murphy's Law was always in effect.

He shrugged the thought away and kept moving, ignoring the November chill in the night air.

CHAPTER 38

Cain Frost sat in a small conference room in the living quarters of the deputy commanding general of Multi-National Forces–West, Brigadier General Travis Thurman. The general was apprising him of the security situation, which had dramatically improved after the surge of 2007. The camp was preparing to close operations and move to Al Asad, which would be the last remaining US military base during the announced drawdown of US forces.

HRI personnel continued to support convoy operations and private security for several of the remaining facilities, but there'd been neither incoming indirect fire to the camp nor IED attacks in almost twelve months. Conditions were radically different from the last time Cain had been in-country.

Fallujah was the first stop on Cain's "inspection trip" to the various camps and bases where his personnel operated. It was the perfect cover to conceal his real objective: get to Haditha and acquire the object.

A break in the weather had afforded them an opportunity to leave Camp Frost early this morning, but another batch of sand and wind was moving in from the west. As a result, he and his forces weren't going to be leaving for Ramadi until tomorrow.

It required all his mental discipline to focus on the general's words, especially when his thoughts continuously looped back to the Syrian treasure buried in the desert, waiting for him to discover it.

He smiled as the general made some comment about how Cain's support would be critical for the transfer of forces and equipment to Al Asad. He was about to respond when his secure BlackBerry buzzed in its holster on his right hip.

He looked down and saw a number he recognized but hadn't heard from in weeks.

Why the hell is he texting me? This can't be good.

"Excuse me, General, that's my chief of operations back in Baghdad. Do you mind if I step outside and call him back? He says it's important." He smiled sincerely as he delivered the lie.

"Absolutely. In fact, I'm going to go grab another cup of coffee. Can I get you one? I didn't sleep well last night, but I still woke up early to hit the gym."

Cain was impressed. The general looked to be in his early fifties, but he maintained himself well. "Sir, that would be wonderful."

"Cream and sugar?" the general asked.

"Just black, sir."

"Aha. A man after my own heart. No man should drink coffee with any of that froufrou shit in it."

Cain laughed at hearing a hardened Marine Corps general use the word *froufrou*. "I certainly agree. Please excuse me, sir."

He stood up, left the conference room, and walked outside. The heat of the day was building, but compared to the summer months, it was downright comfortable.

He opened the text, and what he read turned his blood cold. "Operation under way to capture JB in Mexico. Hours away. Just briefed. President approved."

Short and concise—but it was more than enough to send Cain's mind into overdrive. His source was close to the president, and his information was one hundred percent reliable.

I have to warn Juan, he thought. *I need more time.*

It was a few minutes past eleven o'clock in the morning in Iraq, which meant it was just past two o'clock in the morning in Mexico.

He brought up a new message and typed, "Location compromised. Get out now! Will contact you in 24 hours."

He hit send and waited as the text message was digitally encrypted and sent across the global cellular network.

After a moment's hesitation, he dialed Juan's cell phone number on the off chance he might reach him. No answer. He tried again. Still no answer. He couldn't risk leaving a voice mail.

He ended the call and returned inside to finish the discussion with General Thurman. It was painful, forcing himself to engage in this charade. Even as he smiled and appeared calm, his emotions raged, and his heart pounded at the thought of Juan's potential capture.

Other than Scott, he's the only one who knows everything.

CHAPTER 39

LOS TOROS COMPOUND
0540 LOCAL HOURS

Logan gazed through the night-vision binoculars Commander Vargas had handed to him. Since the team had moved into their final position over an hour ago and assumed a surveillance posture, they'd observed limited movement inside the compound. Logan had seen only three guards, each individually patrolling in the same pattern around the villa. Every eight to ten minutes, one of the them passed directly by the patio rear entrance.

Their final assault position provided an unobstructed vantage point of the entire back side of the villa. The team was hidden near the base of one of the foothills at an elevation slightly higher than the roof. A small copse of trees, bushes, and jagged boulders provided concealment as they waited for zero hour.

Logan's presumption about the compound wall had been correct. It was at least fifteen feet tall, and after further discussion, both Logan and Commander Vargas immediately scratched the idea of trying to scale it. It'd take time they just didn't have, and once the security forces spotted them, they'd be sitting ducks. It was too risky.

That left one option—a hard entry. Fortunately, the team had packed plenty of explosives, and one well-placed C-4 charge would demolish a large-enough section of the wall to allow the team to move in rapidly. Since Bravo Team would be doing the exact same thing—Commander Vargas had coordinated with Lieutenant Commander Concepción to detonate only on his mark—security would likely be confused about the direction of the explosion. Simultaneous explosions might buy them a few precious seconds as they assaulted the villa.

They'd chosen their breaching point directly in line with the rear patio entrance. The initial chaos should provide them enough time to cover the fifty meters from the wall to the glass doors. It'd be close, but Logan thought they'd be able to breach the house before reinforcements arrived.

Logan turned to Commander Vargas, lying prone underneath the bush with him, and speaking in a low voice—whispering carried words farther—said, "Three men? Where the hell are the rest? This can't be that easy."

Commander Vargas watched the compound as one of the foot patrols appeared at the left rear corner of the house, illuminated by the rooftop flood lights pointed down at the perimeter wall at a forty-five-degree angle. "I have no idea. Maybe they keep a minimal security posture at night. Hell, maybe El Fuego is so arrogant he assumes no one would dare attack his home." He hesitated and then said, "Honestly, I just don't know."

"I guess it's a moot point because in four minutes we cover this last hundred meters as quickly as we can, breach, and then we'll find what we find." The foot patrol was now halfway to the rear entrance. "I just pray to God our luck holds out. It looks like we'll have enough cover to reach the wall without being spotted by the cameras."

They'd identified the security cameras immediately, one mounted on a metal rod at each corner of the villa's roof. The cameras operated on timers, but what had shocked both men was the fact that the cameras were synchronized to swivel in a pattern that resulted in all four cameras either facing inward or outward at the same time. More importantly, each camera completed one rotation every sixty seconds.

As soon as the cameras turned inward at 0545, Commander Vargas would radio Bravo Team to utilize the blind spot and execute their final approach.

Logan handed the binoculars to Commander Vargas and made his last-minute preparations. He pulled the charging handle of the UMP to ensure a round was chambered and checked that the safety was still on.

The sense of focus Logan had experienced before every mission during his tenure in Force Reconnaissance returned, his senses heightened in a sharpened state of clarity. His mind welcomed the calm. All thoughts of Sarah, Daly, and the rest of the world disintegrated in his consciousness, his focus solely on the mission.

Showtime, Juan—or whoever the hell you are. I'm coming for you.

———

INSIDE THE LOS TOROS COMPOUND
0544 LOCAL HOURS

Juan Black—whose given name in a previous life was Marcos Bocanegra—stirred from a deep slumber, a headache forming as he opened his eyes.

Shouldn't have had that last glass of wine.

The dinner with Ricardo Ortega had lasted into the early-morning hours. Juan had known he'd be feeling the effects this morning, but he didn't want to be rude to his host.

Wine hangovers are the worst.

The former 7th Special Forces Group member sat up in bed. He still wore his trousers and a white tee shirt from the night before. He rubbed his eyes, stood up, and looked out the curtains of his bedroom window. The dark mass of the foothills filled his view in back of the villa. It reminded him of several counter-drug operations he'd conducted in South America. The irony was that those operations had ultimately led to his current employment.

After he'd washed out of selection school for Delta, he'd been so full of resentment and anger that he'd left the military altogether and contacted a midlevel cartel member with whom he'd once had a standing arrangement. He'd proffered his services for full-time employment, wholly grasping the implications of his choice. As it turned out, his moral flexibility suited the position perfectly, and he'd never looked back.

Still dark outside. What time is it?

And that was when he heard his BlackBerry vibrate.

What the hell?

He grabbed the phone and immediately saw several missed calls and one text message, all from Cain Frost's extremely private and secure personal number.

This can't be good.

Three people on the planet knew the scope of Cain's plan, as well as the real intended target. Juan was one of those men; the other was Scott Carlson, Cain's second in command.

Cain knew Juan was hiding in the Los Toros compound. The original plan had called for him to travel through Mexico and South America, eventually arriving in Venezuela. From there, his ultimate destination was Maracaibo, the Venezuelan city named after its lake. A bank account had been established there in a false name, another identity to which only he had the official documents. He'd planned on remaining in Maracaibo until the looming geopolitical storm blew over.

He opened the message and read "Location compromised," and his military training immediately kicked into overdrive. His mind was already formulating an escape plan as he closed the BlackBerry, holstered it, and grabbed his hiking boots.

He cursed himself for having missed the call and the message.

No point crying over spilled milk. Have to get out now.

As he finished tying the second boot, two simultaneous explosions thundered throughout the compound, shattering the quiet Mexican morning.

He should've realized they'd be coming for him. A slight edge of fear insinuated itself into his thoughts, and as a siren blared throughout the compound, he forced himself to take a deep breath. As he closed his eyes, one word flashed behind them: *escape.*

CHAPTER 40

As Logan crossed the open grass between the breached wall and the sliding patio doors, he looked inside the house for movement, his HK at the ready position, eyes scanning over the top of the iron sights. He preferred the sights for this type of work; there was less chance of error than with a scope.

He knew the guards would be coming soon from either the house or around the sides. He was in front of the right column, next to Commander Vargas, who had the lead for the left column. As Alpha Team quickly covered the distance to the rear entrance, Logan was amazed at the ease with which their entry had occurred.

Once 0545 had arrived, both Alpha and Bravo Teams had synchronized their final movements, covered the remaining distance from their observation posts, and planted the C-4 charges at each location.

As Logan had waited, memories of Fallujah had led to slinking doubts in his subconscious. He knew how quickly these operations could hit a proverbial wall. It was usually then that the bodies started piling up. But when Commander Vargas and Lieutenant Commander Concepción coordinated the detonations—again, without any resistance—Logan's mind immediately refocused, his hard resolve and battle-heightened awareness crushing any lingering uncertainty.

Twenty-five feet to go . . . twenty . . . fifteen . . . His mind ticked off the distances. Then, just as he'd expected, members of the security force finally arrived to counter the assault.

Two men, similarly dressed in dark pants and black shirts, holding modified M4s, appeared in the gigantic kitchen, now full of light from the multiple candelabras hanging from the ceiling. The low-level of illumination outside must have masked the assault forces' movement: the men didn't spot them until Logan and Commander Vargas were less than ten feet away from the back doors.

Logan saw the man on the right squint in disbelief, but even as he tried to react, he was too slow. Logan raised the muzzle of the UMP a few inches, a move that took him less than half a second after practicing it thousands of times in the Marine Corps.

As the man raised the M4, Logan fired three rounds, the UMP set to semiautomatic mode. The first round shattered the right patio door before veering off target as a result of the impact, glass showering the kitchen floor. Even though it missed, the first round cleared the way for the second and third bullets, which struck the man squarely in the chest and stopped him in his tracks as a look of surprise and pain appeared on his face. He fell to the floor, dead from the .45-caliber slugs.

Commander Vargas dealt with the shooter on the left in a similar fashion, but instead of the glass door altering the bullet's trajectory, his first round somehow maintained its course and struck the man in the throat. The man dropped his M4, but as he raised his hands to his neck, the second and third bullets struck him in the forehead and right cheek, shattering the right side of his face as he died.

Both Logan and Commander Vargas stepped through the now-empty doorframes, expecting additional resistance from any of the kitchen's three large, dark entrances.

They were now inside the enemy's lair, susceptible to ambushes and other nasty surprises. Logan knew their success depended on how well the security forces had been trained to defend a direct assault.

Hopefully, not well at all.

Logan and Commander Vargas took positions along a twenty-foot-long marble countertop that ran through the middle of the kitchen. Their weapons were pointed down the main hallway as the remainder of Alpha Team entered the villa. Two members of the FES team remained at the compound wall to ensure no one tried to escape behind them.

"They're either waiting for our next move, or we caught them totally off guard," Logan said quietly. "Either way, we need to go now before they try to coordinate a counterattack. The stairway is in the main hallway. Leave four men here to hold this position. No one gets out."

But even as Commander Vargas moved to issue his orders, Logan thought he heard movement from a distant part of the house upstairs.

We need to move.

Without further delay, Logan strode around the countertop to the right, as Commander Vargas did the same from the left.

The hunt's on now.

As the men entered the hallway, a thunderous explosion shook the entire villa. Logan looked at Commander Vargas. "God, I hope we did that."

Not realizing that the assault had just turned into a ferocious engagement for Bravo Team, Logan turned back toward the hallway, deeper into the villa, praying their luck would hold out.

———

BRAVO TEAM

In John Quick's professional opinion, the initial breach had been as uneventful as a forced entry with explosives could be. The simultaneous detonations must've confused the security forces, since no one intercepted Bravo Team as it infiltrated the compound. All had gone smoothly—at least until they'd reached the garage.

From various overhead imagery and surveillance footage from the Orbiter UAV, they knew the steel-frame garage was as large as the villa, stretching two hundred feet in length and half as wide. It resembled a hangar, with a cavernous open-air second story that occupied the left half. The single-level right side was littered with oversized pickup trucks and SUVs.

As Bravo Team stacked up outside the single-door rear entrance, John thought he heard movement inside. He gave Lieutenant Commander Concepción a hand signal to halt and listen. The team leader paused, but when he heard nothing, he ordered the entry and led the team himself.

As Lieutenant Commander Concepción turned the handle on the door and swung it inward, he stepped through the opening into a dimly lit interior. A second FES member had followed him when a barrage of automatic weapons fire suddenly erupted and struck the Bravo Team commander.

The FES operator behind him leapt backward and launched himself out of the garage as bullets tore into the doorframe where he'd been standing only moments before. He landed on his back and scrambled to the side of the entrance, breathing heavily. He still looked relatively composed for such a close call, or at least John thought so.

These guys are tough.

Lieutenant Commander Concepción wasn't nearly as lucky. John looked down to see the FES leader's body lying on its side, his head a foot away from the entrance. His eyes were open but saw nothing.

The team was stacked against both sides of the doorway, pinned down from the inside. John knew there was no way they were gaining entry to the garage from this location. They needed to find another way.

We need a diversion.

As bullets peppered the entrance, an idea formed. He looked across the open doorway and saw the FES team's second in command, Lieutenant Jorge Garcia. John waited until the Bravo Team members unleashed their salvo, and then he dashed across the opening to the FES lieutenant. He spoke quickly, the FES member now in charge listening intently.

"Lieutenant, there's no way we're going to make it inside this doorway. We have to find another way, but we need a diversion. Right now, they think we're still going to try and force our way inside from here. You need to keep two men here to hold this position and make them think we're pinned down. Then you and I can take the rest of the men and circle around the left side of the building to work our way inside from the front. If we can flank them without being detected, we can take them out and secure the garage, eliminating any chance of escape they might have with the vehicles inside. Once we have the garage, we move to our second objective," he finished, referring to the building attached to the villa.

John stopped talking as the lieutenant quickly weighed his options, finally nodded, and said, "Good idea. Let's do it."

Without a further moment's hesitation, Garcia stepped around the man in front of him, tapped the shoulder of the FES member returning fire through the doorway and issued instructions into his ear.

John watched him point to the HRT member across the open door and issue his orders with several hand signals, which made his intent clear. The HRT member nodded, dropped an empty magazine onto the ground, reloaded, and returned to the firefight.

The lieutenant returned to John and said, "Let's go. You want to lead the way or would you like one of my men to?" There was no condescension or sarcasm in the request. John knew the FES lieutenant was showing him respect by allowing him to make the call, since it was his idea.

"I'll do it." He moved around the left side of the garage, the lieutenant and the rest of Bravo Team close behind him.

Always coming up with the good ideas, aren't you, John?

John knew that if there were anyone inside the garage with any type of military training, someone would likely realize the entrance to the garage was susceptible to a frontal assault. John just hoped that whoever was making the decisions inside would be delayed by the ongoing gunfight for at least another thirty seconds, which was all John and the Bravo Team members needed.

He reached the corner of the building and stopped just long enough to peer around the edge, concealed by the lingering darkness.

Nothing. So far, so good.

He jogged quickly along the side of the building.

Please let it be a direct shot to the front bay doors.

He took a deep breath, exhaled, and leaned around the corner. From his vantage point, John had a direct view of both the attached building, which looked like a large guest house, and the villa. The good news was that there were no security reinforcements coming from either building. The bad news was that lights were turning on in several windows.

We only have a minute or two before they step up their defense. So much for the element of surprise, he thought wryly.

He turned to Lieutenant Garcia and said, "No forces in sight;

however, we only have a minute or two. Lights coming on all over the place. As soon as I turn this corner, I'm keeping my weapon trained on the bay doors. I need you and the other team members to cover the entrances to the villa and that building. Stay close to me. Once we get to the open doors, I'm going in as quietly as I can, and I need you right behind me. Ready?"

Lieutenant Garcia nodded and once again turned and relayed his orders. He looked back at John and said, "Ready."

Even though the run to the first bay door lasted only seconds, to John it seemed like an eternity. He was completely exposed to both buildings on his left.

Move it, old man!

He was fit for forty-two—more so than most twenty-year-olds—but he knew Father Time was gaining ground on him. It wasn't that he'd lost a step: his hand-to-hand encounters in the last few days had proven that. Rather, it was that recovering from those fights seemed to take a lot longer than it used to. As a result, he realized he'd have to rely upon his wisdom and experience. As he ran for the door, he hoped both would serve him well in the next few moments.

He crossed the last few feet to the door as the sounds of the gunfight inside the garage grew louder. He heard multiple men shouting at one another in Spanish. He sensed, rather than heard, the rest of Bravo Team halt behind him.

He glanced around the corner, and with just a glimpse of the interior, his trained eye immediately calculated all options. He knew what he was going to do.

This is going to wake the neighbors.

He turned to the lieutenant, who wore a questioning look as to why John hadn't gone into the garage. He explained his plan and turned back to the door to execute it.

I hope the guys in the back have some cover.

He dropped his pack off his back, rifled through it, and found what he was looking for—the M18A1 Claymore mine. He pulled out the mine, the command wire, and the plastic trigger. He armed the mine and unrolled approximately twenty feet of wire. He looked back to see that the Bravo Team members had withdrawn per the lieutenant's instructions but continued to cover the front of the villa and the attached building.

As soon as the mine was ready, he stepped around the corner and saw six security personnel, arranged in a semicircle behind three large SUVs, still firing toward the open doorway. He bent down and firmly planted the mine in the gravel near the frame of the bay door. He looked up just in time to see an HRT member almost 150 feet away.

Even at this distance, John knew the FBI agent had seen him plant the mine. He pointed and moved both hands apart, indicating that he and the other team member should move away from the doorway and take cover.

Without waiting for a response, John ran back to the rest of Bravo Team, the Claymore's wire dangling from his right hand. All of them were in the prone position and had their weapons trained on the villa.

John dropped down to the ground on his stomach, grabbed the plastic trigger in both hands—memories from Fallujah briefly surfacing in the dark corridors of his mind—and compressed the detonating lever.

KABOOM!

The resulting explosion sent steel balls ricocheting through the garage in a wave of death and destruction. All six security members were killed by the flying steel that caromed crazily inside the structure. John felt the entire building shake with fury as the lethal balls punctured its skin.

As John had hoped, the flying steel also punctured the several-hundred-gallon fuel tank John had spotted on the right side of the garage. The secondary explosion made the detonation of the anti-personnel mine sound and feel like a firecracker.

THUD-whoosh!

With a thunderous roar that rattled John's teeth, an enormous fireball blew through the garage. The tin roof was torn into pieces that were flung in all directions, raining sheet metal and wood all around them. The explosion illuminated the entire compound in a bright-yellow glow as the thunder echoed off the surrounding hills.

With his ears ringing, he turned back to the FES lieutenant. Even as hardened as the young man appeared to be, the look of amazement on his face made John smile. "I think that did the trick," John said. Lieutenant Garcia still just stared at him. "Now for part two."

Giving the young man another moment to relay instructions to the team, John stood up, grabbed his M4, and put it in the ready position. He sprinted across the gravel driveway toward the second building as the rest of the team assumed positions next to him. They moved in-line toward the second objective, with approximately five feet of separation from one to the next.

Let's see what's behind door number two.

———

ALPHA TEAM

Other than the two men in the kitchen, Alpha Team had yet to encounter any members of the cartel's security force. They'd followed two curved staircases that led from the foyer, with its black-and-white marble floor, up to a landing in the middle of one enormous hallway that ran the length of the entire second floor of the villa. The place resembled a small hotel rather than someone's home.

Logan led the team along the right half of the wide hallway as Special Agent Foster took the other part of Alpha Team down the left. Logan moved as quietly as he could down the lengthy corridor. Fortunately, the plush carpet provided plenty of sound suppression—he was virtually silent. Commander Vargas and four Alpha Team members, all from Vargas's FES unit, followed.

Where the hell is El Fuego's security?

At the far end of the corridor stood a large, ornate set of dark wooden doors that occupied the entire width of the hallway.

El Fuego's room, I'm sure. Subtle.

They had already cleared the first two of the four other large rooms that branched off the hall, both empty. Now they moved down the hallway and positioned themselves outside the next two doors. Logan initiated the count. *One . . . two . . .* He never reached *three.*

A salvo of automatic weapons fire burst through the door in front of Commander Vargas, sending splinters flying through the hallway. The Alpha Team members instinctively lowered themselves into a crouching position in case the shooter within decided to spray bullets through the wall as well as the door. Commander Vargas grabbed a flash-bang grenade off his vest, pulled the pin, and held it for what seemed to Logan like an eternity.

The shooting stopped, and Logan heard a man's voice shouting in Spanish, followed by the sound of something metallic falling to a hardwood floor inside.

Bastard's reloading . . .

Commander Vargas must've had the same thought. Rather than wait for the shooter to finish, he grabbed the door handle, cracked the door open, and tossed the grenade into the center of the room. Logan quickly put his hands to his ears for protection. The rest of Alpha Team was already prepared. A moment later, the flash-bang detonated.

Boom!

The confined space of the guest bedroom amplified the explosion as the flash of light shot out the crack in the doorway.

Logan heard a man scream from inside.

Too bad for you, asshole, he thought as Commander Vargas entered the room, his weapon up and searching for the target.

For some reason, the shooter—wearing nothing but a white tee shirt and blue boxer shorts—having been blinded and deafened, still tried to stand and raise the AK-47 he held in his right hand.

Logan saw Commander Vargas, obviously aware of the rules of engagement, lower his UMP and fire two rounds in rapid succession into each of the man's legs.

Pop-pop! Pop-pop!

The bullets shattered the man's right kneecap and his left shin, eliciting a howl of pain that turned into a high-pitched shriek. He dropped the AK-47 and began to writhe on the bedroom floor in agony.

Logan watched as Commander Vargas kicked the assault rifle away from the downed man, grabbed him by his black hair, and screamed, *"Cómo se llama usted!"*

The man was in no condition to resist, but he couldn't hear after being deafened by the grenade. Vargas screamed at him again and pointed at the middle of his chest. The wounded man finally understood and muttered "Eduardo Montanero" between sobs.

Commander Vargas looked at Logan, who shook his head to confirm it wasn't their target's voice.

On to the next room, Logan thought.

Commander Vargas rolled the wounded shooter onto his stomach, ignoring the man's pleas for medical assistance. He zip-tied his hands behind his back and exited the room, closing the door behind him, the man's screams now diminished by the wooden door.

He looked at Logan as he said, "He'll live. The cleanup team can deal with him. He's not our priority."

Logan appreciated the level of cold calculation in Commander Vargas's decision, nodded, and turned back to the last door. Once again, he initiated the silent countdown. *One . . . two . . . three . . . go!* He reached for the handle of the door with his right hand and began to turn it.

Before he could push the door inward, a man's deep voice boomed throughout the hallway, *"Hijos de puta! Me buscas?!"*

Logan didn't understand Spanish, but he turned to the sound of the man's voice originating from the end of the corridor. What he saw turned his blood to ice.

You've got to be fucking kidding me.

Standing in the doorway of the master bedroom was an overweight, dark-skinned Mexican man of average height. He wore an open, dark-red satin bathrobe, his thick black chest hair sticking out in tufts where the front gaped open. His outfit was completed by a pair of navy-blue pajama pants and what looked to Logan like a pair of yellow fluffy slippers. The man had a short-cropped beard and a thick mane of black, wavy hair jutting out in all directions. The look on his face was one of unadulterated outrage.

Uh-oh. El Fuego looks pissed, Logan thought.

Alpha Team momentarily gawked at the cartel leader as the scene suddenly transformed from shockingly comical to imminently dangerous when they saw what he held. The object that had drawn all of Alpha Team's attention was the large, round, hose-shaped nozzle pointed in their direction. Immediately behind the nozzle was a small foregrip, now held in El Fuego's left hand. The weapon also had a second pistol grip, which he held in his right hand. The oddly shaped weapon was connected to a dark hose that snaked its way to a tank worn on his back.

Logan's mental threat-weapons database recognized the US Army M9A1-7 flamethrower from the Vietnam War era, its nozzle glowing with a small blue flame. Before Logan had time to formulate another thought, El Fuego let out an unintelligible roar and pulled the trigger.

The hallway was filled with a tremendous *whoosh!* as liquid flame rocketed toward Logan and the rest of Alpha Team like an angry serpent intent on consuming them all.

———

BRAVO TEAM

The building they'd thought was attached to the villa based on satellite imagery in fact stood alone. A covered walkway with an aluminum roof was all that connected it to the main house. Upon closer scrutiny, it wasn't a guesthouse at all but only disguised as one.

In reality, it was a concrete, rectangular structure with no windows, painted a faded cream color to match the main villa. A large ventilation system ran the length of the entire structure, and multiple chimneys jutted from the rooftop. John knew it was significantly more ventilation than a building its size required.

What the hell is going on inside?

The sounds of gunfire continued from deep within the main house. In the back of his mind, John hoped that Logan and Alpha Team had captured the target. Regardless, he had a big problem of his own to solve.

John and Lieutenant Garcia huddled under the walkway, standing off to the side of a stainless steel metal door professionally installed into the side of the building. A single handle was the only fixture, and it didn't budge when John tried it. The ten-digit key combination lock adjacent to the door only complicated matters. The door was several inches thick, and John knew nothing short of several well-placed charges would remove it from its frame.

John was calculating their options when they suddenly heard a series of beeps from the combination lock.

Someone was coming out.

Fortunately, only he and Lieutenant Garcia would be seen by whoever was opening the door. The rest of Bravo Team was providing security between the two buildings and were spread out against the walls.

Realizing he had nowhere to go, John quickly stepped away from the door, drew his KA-BAR fighting knife, and waited. Lieutenant Garcia reacted similarly. He stood to the left of the door, his assault rifle slung across his back, a curved blade held in his right hand.

John hoped the sounds of battle and the morning dusk would conceal their presence long enough for them to act.

Wait for it, John. Wait for it.

As soon as they heard the last beep, the door swung outward and the barrel of an AK-47 appeared through the opening. John waited until the man's left arm appeared, grasping the wooden foregrip under the barrel.

John lunged forward, snatched the barrel of the weapon with his left hand and violently yanked it down and toward him. The startled member of El Fuego's security stumbled forward out of the doorway and toward John. As his momentum carried him forward, John lunged upward with his right hand, burying the KA-BAR into the man's rib cage. The blade pierced the guard's heart, killing him before he even realized what had happened.

As John guided the dead man to the ground, a second security guard appeared in the doorway, a look of horror on his face as he saw what had befallen his compadre. He raised his AK-47 toward John.

Lieutenant Garcia grabbed the man by the throat and jerked him backward as he slid the curved blade into the man's spine, causing him to arch his back reactively. Lieutenant Garcia plunged the blade in farther until the man shuddered and grew still. He let the dead man fall to the sidewalk as the security door began to close.

John caught the edge of the doorway before it shut.

Well, that's one way to get inside.

He peered into the opening and saw a short hallway that led to a much larger, illuminated space. He heard hurried voices speaking in Spanish, and he looked at the lieutenant.

"They're panicking from the gunfire and explosions and trying to figure out what to do next," Lieutenant Garcia said.

"Well," John said with a wicked grin, "let's not give them the time to figure it out."

ALPHA TEAM

Logan lay facedown on the hardwood floor of the guest bedroom, the one they hadn't had time to clear before El Fuego decided to incinerate them in his ad hoc crematorium. Heat rushed over him from behind.

Screams of pain emanated from the hallway. The other team members hadn't been able to find shelter before El Fuego pulled the trigger on the flamethrower. *I wouldn't be alive if it weren't for whoever's on my back.*

Before Logan could react to the flow of thickened and ignited fuel that had snaked toward him, one of the team members had crashed into Logan, propelling him forward and through the door he'd been about to enter.

He felt the man push off his back. Logan rolled over to his right side to see Commander Vargas regain his footing. Logan likewise scrambled to his feet as the screams continued above the roar of the flames dancing in the hallway. There was no time for a "thank-you."

Logan looked around the room for another way out. He cursed

at the sight in front of them. One of the two large sliding windows was open. A sheet tied to the bedpost closest to the window hung out of it.

"Motherfucker. I'll bet that's our guy," Logan cursed. "He must've heard us coming and squirted. We need air support now, but first we have to deal with El Fuego." He knew there was little chance the other men caught in the firestorm in the hallway would survive, but they had to do something.

He grabbed an M67 fragmentary grenade off his vest and spoke rapidly as he pulled the pin. "He's going to have to stop that blaze shortly. It's a burst weapon. As soon as he does, I'm leaning out and tossing this down his fucking throat. As soon as it goes off, I'll rush down the hall after him. You go left and tend to our wounded. Call the helos and tell them to use their FLIR radar to try and spot anyone outside the compound trying to escape. He'll probably head into the mountains."

No sooner had he finished speaking than the hallway, brightly illuminated moments before, suddenly went dark. In one swift motion, Logan lunged to the door in a kneeling position, his right knee forward and his left leg stretched out. As his knee touched the floor, he released the spoon and flung the grenade as hard as he could around the doorframe and into the hallway. He didn't even look; he didn't want to expose himself to the madman with the flamethrower. Luckily, his aim was accurate.

As the grenade landed down the hallway and bounced toward El Fuego, Logan stood up, his Kimber .45 in his hands, waiting to move. Logan watched Commander Vargas reach around his back for the small medical kit. He pulled out the morphine shots from inside.

Might at least give our wounded men some comfort, Logan thought.

Logan didn't have time to further contemplate his team's fate. The grenade detonated.

BOOM!

Logan was rewarded with a loud scream as the concussion reverberated down the hallway toward them.

Logan broke cover, turned into the hallway, and dashed through the inferno after his prey. He caught a glimpse of four shapes on the ground, but he didn't linger to see if they were moving. There was no time.

The hallway was on fire on both sides of the wall. Smoke crept along the ceiling. Paint peeled and blistered as the heat devoured it.

My own personal version of hell. What a nightmare . . .

Logan moved through the flames, himself a shadow, toward what remained of the doorway to El Fuego's bedroom. Both doors had been blown off their hinges, disintegrating in the grenade blast.

Logan sensed a very large, open space beyond the doorway as he approached. Unfortunately, El Fuego was nowhere near the entrance. Logan hoped the grenade had killed him instantly.

He reached the gaping hole that was now the bedroom entrance. He paused, listening. He heard the sound of metal scraping, followed by a loud crash as something large fell over.

Logan didn't want to give El Fuego any more time to recover from the explosion. He stepped through the opening and into El Fuego's inner sanctum, the Kimber raised in front of him.

On the floor twenty feet away lay El Fuego. He was wounded but still moving. Logan didn't think he was going to expire of his own volition in the immediate future. He quickly scanned the rest of the room and confirmed it was empty.

El Fuego was at the base of a cabinet with built-in shelves. He tried to lift himself up to reach the top shelf, making painfully slow progress. The hose and flamethrower gun trailed behind him. The metal canisters on his back had been punctured by grenade fragments. A dark liquid slowly oozed from several of the holes and flowed onto the back of his red robe and exposed legs. Amazingly, he still wore his yellow fluffy slippers.

His hand was inches away from his objective, a nickel-plated .45 secured on a stand. Logan realized it must be loaded.

Nice. Functional as well as aesthetically pleasing. This guy doesn't quit. I'll give him that much.

Logan lowered the Kimber and fired a single shot into the back of El Fuego's left leg. The man slumped backward to the floor, screaming in pain as he grabbed his shin. He rolled over onto his side, his back up against the cabinet, and stared defiantly at Logan.

Logan quietly said, "I told you not to move . . . or maybe I didn't. Sorry. It's been kind of chaotic out there. Regardless, it looks like you're going to live, depending on what you can tell me about Juan Black." Logan's expression was impassive as he stared into the face of the murderous El Fuego.

El Fuego breathed hard and emitted a short laugh. "Fuck you, gringo. You're not even here for me? I'm not telling you anything, *pendejo.*"

Logan nodded. "I thought as much, but let me tell you what I think." He smiled as he continued, the grin catching El Fuego off guard. "I think Mr. Black was in that guest bedroom we just left, and I'll also bet you have no idea who or what he really is. I can tell you one thing: his name is definitely not Juan Black. As for you, you're done. There's a Mexican army unit on its way to take you into custody. It's your lucky day, asshole. You get to live. I'm going to tie you up first though, just in case you get any more bright ideas."

El Fuego said, "Mexican army? You must be one stupid American. I probably pay half of them. You really think they'll take me in? Or keep me if they do? I'll be back here within weeks or months. It's the way things work down here. You and your country still haven't figured it out yet. You can't *stop* us. There's too much money for the politicians, cops, and military. It's never going to end, *puta. I'm never going to end.*"

Logan ignored the man's rant, despite knowing it was partially—if not completely—true. He started to walk toward El Fuego when he heard a small sound behind him. He whirled and raised his pistol, only to see Commander Vargas standing at the door. The solemn look on his face told Logan everything he needed to know about the fate of the men caught in the firestorm.

Commander Vargas shook his head and beckoned Logan over.

God damn it. Logan had been hoping some of them might live, even though he'd suspected otherwise.

"Logan, they never had a chance. I'm sorry for your men and for mine. We can mourn them later and pay tribute to them on our own time." Commander Vargas looked down at El Fuego, his voice hardening. "But for now, what about this piece of shit?"

"He doesn't know anything," Logan scoffed. "I shot him in the leg because he was trying to reach that weapon on the top shelf. It's a nice pistol, by the way, a collector's item. I bet he keeps it loaded. I was going to leave him for the cleanup team."

Commander Vargas continued to stare at El Fuego. "I called in the air support. The helos should be in the area within minutes. As soon as you get outside, contact the pilots on channel seven. I told them to start looking for movement in the trees and on the hills. They'll relay the information to you as soon as you contact them."

"Thanks. What are you going to do now? Sounds like there's still a hell of a fight going on outside. You reach Bravo Team?"

Commander Vargas smiled faintly. "Yes. Lieutenant Commander Concepción is dead. He was killed as they entered the garage. Lieutenant Garcia is in charge now. John is still alive. He's responsible for the explosion we heard." He paused, shook his head, and said, "Your man blew up the entire garage. There's nothing left. Probably saved several lives doing it."

Logan nodded. "That sounds like John, all right. He's a bit of an overachiever when it comes to explosives."

"So it seems. They're about to enter the attached building. It's apparently some kind of production facility," Commander Vargas said.

"Go figure. Well, at least it's going to be out of service after today. Thank you. And again, I'm sorry about your men. I'm going after Juan Black. Can you tie this piece of shit up for me?"

Logan stepped toward the door when Commander Vargas grabbed him by the arm.

Logan looked up, his eyebrows raised. "Logan, this man is evil. Nothing more. He's responsible for the deaths of hundreds if not thousands. I've seen his handiwork before. If we take him into custody, he might be able to buy his way out with the corrupt officials I know he's connected to."

Logan knew where this was going, but he said nothing.

"Logan, what I'm saying . . . what I'm *asking* is this—from one man of honor to another, do you object if I take care of El Fuego myself? It's the only way justice will be served, especially in Mexico."

Logan didn't hesitate. He'd considered it briefly himself. "I agree. He made his choices a long time ago, and now it's time to pay for them. And if you think he could walk, then do it. Sounds like he's had it coming for a long time now."

Commander Vargas nodded once and said, "Thank you. Now go find Juan Black while I tend to this matter."

Logan was almost at the door when he paused, turned around, and said to El Fuego, "I was wrong, asshole. It's not your lucky day. But even better, you were wrong about that last point. You are about to end." He saw Commander Vargas reach into a cargo pocket and pull out a metallic shape he recognized as a lighter. "I hope you burn in hell, after you burn here." He turned and ran down the flaming hallway to pursue his real target.

A stunned El Fuego sat on the ground, contemplating his imminent demise. He looked from the empty space Logan had just occupied to Commander Vargas, but there was no mercy to be found. His sentence was about to be rendered, the full horror of it slamming him in the gut.

Logan reached the midpoint of the hallway as he heard a loud *whoosh*, followed by screams. He smiled, his righteous outrage and desire for justice temporarily satiated.

That's what you get for playing with fire.

Several moments and screams later, a loud gunshot echoed down the corridor. Commander Vargas had shown El Fuego a small token of mercy at the very end.

That's better than what you deserved, you sonofabitch, Logan thought and kept running. He had more pressing matters to attend to—catching Juan Black.

CHAPTER 41

BRAVO TEAM

Things weren't going as smoothly for John Quick and Bravo Team, which had followed him and Lieutenant Garcia inside once they'd secured the door. As soon as they'd infiltrated the building through the small passageway, they'd been engaged by a security member in a tiny office that served as an observation area for the entire facility.

John had been forced to shoot the man in the chest as they proceeded down the hallway, and as a result, they'd lost what little element of surprise they'd gained during their otherwise silent entrance.

The small office contained few furnishings: a wooden desk with a phone atop it, three folding chairs, and a series of lockers along the left wall. In addition to the minimalist decor, a wall approximately three feet high was connected to the ceiling by a large Plexiglas window. A single door to the right of the glass led inside to the facility. As for the facility itself, the mystery of its true purpose had been solved.

The building was a gigantic, industrial methamphetamine lab. The large ventilation system was the exhaust for the by-product toxic gases produced by the chemical reactions involved when cooking large quantities of crystal meth.

On the far side of the building opposite Bravo Team's entry point was a series of four gigantic stainless steel vats suspended six feet off the floor, which was coated with a clear sealant. Each vat was at least eight feet in diameter and covered with a large cylindrical top. All the vats were connected by a series of pipes and stainless steel ductwork to several large machines, none of which John recognized. But they didn't matter since he was too busy focusing on the concentrated small arms fire they were receiving.

A group of six heavily armed security personnel had positioned themselves behind the industrial equipment and alternated in providing covering fire that had Bravo Team pinned down inside the observation area. The Plexiglas had been shattered by their initial volley. Bullets continued to shred the wooden desk, walls, and lockers.

John had maintained radio silence with Logan until now, but given their current predicament, he knew he had to update Alpha Team. He was about to press the talk button on his microphone when Logan's voice erupted from the Bravo Team channel into his tiny headset, "Bravo Team, we have secured the villa. El Fuego is dead, but the target escaped out a second-story window. Air support is inbound to assist. I'm in pursuit. Treat all remaining security personnel as hostile. Lethal force authorized."

John quickly responded. "Roger, Alpha. Adjacent building looks to be some kind of giant meth lab. We're in the process of securing it. Happy hunting. Out."

"Roger, Bravo. Put it out of commission. Will contact you once I've secured the target. Switching over to the tac air channel now. Call and update the base once you're done. Out."

More bullets hit the walls and remaining pieces of Plexiglas, sending shards cascading onto Bravo Team in cover behind the small wall. Lieutenant Garcia looked over to see John smiling as Logan's transmission ended.

"That's fucking music to my ears. Now it's our turn." He spoke just loud enough to ensure all of Bravo Team heard him and quickly explained his plan.

The security teams inside were well trained. The fusillade of fire continued, four automatic weapons firing in synchronization every time one team reloaded. John was impressed.

Too bad for you guys it's about to end—swiftly.

John pulled an M67 fragmentary grenade from his vest. He watched as both Lieutenant Garcia and another Bravo Team member—one of the FBI's HRT—did the same. He pulled the pin on his grenade and held the metal spoon in place.

"One. Two. Three. Now!" He released the spoon and tossed the grenade over the wall in an arc as Lieutenant Garcia and the HRT operator did the same.

John's grenade sailed over two SUVs and landed near the two-man team on the right side of the facility. The other two grenades landed near their intended marks on the other side of the industrial machinery. All of Bravo Team crouched as low to the ground as possible behind the wall as the security teams realized what had been thrown at them.

John heard one man begin to scream something in Spanish, but his cry was cut short by three successive explosions.

Boom! Boom! BOOM!

Shrapnel whizzed through the air, piercing holes in sheet metal and denting the various equipment. A plastic barrel containing some kind of chemical was punctured, and the leaking fluid ignited. A loud *whoosh!* ripped through the building. The seemingly relentless enemy fire suddenly ceased.

John and Lieutenant Garcia leapt over the wall and ran deeper into the building as three Bravo Team members raised their assault weapons and opened fire in the direction of the security teams' positions. Two other team members went left, completing the other half of their flanking maneuver.

As John drew closer and passed the nearest SUV, he saw flames from the fire in the back of the facility. An acrid smell in the air burned his nostrils.

Time to end this confrontation, he thought, as he prepared for additional resistance from any remaining forces.

The maneuver turned out to be unnecessary.

John circled around a large machine and discovered the carnage the grenades had produced. "Cease fire!" he yelled, and the covering gunfire from the observation area immediately stopped.

Each M67 grenade had a kill radius of five meters, a little more than fifteen feet. Unfortunately for the security teams, they were only two to three meters apart, and the accuracy of the throws had been lethal. All six men were dead, killed by shrapnel from multiple grenades.

The two men in the center team had taken the brunt of it. They'd been hit by shrapnel from all three grenades, their bodies mangled. John stopped and reached for his microphone as the other Bravo Team members confirmed their targets were dead and removed their weapons.

It was time to check in with Mike back at the airport.

"Command, this is Bravo Team. We've secured the secondary building. It's a meth lab—and now out of commission. We also secured the garage. Actually, we destroyed it. We're moving out front to wait for air support. Alpha Team leader has gone after the target, who managed to escape the villa. El Fuego is dead. We have one friendly KIA, and Alpha has at least four."

John heard Mike say, "Acknowledge all, Bravo. As soon as you have the target and are inbound, I'll call the Mexican army in to clean up."

"Roger, Command. Out for now."

John raised his voice to get Lieutenant Garcia's attention. "Time to move out front and establish a security perimeter and wait for extraction once Logan has the target." He looked around at the spreading flames, disgust on his face. "Let this place burn."

As he turned back toward the destroyed office, a loud vibration grew in intensity, rattling the walls and the ravaged equipment. John felt the floor shake and smiled.

Here comes the cavalry, he thought, as the two gunships approached the compound, one intent on landing while the other provided air support to Logan.

———

SPECTER ONE COCKPIT

Captain Anthony Ramirez, copilot of Specter One, scanned the hillside through his Starfire forward-looking infrared radar—or FLIR—camera system. The images were displayed in real time on a small screen directly in front of him on the helicopter's instrument panel. The FLIR had been the last upgrade the crew had installed, and it was working beautifully.

He watched as the gray, desolate images of the foothills below slowly passed underneath them. The gunship hovered directly over the compound in order to gain a vantage point of the entire hillside.

Captain Ramirez was still in disbelief as he surveyed the carnage below. One gigantic structure on the south side of the compound was completely demolished, flames still shooting up into the dawn sky. Another building adjacent to the villa was on fire, a fire that seemed to grow in intensity by the minute. Even the rear of the main villa now had smoke billowing from several broken second-story windows.

He knew that the assault force had suffered several casualties, and he hoped they'd given as good as they got.

As the pilot steadied the helicopter five hundred feet above the compound, Captain Ramirez moved the joystick next to the display. The spherical pod underneath the nose of the gunship turned to face the hillside, and Captain Ramirez zoomed out to gain a wider picture of the area.

There! Movement!

He looked forward out the window, searching for the nearest landmark with his eyes as he said, "Alpha, this is Specter One. Target spotted, approximately one hundred fifty meters due north of the compound and fifty meters west of the breach in the wall. Looks like he's trying to move up into the hills."

He looked over to see the pilot point through the helicopter's windshield, indicating he had a visual on the target as well. "He's crouching near a large outcropping of several boulders. What are your instructions, Alpha?"

"Roger, Specter One. I'm in pursuit on foot." Captain Ramirez heard the pounding of footsteps in the background, followed by fast but controlled breathing when they stopped.

"I'm about to exit the compound. How about providing some direct fire to keep him pinned down while I work my way up? But whatever you do, do *not*—I say again, do *not*—hit him. We have to get him alive. I should be on his location in two to three minutes. Keep your eyes on me and let me know when I'm approximately thirty meters from the target. I'll let you talk me in from there. Breaking cover now. Open fire!"

The pilot of the gunship pulled the trigger on the flight stick, aiming fifty meters above the boulders as he unleashed a volley of 20mm rounds from the GIAT cannon on the port side of the aircraft.

The helicopter shuddered with each shot—*Boom! Boom! Boom! Boom! Boom!*—in rapid succession. Captain Ramirez watched as the rounds impacted north of the moving target, shattering small trees and sending clouds of dirt and debris high into the air.

As soon as the firing stopped, the target changed course and began to move down the slope. "Alpha, target is moving *down* the hillside toward you. I have visual on you both. He's approximately fifty meters from you."

He heard Logan say, "The underbrush is too dense. I can't see him yet. Fire another volley above him and see if you can push him closer to me."

"Roger, Alpha." The pilot opened fire once again, sending another volley of 20mm shells into the hillside below. The resulting impacts echoed off the hillside and had the desired effect. The target moved a little faster down the hillside.

"Alpha, he's only twenty meters from your position, but he's also moving away now. You should be able to intersect him in ten seconds or so."

"Roger, Specter One. Fire off one more ten-shot volley to mask my movement and then hold fire. I should have him by then."

"Roger, Alpha. Good luck. Call us if you need us."

There was no response. Captain Ramirez watched as the pilot opened fire, peppering the hillside. On his display, he saw the two light-gray shapes move in diagonal lines until they intersected and converged on his screen as the last shell exploded. He zoomed in to watch the ensuing engagement, silently cheering on Logan West.

ON THE GROUND

The helicopter's covering fire had masked Logan's movements up the hillside as he weaved his way through the small trees and rough terrain. As Juan Black emerged from behind a large bush directly in front of him, Logan launched himself into the air. He barreled into the unsuspecting man at full speed and slammed his shoulder squarely into Black's side as the last shell from the gunship exploded above them on the hillside, showering them with dirt and rocks.

Logan was rewarded with a grunt of pain as he drove Black into the ground. Before he could make another move, Black, obviously trained in hand-to-hand combat, attacked.

As the two men landed on the hillside, Black tried to wrap his left arm around Logan's head, delivering a swift punch to Logan's left side. Logan ducked under the arm and moved to the right. He countered with his open right hand to push Black's arm away and delivered a vicious punch to Black's face, striking him squarely in the nose.

He heard the distinctive reward of breaking bone and crunching cartilage. Blood burst from Black's nose, temporarily stunning him.

Logan had to find a way to subdue the man without killing him. He used his momentary advantage to mount Black's chest and deliver a series of three punches to the man's face, trying to connect with his jaw.

Black masterfully deflected each blow. As Logan used his arms to shift his position, Black brought both forearms down, forcing Logan to lose his leverage and fall forward into Black's body. Having closed the distance, Black tried to head-butt his assailant's nose, hoping to share his pain and level the playing field.

Logan turned his head to the right at the last second. The top of Black's head squarely struck his left cheek, connecting with the still-healing wound. Fresh blood dripped from Logan's cheek, and he felt Black try to buck him off. Logan rolled away and pressed off the ground with both arms, propelling himself even farther from Juan Black.

Keeping his eyes locked on his target, he cautiously stood. Black did the same. The man's eyes, cold with malevolence, glared at him intensely, and before Logan could speak, Black opened his mouth.

"Mr. West, I was wondering if you were going to join us." His voice was distorted and muffled by his broken nose. "Honestly, I had hoped not, but here you are."

Logan saw that Juan wasn't armed. *Must not have had time to grab his guns. Too bad.*

"That's right, asshole. I know your real name isn't Juan Black, and you already know what I want. So you can make this easy"—he paused for emphasis—"or we can do this my way. It's your choice."

Black leered at him, his teeth flashing white through a red mask of blood. "I always tell my men, 'If you talk the talk, you better walk the walk.' I guess now it's time to put my money where my mouth is. You Force Recon types are always so serious," he said, ignoring his own Special Forces background. "Or maybe it's just a Marine thing. You all think you're special." The contempt was visible on his bloody face. "Regardless, I'm going to remind you right now that you're not."

"So an honorable duel between two professionals, is it?" Logan asked. "But before we do this, you care to tell me which unit you were with? Or do I have to beat it out of you?"

The man laughed out loud. "I'll tell you one thing, Mr. West. My real name is Marcos. That's the only goddamned piece of information I'm going to give you."

"Fair enough, Marcos. Enough chitchat. I'm already sick and tired of your bullshit."

During the conversation, Logan had positioned himself slightly above Marcos on the hillside, hoping to gain the upper hand. Fighting on uneven terrain was especially difficult. The key was balance, and fortunately, Logan's was exceptional.

Now only a little more than five feet away from Marcos, Logan opened the second round of their encounter. Instead of lashing out with a punch or kick, he used his right foot to kick up a small, jagged rock the size of a golf ball into Marcos's face, along with a cloud of dirt.

Definitely not the typical move, but screw it. I need him alive, no matter what.

Logan rushed forward as Marcos tried to wipe the dirt from his eyes. He only succeeded in mixing his blood with the grime, which made it worse. Marcos's eyes burned, and he lashed out with his right fist in a desperate attempt to defend himself.

His punch only struck thin air. Logan easily dodged it and hammered Marcos's left side with a powerful blow.

Even as the punch connected, Logan moved behind Marcos—who roared in frustration—with blinding speed and lashed out with his left foot in a short side kick. He struck Marcos behind the knee.

The blow buckled him, and as he fell, Logan snaked his left arm around his prey's neck, his right arm tight behind Marcos's head and locked into his left bicep. He squeezed and flung himself backward, landing on his back on the hillside.

The fact that he was above Marcos at an elevated angle increased his leverage. He squeezed harder, his muscles flexing and constricting around Marcos's neck, cutting off circulation to his head.

Within seconds, Marcos's writhing suddenly stopped, and Logan knew the fight was over. As he pulled one last time, he growled into Marcos's ear, "When I said 'an honorable duel,' I lied. I don't fight fair. I fight to win. Night, night, sweetheart."

They were the last words Marcos heard before he passed out.

CHAPTER 42

Logan sat in the hangar, watching intently as Commander Vargas questioned Marcos Bocanegra. As the interrogation had unfolded over the last hour, each detail of Cain Frost's lethal conspiracy had been revealed, to the increasing horror of the assembled men.

Once Logan had secured the target, the remainder of the operation had gone according to plan. Both gunships had landed inside the compound—which had been razed to the ground, a smoldering ruin, all buildings, including the villa, destroyed—and loaded both teams, the target, and all casualties before the Mexican army unit arrived to secure the facility.

There'd been no sense of urgency, since a full sweep of the compound had discovered no surviving security personnel. Logan believed in karma, and he figured all of them got what they deserved.

Evil men deserve no mercy. His time in Mexico had reaffirmed that conviction.

Currently, Mike was speaking to his uncle on the phone, trying to secure an immunity deal for Bocanegra. It had been his only demand. The man formerly known as Juan Black was playing his last card, his ace in the hole.

John watched the interrogation on a computer monitor broadcasting the session to the main area of the hangar, which was now empty except for Logan, John, and Mike.

The rest of the assault force was recovering from the intense combat and tending to the wounded and the five dead team members: two FBI HRT shooters and three FES operators. A separate hangar had been converted into a makeshift morgue until transportation could arrive to return the FBI agents home.

Mike had informed FBI headquarters. The Bureau was now in the process of notifying the agents' families. The Mexican navy was doing the same for its fallen warriors.

The interrogation unfolded as smoothly as any Mike had witnessed. Commander Vargas had used no force whatsoever. He hadn't needed it.

Mike had told Marcos from the very beginning that he could offer a presidential pardon in return for a full disclosure of the details and information leading to the prevention of whatever attack was planned.

Marcos, aware of the gravity of his situation, knew it was the only offer he was going to receive, and he'd agreed. He might have been a trained killer and a mercenary for hire, but he was smart enough that self-preservation still guided his actions, especially when he had no other options.

Once the deal had been reached, he'd disclosed what all of them had feared: the plot involved an attack that would change the geopolitical landscape of the Middle East.

Cain Frost planned to launch a tactical nuclear attack on the Quds Force headquarters in Iran? It would start an all-out war and draw the US right back into another massive conflict just as Iraq was beginning to stabilize. It was utter insanity, Logan thought as he watched the live feed.

Mike pushed the end button on his phone. "My uncle is in the process of checking with Cain Frost's staff back at his headquarters in northern Virginia to determine if he's actually in Iraq. And if so, where. My uncle is using some senator's office as a proxy in case Frost finds out about the inquiry: it seems he has a source in the White House. We'll know in a few minutes. If this is true, guys, this is absolutely apocalyptic. And all for revenge . . . unreal."

John stared at the monitor and shook his head in disbelief. "You know, I completely understand his motivation."

Mike and Logan looked at him.

"Think about it, Logan. Hell, we were the ones that found his brother. I still can't believe what I saw. It was horrific and utterly inhumane. I still have visions of it in my head, and I know they'll stay with me until the day I die."

Logan and John had been stunned to discover the identities of the two men they'd failed to rescue in 2004.

Marcos's tale involved one of the most powerful men in the world, a man who'd established an empire in the private security business—Cain Frost.

Cain Frost's older brother, Steven, had been a case officer for the CIA working in US-occupied Iraq to pursue reported weapons of mass destruction.

He and his partner, William Karimi, were lured into a trap by an insurgent group led by the infamous Abu Musab al-Zarqawi. The information al-Zarqawi had received on the American agents had been provided by none other than the Iranian Quds Force, who'd infiltrated the Green Zone and carried out the deception success-fully. The Quds Force agents wanted to bloody the nose of the CIA, regardless of al-Zarqawi's Sunni faith, inflicting damage to America's will to sustain its operations in Iraq. They'd succeeded.

Logan and his men had borne witness to the sinister plan first-hand. It was only a few years later, after Cain Frost had created Hard Resolutions Incorporated—HRI—and used millions to fund his own personal investigation into the death of his brother, that he'd discovered the identities of the Quds Force agents.

The events of the last few days were the result of a blood debt.

Cain and his chief of operations, Scott Carlson, who'd been with Cain since 2005, had personally hunted down the Iranians responsible. Cain had killed one man himself, but he'd left his chief of operations to deal with the second agent.

Scott Carlson had taken his time with the man, methodically inflicting tremendous pain. Marcos had seen the video, and he'd cringed at some of the sadistic techniques Scott had used.

In the middle of the torture session, the man had tried to bargain for his life, offering the most valuable piece of information he'd guarded. It was something an insurgent leader had told him soon after the US began its occupation of Iraq.

It was the location to a tactical nuclear device contained in a briefcase. It had reportedly been designed by the Syrians with assistance from the Pakistanis and North Koreans at a hidden facility in the Syrian Desert.

The weapon had been transported to an insurgent group in western Al Anbar Province. The group had planned to use it in Baghdad to destroy the fledgling Shia government. Fortunately, before the insurgents could strike, they'd been discovered and hunted down by the US military in the city of Haditha.

Before the insurgent commander had been killed, he'd personally dispatched a courier to al-Zarqawi. The trusted courier had in his possession two items. The first was an Iraqi flag. On the back of the flag, a series of numbers had been printed in such a way as to appear as if they were a serial or tracking number.

In truth, the number was a simple code that the insurgent commander had devised in order to hide what the numbers really were—coordinates to the nuclear briefcase he'd buried somewhere in Al Anbar Province.

The second item in the courier's possession was the key to the code. It had been written on a piece of paper and sealed in an envelope to be opened only by al-Zarqawi himself.

The courier had successfully accomplished his mission, but al-Zarqawi, the untrusting and ruthless man that he was, shot the courier dead upon receipt of the flag and the envelope. He wanted to be the only one with the knowledge of the nuclear device.

He kept the envelope for himself. Realizing the flag and the envelope had to be kept apart, he'd given the flag to a local insurgent commander for safekeeping in early 2004.

That insurgent commander had been killed in a US operation, and the flag had been lost, its location unknown. Then in 2008, one of Cain Frost's numerous investigators had stumbled across an after-action report concerning an operation that had gone horribly wrong and resulted in the death of nearly an entire Marine Force Reconnaissance unit.

One note in the report had captured the investigator's attention. "Gunnery Sergeant John Quick took custody of an Iraqi flag and will provide it to the MEF G2 shop for disposition." That one note in a four-year-old report had started the clock on the current chain of events, ironically sending Frost on a search for the very man who'd been dispatched to save his brother's life.

As for the envelope itself, the Iranian had provided its location before he died at the hands of Scott Carlson. Hoping against hope, he'd pleaded for his life. The begging had fallen on deaf ears. Scott Carlson had slit the man's throat. Days later, he found the envelope exactly where the Iranian agent had stated, stored in a bank in Baghdad, still sealed. He'd handed it over to Cain Frost.

Commander Vargas stopped the interrogation. He stepped outside the enclosed chamber into the main hangar to discuss the veracity of Marcos's story.

Logan recalled a reported Israeli air strike in September 2007 on an alleged Syrian nuclear facility called al-Kibar. The reports were speculative and shrouded in secrecy, and neither the Syrian nor Israeli governments had commented on the action. The press treated it as if it had never happened.

"As much as I don't want to believe it, unfortunately, I do. Wars have started for less, and given the resources Cain Frost has at his disposal *and* his motivation, it sounds legitimate."

Mike said, "I agree." He looked at Commander Vargas. "See if you can get him to tell you anything more about the target itself. I can't believe the Quds Force headquarters is going to be an easy target to reach. I need to talk to my uncle to find out exactly where it is."

Logan thought for a moment and then said, "You know, Mike, Marcos may be a trusted agent of Cain's, but it occurs to me that the real target could be somewhere else."

"Come again, Logan?"

"Think about it," Logan said, his voice strengthening. "He goes through all this trouble to obtain a nuclear weapon. He knows Marcos is a loose end he can't tie up. He also knows that if Marcos gets captured—as he did—we're going to interrogate him until we learn everything he knows. I'll bet you anything that he told Marcos what the target was just to throw us off the scent in case he *was* captured."

John said, "What that means is that the only way we're going to confirm the identity of the real target is if we capture Cain before he can leave Iraq. The clock just started ticking faster." He shook his head in disbelief. "This just keeps getting better and better."

"I'll see what I can find out." Commander Vargas turned and entered the small chamber.

It proved to be unnecessary. Marcos didn't have any more information. He'd told them everything he knew.

Commander Vargas joined them at the table moments later. He

looked pale from the weight of the knowledge he now held. Logan sympathized.

So here we are, in a hangar in Mexico, trying to figure out how to stop an egomaniac hell-bent on revenge from starting a war on the other side of the world. This sucks, Logan thought.

Logan looked at Mike, who kept studying his phone, expecting his uncle Jake to call at any moment. He broke the silence.

"Unfortunately, what he's doing is only going to result in more US casualties—if not the fucking end of the world. Iran is going to blame Israel, since everyone knows Israel has an arsenal of nuclear weapons, regardless of what they acknowledge publicly. And considering the rhetoric coming out of Iran to wipe Israel off the face of the earth, they've got the motive. Iran will use it as an excuse to launch a full-scale attack, probably with the support of other countries in the region. The US will have no choice but to defend Israel and respond, and everything we fought and died for will be wasted."

"I agree, man . . ." John's sentence trailed off, then he added, "but Logan, as much as I want to put a bullet in the man's head, he has a point. When do we finally do something about Iran meddling in Iraq and everywhere else? We know they're responsible for hundreds of dead US servicemen from their goddamn EFPs." The explosively formed penetrator was a special type of IED designed to penetrate armor by using an explosive charge to deform a metal plate into a slug or rod shape and accelerate it toward a target, with disastrous effects. It was well-known throughout the Department of Defense and had even been leaked to the press that Iran was responsible for manufacturing and using them in both Iraq and Afghanistan.

John continued. "Cain's just the first one to do something about it. I'd give him credit for it if his insane plan wouldn't end up starting the next world war. Christ, what a mess."

"Unfortunately, nothing's ever black-and-white," Logan responded.

"We should know something soon enough. If Cain has the flag and the key and if he's in Iraq, then he's got to be close to the bomb. The trick is going to be getting both him and the device at the same time," Mike said.

Logan was about to respond when Mike's phone rang. All eyes turned to him as he answered.

Logan and John watched as Mike listened to the caller, taking a few notes and nodding absentmindedly. After sixty seconds, the call ended, and Mike said, "Thank you, sir. I'll let them know." He hung up.

"You want the good news or bad news first?"

"The bad so I know how bad it actually is," Logan said.

"Fair enough. Frost is in Iraq right now. He's with his chief of operations, one Scott Carlson." That fact cemented the underlying truth in Bocanegra's story.

"He left his base in Baghdad yesterday on a trip throughout Al Anbar Province, supposedly to conduct inspections on his security forces at various locations. He was stuck in Fallujah yesterday due to a gigantic sandstorm. He's supposed to be leaving for Ramadi and then finish tomorrow afternoon in Haditha. My uncle is calling the chief of station in Baghdad right now to figure out how to get eyes on Frost. If he has the nuke already, we're fucked."

Logan suddenly sat up, his eyes blazing intensely. "He doesn't."

"How do you know?" John asked. He looked at Logan, who sat smiling, eyes sparkling malevolently.

"Bocanegra. He told us that the insurgent group was hunted down in Haditha. That has to be where they hid it."

Mike nodded. "Good catch."

"So what's the good news, Mike?" John asked, already knowing the answer.

Mike smiled and said, "We all get to go back to Iraq for more fun in the sun."

"You know you seriously suck at this 'good news, bad news' thing," John said.

"Hey, I'm just as excited as you are. My uncle has a C-5 on its way here. It should arrive in an hour. Then we have a direct flight to Baghdad, which should take a little more than twelve hours with multiple air refuelings."

"Change the destination to Al Asad," Logan said suddenly. "It's only twenty-five miles to Haditha. Have your uncle arrange helicopter transport for us. We can beat Frost to Haditha and wait for him. Once we get him on surveillance with a Predator or whatever they're using in Iraq right now, he'll lead us to the weapon."

"That's a smart play, Logan," John said. "But where do we go in Haditha? It's a big-ass city."

Logan already knew the answer. "The largest landmark they have," he said. "The dam."

"Of course. Damn—no pun intended. I should've thought of that already."

"Don't worry, John. It's not your fault. You're just not that smart," Logan jibed, smiling broadly for the first time.

"Yeah. Fuck you too, brother."

Logan looked back to Mike and asked, "What about Bocanegra?"

"That's easy. He stays here in Mexico. If we recover the weapon, Commander Vargas will release him, and he's free to go anywhere except the US. He's never to set foot on our soil again. The president added that condition himself."

"Nice," John commented.

"Well then. I guess someone had better go inform Mr. Bocanegra that he better start rooting for the home team. Otherwise, he'll be remanded to Mexican custody, and right now, they're not too happy with him."

Commander Vargas stood up from the table. "You know, if you

fail because of any bogus intel from him, I'm going to personally see to it our friend in there never sees the light of day."

"Well then, Crisanto," Logan said, "I think you should be the one to tell him that. Maybe he'll think of something he forgot to mention—or at least it'll give him something else to think about over the next twenty-four hours."

Commander Vargas smiled. "My pleasure," he said as he reentered the interrogation chamber.

Logan looked from Mike to John. "I never thought I'd ever go back to that hellhole, ever."

John nodded. "Likewise. But here we are."

"So here we are," Logan echoed. "And now we have to go back to the Sandbox where all this started to finish this, once and for all."

The look of determination in his eyes told Mike and John all they needed to know, and Mike summed it up in one word, "Karma."

John shot back sarcastically, "I prefer the circle of life, or in our case, the circle of death." Then he added cheerfully, "*Hakuna matata*, motherfuckers."

Logan stared at his friend. "You know, John, I'm not sure I ever told you this, but there's something seriously wrong with you."

PART VI

THE SANDBOX 3

CHAPTER 43

Captain West ordered Gunny Quick and his remaining Marines to set up defensive positions inside the building. He and Sergeant Avery were going to exit the south entrance and attempt to flank the insurgents outside the compound.

It was a risky move, but he thought it had a chance of working.

They definitely won't expect it.

Captain West and Sergeant Avery stood by the back door to the building, ready to run on the former's command.

Gunny Quick was moving a thick table along the west wall when they suddenly heard the distant *Thwump!* of mortars being fired once again.

"Get behind the table!" Captain West screamed as Sergeant Helms and Staff Sergeant Hayes scrambled for cover next to Gunny Quick and Sergeant Baker.

Captain West hoped that between the cement wall of the building and the heavy wood of the table, they'd be protected from the incoming mortars and shrapnel. "Prepare yourselves and stay down," West said to them. "This is going to hurt. Let's go!" he shouted to Avery.

As the mortars whistled through the night, Gunny Quick looked at his commanding officer and said, "You're crazier than I thought, sir."

Captain West smiled at him, a glint in his eye, but before Gunny Quick could say anything else, the captain and Sergeant Avery disappeared out the back door at full speed.

I hate indirect fire, Gunny Quick thought moments before the mortar rounds fell on the compound.

———

Abdul Sattar crouched behind his pickup truck as Abu Omar opened fire with the first volley of mortars that he'd requested.

He prayed that Omar's aim was true and that Allah would guide the mortars to the target. If one round fell short of the compound, Abdul Sattar and what remained of his men would likely be killed, not the remaining Americans inside the compound.

He counted the seconds as he waited for the rounds to impact.

One . . . two . . . three . . . four . . . and then all four rounds struck simultaneously inside the compound, four separate explosions that merged into one enormous *Boom!* that sent a gigantic plume of dirt and debris into the air.

He smiled as he waited for the dust to dissipate. It wasn't likely that anyone could survive a direct hit from the mortars, but just for insurance, he'd ordered Omar to fire a second volley.

Abdul Sattar wanted to ensure that whoever was inside was either dead or seriously wounded before he sent more men into another ambush.

He turned to his right to speak to one of his men. The smile fell off his face as his jaw dropped on its hinges and he stared shocked at the scene before him illuminated by the trucks' headlights.

It can't be. No one should've survived!

———

Inside the building, Gunny Quick, Staff Sergeant Hayes, Sergeant Helms, and Sergeant Baker had flattened themselves at the base of the wall behind the table.

Gunnery Sergeant John Quick knew a direct hit would likely kill them all. Even though the table, carved out of a thick, heavy dark wood, had taken three of them to flip, no one survived a direct mortar strike.

He'd wondered where the insurgents had obtained such an obviously ornate and expensive table and when they'd transported it to this torture compound. Then he remembered this was Iraq, and nothing much surprised him anymore except the level of cruelty and violence their enemies displayed on a daily basis.

He prayed silently as the four 82mm mortar rounds landed inside the compound. Two of them were direct hits on the other building. One landed near the south entrance to the compound. The remaining mortar hit the roof of their building, punched a hole through it, and detonated inside their shelter with disastrous effects.

All prayers and thoughts were wiped from his mind as the concussive wave slammed into the table, splintering it in half and knocking him unconscious.

CHAPTER 44

Captain West and Sergeant Avery ran to the south entrance of the compound in seconds. They slowed momentarily as they dashed through the doorway and turned right, only to sprint again toward the western wall.

Captain West was counting on the insurgents focusing their fire on the north entrance, where all their losses had occurred. He was conducting his own personal flanking maneuver and hoped like hell the spirit of Rommel was on his side.

I better be right, or we're screwed.

The two men reached the compound's corner and moved past it into open ground. They looked right as they emerged from behind the wall to assess the situation in front of them. Their movements were concealed by the darkness at this end of the wall.

Thirty meters in front of them were four pickup trucks. One of them near the north entrance was in ruins from the Claymore. The remaining three were parked facing the compound entrance.

Captain West spotted several bodies near the wrecked pickup, but his focus shifted immediately to the bald man with dark sunglasses near the truck farthest from them.

In between the captain and his prey stood six armed men, all dressed in an assortment of dark clothing, all carrying AK-47s. Fortunately for Captain West and Sergeant Avery, none of them faced their direction.

The bold maneuver had worked. The Marines had them dead to rights.

Checkmate, motherfuckers.

As the mortars hit the building, Captain West moved a short distance from the sergeant and transitioned from a run into a combat walk, raising his M4 in a fluid motion. Sergeant Avery, closer to the wall and in stride with his commanding officer, executed the same move. Both men quickly closed the distance, moving parallel to the compound wall.

Captain West had instructed his Marine to hold his fire until he himself initiated contact. He placed the red dot on the back of the head of the closest insurgent, now only twenty feet away, and slowly pulled the trigger.

As the earth shook from the explosions, he watched the man's head jerk forward with the impact of the bullet. His body went limp and fell to the ground.

He moved forward as debris rained down around them. Another insurgent collapsed to the dirt, the handiwork of Sergeant Avery.

Captain West, ears ringing from the mortars, realized that the echoes of the explosions would only mask their fire for a few more seconds. He wasted no time as he stalked the men and pulled the trigger with fatal accuracy.

No quarter. No mercy.

Only seconds later, two more victims standing near the second pickup truck lay dead on the ground with multiple gunshot wounds to their backs.

They closed the remaining distance as the third pair of insurgents turned toward them. They'd recognized the gunfire through the din of the mortar rounds. The expressions of shock and surprise on their faces satisfied the Marines' thirst for vengeance—at least momentarily. Moments later, a hail of gunfire killed both Iraqi men where they stood.

One man collapsed into the beam of a headlamp; the other bounced off the hood of the pickup truck and slumped to the ground, his back against the front tire.

Now it's your turn, Captain West thought as the final echo faded away and the insurgent leader turned and looked directly into his face.

What Abdul Sattar saw was the face of Death, eyes bright with a righteous fury he recognized.

He's chosen a path and will see it to the end, Abdul Sattar thought.

Captain West, maintaining his pace, pulled the trigger and shot Abdul Sattar four times below the waist. Two rounds shattered both bones in Abdul Sattar's lower right leg. The other two rounds entered and exited his left upper quad muscle, tearing away large chunks of flesh.

The bald man immediately dropped to the ground and shrieked in pain, his lower body destroyed.

————

Through agonized tears, Abdul Sattar watched the man who would be his killer slowly approach. The figure appeared out of the darkness, adorned in a one-piece uniform, a weapons vest worn over it.

Abdul Sattar knew it was Allah's will that he die in this place, but he wanted to see the face of the man who would take his life.

Illuminated by the headlights and fire, the man's intense eyes were a bright green Abdul Sattar had never seen before. They looked reptilian, devoid of all emotion except one. *Fury.* The man's jaw was set in determination.

He realized his time was near, and he sighed with relief as he silently prayed for Allah to take his soul to the afterlife.

———

Captain West looked down at the insurgent, controlling the rage that rose inside him like a storm and threatened to overtake his actions.

He'd shouldered his M4 and now gripped his Kimber .45 pistol. He stood over the man that had ambushed and killed at least ten of his Marines. He didn't know the fate of Gunny Quick and the Marines inside.

He growled one word, "English?"

The man nodded and whispered, "You American?"

West replied with a mocking snort and nodded. "You insurgent?"

The man shook his head side to side, spittle flying. He said, "Holy warrior, fighting in the name of Allah. You are the invaders. Iraq is our land, *not* yours."

The last words were uttered with complete conviction.

This was the first time Captain West had come face-to-face with an insurgent leader, a true believer, a murderer, and a terrorist all in one. Even as the man bled out from his wounds, he still insisted his actions were justified. It was the certainty of the insurgent's absolute belief that suddenly shook something loose in the foundation of who Logan West was as a man and a Marine.

We can't win here—at least not until we take off the kid gloves and get in the trenches with these bastards.

The realization froze him to his core more than the incoming mortar rounds had.

He pointed his pistol at Abdul Sattar's chest. "My name is Logan West, First Force Reconnaissance Company. You killed my men, executed some of them." He paused as the finality of the battle sank in and the words caught in his throat. "And now, I'm going to send you to whatever hell awaits you, you evil sonofabitch."

He pulled the trigger, and the .45-caliber slug punched a hole in Abdul Sattar's chest, tearing apart his heart.

Captain West looked up at Sergeant Avery, who stood watching him and nodded his approval. The sergeant understood the necessity and righteousness of what his captain had just done.

Finally, Captain West spoke. "Let's get back inside and see how they are. We're not done just yet."

He holstered his sidearm, and both men jogged into the compound. Sergeant Avery wondered what his commanding officer meant by that last cryptic statement.

Yet?

CHAPTER 45

Captain West entered the building where Gunny Quick and his Marines had sought refuge. The carnage from the direct hit was devastating.

Fortunately, the mortar round had landed at the other end of the building, but the shrapnel had torn out chunks from the walls and floors. Two of the ceiling support beams were split in half, one end of each hanging down to the floor, the other still attached to the roof. All the windows and both doors had been blown out.

He spotted Gunny Quick as Staff Sergeant Hayes tended to Sergeant Baker, who was bleeding from a wound to his torso.

The table they'd used for cover was in pieces.

It's a wonder any of them are alive, Captain West thought.

The gunnery sergeant was bleeding down the right side of his head, but the wound looked superficial. Captain West knew head wounds bled profusely and often looked worse than they were. Gunny Quick ignored the blood, which reassured the Marines it wasn't life-threatening.

"How's Baker?" Captain West asked.

"He took a piece of shrapnel to the abdomen, but he should be okay. Fortunately for him, he was knocked out when he hit the wall.

So he's not feeling the pain that's going to come when he wakes up. Hayes already gave him some morphine."

Captain West nodded, relieved he hadn't lost another Marine. He was dreading the letters he'd have to write notifying the families of the loss of their loved ones. He pushed the thought away since there was one more piece of unfinished business.

"What about you?"

Gunny Quick looked up. "I got knocked out, too. Fortunately, it's just a small cut. You know how these things are." He shrugged. "I'll live. What happened out there?"

Captain West responded matter-of-factly. "Avery and I got 'em all. Saved the sonofabitch who led the ambush for last. Hopefully, he's in hell with the rest of 'em." His voice wavered slightly with the fury he felt, suppressed emotions he wasn't sure he'd be able to contain for long.

Before he could continue, Sergeant Helms spoke up. "Sir, the cloud cover is abating. Fixed-wing support is minutes away, and the CASEVAC is about fifteen minutes out. Your orders?"

"Tell the fixed-wing to maintain an altitude of twenty thousand feet. We have the situation under control. Helms, contact the COC and tell them we have eighteen EKIA, but we have one last target to take out before we're done."

Captain West looked at Gunny Quick and said, "John, there's one more thing we have to do."

Gunny Quick interrupted him. "I know, sir. The fucking mortars. Already thought about it. We can't leave the bastards using them alive, or they'll do this to someone else. What's your plan?"

Captain West outlined his intentions, and as Gunny Quick listened, a wicked smile formed on his face, a line that cracked the mask of blood he wore from the head wound.

This is actually going to be fun, Gunny Quick thought. He looked forward to delivering the justice his fallen comrades deserved.

CHAPTER 46

Abu Omar hadn't heard from Abdul Sattar in the last ten minutes. He was growing concerned. Once they'd launched the last volley, he'd tried to raise him on the radio to find out what the results had been. He prayed to Allah that his instructions had been accurate and their aim true.

The two-man teams looked at him, waiting for further orders. He tried to contact his leader again. This time he received a garbled response, and he couldn't understand what Abdul Sattar said. The push-to-talk Motorola handheld radios were often unreliable. Abu Omar didn't understand why they continued to use them. He thought it might be for operational security purposes, but he knew better than to question Abdul Sattar.

He was pressing the button on the radio to speak again when he looked up to see two sets of headlights moving quickly across the desert floor from the direction of the compound.

Praise be to Allah, he thought. He smiled. The operation must've been successful.

He put the radio down on the back of his pickup truck and walked to the front of the vehicle, eager to hear the details about Abdul Sattar's latest victory over the infidels.

———

Captain West had turned on the high beams in the Toyota pickup, hoping they would provide the element of surprise they needed.

Sergeant Avery stood in the bed of the pickup, manning the DShK heavy machine gun. Both men wore dark clothes they'd scavenged from two dead insurgents. The clothes stank of sweat and blood, but Logan knew the clothes might buy them an extra few seconds that could be the difference between life and death. This was a game of inches, and one miscalculation could end it, permanently.

He looked right to see Gunny Quick driving the other Toyota, Staff Sergeant Hayes manning the DShK in the back. Even this close, he couldn't tell they were US forces. Both Marines still had camouflage paint on their faces and wore dark clothing as well.

Captain West focused on the desert floor and concentrated on his driving. He looked across the black horizon behind their objective, the building they'd seen a little less than a kilometer from the compound.

He knew the mortar teams were using it for cover, but he recognized that until he saw the men themselves, the best course of action was to drive toward the building. If the insurgents observed him driving in the wrong direction or in an erratic manner, they'd rightfully become suspicious. He and his Marines would lose their tactical advantage if that happened.

At forty-five miles per hour, the building grew larger by the second. The pickups closed the distance quickly, but Captain West still saw nothing.

Damn it! They have to be here!

The Toyotas kicked up plumes of dust behind them as they barreled forward.

Please, God, let there be something.

Just as doubt crept into his mind, he saw a very low light emanating from a clump of shrubs and small trees two hundred meters past the building. He realized that the building itself was actually an old barn.

Who the hell is dumb enough to farm in this country?

He targeted the lights and decided to circle around the right side of the barn to approach the mortar teams, even though the left side had a more direct route.

He radioed Gunny Quick. "I'm going right. Get behind me. It should provide us an extra few seconds of surprise. We'll hit them on their left flank. As soon as I stop, pull up on my left side. Avery and Hayes will take it from there. This should be over quickly."

He'd given instructions to both Sergeant Avery and Staff Sergeant Hayes to open fire once both vehicles had stopped, and not one moment sooner.

Death was coming for these men, and try as he might to emotionally detach himself from it, he looked forward to wiping these twisted, sadistic murderers from the face of this country. A focused anger burned brightly through every fiber in his being. The hairs on his arms and the back of his neck were raised. His mind was on autopilot. Although he processed everything he observed—the light growing brighter, the outline of mortar teams, the city lights from Fallujah—he also saw precisely in his mind's eye how this fight would unfold in the next few minutes. And it didn't involve any of the enemy breathing after it was over.

Both vehicles passed the barn and adjusted their direction for the final approach to the mortar positions.

Through the headlights, Captain West spotted the outline of four teams. Their positions were staggered: two mortars in front, and two mortars in back. The rear mortars were approximately twenty meters away from the front positions.

Standing in front of another pickup truck was a smiling man with his arms crossed. He wore a dark baseball cap, glasses, and a short beard.

He must think I'm the conquering hero returning in victory. Don't worry, friend. I'll wipe that smile off your face in just a second.

———

When both trucks had driven around the right side of the barn, Abu Omar became momentarily concerned.

What is he doing?

He was also disturbed that there were only two trucks. Did Abdul Sattar need something from him?

It never crossed his mind that Abdul Sattar's men had lost the battle. All their previous ambushes and attacks had been successful. Why would this one be any different?

The lead vehicle skidded to a halt. The one behind it pulled up beside it and slammed on its brakes as well.

What's the hurry? We dealt another blow to the Americans.

CHAPTER 47

At a distance of thirty meters—a distance that Captain West determined would afford Sergeant Avery the best fields of fire—he slammed on the brakes and stopped the pickup in line with the rear two mortar positions. He watched in the rearview mirror as the momentum pushed Sergeant Avery forward against the cab of the truck, but he somehow maintained his balance.

Moments later, Gunny Quick stopped the other Toyota twenty meters away, in line with the front two mortar positions.

Captain West waited for the roar of the machine guns to shatter the silence.

Now.

As the dust rose in front of the pickups from the sudden stops, Sergeant Avery and Staff Sergeant Hayes pressed the butterfly triggers on the DShK machine guns, and Captain West sat back to watch the slaughter unfold. As 12.7x108mm shells cascaded off the roof of the pickup and down the front windshield, his face remained impassive through the flickering light of the gunfire. He felt no emotion or sympathy for these men.

Who knows how many Americans and innocent Iraqis have died at their hands?

All he felt as his gunners delivered death was a sense that he was righting one of this country's many wrongs.

The first burst of fire from Sergeant Avery cut the smirking man in half. His expression changed only slightly as the top half of his body toppled forward. With the mortar teams' leader dead, Sergeant Avery then strafed the first mortar position. The rounds impacted men, the mortar tube, and the box of mortar rounds, in quick succession.

One man's arm was shot off by fire, but he was killed by a round that punched a hole in his chest the size of a fist and severed his spine. His partner was struck in the head, which disintegrated in a shower of blood and bone. Another bullet struck the tip of an exposed high-explosive mortar round. The mortar detonated and propelled the dead bodies of both men into the air like rag dolls.

Sergeant Avery elevated his gun slightly to target the second position. The two insurgents on that team reached their weapons, managing to grab their AK-47s—but that was as far as they got. The sergeant's fire killed both men before they had a chance to pull the triggers, their bodies torn apart.

As soon as he was certain the last two of his targets were down for good, he swiveled the DShK to provide additional fire on Staff Sergeant Hayes's objectives. He was too late though. Staff Sergeant Hayes had been just as accurate and lethal. Both front teams were dead or lay dying.

The surprise attack had succeeded. The battle was over.

Inside the truck, Captain West paused to survey the horrific yet satisfying scene in front of him.

It's still only a Pyrrhic victory, he thought. *No number of dead insurgents will make up for the losses of the good men that died tonight.*

He opened the door to the Toyota, and the smell of cordite overwhelmed his nostrils. He grabbed his M4 and walked toward the mortar positions. There were no sounds or movement.

This part of the night had been easy, but he reminded himself it was better to be easy than hard. Hard was what this entire mission had been. He'd lost ten Marines. Hard got men killed.

Gunny Quick exited his pickup. He walked over to join his leader and friend. Both Sergeant Avery and Staff Sergeant Hayes jumped down from behind their mounted weapons and picked up their M4s.

Sergeant Avery was the first to speak. "Wow."

Captain West broke the silent reverie that had fallen over them as a result of what they'd just accomplished. "Excellent shooting. Now let's check their bodies for IDs or anything that can tell us who they were. Once we're done, get back in the trucks, and we'll head over to that barn. There has to be something they're protecting. Otherwise, they wouldn't have set up here."

He grabbed the radio handset from Staff Sergeant Hayes and called Sergeant Helms back at the compound to inform him they'd killed the mortar teams but needed fifteen more minutes on site before they returned.

"Sir, there's also a QRF inbound from Fallujah," Sergeant Helms said, referring to the camp's quick-reaction force. "They activated it when we made the initial call. I think I see their lights off the main road. They'll be providing security for the helos on site."

Captain West heard the sound of rotors in the distance. The CASEVAC was getting close. They were going to need time on the ground to retrieve his men.

"Roger all. Tell the QRF commander we'll be back in fifteen mikes. We're moving to investigate the building. I'll get back to you."

"Roger, sir. Also, Sergeant Baker's stable and still unconscious, but that's because of the morphine. Out here," Helms signed off.

Captain West looked up at his men and said, "Let's get this done and get the fuck out of here. This place is really starting to suck."

The other three men raised their eyebrows at the comment, aware that the mild vulgarity and huge understatement was intended to lighten the dark mood that threatened to suffocate them. Killing the insurgents had served justice swiftly and satisfied their vengeful bloodlust, but it still couldn't bring their brothers and friends back. The harsh reality of the price they'd paid was painful.

Their search of the bodies turned up nothing: no identification of any kind, just clothes and weapons.

Captain West ordered Sergeant Avery and Staff Sergeant Hayes to destroy the remaining mortar tubes and rounds. With a few well-placed grenades, the task was easily accomplished in minutes.

The men returned to the Toyotas, and the team looked back one last time to see if there was something they'd missed. Satisfied, they drove to investigate the barn.

The barn stood two stories high with a lean-to roof that sloped down from the back to the front of the building. The front was approximately thirty meters wide; the sides, twenty meters deep. Two gigantic sliding doors appeared to be the only entrance. The exterior wooden walls were painted sloppily—none of them could tell the exact color in the darkness.

Iraqi craftsmanship at its finest, Captain West thought.

He walked to the sliding doors and pulled a wooden beam out that was secured through two metal latches, one on each door. He slid the left door open and revealed a large space that was mostly dark.

In the back of the barn below the ceiling of an open-air, three-sided loft, they saw a soft glow.

The barn has electricity.

They entered the building and moved slowly to the back. Staff Sergeant Hayes searched the left wall near the entrance. "Sir, found a switch," he called out.

He flipped it upward. "Holy shit," Gunny Quick said. "Jackpot."

Captain West couldn't believe it. They'd discovered an insurgent command center.

Three tables were lined up side by side. On each one were two computers and a radio, which looked like some type of Iraqi high-frequency system. In addition to the computers and radios, plywood had been erected behind the tables. Taped to the plywood were maps and photographs of both the city of Fallujah and the camp the Marines were using as a base of operations.

Captain West walked over to the center of the table.

No fucking way . . .

He was riveted by one particular photo, which had been taken from the ground. It showed a building complex surrounded by concrete walls. There was only one entrance to it, which was guarded by a Marine and surrounded by concertina wire. It was the Tactical Fusion Center in the middle of Camp Fallujah.

"Sir, you're not going to believe this," he heard Gunny Quick say. He looked over to see the Marine holding multiple ID cards that were provided to Iraqi contractors for access to the Marine camp.

"Damn." Captain West turned to Staff Sergeant Hayes. "Tell Helms to contact the COC. Tell the watch officer to find the division G-2, Colonel Gifford. Tell him to wake him up if he has to. It's an emergency. Give him our frequency and channel and have the colonel call me as soon as he can. Tell them we hit the fucking insurgent intelligence lottery. We're not going anywhere right now."

He heard Staff Sergeant Hayes relay his instructions. His peripheral vision caught some movement, and he looked to see Gunny Quick folding something, about to place it in his backpack.

"Gunny, what'd you find?"

Gunny Quick turned his head toward him, an odd look in his eye. He nodded his head to the right of the tables.

"These fuckers were using that area to film beheadings. There's blood all over the floor . . . lots of blood . . . and this."

He held up an Iraqi flag with both hands.

"It was hanging in the background. I'm taking it as a reminder and to ensure that no one ever again uses this particular flag as a symbol of torture and evil. This operation is now closed, but I want to remember what we did here. And this will remind me."

Captain West understood, although he knew he wasn't going to need a trophy to remind him of any of this night's events. He had a feeling they'd be far too vivid for way too long.

"Fair enough. Just make sure you let the G-2 know. If he gives you any grief about it, I'll take care of it." He paused, then added somberly, "You know, this intelligence could save a lot of lives, both American and Iraqi. We paid a high price for it, but no matter what's here, it wasn't worth it to me."

The enormity of the night's events weighed heavily on both men. They were trained professionals, elite hunters of men, but this mission was something altogether unlike anything they'd ever encountered.

"I agree, sir, but at least this intel might bring just a little bit of value to this entire fiasco. I still can't believe we were used to do the CIA's dirty work. I don't want to 'what if' this one to death, but more prep time might have avoided some or even all of our casualties. What a fucking nightmare . . ."

Gunny Quick's voice trailed off.

Captain West remained quiet. Finally, he said, "I know. And I'll tell you one more thing—and you can take it to the bank—if I ever see that motherfucker James again, I'm going to kill him. I don't care who or what he is, he's a dead man for setting us up like this. You hear me? A fucking *dead* man."

The conviction in Captain West's voice was unmistakable.

As determined as his commanding officer and leader was, Gunny Quick realized that James had likely left Camp Fallujah as soon as they'd stepped off for this mission. He was certain Captain West knew it as well.

He also knew that somehow, no matter how long it took, his boss would see the man again. He only hoped he'd be around to witness that reunion.

You're a dead man walking, James, and you don't even know it.

PART VII

RECKONING

HADITHA DAM, IRAQ

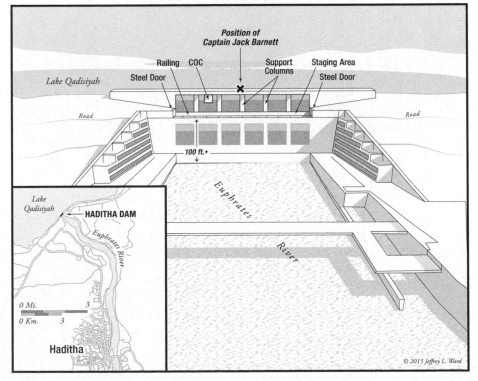

Position of
Captain Jack Barnett

Railing   COC   Support   Staging Area
Steel Door   Columns   Steel Door

Lake Qadisiyah

Road   Road

100 ft.+

Euphrates

River

Lake
Qadisiyah

HADITHA DAM

Euphrates River

0 Mi.   3
0 Km.   3

Haditha

© 2015 Jeffrey L. Ward

CHAPTER 48

HADITHA, IRAQ
2 NOVEMBER 2008

The city of Haditha—home to some one hundred thousand Sunni Iraqi citizens—was located approximately 140 miles northwest of Baghdad. It had been center stage for several major events in the aftermath of the US invasion in 2003 as a result of both its location and its single-largest piece of key terrain—the Haditha Dam.

The dam sat on the Euphrates River and supplied water through an extensive system of regulation and pumping stations, and irrigation and drainage canals. It was an enormous, earth-filled structure over five and a half miles long and 187 feet high. It contained more than sixteen floors of rooms and chambers that housed not only the power plant itself but also the Marines who currently ensured its security.

US Army Rangers had seized the hydropower complex in April of 2003 to prevent its possible destruction by Iraqi forces. Destroying the dam would've resulted in an immediate lack of water during the sweltering summer months, massive flooding from the enormous artificial lake the dam created, and the loss of a major source of electricity.

Haditha proper, which actually lay a few miles south, had been a center of insurgent activity after US forces took control of the dam. Multiple operations had been launched against the insurgents holding the city until tensions between US Marines and civilians had finally boiled over, ultimately resulting in the controversial killing of twenty-four Iraqi noncombatant civilians in 2005.

International news coverage and an outcry from politicians, using words like "murder," only inflamed the volatile situation until the US changed its strategy in 2006 and drove out the remaining insurgents by the end of 2007.

Now, nearly one year later, things had quieted down dramatically, so much so that Cain Frost's private security contractors augmenting the dam's security hadn't come under attack in almost six months. Cain wouldn't have believed it himself if he hadn't been out here on another site visit three months ago, when he'd been provided a guided walking tour of the city by the chief of his security forces.

So much change in so little time. And I'm about to change it all some more, he thought now as he looked at the dam through the tinted window of the Cougar HE armored fighting vehicle in which he rode shotgun. His convoy had already passed the city, having left Fallujah late in the morning.

The fact that he'd lost contact with Juan Black—Marcos Bocanegra—yesterday concerned him. His source in DC had gone off the grid as well, indicating that events were escalating not just for Cain but also for the organized forces pursuing him. If US law enforcement were close on his trail, his source wouldn't have the time to contact him again. It didn't matter. The finish line was in sight.

Cain knew that the secrecy and sudden lack of information—especially with such a highly placed source—meant one of two things: the assault had gone disastrously wrong, or the US had succeeded in capturing Marcos and now knew Cain's intentions, if not the exact target of them. He hoped it was the former and that the aftermath would provide him enough time to retrieve the nuclear device and leave Haditha tomorrow morning. If it were the latter . . . well, he'd deal with it at the appropriate time. There was no point in dwelling on it. He was past the point of no return.

As a precautionary measure, he'd contacted his home office. No law enforcement or Department of Defense officials had called for him, but his office had received a phone call from some senator's office looking into the future of his Iraq contract.

Fucking politicians. Always about money with those corrupt bastards. He had no plans to call him back, ever.

Cain looked at the GPS-enabled laptop computer in front of him as his convoy approached the coordinates he'd preprogrammed into it. They were almost there.

"Scott, make the call," he said to his chief of operations, the driver of the Cougar.

"Roger, sir," Scott Carlson responded. He picked up the transmitter on one of the vehicle's tactical radios, already programmed with the radio net frequency for the dam's combat operations center.

"Haditha COC," he called out, "this is HRI Actual about a mile and a half southwest of the dam. One of our vehicles just stalled—if you can believe that," he added for good measure. "We're going to stop all the vehicles. The boss doesn't want to leave one out here alone, even though the threat level is low. As soon as we ID the problem, I'll call you back. How copy?"

"Roger all, HRI Actual," responded a youthful-sounding Marine. "Radio if you need us. We can be there in minutes."

To have Marines respond to their location was *exactly* what Cain didn't need, especially at this stage of the game.

Scott and Cain exchanged glances, and Scott said, "Appreciate the offer, COC, but I think we have enough firepower to take on a small army. We've got the boss with us, you know?"

Cain shook his head in mild exasperation, but the banter seemed to strike the right chord with the Marine. "I hear that, sir. You should see what we take when we escort visiting generals on sightseeing tours of the city. Insurgents would be crazy to attack us. Anyhow, we're here if you need us. Good luck. COC out."

"Roger, COC. Thanks. HRI Actual out."

Cain said, "Nice job. Hell, I'd have believed you myself."

Then just as quickly, Frost's face donned the mask of intensity only his inner circle ever glimpsed. "Now let's get down to business. We have a country to attack."

The entire convoy of five vehicles stopped as one, pulling over to the side of the asphalt road. The doors of each vehicle opened in unison, and Cain Frost's personal security force of fifty highly trained operators exited the vehicles to set perimeter security.

Each man had been chosen specifically for this mission, and each one was committed to its success. Several had lost friends to IED attacks that had been linked to Iran. But just to ensure their loyalty, Cain had promised each one a $400,000 bonus, a small sum considering the vast wealth he'd protected in numbered accounts in the Caribbean.

Cain stepped out of the lead vehicle and looked east across the road. There was nothing but flat desert sand that dropped away to the Euphrates River approximately a quarter mile away. A lone tree stood guard at the edge.

Good.

He checked the coordinates on the laptop one more time and scanned the desert floor. His heart beat rapidly as he saw the rock formation one hundred yards ahead.

It dumbfounded him that a nuclear device was buried so close to where he stood. He felt a surreal sense of calm wash over him as he focused on what he had to do in the next few minutes.

Have to remain calm. Stay focused, Cain.

He looked back to the dam and counted to sixty. *No reaction. Looks like we're in the clear.*

"Scott, grab four men and follow me. Let's get this over with."

Cain moved toward the rocks, holding a small, portable GPS. Scott Carlson and the small security detachment followed, carrying an assortment of shovels and pickaxes.

Two minutes later, Cain stopped and said, "This is it. We're on top of it."

He looked around and confirmed that he stood at the precise intersection of the five large boulders that marked the spot. He glanced down, and his handheld GPS also confirmed it.

"Start digging. We need to be out of here within minutes."

All four men dug furiously as Cain and Scott silently watched.

After a few minutes, as a hole slowly materialized in the desert floor, Cain finally spoke. "Scott, we're about to take possession of a tactical nuclear device built by a tyrannical Middle Eastern country that was aided by North Korea, all in violation of international law and UN sanctions." He paused.

His chief of operations said nothing.

"When I say it out loud, it sounds ridiculous. I still can't believe this day has finally come to pass."

"I know, sir, but it has, and within forty-eight hours, you'll have your justice, and the rest of the world will know that your conviction has done what the rest of the international community could not."

"Well, Scott," Cain said thoughtfully, "that's one way to look at it, but unfortunately, I don't think the rest of the world will see it that way. Some will, but our own country *most definitely* will not."

Before Scott could respond, there was a metallic *clang* as one of the shovels suddenly struck a buried object.

"Sir, you may want to take a look at this," said the man who'd swung the pickax.

The rest of the team brushed the dirt away as Cain approached and looked into the shallow pit. He revealed no emotion as he mentally reviewed every action he'd taken—the lives he'd ended, the lies he'd told—over the past few years to reach this point. It was all worth it.

Steven—it's almost time, brother.

One side of a large, aluminum suitcase was exposed, covered in a fine coat of dust and dirt. Cain immediately identified it as a Zero Halliburton, one of the most widely recognized suitcases in the world. In addition to being featured in dozens of Hollywood movies, it was incredibly sturdy and extremely airtight in dusty conditions. *Such as this godforsaken desert . . .*

"Congratulations, sir," one man with a shovel said.

"Thank you, Jackson. Now please get it out of there and place it in the container in the back of my vehicle."

Jackson nodded, and the four men cleared the remaining sides of the suitcase. Within seconds, the tomb of dirt and sand was no more. In one anticlimactic move, Jackson bent over, found the handle, and hoisted the nuclear device out of the Iraqi ground that had been its home for the last few years.

None of the men uttered a word as they returned to the vehicle and loaded the suitcase into the back of the lead Cougar, securing it in a large, dark-green, rectangular container lined with black foam.

Scott issued a signal to the rest of the security force, which then entered the vehicles and waited for the lead Cougar to move.

Cain nodded at Scott, who once again picked up the radio transmitter and said, "Haditha COC, this is HRI Actual. Over."

The same voice as earlier responded. "This is Haditha COC. Go ahead, HRI Actual."

"COC, turns out it was just some loose wires on the engine. I'm not a mechanic, but our men can fill your maintenance guys in, if they're willing to take a look. Regardless, we're inbound with an ETA of less than five minutes. Over."

"Roger, HRI Actual. I'm sure our guys would be happy to help. See you shortly. Out."

"Roger, COC. Out here."

Cain turned to Scott once more. "One last item before we move . . ." He pulled out a secure phone, typed a short text message, hit send, and said, "Okay. Let's go."

Just as quickly as they'd stopped, the convoy moved out, its mission accomplished, Cain confident that his plan was on the brink of success.

Now for the hard part.

He was comforted by the fact that he was a superb liar. He'd be utilizing that skill to push through the remainder of the day to tomorrow morning, when his security force would finish its site visit and begin its return to Camp Frost—without him or his chief of operations.

As the convoy departed, none of them heard the sound of engines on the Euphrates as a single rigid-hull boat powered up and crept back up the river toward the dam.

CHAPTER 49

A mile and a half away on top of the Haditha Dam, five men in Marine Corps desert digital camouflage uniforms lay prone, observing the convoy's actions.

A sixth Marine sat fifteen feet behind the men on the concrete, a military radio in a backpack at his feet. A Marine captain and forward observer—FO for short—for the artillery unit deployed in direct support of the 7th Marine Regiment, he was particularly skilled in calling in artillery support and had recorded over fifty call-for-fire missions in the Battle of Fallujah. It was more than any other FO in the Marine Corps.

He'd just conveyed the convoy's status to the group, the COC having immediately relayed it to him.

Colonel Anderson Walker, a fit, midfortyish man from Texas who wore a boonie cover on his head, pulled back from a pair of military binoculars and said, "Looks like they got what they wanted, gentlemen, and they're heading here."

"That's good for us, colonel, as insane as it sounds," Mike Benson replied. "Once they arrive, we stick to the original plan. Once you separate Cain and his deputy from the rest of the men, your Marines take them into custody and then secure the nuclear device."

Logan, John, and Mike had arrived at Al Asad earlier in the morning. They'd caught a headwind across the Atlantic and refueled in the Mediterranean, completing the flight in a little more than ten hours.

The secretary of defense had personally called Colonel Walker on a secure telephone and briefed him on the situation. He'd ordered him to provide any and all support to the small contingent of guests he now hosted.

In Logan's opinion, the colonel was doing everything he could to assist them, even enthusiastically so. He hadn't needed the secretary of defense to emphasize the gravity of the situation. This was Colonel Walker's third deployment to Iraq. He'd lost thirty-four Marines under his command. As he put it, "This asshole wants to start another war that will only get more Marines killed. That's all I need to know. Hell. If I get the chance, I'll put a bullet in his head myself."

"Mike," Logan said, "you know there are some highly trained operators with him. Just remember, this could go south fast, especially if they understand what they're doing is considered treason."

John added, "Which is why the colonel's quick-reaction force is currently staged in a locked garage adjacent to the large bay the convoy will enter once it arrives. It's as good a place as any in this facility to seize them."

The bay was actually an enormous staging area over two hundred yards long and sat directly atop the multiple gates that fed the Euphrates when opened up to the reservoir. It was segmented by five gigantic concrete pillars, which created multiple openings from the bay to the concrete railing. Beyond the railing was a straight drop into the waters of the Euphrates, one hundred and twenty feet below.

It would be closed off at both ends by two infantry companies—

also staged and out of sight—once the convoy entered the bay. There would be no escape.

"Captain West," said a grizzled, hard-looking man, the regiment's sergeant major—he preferred to use Logan's former rank as a sign of respect—"our Marines are ready. They've been briefed on the seriousness of the threat to our national security these men pose—without mentioning the details of the nuclear bomb, of course. No matter what happens, they're good to go."

"Sergeant Major, I appreciate that. I know the resolve. I still have it. But again, these are professional killers hell-bent on attacking a foreign nation. Cain Frost and Scott Carlson are just as dangerous as anyone on our side. Any tricks they might have up their sleeves will be lethal."

"Well then, Logan, we're just going to have to see how this thing shakes out. It's going to go one way or another, but I'm betting on the home team." Colonel Walker had been a high school football star in Texas and was known for his sports references, as were many Marine Corps officers.

"Gentlemen—and that includes you, Sergeant Major, no offense," the colonel said, referring to the fact that senior staff noncommissioned officers took pride in their enlisted status and jokingly "worked for a living," as opposed to the officers above them, "I believe it's time we head down to the COC and wait for our guests to arrive. There's nothing more we can do up here."

The colonel turned to the FO and said, "Jack, you stay up here until this is over. If this goes wrong, be prepared for anything, got it?"

The Marine captain wasn't fazed. He'd seen too much combat in Fallujah to be surprised by anything, even a nuclear bomb.

"Sir, if they try to make a break for it, I'll rain death from above and send them all to Kingdom Come."

Colonel Walker smiled. "That's what I like to hear, son."

He turned to the group and gestured to an opening in the roof that led to a ladder. "Shall we?"

Mike looked at Logan and said, "I really can't wait until this shit is over."

"I hear you, brother, but we have one more job to do before we can go home."

"No kidding. Let's just make sure we do it right," John said.

The men climbed down off the roof, leaving Captain Jack Barnett to watch over all of them.

CHAPTER 50

The five Cougars pulled into the staging area and rolled to a complete stop on the left side of the enormous bay. Two steel doors twenty feet wide and fifteen feet tall rolled toward each other.

Clang!

The doors shut, sealing the convoy inside the bay. Another set of doors closed at the opposite end.

A group of Marines in overalls were hunched over two Humvees halfway down the bay. One Marine was inside on the floorboard, while another aggressively looked for something under the hood. They glanced up as the vehicles stopped, acknowledging the private security force with a few nods, and returned to mechanical work in progress on the nearest vehicle.

Cain Frost spotted Colonel Walker near a large, closed metal door that led deeper into the dam. He'd obviously been waiting for his visitors, his sergeant major at his side.

The colonel waved at Cain, and the two Marines walked in the convoy's direction.

The security force dismounted the Cougars, exiting from the rear of each vehicle and forming a loose perimeter.

From inside the lead Cougar, Cain spoke to Scott Carlson. "No matter what, Jackson's team stays with the vehicle until we can unload our gear. If anyone asks, the suitcase is secure communications gear for us to talk to our headquarters back in Baghdad. Call or text my cell if something changes. Got it?"

"Roger, sir."

"Good. Now let's put on this dog and pony show and try to act gracious at the warm welcome of the good colonel here."

He looked at Scott through Oakley sunglasses covering eyes that revealed no emotion. "In other words, lie."

Cain opened the passenger door and stepped down. He carefully used the large step to reach the ground several feet below, bending his knees as he landed.

As he straightened up, he glanced over at the Marines working on the Humvee. Two of the Marines now stood on the other side of the Humvee, glancing more frequently at Cain and his security force.

What? Never seen actual professionals before?

What Cain didn't see were the other four Marines in the back of each Humvee quietly checking their weapons.

Cain turned his attention back to Colonel Walker. He'd almost reached them, a broad welcoming grin on his face.

Cain moved around the front of the Cougar and looked to his left to see Scott conferring with Jackson and his security detail. All of his men had exited the vehicles. He noticed their guns were still in their hands, gripped casually but firmly and aimed toward the ground. He knew his men could go weapons hot in seconds. The thought eased some of the tension he felt.

"Mr. Frost," he heard in a warm southern accent. "I'm so glad the weather broke, and you were able to make it." Then the colonel was directly in front of him, extending his hand in an enthusiastic greeting.

Cain immediately assessed the man's character, noting the fit physique, the short, Marine haircut, and the confident stance of a serious man.

The colonel smiled, but Cain saw the glint of something else in his eyes. It flashed momentarily and was gone, the grin once again the dominating feature on his face.

Was that contempt? No way. It's just your nerves. Calm down or you're going to make him suspicious, even though he has no reason to be. You've come too far to screw this up at the end.

"I appreciate the hospitality, colonel. It's been a long few days, and this is the last stop on our little tour. Are my men around? I don't see any of them here." Cain looked around the bay, noting again the Marines that were now watching his men intently.

"They're actually on a perimeter sweep today. I figured they'd want to double-check the fence line since their boss was coming. And your boat crew should be returning from a patrol on the river. I thought you'd link up with them after we had a chance to grab some chow and chat awhile. I hope I wasn't being presumptuous?"

Cain smiled, gnawing skepticism beginning to erode his confidence. The hair stood up on the back of his neck. "Not at all." He already knew the location of his boat crew. "Makes sense to me."

"In that case, Mr. Frost, let's head to the COC, grab that bite to eat, and I'll take you on a tour of the facility. I'll have my sergeant major here"—he paused as he nodded at the man to his right—"show your men to their billeting."

He gestured toward the closed vertical door in the back of the bay wall and said, "Shall we?"

Cain heard Scott order the men to unload their gear. He turned and gave him one final nod and fell in next to the colonel as he was led away toward the back of the bay.

Cain scrutinized the environment, his senses highly trained and acutely aware, rapidly processing information from his surroundings. Nothing seemed out of the ordinary. Then for no other reason than professional curiosity, he glanced down at the colonel's sidearm in a quick-draw holster on his right hip. Two facts immediately registered, and alarm bells began to ring loudly in his head.

Why is he wearing a quick-draw? It's uncomfortable and intended for combat. Shit. His weapon's loaded. The magazine was inserted into the bottom of the pistol grip. *No reason for him to carry a loaded weapon here. The security threat is minimal, even nonexistent. There's a greater threat of a negligent discharge by a careless Marine than an attack. Unless—*

Before he could finish the thought, his cell phone vibrated. He stopped midstride and grabbed his BlackBerry from its holster on his belt as he said, "Excuse me, Colonel. Give me a sec. It's my home base in Baghdad."

"It's an ambush. They know."

The short message sent his cognitive processing into overdrive. His mental calculations returned with only one option, no matter how many times he ran the scenario.

He calmly replaced the phone back in its holster. Colonel Walker looked quizzically at him. "Is everything okay, Mr. Frost?"

Cain's face was expressionless. "Unfortunately, Colonel Walker, I'm afraid not."

Without uttering another word, Cain withdrew his own HK .45 pistol in a blindingly fast movement and shot the colonel point-blank in the chest.

As the shot echoed off the concrete walls and pillars, one lone moment of silence stretched across the bay like an eternity. Then it was shattered by explosions and gunshots as the enormous staging area on top of the Haditha Dam was turned into a war zone for the second time since the United States had invaded Iraq.

―――――

THE EUPHRATES RIVER

Tom Denton had secured his small-unit riverine craft—or SURC—to the concrete pier along the base of the dam. The flow from the dam was turned off to allow his HRI patrol boats to use the dam as a staging area for riverine operations. As far as the Marines in the COC were concerned, Tom and his four other HRI security personnel had just concluded another patrol on the Euphrates.

Tom Denton had also fulfilled one other function that only he knew about—be prepared to evacuate Mr. Frost if he contacted him on his cell. He'd been given precise coordinates and told to stage his boat and wait. Tom had told his team they were providing escort for the HRI convoy in case anything happened on the road to the dam. If needed, they could beach the SURC and move to support. Fortunately, no order had come, just a text informing him that his boss was clear.

The rest of the riverine unit hadn't been briefed on the real intent of their employer's visit: only Tom had a need-to-know for that information.

So when he'd received the "all clear" signal, he'd assumed the mission was still a "go," absent any unforeseen obstacles. His instructions had been to act normally and link up with Mr. Frost this evening. He intended to keep his appointment. He was being paid an exorbitant amount of money to do so.

As he threw the boat's line to a young Marine, he heard another Marine speak to someone on the dock. His crew had already disembarked and were walking away down the concrete pier. He'd told them he'd tie up.

"I don't know what's going on up there, but the place is locked down. I couldn't get to my Quadcon on the other side. Was going to use the bay to cross but was told to find another way around."

Tom's ears perked up, and he looked up to see the Marine engaged in a conversation with a fellow team member. They were part of the Marine's own Riverine Squadron, but their boats were tied up farther down the dock.

"You serious?" the second Marine asked.

"Abso-fucking-lutely. Hell, I even saw part of our quick-reaction force head into the COC as the gunny shut the door in my face. Fucking crazy, man."

That was all Tom needed to hear.

He grabbed his cell phone from his cargo pocket and sent Mr. Frost a text message to warn him. The message sent, he waited.

Come on, sir. You better see it. He knew Cain and his men were fish in a barrel up there.

Suddenly, the sound of gunfire poured across the dam like crashing waves.

He didn't hesitate. He yanked the line back from the dock and started the engine.

This is going to get ugly.

He had no idea how right he was.

CHAPTER 51

HADITHA DAM STAGING AREA

Cacophonous gunfire roared through the enormous space. Even as the first shot ricocheted off the walls, Marines poured into the space from hidden staging areas behind doors at both ends of the bay, weapons up and searching for targets.

Cain Frost screamed, "It's an ambush!" and pivoted to run back toward his Cougar, determined to reach his vehicle and the nuclear suitcase.

His men reacted instantly, opening fire on the Marines as the Marines found cover behind large stacks of crates sitting on pallets scattered at both ends of the bay.

Cain didn't look back as he heard the door to the COC—his initial destination—raise on its vertical rails. Footsteps pounded on the floor as someone screamed, "Grab the colonel!"

Cain reached the front of the Cougar and suddenly came face-to-face with Scott Carlson, who pointed his HK G36C Commando assault rifle toward Cain and fired past him.

Cain turned and saw one of the Marines who'd been pretending to be a mechanic fall to the floor as Scott's rounds found their target.

"Sir, we have to get out of here, or we're all going to get slaughtered." He spoke loudly but didn't yell. Scott was not a man disposed to panic, even in situations like this one. It was one of the main reasons Cain had chosen him as his second-in-command years ago. He'd heard about the chameleon who worked for the CIA in the Green Zone. His reputation as a master manipulator had preceded him. It was a skill Cain valued more than any other.

"They have the entrances at both ends blocked." He stopped talking to fire the G36C again. Cain didn't bother to turn as he heard a Marine scream in pain behind him. Scott usually hit what he aimed at, unfortunately for the Marine he'd just shot.

"Tell the men to load the vehicles. Get the .50-cals up. Once they're providing covering fire, grab a SMAW from the back and take out the door at the far end," he said, referring to the shoulder-launched multipurpose assault weapon. "We're driving out of here. We'll figure out the rest once we get outside."

Scott acknowledged the orders with a nod and moved toward the back of the vehicle so that he was in earshot of the closest man at the next Cougar. He barked the instructions as bullets bounced off the concrete floor between his vehicle and the next.

Each member of the HRI security force had found cover, either behind the Cougars' enormous wheels, his back to the open air and the river below, or near one of the gigantic columns of concrete that served as a partition and support.

Cain saw a few of his men lying motionless near their respective Cougars, victims of the assaulting Marines.

He grabbed the passenger door and leapt into the front seat. Inside the vehicle was the safest place at the present moment. He kept the door open in order to provide Scott with additional cover as he yelled orders to the men, who relayed them all the way back to the last vehicle.

So close . . . No matter what, have to keep trying. His only thought was of his brother. Nothing else mattered, even as men were killed and wounded on both sides of the battle. *Nothing else matters!*

The firefight rose to a fevered pitch. Automatic and semiautomatic fire joined in one endless cacophony of sound. Bullets pinged off the Cougar's armor and windshield.

It's going to take more than that, Cain thought, managing a malevolent grin.

He heard the roar of five .50-caliber Browning machine guns open fire. Inside the cavernous space, the heavy weapons turned the tide of the battle in Cain's favor in a matter of seconds.

This might actually work, he thought as his men unleashed steel hell all around him.

———

INSIDE THE COC

On the other side of the vertical, corrugated steel door, Logan West and John Quick reacted instinctively at the sound of the first gunshot.

Neither man contemplated what might've tipped Cain to the ambush. It was irrelevant. As all professional soldiers knew, no plan survived first contact. The only thing that mattered now was securing the nuclear device.

"Get the door up!" Logan shouted at a Marine major who stood next to a control panel along the right wall. He pushed a button, and the door slowly slid upward on its rails, revealing the unfolding chaos beyond.

Logan and John were crouched behind a heavy metal desk, one of many arranged throughout the large operations center. The furniture was currently being used as cover by the Marines, all aiming M4s toward the opening door.

Logan and John were closest to the door and the first ones to spot

Colonel Walker's form, motionless on the floor. His sergeant major was trying to drag him to safety inside the confines of the COC.

"Choose your targets and watch for friendly fire!" Logan screamed above the din. He opened fire with his M4 at the nearest HRI man aiming an assault rifle toward the sergeant major. Unfortunately, in his haste, he'd moved from cover, and a short burst from Logan's weapon struck him squarely in the chest. He fell to the concrete floor.

Logan was looking for his next target when John yelled, "Cover me!" and jumped over the desk, sprinting toward the sergeant major.

As John ran, a platoon of quick-reaction force Marines that had been lined up along each wall dashed through the door. They peeled away out both sides of the entrance in search of cover and enemy combatants.

Logan watched as John reached the sergeant major. He grabbed the commanding officer's left arm as the sergeant major gripped the right one. Both men pulled the fallen Marine along the smooth, cold floor toward the COC, a small streak of red trailing behind.

Logan spotted another mercenary at the rear of the lead Cougar. He aimed through his reflex sight and unleashed three quick rounds. Only the first bullet was necessary. It struck the man in the forehead, snapping his head back and killing him.

Two down. This is going to get messy.

Logan looked to his right to see Mike firing an MP5 10mm submachine gun, his personal weapon with which he'd trained within the FBI.

John and the sergeant major dragged the colonel until they reached cover behind a desk. Logan looked down and saw the commanding officer was gone, his open eyes rolled back in his head.

Motherfucker . . . Another innocent casualty to add to Cain's rising death toll. He breathed deeply to control the rage that coursed through his veins.

John saw the anguish on the sergeant major's face, and he said, "I'm sorry, Sergeant Major. He's gone."

Logan watched as the other man's grief quickly turned to a mask of vindictive hatred. The sergeant major said, "I'm going to kill as many of those fuckers as I can. No way they get away with this shit. No fucking way!"

The gunfight outside the COC ebbed back and forth. Bullets entered the COC as the hostile security force realized there were Marines inside firing at them. Rounds bounced off the walls and careened off the ceiling and floor.

Logan calculated his options, looking for any tactical advantage he could exploit.

It's turning into a Mexican standoff. Christ . . .

He watched as the HRI personnel worked their way toward the rear of the two Cougars closest to the COC. Some of the men provided cover as the rest loaded up into the back of the two vehicles.

What the hell are they doing? Logan wondered. *There's nowhere to go.*

The Marines concentrated their fire on the vehicles, but the bullets had no impact. The vehicles' heavy armor easily deflected the well-placed shots. Nothing short of a direct hit with a tank round would stop one of them.

He looked at John and opened his mouth to speak. Suddenly, the deafening sound of .50-caliber gunfire drowned out the small-caliber automatic weapons.

Logan ducked his head under the desk as the gunner in the lead vehicle swiveled the Browning toward the COC and opened fire.

This is going to hurt.

Boom! Boom! Boom! Boom! Boom!

The inside of the COC was transformed into a whirlwind of shattered furniture, computers, and electronics as .50-caliber rounds impacted everything in sight. Those who dove to the floor survived.

An unlucky few were killed instantly, their bodies suffering grievous wounds from the heavy-caliber machine gun.

The gunfire continued for at least fifteen seconds. Chunks of concrete were torn from the walls; racks of electronics and radios exploded in sparks and flame. The COC was turned into a scene of utter devastation.

So this is how it ends, Logan thought.

BOOM!

A tremendous explosion shook the entire facility as Scott Carlson fired his SMAW—the loudest weapon in the Marine Corps arsenal—at the metal doors at the far end of the bay.

The 83mm rocket sailed through the air toward its target, streaking only feet above the heads of several Marines near the decoy Humvees.

The rocket struck the sliding metal doors, and a second explosion shook the dam. The doors were blown outward, and an enormous, gaping hole appeared, allowing sunlight to stream into the bay.

The Marines shook their heads to clear the silence most of them were suddenly experiencing. The SMAW and the resultant explosion had temporarily deafened them.

The .50-caliber fire stopped.

At least that's one small mercy, Logan thought as he leapt up from behind cover and edged to the right side of the door, finally gaining a vantage point of the entire scene.

Amid the carnage of bodies and ammunition shells, Logan immediately recognized what Cain's plan was. Most of the gunfire had subsided. Cain's men were almost completely loaded into the vehicles.

John appeared at Logan's side and saw it as well. "Christ. He's going to drive his way out of here, and we don't have anything that can stop those beasts."

"Yes, we do. Cover me." Before John could object, Logan West shot out of the COC and sprinted along the back wall toward the far entrance.

John was shocked at his friend's sudden move, but after years of training and shared combat, he instantly intuited where he was going and what he planned to do.

Oh my God. He's completely insane. Still, he opened fire, hoping to draw attention away from the fleeing figure of Logan West.

————

As the Marines recovered from the explosions and .50-caliber onslaught, Cain yelled, "Scott, we need to move now! We only have seconds left before they recover! *Go! Go! Go!*"

As Scott started the 330 hp engine, Cain glimpsed a flash of movement from the left. Was that Logan West, sprinting at full speed along the back wall? *What the hell is he doing?*

As Cain watched, Logan dodged in and out of cover, never slowing his stride, working his way toward the far end of the bay.

Then Cain saw the finish line of Logan's run, and like John Quick had, he realized what the next move was. *Oh no you don't, you sonofabitch!*

"Scott," Cain said calmly, "if you don't punch it now, we're not getting out of here." He suddenly raised his voice and screamed, "Move!" as if kicking a stubborn mule in the side. It had the intended effect, and the Cougar lurched forward, grabbing at the concrete floor as it gained traction, screeching along the way.

It was a good old-fashioned footrace, but Logan West had set his high school record for the forty-yard dash while on the football team his sophomore year. Man versus Cougar. It was an even match, but this was no game, and Logan intensely focused on his objective. He breathed heavily and deeply but in control. *This is going to work. I know it.*

He visualized every action he had to execute once he reached the end of the bay. It was going to be close.

Eighty yards . . . He saw a few Marines from this end of the bay turn toward him from behind cover as he moved past their positions, a blur of speed.

"Open fire and slow the Cougars down! They're coming your way!" he barked through gasping breaths. He didn't wait for their reaction.

Sixty yards . . . Logan heard the convoy moving through the carnage toward him. Cain had taken advantage of the lull in the battle to get his vehicles running.

The sound of gunfire once again filled the top of the dam. Marines directed their fire at the convoy as the vehicles weaved their way in and out of the gigantic stone pillars, entrenched Marines, Humvees, and trucks strewn throughout the bay.

Thirty yards . . . He'd be there in seconds. The Cougars were still three pillars away—at least 130 yards.

Ten yards . . . *Get ready, this is for keeps . . .*

He reached his destination and leapt into the air. His right foot struck the passenger-side running board as he launched himself into the open cabin of a lone, twelve-foot high, seven-ton truck. The behemoth was a six-wheel-drive all-terrain vehicle used by the Marine Corps to tow anything from water and fuel supplies to howitzer cannons.

Logan had a different purpose in mind for this one, as his momentum carried him across the small gap between the seats, and he landed squarely in the driver's seat with a jarring thud.

He spared a glance through the two-inch bulletproof glass. The convoy had gained speed and momentum, even as the entire assembled force of Marines concentrated their fire on it.

Unlike a commercial vehicle, the seven-ton truck Logan had chosen had no key ignition. Logan turned the silver ignition switch and was rewarded with a series of beeps, indicating the battery switch on the back of the cab was on. *Thank God . . .*

He remembered a staff sergeant once told him that Marines were prone to leave the battery switches in the up and "on" position. It allowed them to get the hell out of sticky situations a few seconds faster. Logan had counted on it.

As soon as the beeps stopped, Logan turned the switch, and the 425hp engine roared to life.

Now for the fun part.

Logan slammed the gearshift into drive, released the clutch, and pinned the gas pedal to the floorboard. The truck lurched forward, quickly gaining speed.

Logan was fifty yards from the hole blown into the bay doors by the SMAW.

Cain's convoy moved faster.

Logan watched all five vehicles approaching from the right. He aimed the front of the seven-ton directly toward the opening and revved the engine, shifting gears as rapidly as he could. The seven-ton gained ground and power as it moved to intercept the escaping Cougars.

This is going to be close.

The convoy was only thirty yards away and approaching fast. Logan didn't have time to think as he braced himself for the impending impact.

The truck was fifteen yards from the opening when Logan finally realized he'd calculated correctly. He was going to make it. He looked through the windshield at the lead Cougar and saw its two occupants staring at him, mouths agape.

Logan managed a smile, but then the smile was wiped away as his seven-ton truck struck the front left quarter of the Cougar at forty miles per hour. The violent impact threw Logan toward the steering wheel, the wheel itself whipping to the left. Logan never let off the gas. As he tried to control the steering wheel, he kept the pedal pinned to the floor.

The force of the seven-ton, magnified by the several layers of armor, threw the Cougar off course and to the right, even as Scott tried to slam on the brakes. Logan paid no attention as the remaining four vehicles drove past them through the hole in the bay doors. This was the only one that truly mattered.

Logan, now in control of the seven-ton, blinked his eyes as blood poured into them. *Must have hit my head . . .*

He shifted again, leveraging the lower gears for more power. The truck pushed the wounded Cougar sideways.

Logan was only ten feet from the cab of their windshield. He saw Cain—he recognized him immediately since he was one of the most powerful figures in the global private military-industrial complex—in the passenger seat screaming at the driver, who fought to regain control of the Cougar. *Good luck, asshole.*

Logan looked hard at the driver, images from Fallujah surging from beneath the surface of his memory. *It can't be.* But it was. The cold certainty of it gripped him momentarily like an ice-cold vise.

The driver of Cain Frost's Cougar was none other than James, the treacherous CIA agent who'd set his Marines on a path to their deaths. *The sonofabitch must be Scott Carlson, Cain's second.* Logan didn't know how James—now Scott—had come to be in the employment of Cain Frost, and he didn't care. He stared momentarily at the man who had haunted his nightmares, a man he'd vowed to kill. *It's almost time, motherfucker.*

Logan averted his gaze from Scott's face and locked eyes with Cain. Then Logan did something unexpected. He smiled at Cain and pointed straight ahead, gesturing with his index figure as he did so.

Cain stared back, confused. The seven-ton continued to grind, bullying the Cougar sideways at will.

A sudden look of horror appeared on Cain's face. Cain shouted something to Scott, who jerked his head to look at Logan.

Logan made a "bye-bye" gesture with his right hand, smiling the entire time. Knowing that his enemy understood what was about to happen, Logan put his hand back on the steering wheel and gripped it with all his strength.

The seven-ton pushed the Cougar ten more feet. Logan heard a metallic *pop,* the sound of steel bending.

Logan revved the engine one last time, pushing forward. *It's done.*

The front of the Cougar tilted upward as the vehicle breached the railing at the edge of the bay.

Logan yanked open the driver's door, keeping his foot on the gas as long as he could. The Cougar passed the tipping point, and Logan stole one last look into its cab. He thought he heard screaming, but he wasn't sure and didn't care. The Cougar disappeared over the edge.

Logan didn't hesitate. He dove from the cab of the seven-ton as its momentum carried it through the gap in the railing, chasing after the Cougar. He landed on the hard concrete and rolled several times.

Oh no, he thought as his momentum carried him directly toward the open air. He heard two huge splashes as the Cougar and seven-ton landed in the river below. He was certain he was about to follow them over the edge, but then his roll was stopped as his back slammed directly into a pole in part of the railing that remained intact. His breath was knocked out of him, and he steadied himself against the sensation that he was about to pass out.

He opened his eyes. The gunfire inside the bay had stopped. *Blessed silence . . .*

He lay on his stomach, his face resting on the concrete edge of the bay, squinting as the Iraqi sun poured down on him. He looked down into the river, and he saw the back of the seven-ton bobbing in the water. The Cougar was on its left side. There was no movement around the vehicle. Whether the men in the back of the Cougar had been killed or knocked unconscious, the end result would be the same. The vehicle began to sink into the dark Euphrates water.

Logan thought he heard someone shout his name: his ears still rang from the sounds of the battle.

He was about to turn toward the main part of the bay where the firefight had begun when a sudden glint of metal flashed in his eyes from the water below. He put his hands over his eyes to shield them from the sun and searched for the shining object in the murky water below. He found the source of the reflection thirty yards away from the sinking Cougar and seven-ton.

Oh, fuck . . .

Both Cain Frost and Scott Carlson had survived the fall and were swimming away from the dam. A large, metallic briefcase trailed in the water behind Cain, held in his left hand. To Logan's surprise, he saw a SURC moving toward the survivors.

He's going to rescue them. I need to get someone to radio that patrol boat. The sound of footsteps stopped next to him, and Logan turned to see John Quick staring at him in amazement.

Before he could speak, Logan said, "It's him. I don't know how, but's it's him."

"Who, Logan?" John asked.

"Scott Carlson, Cain's chief of operations. I'm assuming that's who was driving Cain. The motherfucker is James, our CIA friend from Fallujah."

"Christ, after all this time . . ."

Logan looked into his friend's eyes and saw the pain from old memories. "I know. It's crazy. We'll figure it out later, but first someone needs to radio that boat and tell that operator the men he's about to rescue are the ones we're trying to stop. Looks like Cain's got the bomb too."

Logan stood up, almost falling over as John steadied him. He saw three Marines approaching. "Any of you have a radio?" he asked.

Before they could answer, John said, "I don't think we have to worry about the driver's safety anymore."

"What are you talking about?" Logan snapped his head back toward the river, only to see the driver helping Cain Frost out of the river and onto the SURC. Scott was already on the deck. All three men shook hands and smiled warmly at one another in recognition.

"Oh shit. He had a backup plan." They watched as the small patrol boat turned around and sped down the Euphrates River, moving toward the city of Haditha itself, five miles away.

"John," Logan said slowly, "can someone please get me a helicopter? This isn't over just yet."

CHAPTER 52

TOP OF THE HADITHA DAM

Captain Barnett had lost contact with the COC at the first sounds of the intense firefight below. He knew something had obviously gone wrong, but Colonel Walker's orders had been specific.

"If something happens and this goes sideways, it's your job to make sure none of the bastards get away. You understand, Jack?"

Captain Barnett understood. Other than the sergeant major (who didn't really count since he was the colonel's right hand and wielded more power than any captain in the Marine Corps), he was the lowest-ranking officer to be fully briefed on Cain Frost and his sociopathic intentions. There was no way in hell he would let Frost get away with this madness if he had anything to say about it. He'd seen enough death and mayhem—hell, been responsible for plenty of it himself—to last several lifetimes. Another war would only lead to more of the same.

The explosions rattled the concrete roof where he sat atop two large olive-green boxes. He fought the urge to climb down into the heart of the dam. As much as his instincts and training urged him to run toward the fight, he knew that for right now, for this moment, his job was up here. So he silently prayed for the Marines below and waited as the battle raged on. It was one of the hardest things he'd ever done.

The gunfire picked up in intensity, and he would've sworn he heard several .50-caliber machine guns firing simultaneously.

That's not good for someone.

Then the firing stopped as abruptly as it started, the silence followed moments later by two thunderous explosions, the second one coming from his left.

He spoke into the handset on the AN/PRC-117 VHF manpack radio at his feet. "FSC, this is Black Sky. Anything from the COC yet?"

The Fire Support Center responded, "Not yet. Sounds like things are getting crazy up there."

"No kidding, FSC, I'm about—" was all he had time to say before he heard a splash in the river below. A second dramatic splash followed moments later.

"FSC, wait one." He dropped the handset, slid off the olive-green containers, carefully avoiding the large weapon lying on the roof, and ran over to the edge of the dam.

Good Christ almighty. One of HRI's Cougars was slowly sinking below the surface of the water. Then he saw the truck. *Is that a seven-ton?*

Captain Barnett knew it was. He just hoped the crazy driver had escaped before plummeting over the edge. He saw movement in the water, but his attention shifted as he heard the roar of powerful engines to his left.

Four Cougars sped down the dirt road away from the dam, weaving in and out of the tactically positioned Jersey barriers. Marines manning the checkpoints along the half-mile road to the main gate opened fire. The assault rifles and 7.62-caliber machine guns had no effect on the powerful antimine vehicles. The rounds ricocheted off the bulletproof glass and armor.

That former captain must've known something like this would hap-

pen. The colonel had told Barnett that it had been Logan's idea to place him on overwatch.

Here was the moment he'd trained for, happening right before his very eyes. *The bastards were trying to get away.*

Captain Barnett sprinted back to his position, leaned down, and picked up the heavy FGM-148 Javelin missile he'd prestaged on the roof of the dam. He jogged as quickly as he could to the edge of the roof, the nearly fifty-pound weapon slowing him down slightly.

He was proficient in the use of the Javelin. Normally, a two-man crew was required to operate it, more for stability than anything else. Fortunately, his two-hundred-pound frame was all muscle, and he'd trained to fire solo on multiple occasions. Now he was going to get the chance to see if that training paid off.

He crouched and sat down on the roof, bending his knees in front of him. He raised the command launch unit—the CLU—over his right shoulder, balancing the weight of the missile tube carefully.

He looked through the viewfinder and found the four Cougars outside the camp. They were already more than six hundred meters away. The small convoy had somehow blasted its way through the main gate on the side of the dam.

The CLU's infrared mode searched for the heat signatures of the fleeing vehicles. Captain Barnett flipped a switch, and a box appeared in the viewfinder. Seconds later, he was rewarded with a steady tone as the CLU locked on to the lead Cougar. *Bingo.* He pulled the trigger.

WHOOSH!

The warhead shot out of the missile tube toward the Cougars, and the missile's main ignition system ignited. The warhead streaked upward into the sky at a steep angle, the sophisticated tracking system choosing the best angle of attack.

Captain Barnett's part of the job complete, he dropped the heavy CLU and watched as the missile reached its zenith, seemed to stop in midair, and then rocketed earthward in a direct line at the lead Cougar now eight hundred meters away.

Even after seeing the Javelin used several times in combat, the technology of the weapon never ceased to amaze him. It'd been designed to maximize a top-attack angle in order to defeat heavily armored vehicles, including tanks and armored personnel carriers.

The Cougar never had a chance.

In an instant, the high-explosive antitank warhead slammed through the top of the armored vehicle. The first explosive-shaped charge cleared a pathway through the armor, allowing the main warhead to detonate inside the confines of the Cougar.

The result was spectacular—and horrific for the men inside.

The vehicle exploded outward as if trying to expand on its frame. The lumbering behemoth rolled onto its side and flipped several times down the road before grinding to a halt.

The first two vehicles behind it had been following too closely. The second Cougar tried to stop as the driver slammed on its brakes. His reflexes were too slow. The personnel carrier smashed into the burning hulk of the first and was launched into the air as it broke through the other vehicle's remains. It tilted in midair and then fell over, almost in slow motion, as it landed on its right side.

The third Cougar's driver had more time to react, but not much more. The driver avoided the wreckage and veered to the left but quickly lost control as a result of the high speed. The Cougar fishtailed wildly down the road and went right over the edge. Captain Barnett watched as the Cougar rolled onto its left side and suddenly dropped out of sight.

One shot, three kills—not too shabby. One more to go . . .

The fourth vehicle swerved around the wreckage, and its driver accelerated past the carnage, obviously hoping to place as much distance as possible between him and the dam.

Captain Barnett reached down and grabbed the spare warhead

he'd brought. He detached the spent tube and connected the new missile, assuming a sitting position once again. Looking through the viewfinder, he saw that the surviving Cougar was already almost a thousand meters away.

You may as well just park it, buddy. There's nowhere to go, he thought with a wry smile.

Seconds later, the beeps transitioned to a steady tone as the CLU locked on to the remaining vehicle. He pressed the trigger once again, and the second missile launched into the air, quickly covering the distance as it greedily streaked toward its prey.

He put the CLU down and stood up. There was no doubt it would be a direct hit. Nothing could stop the warhead now.

Moments later, the missile impacted the rear of the Cougar, tunneling through the armor and striking the gas tank. The detonation of the warhead and the gas tank's explosion were nearly simultaneous.

B-BOOM!

The vehicle flipped forward onto its roof, flames pouring out of it as it skidded down the dirt road. It finally ground to a halt, a burning cauldron of death.

Barnett saw no movement on the road from his vantage point, which was fine with him. He turned around to radio the COC once again only to find one bloody Logan West covered in dirt and grime smiling at him.

"Nice shot, Captain. They got what they deserved."

Captain Barnett opened his mouth to ask what had happened below, but he never got the chance. A loud vibration suddenly shook the roof of the dam.

He looked past Logan West and saw the FBI agent and the retired gunnery sergeant standing behind him. They turned around to face the back of the dam, toward the lake.

The thrumming sound grew louder, filling the air around them.

"Get downstairs and see the sergeant major!" Logan shouted. "That's our ride!"

Like a specter emerging from the darkness, a Bell UH-1Y Venom helicopter rose into view, a 7.62mm Gatling minigun mounted on each side.

The Super Huey hovered for a moment and then touched down on the concrete roof fifty feet away.

Captain Barnett stared as Logan West, John Quick, and Mike Benson raced to the open compartment in the middle of the helicopter and jumped aboard, sliding onto the two leather benches that faced each other.

He saw the men pull on headsets and watched as the pilot lifted off. Captain Barnett said to no one in particular, "Nice ride," as the pilot angled the nose forward toward the front of the dam. The Super Huey shot forward, leaving Captain Jack Barnett alone once again on the roof of the Haditha Dam, wondering how in the hell this day was going to end.

CHAPTER 53

OVER THE EUPHRATES RIVER

The pilot of the Super Huey concentrated on the small speck in the river a mile and a half downstream. The boat had opened up a sizable lead in a short amount of time.

The pilot spoke into his headset to his passengers. "Thirty seconds until we're on them!"

He heard a man say, "Roger," and then to the crew chief, "Use the Gatling, but do not—I say again, do not—hit the boat, at least not until I give the word. Understand?"

His crew chief said, "Roger, sir. I'll only try to scare the shit out of him—or at least make him think about stopping."

The river below flashed by in a blur. At two hundred feet, the sensation of speed was magnified exponentially. Buildings appeared sporadically on both sides of the river, and small copses of green trees grew in density.

We're getting close to the city. Not good. Logan thought of the potential for civilian casualties, knowing this city had seen more than its fair share of bloodshed since 2003. He didn't want to add to it unless he had no choice.

The boat moved dangerously fast, but the Super Huey had almost reached it. A few more seconds . . .

"Stand by. I'm going to pass him and set up a blocking position a quarter mile downriver."

Logan wondered how long Cain would drag this out. "Guys, I don't know what he's planning. Unless he has another escape route, he has to know we're going to get him."

Over the roar of the rotors, he heard Mike say, "Honestly, Logan, I don't know, and I don't care. All I know is that we have to get that bomb at all costs. If he gets desperate, he can always trigger it."

Logan heard John say, "I don't think so. I think—" but he was cut off as bullets ricocheted off the side of the Super Huey as it passed the port side of the patrol boat. A few rounds struck the inside of the helicopter, and sparks sprayed the passengers.

The crew chief opened fire with the Gatling minigun. Logan watched as two streams of 7.62mm bullets lashed out from the Super Huey with a *burrrp! burrrp!* cutting across the front of the patrol boat, the impacts creating small geysers in the river.

The pilot increased the throttle, and the Super Huey shot forward, racing ahead of the SURC. Within seconds, the bird was out of range of the SURC's mounted machine gun. Logan heard the pilot mumble something, but he couldn't distinguish the words. *I can only guess he's as eager to end this as I am.*

He looked south and saw they were near a small island that divided the river. It was connected to the city by a short bridge.

The pilot suddenly brought the nose of the helicopter up and turned hard to the right, slowing down as he executed the maneuver. He lowered the Super Huey to an altitude of twenty feet. The side of the helicopter squarely faced the approaching SURC, less than a quarter of a mile away and closing fast.

Logan realized that during their brief trip in the air, they'd somehow covered the five miles from the Haditha Dam and were now in the heart of the city.

Christ. Cain could kill tens of thousands if he detonated now.

"Gunny," Logan shouted at the crew chief, "if he opens fire again, sink him. The suitcase is protected, and even if it's punctured, only the explosives should detonate. The nuclear payload itself shouldn't—at least I hope not." *Or we're all fucked,* he didn't add.

"Roger."

The boat came at them, now less than one hundred meters . . . ninety . . . eighty . . .

It wasn't slowing down. What the hell is he doing? Logan didn't get a chance to voice the question.

Suddenly, the SURC veered to the right, exposing its side to the attack helicopter.

Logan realized what was happening a moment too late as Scott Carlson aimed an RPG at the Super Huey. The driver of the SURC had waited until he was within fifty meters and then turned to provide Scott a clear line of sight. Scott pulled the trigger, and the RPG streaked toward its hovering target.

The Super Huey's crew chief reacted and depressed the trigger on the minigun. The fusillade of bullets crossed the Euphrates toward the boat. Unfortunately for the Super Huey, Scott Carlson's aim was precise, and the result was disastrous.

Logan initially thought the RPG would tear into the cabin of the helicopter, but then he heard a loud *bang! thwack!* as the rocket-propelled grenade struck the rotor above them, splitting one of the four blades in half.

Logan's only thought was, *Smart bastard,* and then he braced himself for impact as alarms sounded inside the cabin and the cockpit.

The cabin shuddered violently as the remaining rotor tore itself apart. The Super Huey turned to the left but then suddenly straightened up, hovering for a brief moment, suspended in midair.

The pilot seemed to regain control. Logan looked back at the river to see the SURC speeding for the bank of the Euphrates and the expansive city beyond the gradual slope of the shoreline. *Not so fast, asshole.*

"Gunny, open fire again. Don't let him—" He was cut off by the sound of shrieking metal, as the rotors completely disintegrated. The Super Huey dropped nose down and tilted to the right.

There was no way the pilot would recover this time. He shouted, "Brace for impact!" As Logan watched the surface of the Euphrates rise up to meet the plunging helicopter, he thought, *If Cain makes it into the city, we'll never catch him.*

Then the Super Huey slammed into the water, sending plumes of smoke and mist high into the air, and as water rushed into the open cabin, Logan's only thought was of their survival.

CHAPTER 54

Cain did have a backup plan. It was his last resort. During the final weeks of the operation, he'd used his considerable resources to contact a local insurgent commander in Haditha. Scott had led the effort, and it was only after multiple attempts that the insurgent leader had allowed one of his deputies to travel to Baghdad to meet with Scott.

The offer had been simple: "Provide us with a way out of Haditha on the day of our choosing. It has to be undetectable by the US military. They'll be looking for us. Do this one thing, and we'll fund you with all the weapons and equipment you can handle."

The insurgent deputy commander had been so dumbfounded by the offer that he'd been speechless.

"It's a real offer. Don't ask why. But here's the catch. We're not going back to Baghdad. We need to get into Syria." The insurgent had raised his eyebrows.

"So, we'll help an American willing to help kill his own people and who needs to get smuggled into Syria, correct? *Inshallah*," the insurgent had said.

It sounded preposterous to Scott when the man had stated it so bluntly, but it was the truth. Their goal was larger than a diminishing insurgency or any American lives that might be lost because of their actions. They were about to make a statement that would transform history.

The agreement had eventually been reached, and in a remote building just one hundred meters west of an old soccer stadium more than a mile away from the SURC's current position, four men waited to honor their end of the bargain.

As Cain watched the helicopter sink into the Euphrates, he turned his attention to the riverbank. The driver aimed the craft toward a gradual slope forty yards away.

Within seconds the patrol boat reached the shore, and Cain felt the bottom scrape the bank below.

Cain looked back at the helicopter one more time. He thought he saw a flash of movement near the remnants of the hulking machine above the surface. He couldn't be sure, but he certainly didn't have time to wait and see.

Scott and the driver both jumped out of the boat, boots crunching on the gravel surface. Scott carried the nuclear suitcase.

"Let's go, sir. We've got a bit of ground to cover before we're in the clear."

"Nice shot with that RPG, Scott. I knew I paid you well for your skills," Cain said.

"Honestly, I'd have done that one for free. I can't stand that smug West bastard or his fucking sidekick." Scott wasn't smiling.

Cain nodded. He shared the same sentiments. "If nothing else, it should buy us some time. Let's go."

He turned his attention to the driver, Tom Denton, as he walked up the short slope to the streets above. "Tom, nice job. I knew I could count on you."

"Sir, I'm in this till the end. I lost a cousin to an IED attack in Sadr City, and I know those assholes were funded by the Iranians. So if we can hit them back, I'll do whatever needs to be done," Tom said.

Cain nodded. "Scott, hand him the suitcase. You and I are on point."

Scott turned over the nuclear weapon to Tom, who, though surprised by the move, didn't appear to be afraid of the bomb.

Good, Cain thought. *Maybe I really can count on him.*

It was down to just the three of them, and it was all or nothing. If they reached Syria, the rest of the operation was already in place. He'd paid heavily for an Iranian visa, and after a substantial weapons shipment to Damascus, the Syrian government had guaranteed him a private flight to Tehran. All the Syrians knew was that he wanted to meet with the Iranian government.

It had taken over a year and a half of clandestine meetings and worldwide conversations to secure a two-hour meeting with a representative of the Iranian regime. The meeting was scheduled for two days from now in a hotel in downtown Tehran. The hotel itself was unremarkable; however, its proximity to the Iranian Parliament building near Baharestan Square was crucial. In two days, the supreme leader of the Islamic Republic of Iran would speak to Parliament about the future of Iran's nuclear program. *That is, unless I have something to say about it.*

Cain didn't know if the Americans had found his map of the Quds Force headquarters at Fajr Base. He hoped they had. It was intended as a decoy to throw them off his scent once he dropped off the grid in Iraq.

His real targets were the supreme leader of Iran and the entire Iranian Parliament. He was going to kill them all.

Once his meeting with the regime was concluded, he planned to set the nuclear device to detonate during the speech. He'd flee south of the city to escape the explosion.

He'd established a network in southern Iran, one that wouldn't ask too many questions, even in the wake of the country's political collapse. This network controlled the final piece of the puzzle—

smuggling him into South America to a nonextradition country of his choosing. Iran had been involved for years in shady deals with various South American dictators. Guaranteeing his sanctuary had been the easiest aspect of the whole operation.

"All right, then. Let's go before any survivors from the crash or their reinforcements show up. We'll stick to the alleys and side streets."

The three men climbed the slope and disappeared, their new objective more than a mile away.

CHAPTER 55

Logan pulled the pilot's unconscious body toward the shore, acutely aware that with each stroke, Cain Frost and Scott Carlson moved farther away and into the urban maze that was Haditha.

John assisted the copilot, who was conscious but had two crushed legs and couldn't swim on his own. He clung to John's back as the shoreline grew closer, the contingent of men laboriously working against the flow of the Euphrates.

It was a miracle that none of them had been killed in the crash, especially Mike, whom he'd seen flung against the side of the Super Huey like a rag doll. Mike had complained about pain in his right ankle and foot, but he swam with the rest of them.

The gunner and crew chief had surfaced from the wreckage unscathed. *Some Marines have nine lives,* Logan thought.

The men didn't speak. Their common focus was on one thing—reaching dry ground.

Logan had seen less violent crashes do more damage to life and limb. Maybe the Big Guy upstairs really was looking out for their welfare. He didn't have time to contemplate it. In his mind, the clock was ticking, and when it reached zero, the Middle East became a powder keg.

Logan redoubled his stroke, drawing strength from a place he had almost forgotten he possessed. Suddenly, he felt the shifting dirt and silt of the riverbank. The last few steps were the hardest, but he finally emerged from the river, soaked and filthy, but alive.

He pulled the pilot up onto the wet earth, took off his helmet, and checked his vitals as the rest of the group emerged from the murky water.

Thank God. He's still breathing.

"Jesus Christ," he heard John say, "I never liked helicopters—no offense, Captain," speaking to the injured man he'd just rescued from the crash.

"None taken," the young copilot said, grimacing in pain and wincing as he lay on the ground. "I've got bigger problems right now than your fear of flying."

He pulled out a portable PRC-434G personal survival radio from a zipped cargo pocket in his flight suit. He pressed two buttons, activating the GPS transponder and personal locator beacon, and turned the selection dial to voice.

"Haditha COC, this is Raven Six. We are down in Haditha. I say again, we splashed down in the river. Current location is the riverbank inside the city. The helo is in the river underwater. All onboard alive. Request immediate QRF support."

Logan interrupted him. "Captain, if we have any chance in hell of catching Cain Frost and his men, we need to leave now." He looked at Mike, who sat and examined his right ankle. It was swollen to almost twice the size of his left one. It was either severely sprained or broken. Regardless, Mike shook his head, silently confirming to Logan what he already suspected—he was out of commission.

It's just John and me.

Logan turned to the crew chief and his gunner. "Gunny, can I take your radio? They have a head start, but in the event that we catch them, we're going to need support. We'll contact you as soon as we can."

John checked his 1911 .45-caliber pistol, pulling the slide back to allow any trapped water to escape. He ejected the magazine and inserted a fresh one; he did the same for his M4, which had survived the crash slung across his back. He looked up at Logan once he was finished. "Ready when you are, boss."

Logan nodded. "Gunny, the people of this city aren't exactly friendly to Marines after what happened here. Be careful. Call us if you have trouble, but understand one thing—finding Cain is our number one priority."

"Roger. Good luck, sir. If anyone tries anything, Sergeant Cruz and I can handle it. It's not our first Iraqi rodeo. Hell, it's not even my first crash," he added, somehow managing a smile as he said it.

Mike stared at the pilot. "Fucking Marines—you're all nuts. Stop dicking around, Logan, and go get that sonofabitch. We'll be fine."

"See you soon, Mike." Without another word, Logan unslung his M4, and he and John sprinted up the slope and disappeared into the city.

CHAPTER 56

The three men worked their way through the convoluted maze of Haditha. Each Iraqi they passed stopped and stared at them. It didn't help their conspicuousness as Westerners that they carried assault rifles and a large metallic suitcase as they ran.

The buildings were no more than a few stories tall, but they were tall enough to confuse the casual traveler. Streets intersected at odd angles, with no discernible pattern. Some were paved; others, just dirt and rock. Old cars and pickup trucks sped by in the streets. Some slowed down as they spotted the foreigners but then sped off at the sight of their weapons. The afternoon commotion added to Cain's confusion.

Spotting an alley only a few feet away, Cain said, "I need to check our location." They moved off the main road to the unpaved side street.

Cain pulled out a thick, laminated map and his Garmin GPS. He cross-referenced the map with the coordinates from the GPS and said, "Okay. We're still a little more than half a mile away. We need to keep going down this main road, and in about three hundred yards, veer left into what looks like a residential neighborhood. The soccer stadium should be on the other side. Let's move."

We're almost there. If our luck holds out, we'll be in Syria by this evening.

Logan and John raced through the streets in hot pursuit. Logan had no frame of reference for Haditha since neither John nor he had spent any operational time there. Street vendors and pedestrians moved away from the rushing Americans, fear and doubt visible on their faces. A young Iraqi woman shielded a small boy ahead of them on the sidewalk.

Logan tried to crack a friendly smile as he dashed past her, but they shied away.

They moved down the main thoroughfare of the city, but there was no sign of Cain and his men. Finally, they stopped at a large intersection with traffic moving in all directions, each driver exercising his own version of traffic rules and etiquette. Iraqis on all four corners turned and looked at them. The contempt was obvious, but Logan felt no threat. *They've just seen too many Americans in uniform.*

"I don't mean to be a buzzkill, but this isn't looking good. They've got a head start and know where they're going. We don't. This is turning into a wild goose chase. Hopefully, we can get a UAV or direct air support to try and pick them up again. Otherwise, brother, we're just shooting in the dark."

"Just give me a second." Logan continued to scan the streets. *Come on. Give me something, anything.*

He looked back and forth across the intersection. He was about to give up when something caught his attention.

"Bingo," he said in a low voice. "Across the street on the far corner. Let's go."

John looked and finally spotted what Logan had seen. On the far corner was a young Iraqi teenager, waving for their attention as he repeatedly pointed down the main road that continued on the other side of the intersection.

"I'll be damned . . ." John said.

Both men sprinted into the street in pursuit of their prey. *It's not over yet, asshole.*

———

Cain stopped again at the end of the main road, which curved away to the north. They moved into what was in fact a small suburb of densely packed homes, although the mazelike streets were not laid out in any sort of grid. The street they were on ended in an intersection 150 meters away, where it branched left and right in a Y.

"Once we're through these streets, we should see the soccer stadium." Cain turned and faced the two men. Both were breathing heavily, but for Scott and Cain, who were in superb physical shape, this run was a moderate exertion. Tom, on the other hand, was breathing hard, hands on his knees, trying to catch his breath.

Cain and Scott looked at each other and then back at Tom. "Tom, are you going to make it? We can't slow down. You understand?" The words were casual enough, but Tom understood the threat behind them. *Keep moving, Tom, or we'll leave you behind.*

"I'll be fine, sir. Just had to catch my breath. I can keep up."

Tom saw another glance exchanged between Cain and Scott, and then Cain said, "Okay, then. Let's go." Tom had received a brief reprieve.

Cain and Scott turned to enter the neighborhood when *crack! crack! crack!* shattered the relative afternoon calm.

Cain whirled around, assault rifle up as he searched for targets. Tom Denton lay in the middle of the street, the suitcase on the ground, blood leaking from two bullet holes in his back. Then Cain saw the shooters.

"Three hostiles, one o'clock! Grab the suitcase!" Cain returned fire at a group of three Iraqi males pointing AK-47s in their direction. The man who'd dropped Tom was on one knee.

As the other two men opened fire from standing positions behind him, a quick burst from Cain's HK Commando assault rifle caught the kneeling man in the chest. He immediately fell forward, his face striking the concrete, the AK-47 skidding across the pavement.

His friends saw their comrade fall and shouted in Arabic. They then did something Cain hadn't expected. They ran *toward* Cain and Scott, firing wildly as they moved across the street.

Cain fired another burst; he missed but provided Scott enough time to retrieve the nuclear weapon. He watched as more Iraqis appeared from around the corner of a house, AK-47s in hand.

Uh-oh. Now we're outgunned.

"Scott, we need to leave! Three more hostiles! Follow me!"

Scott, suitcase now in his left hand, turned back and fired his HK with his right. He didn't hit any of the men, but his fire had the intended effect—all five Iraqis dove to the street for cover. He'd bought them a few precious seconds.

He turned and followed his boss into the once-quiet Haditha suburb.

————

The sound of gunfire echoed across the city. Haditha's citizens stopped wherever they were to listen. Each man and woman calculated his or her distance from the battle. Those closest to the gunfight sought refuge inside their homes. Experience told the others, even those on the streets, they were far enough away to be relatively safe—at least momentarily.

Logan and John's reaction was slightly different. Both men looked at each other and then picked up their pace, sprinting toward the sound of automatic weapons fire.

What the hell was going on? Logan hadn't expected to hear a gunfight. He hadn't expected to hear anything, for that matter. *Something must've gone wrong. Bad for them; good for us.*

They ran on, noticing Iraqis on the sidewalk looking down a side street out of view at the next intersection. They ran to the corner and stopped, M4s at the ready, absorbing the scene in front of them.

They were near the entrance to a neighborhood. The street they were on continued for at least 150 meters, ending in front of a row of homes where the road split in two directions. Logan saw a group of men with weapons disappear up the right branch of the road.

Thirty meters in front of them, one man lay lifeless on the pavement, blood pooling beneath him. Two more Iraqi males knelt beside him. One of the men talked on a cell phone as he looked farther down the street.

Logan saw another body in the middle of the street. Logan realized it had to be one of Cain's men. He didn't see the weapon. *They're still alive.*

"Umm, Logan. They know we're here."

Logan looked back at the two Iraqis. The man on the cell phone was pointing at Logan and then back at his phone. The other man stood up, but he didn't raise his assault rifle toward them. *That's a good thing, I think.*

"Logan, were you expecting a call?" John said incredulously. "Because these guys seem to know you."

Logan sensed no threat from the two Iraqis. "How's your Arabic? Mine's rather rusty."

"That's better than mine, which is nonexistent."

"Well, then, this should be a short conversation."

Logan and John jogged over to the man on the cell phone. They nodded in greeting, and the man on the cell phone began speaking rapidly in Arabic.

The man realized they had no idea what he was saying. He spoke again into the cell phone and then thrust it toward Logan.

"This should be interesting," John said.

Logan accepted the phone, put it to his ear, and said, "This is Logan West."

"Logan! It's Gunny Branch back at the crash site!" Logan was surprised to hear his voice, and his face broke into a grin of stunned disbelief as the crew chief explained the situation.

"You're not going to believe this, but after you left, a group of Iraqis approached the riverbank to see what happened. There was an English teacher with them. So I started talking to him and told him what was happening. Turns out he was an officer in the Republican Guard and returned here to live with his family after the war started."

"Gunny, get to the point. We're running out of time."

"Actually, you now have more time than you thought. I had an idea. I told him that we were chasing three very dangerous men who had a weapon on them that would kill a lot of people in Haditha if they got away. I also told him you and John were on foot trying to catch them. And this is where it gets crazy—he offered to help. Turns out his brother and his cousins were also in the military. They have a sort of militia here to help preserve the safety of their neighborhood from any remaining insurgents. He called his brother, Ahmed—that's who you're looking at—and his brother got the gang together and started looking for Cain and his men. And obviously, they found him. They think they know where he's going, and when I'm done talking, Ahmed will take you to go after him. They also have his cousin and a group of men on the other side of the neighborhood you're in to keep them from squirting out."

"Gunny, that's a brilliant piece of thinking. When this is over, you'll hopefully have helped save thousands of lives. We're going now, but before you hang up, please tell Ahmed we're sorry for the loss of his friend. They already took one casualty helping us. Thanks, Gunny."

"Good luck. Get that sonofabitch."

"Roger. Out here." Logan handed the phone back to Ahmed.

Ahmed spoke into it briefly and hung up. He looked into Logan's eyes and saw the empathy for the loss of his comrade. He scrutinized Logan and then nodded, breaking through the language barrier, as if to say, *I appreciate your condolences.*

The moment passed, and Ahmed pointed down the street.

Logan extended his left arm in the universal gesture of "lead the way."

Ahmed nodded again, spoke to the other armed man, and jogged down the street to where the others had disappeared.

This is starting to break our way—finally.

———

Cain and Scott moved deeper into the labyrinth of the neighborhood. They used the narrow streets to try and put distance between themselves and their pursuers, but the convoluted layout of the area made it easy to become disoriented. Cain thought they were heading west, in the right direction, but he couldn't be sure.

They snuck down an alleyway between two houses. At the end, they paused, and Cain peeked around the corner. He saw a deserted street stretching in both directions. Another row of houses was on the other side of it, but he sensed a large, open area beyond.

We have to be close.

"Hold here. I need to check the GPS to make sure we're where we're supposed to be. If not, whoever that was is going to get to us before we can get the hell out of this mess."

"Who were those guys, anyhow? We should've had a clean get-away."

"Who knows? But it doesn't matter." He looked down at the Garmin device once more. They were closer than before—a little more than a quarter mile away, but they'd somehow drifted south.

"We need to cross this street, get to the other side of those houses through that alley down there, and then turn back to the north to get to the stadium," Cain said.

Scott looked in the direction Cain indicated. On the other side of the street were three parked cars and an old white pickup truck. Scott guessed it was at least eighty meters away.

"I don't like this one bit. We're exposed until we cross that street. If any of those guys come around a corner, we'll be caught in the open. And who knows what's through that alley."

"We don't have a choice. We can't go back, and the longer we stay here, the greater the chances we get killed or caught. It's our only option."

Scott knew Cain was right. "Well, then, what are we waiting for? Ready when you are."

Cain nodded, turned around, and exited the alleyway, exposed in the waning Iraqi daylight.

Scott quickly followed on his heels, his eyes scanning up and down the street. A dog barked in the distance. A door slammed in a nearby home. A loud metallic clang came from somewhere behind them. Scott felt eyes crawling over his skin. *We're being watched. We're not going to make it.*

But just as the doubt began to blossom into something akin to panic, they were across the street and jogging between the pickup and another car. The alley—and safety—was now only ten meters away.

Cain knelt behind the bed of the truck and looked down the alley, which was at least thirty meters long. The homes might not have appeared to be that big from a distance, but up close was a different story. They were much longer than he'd thought.

He saw a few metal trash cans, some bottles on the ground, but nothing else. A door was positioned midway in each exterior wall of the two houses facing each other across the alley.

The alleyway itself was empty. Through the gap at the other end of the alley, he saw more open space. *We have to be close.*

"Let's go."

They broke from cover and sprinted toward the passage. Cain immediately slowed to a crouching walk once they were between the buildings. He looked at Scott and raised his right finger to his lips in a "quiet" gesture.

They could hear a television inside the home on the left. Scott thought he heard movement on the other side of the wall in the house to their right.

They crept down the narrow opening, cautious with each step. When they reached the end, Cain once again peered around the corner of the house, looking north. Each house had a dirt backyard that was about twenty meters deep, ending in a four-foot stone wall that ran the entire length of all the properties. What he saw past the wall turned his blood cold.

Cain immediately motioned for Scott to retreat back down the alleyway. Cain risked one last glance and then rejoined Scott.

"The good news is that we're almost there. The soccer stadium is just north of here, across a small field of weeds and rubble. The bad news is that there are six Iraqis with AK-47s fanning out and moving across the field toward us. They're only a hundred meters from here. I don't know if they're going to come inside the neighborhood or wait us out, but they don't look like amateurs."

"Shit," Scott swore violently under his breath. "What now?"

"We go back and try to work our way up the street and see if we can sneak past them."

"Sounds good."

Scott turned around and worked his way back up the alley. They were only halfway through it when they heard voices and shouting coming from the street out front.

This can't be happening, Cain thought. *Not now. Not this close.*

Unfortunately, it was. They were trapped between two groups of armed gunmen, and there was no way out.

Cain thought for a moment. *We need a distraction, or we're never getting out of here.*

"Call your insurgent contact," Cain ordered. "Tell him we're trapped in the row of homes at the edge of the field. Tell him we need them to somehow distract the men in the field, or we're never getting out of here. And if we don't get out of here, his supply of money and weapons runs out."

Scott was already dialing the number.

There was only one place to hide. Cain checked the doorknob on the right. It was locked. He heard Scott speaking Arabic as he moved past him to check the door on the left. He turned the knob, and it began to open. *Bingo.*

He looked back at Scott, who'd just hung up the phone. "We're good. He said we'll hear his signal in three to four minutes. He told us there's an SUV waiting for us, but no matter what happens in the field, we have to get to the other side of the soccer stadium. He can't risk sending all his men here."

"Okay. We're going in here until then. Be ready, but no matter who's inside, no shots. We can't risk drawing them right to us."

"Roger, boss."

Scott slung the assault rifle across his back, drew a Glock pistol from a hip holster, and picked up the nuclear weapon.

Cain slowly turned the knob all the way and pushed the door

inward. The sounds of the television were more distinct. He stepped through the opening into a dimly lit kitchen, the light from the back windows the only source of illumination.

Scott entered behind him. The kitchen was clear. *That's one small blessing,* Scott thought.

The two men moved quietly from the kitchen into an adjoining living room and family area. Two worn couches were arranged in an L configuration, facing the television. Neither man paid attention to the Arabic soap opera unfolding on the small screen. It was the occupants of the house which drew their attention.

A young boy no more than ten sat on one of the couches, staring at the intruders. He was too shocked to speak. An older Iraqi woman, in her sixties at least, sat on the other couch. Before she could speak, Scott began to whisper in Arabic.

"We'll be out of here in a few minutes. We're being hunted by some bad men, and we need a place to hide. Please don't shout, or they'll come in here and kill all of us. We'll be gone shortly."

The story sounded plausible to the old woman, who knew there were still insurgents in the city. She'd heard the stories of what they did to their own people. There was no way she was going to bring them to her home.

She nodded, moved over to the couch with her grandson, and put her arm around him, as if to shield him from these two intruders and the horrors outside.

Scott whispered, "Thank you," trying to make the lie sound sincere, and turned back to Cain. "What now?"

"Now we wait. Let's go to the kitchen, but keep these two in sight just in case they do something foolish."

They didn't have to wait long: several automatic weapons suddenly fired in the field outside.

"Let's go! That's our cue," Cain said.

CHAPTER 57

Ahmed had led them through a series of narrow alleys and small streets. They'd linked up with the group of Iraqis they'd spotted disappearing down the street when they first encountered Ahmed. They now numbered seven.

Logan was beginning to like the odds.

They moved swiftly, a single column of men weaving between the houses. Logan knew they were getting close when the sound of gunfire erupted. Logan estimated it was only a block or two over, toward the western edge of the neighborhood.

The street's residents must've sensed something dangerous unfolding near their homes. They hadn't encountered a single civilian on the streets. *Smart people.*

The gunfire increased in volume and intensity, and Logan heard the sound of at least one light machine gun.

The group emerged from another alleyway onto an abandoned street. Ahmed suddenly halted next to an old white pickup parked on the street. He turned to Logan and pointed toward the row of houses that faced them, raising his hand as if moving up and over an invisible obstacle.

Logan nodded and spoke as he studied the houses. "John, this is it. The field is on the other side. We still have an element of surprise. Let's use it."

Logan gestured to himself, Ahmed, and John and then toward an alley two houses up on the other side of the street. He next gestured to the four remaining men and pointed to an alleyway directly across the street and another one two houses down. They understood; two men would cover each avenue of approach, while Ahmed would follow the Americans.

Ahmed issued instructions to his men. Within a matter of seconds, the group divided and jogged quickly to their respective objectives. Logan hoped his newfound Iraqi companions would be safe.

We'd better find the bomb, or this whole country won't be safe.

This time Logan entered the alleyway first, scanning the narrow terrain for any threat. John followed closely; Ahmed entered last.

More gunfire—followed by the sound of screaming. Logan moved faster. He reached the end of the alley and held up his right hand in a fist.

Freeze.

He slowly craned his head around the corner of the house to gain a vantage point of the unfolding battle in the field. A moment later, he returned to cover and huddled with John and Ahmed.

"Good news; bad news. Good news is that Cain and our friend Scott are four houses down, fifty meters away. Scott is carrying the suitcase. They're crouched in front of a low wall that runs along the back of all these yards. They're creeping along it, moving in this direction. The bad news is that there are two pickup trucks one hundred thirty meters away with mounted light machine guns. They must be helping Cain because they're shooting at a group of Iraqis—must be Ahmed's cousin and his friends—in the middle of the field. I couldn't tell how many men were in the trucks, but at least two of our friends are down. The rest are hiding behind a cluster of small boulders, holding up their weapons and firing blindly. They're pinned down. The second they move from cover, they'll get torn to pieces."

Logan looked at John and went on. "We have to help them, but the second we expose ourselves, there's a good chance Cain and Scott will see us. I want Cain alive, but Scott can burn in hell. It's about time he paid for what he did to us in Fallujah. We need to take down the gunners and Scott at the same time. You ready for some sharp-shooting, John?" Logan asked.

"Always," John replied, a hard edge to his voice.

"So when I break left, you step out to the right. Make the shots count. Once they hear them, it will only be seconds before they figure out where they came from."

Logan pointed at Ahmed and gestured for him to remain behind John. "I hope he understands me."

"So do I," John said. "I don't need to get shot in the back."

"Ready? We do it on three. Once this starts, it doesn't stop until we either have the suitcase or we're dead, understand?"

"I'm all in, Logan." Now, he smiled. "Enough with the pep talk. Let's finish this."

"All right, then. Here we go."

Logan turned back to the edge of the alley and raised his M4 to the ready position. John and Ahmed moved to the other side of the alley and did the same, John with his M4, Ahmed with his AK-47.

The gunfire picked up once more, and then . . .

"One . . . two . . . three!"

Logan turned in a crouch and stepped from behind cover, his eyes now looking through the reflex scope of his M4. He spotted Scott Carlson, the man he'd first encountered as "James" in Fallujah, now only three backyards away. The red dot swayed slightly as Logan moved closer.

John emerged behind Logan. He saw the two pickup trucks

parked near each other at an angle, mounted machine guns firing at the boulders in front of them.

Oh shit, John thought. There were now four more bad guys moving toward the boulders on foot, two from the other side of the trucks and two from this side. John didn't know where Ahmed was, and he didn't have time to look. The new threat captured his attention.

Still have to get the gunners first, John thought, as he placed the dot of the scope on the forehead of the closest man.

Meanwhile, Logan exhaled as he prepared to depress the trigger. *Bastard must've caught our movement with his peripheral vision.* Scott was now looking directly at Logan, his face captured perfectly in an expression of surprise. *Too late, you arrogant prick.*

Logan and John pulled their triggers at the same time, perfectly synchronized after years of training and fighting side by side.

Logan's bullet struck Scott Carlson in the center of the forehead, just above the eyes. Logan saw his head snap back. Scott fell to the dirt, his torso coming to rest on its side, the weapon pinned between his body and the wall. The man that Logan had vowed to hunt down for leading them to an ambush in Iraq was finally dead. *That's for all the widows and fatherless children you created, you sonofabitch. Burn in hell.*

Logan sprinted toward Cain, who scrambled toward Scott's body and the weapon. He hadn't seen Logan yet.

John's first shot was just as accurate as Logan's. The bullet struck the gunner in the side of the head. The dead man pitched sideways off the truck, falling to the ground.

The two insurgents closest to their position turned, searching for the origin of the shot.

John didn't have time to focus on them. *First things first . . .*

He moved the scope to the second light machine gunner. *Gotcha.* He pulled the trigger a second time as he heard Ahmed's AK-47 open fire a few feet away.

John's second shot struck the other gunner in the throat, his aim slightly thrown off by the sound of the AK-47 firing in such close proximity. The gunner raised his hands to his throat and fell to the bed of the pickup. Both light machine guns finally went blessedly silent.

John spared a glance to his right. Ahmed was firing his rifle from a kneeling position. John looked back at the battlefield and saw the two insurgents who had turned toward them—the ones John had ignored—lying motionless in the dirt.

That's four down. Nice shooting, Ahmed.

Logan ran through the yards toward Cain. Their eyes locked as Cain glared at him with utter contempt.

Cain pushed Scott's fallen body away from the wall and raised the G36C assault rifle as he grabbed the suitcase from the ground. He pulled the trigger.

Logan dove to his left, hit the ground, and rolled away—from nothing. He leapt out of the evasive maneuver and looked up to see Cain toss the weapon to the ground. Cain grabbed the suitcase, leapt over the low wall, and ran.

Logan smiled. *Jammed . . . tough luck, shithead.*

Logan broke into a dead sprint, twenty meters behind his prey. *No escape this time.*

John and Ahmed watched Logan pursue Cain. Ahmed aimed his AK-47 at the fleeing figure with the suitcase, eager to shoot the American who'd brought this violence to his city. The barrel was knocked up and away at the last second as he pulled the trigger, the bullets firing aimlessly into the sky.

Ahmed turned in anger, only to see John shaking his head from side to side. John pointed to Logan, who was fast in pursuit and almost across the field, moving closer to the abandoned soccer stadium.

John said, "He'll get him. Trust me on this one." He put his hand on Ahmed's shoulder and pointed toward the pickup trucks.

The gunfight was almost over. Without the cover of the machine guns, the remaining two insurgents realized they were now out-manned. They turned around and ran toward the soccer stadium. Unfortunately for them, there was too much open space to cover.

John and Ahmed watched as the four Iraqi men that had helped them stepped out from behind the boulders, aimed their weapons at the fleeing insurgents, and opened fire. The fusillade struck both men in the back, and they pitched forward into the dirt.

Well, John thought, *that's one way to deal with insurgents.*

CHAPTER 58

Cain was fast, even for the CEO of the world's largest private army. Logan was surprised at how quick and sure-footed his movements were. Fortunately, Logan was faster.

The soccer stadium loomed closer as the foot chase continued. The distance between the two men shortened. Logan was only fifteen feet behind and closing rapidly.

Have to get him before he gets to the other side.

The grassy field suddenly gave way to tougher terrain below his feet. They'd reached the perimeter of the stadium.

A wall encircled the entire facility. Cain dashed through an opening, and Logan realized it was an entrance. The stone wall wasn't a wall at all, but the back of concrete steps that served as bleachers. Logan thought the stadium resembled a high school track with solid seats instead of aluminum stands.

Cain raced across a dirt walkway before entering the field itself. Logan ran harder, pushing his muscles to maximum exertion. The gap between the two men closed to only a few feet.

The field was now abandoned to rocks, dead grass, and trash, though Logan imagined the turf had once been full with a short, manicured grass. Once used by insurgents to execute Iraqi policemen, the stadium was merely a ghostly shell of its former self.

Have to pick up the pace.

Logan breathed rapidly and pushed himself beyond his limits. He was almost upon his target. He prepared to surge one last time when suddenly Cain's left foot landed on an old bottle that lay hidden in a patch of grass, and he lost his balance. His feet flew out from beneath him, and he sprawled facedown into the earth, the suitcase bouncing end over end, coming to a sudden rest a short distance away.

Logan stopped short and stared at the man he'd chased across the world, now lying only a few feet away. He slowed his breathing as he waited.

At least the running is over, Logan thought. *Now for the hard part.*

Cain pushed himself off the ground, stood, and turned to face Logan. As he brushed dust and dirt off his shirt, he stared at Logan, expecting the former Marine Force Reconnaissance captain to speak. Logan just looked back at him, fierce resolution on his face. The cut from the first day's events had opened again, and a thin trail of blood trickled down his cheek.

Cain finally broke the silence.

"You do see the irony here, don't you, Logan?"

No response.

Cain continued. "If you stop me, you'll only delay the inevitable. Iran *will* get a nuclear weapon. It may not be today. It may not be tomorrow, but it will be soon. I guarantee it. And when they do, *and* when they choose to use it—as they've said they would—the resulting war will make Iraq look like a field exercise. The US will get sucked into it like we always do. We'll commit our forces, maybe not in the most effective manner—depends on the administration in the White House—but we'll commit. And depending on what the Quds Force does globally and how committed the Iranian military is, our casualties will be catastrophic, to both the military and to the public's resolve." He paused for a moment and laughed.

"What's so funny?" Logan asked quietly.

"I was remembering something the secretary of defense once told me. He said, 'Cain, privately, we call it the SGLI plan.' You know what that means?"

Logan nodded, morbidly amused at the dark humor. SGLI was Servicemembers' Group Life Insurance, the insurance policy that protected all men and women serving in the armed forces. If the casualties were high, the insurance plan would pay out hundreds of millions of dollars to the families of the fallen. And a war with Iran would definitely result in enormous casualties.

"It's an appropriate moniker, albeit sick and twisted," Logan said.

"So you see, Logan. If you take the long view—and I always do—something has to be done now to let the Iranian regime know that they're vulnerable. That their aggression can be stopped. That using their Quds Force to facilitate IED attacks against US forces in Iraq and Afghanistan will not be tolerated. That those responsible for the loss of American lives, for the savage murder of my brother, will be held accountable and brought to justice."

His voice rose, his emotion no longer suppressed by cool logic.

He's coming unhinged. Wonder how far I can push . . .

"They need to know that not all of America will sit idly by while Iran pursues a course of action that will ultimately cause even more harm later than offensive action by *us* does now. I've watched this farce develop over the last several years, and it sickens me. I can't take it."

"I agree," Logan said. "It is completely and wholly fucked up." The raw bluntness of his statement had the effect of a slap to Cain's face.

Cain shook his head, stupefied. "If that's true, then why would you *stop* me? I can strike a blow that will do everything I said—that will save more lives than we stand to lose. But here you stand, ready to fight for a country that can barely take care of itself." Cain's eyes narrowed visibly. "Why?" The last word was almost a hush, barely audible in the Iraqi air.

"Because *you* don't get to make the rules," Logan snarled at him. "You are not above the law, no matter what your motives are." He paused, choosing his next words carefully.

"But it's not about geopolitics, is it, Cain? I know about your brother. I know what the Quds Force did to him. Hell, I found his body, remember? I still have nightmares about it." Cain's eyes glazed over for a minute, as if a memory of Steven slipped across them. "No man deserves that. But guess what? Here is the hard truth, Cain: it's not *your* decision to make." Logan let the words sink in. "Unless someone elected you president in the last few hours, it will *never* be your decision to make. You talk about bringing the Iranian regime to justice for all the American lives they've taken. That sword cuts both ways, Cain. What about you? What about all the lives you've taken in your personal vendetta? All the horror and violence your blind quest for revenge has caused?" Logan spoke forcefully, emphasizing his point.

"You have to pay for your sins, Cain. Once you started all this, you became just like them. You lost the fight as soon as it began. You're *no* better than they are."

Cain trembled with outrage.

I'm pushing him over the edge. Maybe I'll force him to make a mistake.

"I may be disgusted with some of the things our government does," Logan went on. "How it shies away from making the hard choices, sticking with an unpopular course of action out of political expediency. To be honest, it's one of the reasons I left the Marine Corps. But even though I don't wear a uniform anymore, I took an oath. And that oath stated that I'd act 'against all enemies, foreign *and* domestic.' Like you, Cain. Even though you may see yourself as some kind of patriot, you're not."

Logan saw the veins on the side of Cain's neck pulse with rage, reaching a crescendo in concert with his elevated heart rate.

"You asked me why, and I'll tell you." Logan paused one more time. "Because you have to be held accountable, and I happen to be one of the few men on this planet who can do it. Justice has to be served, and I intend to see that it is." Then he added, "Which is why I'm taking you back to expose you to the world for what you are—a traitor and a murderer."

Logan steeled himself for what was coming. He knew the moment was upon them both.

Cain hissed at him, "Then I guess there's really nothing else to talk about."

"I guess not."

"Then let's get this over with quickly," Cain said as he glanced at the suitcase, his prize waiting to be reclaimed. "I have a ride to catch."

Cain immediately dropped into a low fighting stance, his left foot forward, his left hand open in front of him at chin level, right hand cocked in a fist. He moved forward in a zigzag pattern toward Logan, his movements fluid and effortless. The anger on Cain's face turned to something else Logan recognized—fierce determination.

This isn't going to be easy, Logan thought.

He stepped backward into his own conventional fighting stance, hands raised in front of him. *Give him a few more feet.*

Cain switched stances, his right foot forward, and moved within striking distance.

Logan lashed out in a low roundhouse kick intended to knock Cain off balance. But Cain lifted his right leg, causing Logan's kick to sail through the air between them.

Crack! Crack! Cain delivered two powerful punches with his left fist, striking Logan first on the side of his nose and then the right cheek.

Logan's eyes watered from the blows, and a jolt of pain flashed through his head.

My God, he's fast.

Unlike most people when struck violently in the face, Logan

fought through the initial shock and allowed his momentum to carry him past his nemesis. As he turned, he lashed out with a spinning back fist with his left hand. Cain dodged it easily.

Logan regained his footing and faced Cain once more. Cain smiled, a sadistic, confident look in his eyes. Cain sensed Logan's surprise at his fighting skills.

"What did you think, Logan? That this would be easy? That I'd fall over and beg you for mercy?" Cain shook his head from side to side. "Rule number one, Logan. If you plan to attack a fundamentalist Islamic nation, you'd better be able to defend yourself. You're not the first person who's opposed me, and from the looks of it, you're not going to be the last."

Logan knew he was right. For the first time during this entire ordeal, legitimate doubt crept into the back of his mind. It wasn't panic. Logan was *trained* not to panic, knowing he couldn't afford to no matter how dire the situation seemed, but he instinctively realized that he might not emerge victorious. Cain was—apparently—that good. Logan hadn't even sensed his strikes coming.

I'm going to have to switch tactics somehow. He has to have a weakness.

That was as far as his thoughts progressed before Cain launched a vicious assault at him. Several blows struck Logan in the ribs and face in blinding succession as he tried to defend himself. He tucked his arms in to his sides, leaving his face exposed.

Cain lashed out with a hammer fist to Logan's left temple. The blow staggered Logan backward. Logan shook his head to clear the thrumming sensation inside his skull.

The onslaught would've incapacitated any other man, but Logan's fitness and training saved him. He was battered and bruised but still standing.

Cain stood back, appreciating his handiwork. He looked fresh and ready for more.

Logan immediately knew his only chance of winning lay elsewhere. *There's no way I can beat him on his feet.*

Without wasting another moment, he lowered his head and launched himself at Cain, executing a double-leg takedown, his chest slamming into Cain's lower torso. He lifted Cain off his feet and propelled him to the hard dirt below. He was rewarded with a guttural exhalation as the wind was knocked out of Cain's lungs.

As fast as Cain was, the maneuver surprised him. He struggled to push Logan off his chest. Logan responded by raising himself up and away from Cain, which provided him with enough space as he punched Cain on both sides of his rib cage. *Thud! Thud! Thud! Thud!*

Cain, realizing he couldn't withstand a continued onslaught of ferocious body shots, brought his right leg up between their bodies. He snaked the leg around the right side of Logan's torso and twisted, gaining enough leverage and momentum to send Logan sprawling to the ground next to him.

Logan rolled away to avoid any further counterstrikes. As he scrambled to his feet, he watched Cain kick his legs straight up into the air, the momentum lifting his upper body upward. He landed squarely on both feet and faced Logan.

Motherfucker thinks he's Bruce Lee.

The men faced each other, both fueled by adrenaline. Cain breathed hard as a warm wind kicked up the fine sand and desert dust, coating both men with it.

Logan remained motionless. Cain moved forward, a predator stalking his prey. The smile was gone, leaving only a mask of unadulterated hatred. Logan expected another assault of punches.

Instead, Cain spun around completely on his left foot and delivered a back kick that caught Logan squarely just below the sternum. The kick knocked the wind out of him, and the force of the blow partially doubled him over. He knew he had to move away, but he wasn't fast enough.

Cain smoothly transitioned into his normal fighting stance once again. He lashed out with a roundhouse kick from his right leg that struck Logan on the left side of his face, sending blood from the wound splattering across the dirt. Logan crashed to the ground like a fighter on the verge of being knocked out.

Logan struggled to regain his balance, but his equilibrium had been destabilized by the kick. He managed to lift himself up on both hands and knees. *Have to get away. Can't take much more.* He willed himself to move, but it wasn't enough.

Cain delivered a powerful kick that cracked two ribs on Logan's left side and flipped him onto his back, where he lay broken and in pain. He coughed and tasted the copper flavor of blood. *Might've punctured a lung. Fantastic . . .*

He focused his eyes on Cain, who stared at him from only a few feet away.

Cain sensed victory at hand. He stood directly over Logan. "I told you, but you didn't listen—you can't beat me. Now it's time to finish this little dance once and for all. I'd be half-tempted to let you live if I thought you'd go back to drinking yourself into oblivion, but I don't think you'd let this go, and I don't need you or anyone else coming after me. So it's lights out." He paused for a moment and looked down at Logan one last time. "Good-bye, Captain West."

Come on. Get it over with. Logan waited for the final blow to come, knowing it would be fast and lethal. He was right on both counts.

Cain raised his right leg and viciously brought it downward toward Logan's throat, intent on crushing his windpipe.

Although in excruciating agony from the broken ribs, Logan summoned enough strength for a last-chance defense. He brought both hands up and caught Cain's boot inches away from his face, then violently twisted his hands 180 degrees to the right.

He felt something pop in Cain's ankle, and Cain shouted in pain as Logan jerked his foot down.

Cain was thrown off balance and fell forward across Logan's body, landing at an awkward angle on top of his already damaged ankle. There was a loud crack as at least one bone broke. This time Cain shrieked in pain.

Now it's my turn! Logan's mind roared in fury.

Logan rolled toward Cain, who writhed in agony from the shattered bone. He sensed Logan near him and tried to hit him with a left-handed back fist. Logan caught the arm in both hands. *You just sealed your fate. Thank you.*

Logan maneuvered his body so that he held Cain's left arm—fully extended—between his legs. His right leg lay across Cain's chest and pushed him against the ground; his left, across his stomach. Logan's feet were interlocked. There was nowhere for Cain to go.

Stand by, asshole. Here comes the real pain.

Logan leaned back and pulled Cain's arm with all his strength, the megalomaniac's elbow now past the point of normal flexion. Cain screamed louder; Logan only pulled harder. A cold fury filled his head. Cain's screams dimmed in intensity. Logan lurched backward one last time. It was enough.

Crack! The humerus in Cain's upper arm snapped like a rotten tree branch. The tendons in the elbow ligament ruptured, and the cartilage tore away from the bone. Cain's left arm was rendered useless and permanently damaged.

I hope it hurts like hell. You deserve it.

Logan released the arm and closed in on Cain as his adversary coughed in agony. Cain's world had become nothing but blinding pain. All rational thought and reason fled his mind. He babbled incoherently, but Logan didn't care. He wasn't done with him just yet.

Logan positioned himself behind Cain and snaked his right arm around his throat. He locked his left hand behind Cain's head and his right hand inside his left elbow. Cain couldn't resist. Logan squeezed.

As his arms cut the blood circulation to Cain's head, Logan thought, *This is more merciful than you deserve.*

The chokehold sliced through the panic in Cain's head, and he realized too late what was happening. He resisted, flailing at Logan with his remaining good arm.

Logan only squeezed harder. Cain's attempts to free himself subsided. *Almost done . . .*

He felt Cain's body go limp as he finally passed out. He was about to remove his arm from Cain's throat, but he never got the chance.

From across the soccer field, two Iraqi men with AK-47s appeared from one of the dark walkways, pointed at him, and began to run. Logan hadn't seen the two men before, either with Ahmed or his friends, which meant they were likely here to help Cain.

You've got to be kidding me, Logan thought. *After all this . . .*

He knew as soon as they reached him they'd shoot him in the head and take both Cain and the bomb. His mind searched for options, but it seemed that his had all run out.

The two men closed the distance, weapons raised, shouting in Arabic.

Logan did the only thing he could think of—he used Cain's body as a human shield, trying to prevent the inevitable for as long as possible. He knew they wouldn't shoot him while he held their valuable asset.

The shouting grew louder. Both men were now only twenty yards away and realized what Logan was doing. One of the men said something in Arabic Logan didn't understand. The two men split up and moved away from each other, intent on flanking Logan from both sides to get a clear shot.

Nice. At least I won't be killed by stupid men.

Logan tried to keep Cain between them and him. His ploy wouldn't last much longer. The man on Logan's right was now only ten yards away, close enough that Logan had nowhere to hide.

Logan realized it was over, and the finality of it slammed into his chest like one of Cain's strikes. There was nothing left to do. He prayed that he'd done enough to give the US time to hunt these men down after he was dead. He'd done everything he could, but the game was now out of his hands. His thoughts drifted toward Sarah. *I'm sorry, babe. I love you.*

The man raised the rifle and pointed it directly at Logan's head. At this distance, he couldn't miss. He said something to Logan, but it didn't matter.

Logan opened his eyes, looked at his would-be killer, steadied himself, and replied, "Fuck you too." He closed his eyes and waited for the end to come.

Crack! Crack! Crack!

Three shots rang out across the soccer stadium.

Logan realized none of them had killed him, and he opened his eyes. The gunman pointing the AK-47 at his head was in the midst of crumpling to the ground, the rifle dangling from his right arm.

Logan spun his attention to the second attacker, who looked past Logan and began to raise his own AK-47. He was too slow.

Crack! Crack!

Two bullets struck the second gunman in the center of his chest. Logan watched as the man turned toward him, looked down at his chest and then back at Logan, an expression of confusion on his face. His eyes rolled up in his head, and he fell forward, dead before he hit the ground.

Logan lay back against the dry Iraqi earth. *Thank you, God. I really didn't want to die here today.*

He looked up at the sky, exhausted. The daylight was finally starting to wane as the sky turned a deeper shade of blue. His ears registered more sounds. Men shouted as nearby vehicles skidded to a halt. He heard rapid footsteps and then the sky was blotted out by the looming figure of John Quick. Logan couldn't speak.

John looked down and quickly assessed the situation, figuring out what had transpired on the soccer field of battle.

Logan finally pulled himself back to the moment. "Could you have seriously cut it any closer, John? A few more seconds and you'd have been speaking at my memorial . . . Christ . . ."

Logan heard more men approaching, but he didn't look to see who they were. It was over. That was all that mattered.

John smiled at him. "Better late than never. Jesus, Logan. You look like shit."

"Thanks, John, I feel like it too," he said, trying to smile before his breath caught in his lungs as his broken ribs sent pain coursing through his body. "But I think our good friend Cain here is the worse for wear."

"Good. Just between us, looks like you let him off easy. He doesn't deserve to live."

Logan nodded. "I agree, and I thought about it, but as I told him, I want him to pay for what he did. Killing him would've let him off the hook."

Logan finally shoved Cain Frost's unconscious form away from him. John reached down and helped him up.

"Now the entire world will know what he did. He's a traitor, John, and I want everyone to see him for who he is."

John nodded. The sound of rotors grew louder in the desert air. A faint vibration shook the ground beneath them.

"You got helos?" Logan asked.

John was still grinning. "Absolutely. Only the best for you."

Logan tried to laugh, but it hurt too much.

"Sorry. No more jokes," John promised.

"I'm going to hold you to that. Will probably last all of two minutes," Logan said.

Logan carefully walked over and picked up the briefcase.

All of this death for something so small.

He blinked in disbelief, the enormity of what he held in his hands becoming a reality.

"At least it's finally over," John said, gently clapping him on the back. The helicopters grew closer, and Logan saw two CH-53Es appear on the horizon. "Now, let's go home."

"Amen to that, brother. I've had enough of Iraq for two lifetimes." He shook his head, adding once more, "Amen to that."

EPILOGUE

FOUR MONTHS LATER

Logan drove west on Route 40. His AA meeting had lasted a little longer than he'd expected. He'd finished his "ninety in ninety"—the newly recovering alcoholic's goal of attending ninety meetings in ninety days. Old-timers said it built a foundation of sobriety, and Logan knew it to be true. He just hoped his foundation didn't crumble to pieces this time around. He didn't think it would. The hunt for the flag had fundamentally changed him, and he'd begun to fill the void that had slowly gnawed away at his soul. But only time would really tell. *Which is why it's only one day at a time,* he thought.

He looked at the dashboard clock. It was almost five o'clock. He was going to be late. *Sorry, hon.*

He was only twenty minutes from Sarah's house. He'd stopped calling it his place after he returned from Iraq. Something inside him had finally accepted the fact that their life together could no longer exist in its former state.

His relapse, the events that had transpired, the loss of Daly—all of it had forced them to evaluate their lives through a different lens. Their love was strong but shaken. It would take time to rebuild.

And I'm the one responsible, Logan thought.

He shook his head. Blaming himself didn't help; it only added to the guilt he still struggled with on a daily basis. What did matter was that there was still a chance. Both he and Sarah were committed to it.

Logan reached for his wireless earpiece and inserted it into his right ear, but before he could dial Sarah's number, his cell phone rang. He wasn't expecting any phone calls.

He looked down. It was Mike Benson. *What could he want?*

He hadn't talked to Mike in two weeks. They were as close as brothers, but it was common to go as long as a month without speaking to him. Cain's trial wasn't scheduled to begin for another two months. So it must be something else.

Logan answered the phone, "Mike, what's up? I'm on my way to meet Sarah at her place for dinner. Just left a meeting in Laurel."

"You're in your car?" There was urgency to his question.

That isn't good. "Yes. I'm in my car. Like I said, I'm on my way to Sarah's. What's going on? I can tell something's wrong."

"You have satellite radio in that Land Cruiser, don't you? Turn on CNN or Fox News. It's on every channel."

"What is, Mike?"

"There was an explosion outside the district court in DC less than thirty minutes ago. Looks like some kind of VBIED. Multiple casualties." Logan heard the anger and sadness in Mike's voice. "It's bad, Logan."

"Jesus . . ."

"But here's the really bad part. Brace yourself for it. Looks like the target was Cain Frost. He's dead, Logan. We just confirmed it."

Logan felt temporarily disoriented. He realized his heart was racing. "Hold on a sec, Mike," he said as he slowed the SUV and pulled off to the side of the road.

Moments later, the Toyota in park, he said, "We always thought he had outside help, but we couldn't prove it. We knew he managed to warn Juan Black before we got to the compound."

"I know, Logan. The FBI and the Secret Service did a full investigation, which resulted in nothing. Only the president's national security advisor and a few others even knew about it." Mike paused. "It doesn't matter right now. Let me tell you what does."

I don't like the sound of this.

"The president has ordered a task force to investigate who was behind the assassination of one of our country's most notorious traitors. He's furious. Like you, Logan, the president wanted Cain to pay publicly for trying to start a war."

"Good for him, but what does this have to do with me?" *Although I think I already know the answer, God help me.*

"Well, as you know, my uncle Jake is now the deputy director of the entire FBI, and I have his old job as the assistant director for counterterrorism. As a result, I'm leading the task force." Mike had been elevated to senior executive and promoted less than a month earlier.

"But I also get to choose who I want on it."

"Mike, I told you—"

Mike cut him off. "I know what you told me after we got back. You'd testify and then you wanted nothing else to do with it. But guess what? Someone decided to take care of Cain before our courts could, and you know what that means, don't you?"

Logan did. "It means something else is still going on, and it's larger than just Cain and his personal army." HRI had been disabled as a corporation weeks after Cain's capture, its holdings seized by the government, pending the trial.

The words hung in the air. Finally, Mike said, "Exactly. And there's something else I need to tell you."

"I can hardly wait. What is it?"

"I reached out to John first. I figured you'd be more inclined to say 'yes' if I had him on board."

"Smart bastard. What did he say?"

"What I expected. He's in if you are, which I assume means you're in if he is, kind of like a catch-22. So you can't say 'no.'"

"You're an asshole."

"I know, but you still love me. Seriously, Logan, I need you both." Then he asked for confirmation. "So what do you say? Are you in?"

Logan watched the traffic on Route 40 speed by, jealous of the drivers who led normal lives. It amazed him how quickly events could change the course of a single life. Nothing ever turned out the way it should.

How did I come to this? he pondered.

Yet it didn't matter. What did was that there'd been a major attack on US soil, innocent lives had been lost, and now one of his closest friends was asking him for his help.

Logan suddenly had a vision of Captain Jack Barnett on top of the Haditha Dam, in tactical overwatch at Logan's recommendation. It'd been the right move at the time, and he'd been right to suggest it. And here was Mike, asking him to do the same thing, in a sense.

"Overwatch," Logan said.

"Say again, Logan?" Mike asked, obviously not understanding.

"You're asking us to go into overwatch, except it's not tactical, it's strategic—for the entire country," Logan replied quietly.

A moment of silence engulfed them as Mike processed the analogy.

"That's a good way of putting it, brother," Mike finally said. "More importantly, are you in?"

"What do you think, Mike?" Logan said, finally.

"Good. In that case, call Sarah and reschedule dinner. Tell her I'm sorry and drive down to FBI headquarters. Security will be waiting for you."

"Sounds good. See you shortly."

Before Logan could hang up, Mike added, "Logan, one more

thing, and I mean it. Thank you. I know how hard this is for you after everything that's happened."

Logan heard the appreciation in Mike's voice and understood the strength behind the words that bound them together as friends.

"Always, Mike. It's what brothers are for. I'll see you soon." And somehow, that said it all.

ACKNOWLEDGMENTS

Writing this novel was unlike anything I've undertaken in my life. It was truly a collaborative effort, and there are countless people who deserve my utmost thanks and sincere appreciation. First, thanks to you, the reader. I wrote this story thinking of you. As a fan of this genre, I placed myself squarely in your shoes and thought, *What do I really want to read? What won't bore me to tears?* I hope I've succeeded in answering those questions, but ultimately, you'll be the judge of that. Enjoy the ride. Second, to Mark Cronin, my first beta reader, good friend, and mentor, who read *Overwatch*'s first draft, told me I had a great story on my hands, and kept encouraging me through the countless rejections, telling me, "It's just a matter of time": thank you. Third, to all of my other beta readers—including author Betsy Harigan—who provided edits, suggestions, and general comments: thank you. Your feedback was critical. Fourth, to my agent, Chris Frank, of Simenauer & Frank Literary Agency in Naples, Florida, without whose determination and perseverance this novel would not have been possible: a big thank you. Fifth, to my editor, Meg Reid, whose edits really make the pages hum, and the team at Emily Bestler Books: thank you. Finally, and most importantly, to Amy, my wife, partner, and mother of our two wonderful children: a huge *thank you!* Without your love, support, and encouragement, as well as the time you gave me amid our busy lives to embark on this adventure, none of this would be possible. Now the real journey begins.